SISTERS OF
SORROW

Axel Blackwell

To the 796 children who died in the care of Sisters of Bon Secours at The Mother and Baby Home of Tuam, Ireland. May their souls finally find peace.

Part One:
Into the Night

Chapter 1

ANNA DUFRESNE SAT ON THE edge of her cot in the predawn hour, staring down at her mummified pinky finger. It lay in a stained hollow beneath her pillow, like the baby teeth she used to hide for the Tooth Fairy. Anna sighed. Once, she had fantasized about waking to find that the Finger Fairy had replaced her pinky with a key. But that was last year, when she had been a little girl.

Anna lifted the finger and dangled it by its leather thong. Misty gray light drifted through the high windows, settling over the dormitory hall like fine dust. In the gloom, her finger could have been a gnarled twig or a bit of root. The nail had fallen off. Only the tiny knob of bone, at its knuckle end, distinguished it as having once been part of her.

Anna dropped her hands, and the finger, into her lap. Jane, the other head girl in the room, stirred. She rolled over and faced Anna.

"Morning, Pinky," Jane said.

Anna didn't reply.

"Sister Eustace says we're getting a new little rat today," Jane said, wiping her nose.

"Yes, I heard. She's only six. Her brother is coming too, I think," Anna said. "And they are not rats."

Jane snorted. "Well, whatever she is, she will be sleeping on your side. I have more than enough vermin over here already." She yawned, stretched and sat up on her cot.

"She will sleep where ever Sister Eustace places her, Jane." Anna tied her pinky finger around her neck by its leather thong, her remaining fingers moving with practiced ease.

"Oh, what a lovely pendant," Jane cooed. "Such finery for M'lady."

"Ah, my dear Jane," Anna said in a tired voice, "the ivory around my neck is simple next to the radiance of the rubies on your cheek."

Jane's cheeks flared with angry color. Her bright flush eclipsed the infected red pimples covering her face. She leapt to her feet and balled her fists. "I'll put some rubies on you, Anna Dufresne!"

Jane lunged. The iron legs of her cot screeched against the cold stone floor, echoing up and down the dormitory hall. Anna flinched. Jane shoved Anna backward onto her cot, pinned her shoulder, and raised her right fist.

"You tell me you're sorry, or I will make you sorry!" Jane said. She was sixteen, two years older than Anna. And Jane could hit – hard.

"I'm sorry, Jane," Anna said.

Jane hesitated, some of the anger deflating.

"Jane," Anna said, "the bell..."

A mean smile replaced the rage on Jane's face. She gave Anna a light slap, then released her. "Well then, you had better start getting ready, hadn't you?" She grabbed one of Anna's shoes from under the cot and flung it into a dark corner of the hall. There was a muffled *thonk* and a child cried out.

"Oops," Jane said and giggled.

Anna scrambled off the opposite side of the cot, toward the shoe.

Behind her Jane called, "That new rat is sleeping on your side."

Anna said nothing. She waded through the piles of straw that served as bedding for her fifteen wards. The younger girls, roused by the commotion, woke, rubbed their eyes, picked straw out of their hair.

"Who cried?" Anna asked.

"I didn't cry, Miss. I just...I just..." It was Mary Two. "I found your shoe," she said, holding it aloft. Mary could be whiny sometimes, but she was a good worker. Her dad had been hanged for rape and her momma ran off to be a prostitute in Chicago, according to Sister Eustace. Mary had been here since she was seven.

"Did it hit you in the face?" Anna asked, taking the shoe.

2

"No Miss, just my arm." Mary held out her right elbow.

Between the dim light and the scrim of filth on Mary's arm, it was impossible to tell if the shoe had left a bruise. "You'll be fine, Mary, get dressed."

"Yes, Miss."

"Somebody make sure Lilly is ready when the bell rings or you all get half rations at breakfast," Anna said, surveying the heaps of straw. Lilly was her youngest charge, a five-year-old waif. Sister Eustace hadn't told Anna her history.

Ashen morning light strengthened through the narrow windows. Behind her, one of Jane's girls lit the candles in the chandelier. Anna's girls all appeared to be awake and moving. Jill was the only one who tended to over sleep, but she had been curled up against Mary Two when the shoe hit. She had scrambled to her feet as soon as Anna started moving in their direction.

Anna returned to her cot and dressed, slipping a rough-cut work dress over her nightshirt and pulling a shawl around her shoulders.

"Thank you for not throwing my other shoe, Jane," she said.

"You are welcome, Anna," she paused, "and I am sorry I hit you. That wasn't necessary."

"Oh, did you hit me?" Anna asked, pulling on her shoe. "I didn't feel anything."

"Well, then I'm not sorry!"

Anna looked up at her, smiling. "Me, neither."

Jane's face hardened, and her flush returned. Then, high up in the single stone tower of The Saint Frances de Chantal Orphan Asylum, the bell rang. All emotion dropped from Jane's face. Both girls ran to the arched oak door at the end of the hall and started calling the names of their charges.

Anna: "Elizabeth, Mary One, Lilly..."

Jane: "Miriam, Sarah, Norma..."

As they called each name, the girl belonging to it fell in line behind either Jane or Anna. The bell pealed out its third *bong*.

Jane called, "Joan?"

Joan, the oldest girl on Jane's side, called back, "All here, Miss."

The bell struck four.

Anna called her oldest, "Lizzy?"

Lizzy called back, "All here, Miss…"

Fifth *bong*.

"…and Betty's shoes are on the right feet."

The girls tittered with nervous laughter. Many of them making quick inspections of their own shoes. Anna glared at Lizzy, who pretended to ignore her. Then, the bell struck its final note. The laughter ceased and the girls froze, standing straight as soldiers. Keys jangled in the lock beyond the oak door. Anna heard Lizzy's harsh whisper, "Breathe!" then Mary Two's quick gasp of inhalation.

The lock clicked. The door swung silently open. Sister Eustace and Sister Martha strode into the hall. Another sister, one Anna did not recognize, stood in the open doorway, covering her nose with a handkerchief.

Sister Eustace and Sister Martha walked between the two lines of girls. When they reached the end of the line, they turned and walked back to the doorway. After conferring with Sister Martha, Sister Eustace addressed the girls.

"Ladies, your hands."

Jane and Anna held out their right hands, knuckles up. A leather crop appeared in Sister Eustace's hand, slipping out of her sleeve as quick and smooth as a gambler's draw. She tapped Anna's hand with the crop. Then, she struck Jane's hand, but only hard enough to produce a light *snap*.

"Your cot is out of place, Jane," she said. "Other than that, all is in order. Before you leave for breakfast, let me remind you that today is laundry day. We will be collecting your bedding this afternoon while you are at the factory. The blankets will not be dry until tomorrow. I have asked Abbess McCain to turn up the boiler for this wing tonight. She said that she would base her decision upon your performance at the factory today. Therefore, I strongly recommend that you meet your quota. Anna, after you feed your girls and take them to the factory, you will report to my office."

"Yes, ma'am."

"Oh, I almost forgot, we have a new sister with us." Sister Eustace turned to the woman standing in the hall. "This is Sister Dolores. She has come all the way from Florida. I expect you to remember her name, and to make her feel welcome here."

Sister Dolores lowered the handkerchief from her nose. She nodded a greeting at the girls, but said nothing. Her hands fidgeted, wringing her handkerchief. She looked terrified. St. Frances was a very long way from Florida. She had probably come to the orphanage as voluntarily as any one of the orphans had.

"Well, then," Sister Eustace said. "Off with the lot of you!"

***

Anna and Jane sat at the table with the four other head girls. Two hundred or so younger children sat in little circles on the stone floor. Across the dining hall, five head boys huddled around their own table. The sixth chair at the boy's table sat empty. Daniel Seabrook, who had occupied that seat for as long as Anna could remember, had been killed last week when a column of poorly stacked crates toppled. Looking at Daniel's empty chair, Anna suddenly understood why the little ones sat on the floor, why they were not assigned seats. Seeing a new empty chair every time the factory took a child might make the sisters uncomfortable.

Anna turned her attention back to her own girls. Sister Evangeline had kitchen duty this morning. She hauled a cauldron of weak porridge from one cluster of children to the next. Lizzy called Sister Evangeline *The Woodpecker*. Frizzy red hair sprang from beneath her coif and jetted over her bandeau in little puffs. Her nose jutted out of her face like a sharp beak.

The Woodpecker dumped a ladle full of porridge into Anna's bowl, then stooped down close and said, "You best be certain to be upstairs soon as the bell strikes seven."

"Yes, ma'am," Anna replied.

After Sister Evangeline served the remaining head girls and moved away, Jane leaned over and whispered, "What have you done now, Anna?"

Anna slurped thin gritty gruel from a tin spoon and shrugged.

"We need you at the factory. Today of all days. When you get in trouble, we all suffer."

"I didn't do anything, Jane. I do not know why Sister Eustace wants to see me. Maybe I am to be adopted," Anna said with a wry grin.

"Who would want you?" Jane asked. "And, this is not a thing to joke about, Pinky. If we miss quota we will *freeze to death* tonight."

"Stop calling me Pinky, pimple lips," Anna said.

"If you mention my complexion one more time, Pinky, I swear to Christ, I will smother you to death with your own pillow!"

"We will not have any pillows tonight, Jane, and you will have forgotten by tomorrow." Anna lifted the tin to her lips and drained its contents. The bowl hid most of her face, but she continued to smile at Jane with her eyes.

Jane wanted to stay angry, but the older girl couldn't help grinning a little. Finally, she said, "What are we going to do, Anna?"

"You, Jane, are going to make quota. You are going to scream and yell and beat on your girls until they pound out enough Frances de Chantal shoes to keep you alive for another night." Anna snapped her fingers at Lizzy, who was laughing a bit too loudly. "*I* am going to go to

Sister Eustace's office and likely get screamed at and beaten, too. Then I'll come help you make shoes."

Jane sighed. "I think we should form a coup."

"Ha. We could mutiny, like on the Bounty," Anna said. "You would make a wonderful Abbess McCain."

"If I were the Abbess, I wouldn't make you wear that awful finger around your neck."

"No, you'd cut off my other pinky and make me wear them both as earrings."

"And you'd deserve it," Jane said, scraping the last of her breakfast out of its bowl.

Sister Elizabeth blew her whistle. The children rose, lined up, and filed out of the dining hall, depositing their bowls and spoons in a washing trough as they went. Jane and Anna walked side by side down the corridor to the stairway. Their girls trailed them in neat lines.

"Listen, Jane," Anna said, "I honestly don't know why I have been called to see Sister Eustace."

"It can't be anything good."

"No," Anna said, "it can't."

"I'll make sure Lizzy gets your girls out tomorrow morning if…if you haven't returned."

"Thank you." Anna smiled at her. She paused, then added, "If you get behind today, tell Lizzy I said to call out the reserves."

"The what?" Jane asked.

"You have to say it just like that. *Call out the reserves*. That's our little code."

They had reached a broad stone staircase that descended into the factory. The air was heavy with the scents of leather and dye, hot copper and burning coal. The presses and stitchers and cutters and mills thrummed, pounded, hissed – hungry machines, eager to devour their young operators. The industrial din would soon make conversation impossible. Anna finished quickly.

"We always put a pair of shoes aside when we are ahead of quota. There's a stash — a couple dozen pairs. Lizzy knows where. If you are not going to make quota honestly, tell her I said to call out the reserves. She will find you enough shoes to buy some heat tonight."

"Why, Anna, you are a little devil."

"And you see where it has gotten me?" She reached out and squeezed Jane's hand. Jane startled, but squeezed back.

The bell began to strike seven as they passed into the factory. The roar of machinery drowned out whatever Jane said next, which was fine by Anna. She yelled for Lizzy to get the girls to their stations, then turned and fled back up the stairs toward Sister Eustace's office.

Chapter 2

THE SAINT FRANCES DE CHANTAL Orphan Asylum was a fortress-like structure consisting of two long wings joining at a center rotunda. The factory occupied the entire lower floor of the south wing. The top floor housed the dining hall, kitchen, and the nuns' living quarters. The orphans slept in the dormitory halls of the north wing. The north wing stood as tall as the south but was only a single story, with high, vaulted ceilings. Anna had heard tell of a basement below the north wing, but she had never seen it.

All the offices were located in the rotunda, the Great Round Room. It served as the main entrance to Saint Frances de Chantal, featuring massive oak double doors, and a high domed ceiling and mosaic marble floor. A wide balcony wrapped around two-thirds of the rotunda's mezzanine level, terminating on either end in broad staircases that swept down to the double doors. Sister Eustace's office was on the mezzanine level.

Anna could have entered the Great Round Room directly from the factory, but the orphans were not allowed to use the formal staircases. Instead, she climbed the back stairs from the factory to the kitchen, then exited the kitchen onto the mezzanine's balcony through a narrow service door.

Anna sat on the wooden bench outside Sister Eustace's office, waiting to be summoned. She stared over the railing and out across the empty dome of the Great Round Room. Pairs of sisters hurried up and down the stairs, or back and forth over the balcony, carrying boxes or files or stacks of linen. They chattered in hushed tones, until they saw Anna, at which point they fell silent and hurried past.

Anna felt she had been sitting on the very hard bench for hours when the bell struck a single note, indicating the time was seven-thirty. The bell hung in its tower, sixty feet above the center of the rotunda. Anna liked to stand on the star at the middle of the Great Round Room and stare up at the bell, imagining the view from up there. She liked to watch the pigeons that occasionally flew in through the openings at the top of the tower.

What would it be like to be one of those pigeons? Anna wished she could flap noisily around the enormous dome until Abbess McCain herself came out to see what was causing all the commotion. Then her pigeon would fly up to the bell, plop a dropping on it just for spite, and soar out of the fortress to discover whatever may lie beyond its walls. She especially wished that right now. Her breakfast was not sitting easily in her stomach. Her underarms were damp, despite the morning's chill, but her mouth was quite dry.

When the call finally came, Anna stood so quickly her head buzzed, and her vision clouded over briefly. One knee popped. She straightened her dress, opened the door and walked into the office.

She stood before Sister Eustace's expansive desk, hands clasped behind her back. The sister fussed over a stack of papers, ignoring Anna. Beyond the old nun, double glass doors opened onto a white stone patio, providing a glimpse of the grounds around Saint Frances. Anna had arrived at the orphanage when she was nine and had not seen the outside since that day, five years ago.

Through the doors, she could see a luxurious grass lawn surrounded by a dense forest of fir trees and madronas. On the right edge of the view, the lawn dropped away over a steep hill. A thin ribbon of blue lined the edge of the horizon just beyond that drop, the Strait of Juan de Fuca. The Strait connected the Puget Sound to the Pacific Ocean. The Pacific Ocean connected to every other place in the world.

More than anything else, Anna wanted to see the ocean, maybe even swim in it someday – if she ever learned to swim.

"Anna!" Sister Eustace said.

"Yes, Ma'am." Anna snapped her eyes back to the nun.

"Stop gawking."

"Yes, ma'am."

"Why are you here?"

"You called for me, ma'am."

"Of course, I called for you, child! But why? What have you done that has necessitated me calling for you?"

Anna wrung her hands behind her back. "Ma'am, I'm sure I don't know, ma'am."

"Come, now! You are at all times up to some wickedness!" Sister Eustace snatched up the leather crop and pointed it at Anna. "Have you been hoarding blankets again? Or trying to climb out the dormitory windows?"

"No, ma'am. I promise. The windows are much too narrow for me to squeeze through."

"Ah! So you have tried it."

"Just once, ma'am, and that was long ago."

"Whatever for?" Sister Eustace nearly sprang out of her chair. "Don't you know a fall from that height would kill you? The wolves would have eaten you right there on the lawn." Blood drained from Sister Eustace's face, and she settled back into her chair. "The wolves or something worse."

Anna said nothing, trying to keep her eyes from wandering back to the glass doors.

"No matter," Sister Eustace said, recomposing herself. "No matter. The Church has seen fit to entrust us with the care of the most incorrigible and deviant urchins, and I am sure we are up to the task. Whatever mischief you have sought out has certainly come back to you today, child.

"There is a decidedly nasty bit of work that needs doing, and Abbess McCain named you as the girl for the job. You will be cleaning the cistern overflow pipes today, Anna," Sister Eustace concluded with a hint of triumph in her voice.

Anna looked at her with blank confusion, which clearly disappointed Sister Eustace.

The nun grunted, then elaborated, "The storm we had three weeks ago washed a great quantity of debris into the overflow pipes. With the constant rain, all our cisterns are nearly full. If the debris is not removed from the pipe, soon we will have rain-water flooding the factory."

"I'm sorry, ma'am, I don't understand."

"Of course not. But there's not much *to* understand, and the job is simple enough. You do know that The Saint Frances de Chantal Orphan Asylum stands on an island, don't you?"

"No, ma'am."

"Well, why else would we have brought you by boat?" Sister Eustace demanded.

"I don't know, ma'am."

"That is right, you don't know. There is much you don't know. And you'd do well to keep that in mind.

"But as I was saying, because we are on an island, we have no fresh water but the rain which we collect in underground cisterns. It is our good fortune that it rains so frequently here. We seldom want for water, but sometimes the excess is a problem. As it is now. There are pipes that drain this surplus into the sea. But, as I said, these pipes have become blocked.

"The cisterns lie directly beneath the factory and the rotunda. If the blockage is not removed, the factory will flood, and you and your little charges will not be able to work." Sister Eustace pointed her crop at a framed bit of needlework that hung on the wall behind her desk. *If a child will not work, neither shall he eat*, it proclaimed in dainty little cross-stitched X's.

"You will need to crawl down the pipe and clear the blockage. I would have preferred to select one of the boys, but any that are competent to handle the task are also too broad in the shoulders to fit down the pipe.

"You, Miss Anna, have proven yourself quite capable of squeezing into tight spaces and operating under cover of darkness. Abbess McCain specifically requested you for this assignment. She thought it would be a natural match for your talents. She also thought it would serve as a reminder that she still has her eye on you." Sister Eustace said this last piece sternly, pointing the crop at Anna.

"Yes, ma'am," Anna said, looking at the floor.

"Very well, then. Sister Elizabeth will take you below and show you the cisterns. But first, this is Maybelle Lawson." Sister Eustace motioned to a girl seated in the corner. She looked to be about six years old. Her eyes were red and swollen. She had apparently been seated there the entire time Anna had been in the room but had not made a sound.

"Maybelle is to be one of your charges. Her parents have been jailed for some depravity which was particularly embarrassing to their extended family, none of whom felt obliged to care for little Maybelle or her unfortunate brother. Her brother, Donald, was also to be housed here, but he passed away quite suddenly, leaving little Maybelle truly alone."

Anna nodded at the girl. Maybelle stared back but did not acknowledge her in any way.

"She hasn't spoken since her brother passed," Sister Eustace said. "But she seems bright enough, not an idiot, anyway. We certainly do not lack for idle chatter around here, do we Anna?"

"No, ma'am."

"So, if she does remain a mute, perhaps I will consider it a blessing. In any case, she will be in your care during her stay with us. I will have Jane situate her tonight, as you will likely still be working in the pipes, but after that, she will be your responsibility."

"Yes, ma'am."

"Sister Elizabeth!" Sister Eustace called. Sister Elizabeth appeared in the doorway, holding a burlap potato sack. "Would you be so kind as to show Miss Anna to the work I have assigned her?"

"I would be delighted, Sister Eustace," Sister Elizabeth said with a sardonic grin.

Anna followed Sister Elizabeth out onto the mezzanine balcony and back to the narrow service door. The service door was a flat panel set flush into the walls around it. When closed, it blended with the surrounding walls and almost disappeared. Though everyone at the orphanage knew of it, Anna liked to imagine it was a secret door. In a structure as old and eccentric as The Saint Frances de Chantal Orphan Asylum, Anna imagined there must be many secrets.

After descending the back stairs into the factory, Sister Elizabeth led Anna out through a riveted iron door, into rooms forbidden to the orphans. A warehouse and loading area lay beyond. Wooden crates stood stacked to the ceiling on one side of the room. Ream after ream of shoe leather lined the other. At the far end, two carriage style doors opened to the outside.

Anna stood mesmerized. Out these doors, the bright blue sea stretched to the horizon, flashing in the early morning sun. A pier and dock dropped down the beach and into the water. A boat of some sort bobbed alongside it. Black smoke wafted out the top of the boat's stack. Seagulls wheeled in the air above the boat and squabbled over prime perches on the dock's pilings. The sea air smelled fresh. Waves splashed under the dock and lapped the shore.

Then, *SNAP!* and a fiery sting bloomed across the back of her thigh. Anna spun to face Sister Elizabeth. Before she could beg forgiveness, Sister Elizabeth struck her across the face with the crop. Anna staggered backward and fell into the wall. Blood filled her mouth. Her tongue found a gash on the inside of her cheek.

"Get up!" Sister Elizabeth bellowed. "What is the matter with you? Do you think you are on a tour? Sightseeing? Slothfulness is a sin. The worst sin there is here at Saint Frances."

Anna got to her feet, cowering against the wall. "I'm sorry, Sister..."

"Lying is a sin, as well. You are not sorry for anything you have done. I tell you what, you little demon, if I was the one who caught you trying to climb out that window, I would not have pulled you back. I'd have shoved you right through!" Sister Elizabeth advanced on Anna, raising the crop. "And if I had been the one with the knife when we caught you and Rebecca, I wouldn't have stopped with your little finger."

She swung the crop in a quick forehand *SNAP* backhand *SNAP* at Anna's face. Anna threw her hands up, catching both lashes on her forearms. She sank into a half squat.

Sister Elizabeth raised the crop again, then lowered it. "Stand up."

Anna stood.

"I should beat you more, you deserve it, but there is work to do, and I am tired. If you give me any more trouble today, even the least bit, I give you my holy oath, I will drown you in that pipe." She thrust the crop at Anna. "Do you doubt me? It is not the *righteous* nuns who get sent to Saint Frances de Chantal. Don't you know that by now?"

"No, ma'am," Anna said, her eyes wide, her back still pressed into the wall.

"Then you are a fool," Sister Elizabeth sighed. "And I have no patience for fools. But, take me at my word, Anna, you wouldn't be the first little rat to drown in that pipe... or to be eaten by whatever lives down there. You do as I tell you and give me no sass. Have I made myself clear?"

Anna nodded, slowly, keeping her eyes fixed on the sister, "Yes, ma'am."

"Very well, then. Carry that." She nodded at the potato sack she had dropped. "Walk in front of me. It's not far now."

***

They exited the warehouse through a low arched passage. Before closing the warehouse door, Sister Elizabeth opened a box on the wall and withdrew an odd contraption; a round, concave mirror – slightly larger than a baseball – attached to a brass cylinder. She shook what looked like gray pebbles out of a paper sleeve and dropped them into the cylinder, then poured a bit of water in as well.

"It's a miner's lamp, child. Watch carefully. This will be your only light down there." She pointed to a small metal wheel on the inside of the concave mirror. "This is how you relight it, if it goes out." Sister Elizabeth flicked the little wheel. It spat sparks and a yellow flame popped to life at the mirror's center.

Anna nodded.

Sister Elizabeth grinned. "After you."

The passageway slanted downward, its angle increasing until the floor broke up into steps, a stairway that curved and then spiraled around itself as it descended into the lowest foundations of the structure.

The stairs ended at an iron door with a large lever in its center and a peep window near its top. Sister Elizabeth slid open the peep and peered in. After a brief hesitation, she snatched the lamp from Anna and shone it through the peep window, trying to see around it into whatever lay beyond.

"Looks clear," she said at last, handing the lamp back to Anna. "You go first."

Sister Elizabeth pushed down on the lever. Four bolts, one at each corner of the door, slid free of the door's frame. Flecks of rust drifted down from each bolt hole as they slid. The door was heavy, and its hinges rusted. It screamed like a banshee as Sister Elizabeth pushed it open.

Anna shone the lamp into the room beyond. It was hardly four feet on each side and very short. She could have touched the ceiling if she stood on tiptoe. Three of the walls were stone, like most of the orphanage's walls. But the wall to her right was made of iron. It looked like one of the older machines in the factory. A system of large gears and ratchets lined one corner of the iron wall, and a heavy chain hung from the ceiling, a lift chain of some sort, Anna guessed. A riveted iron plate covered the top half of the wall. Water dribbled around its edges.

Dripping echoed through the chamber. Other sounds echoed as well. Some from behind the iron wall, others ambient, seemingly without source – distant voices and the sounds of the factory, the surf on the beach and the eerie cry of seagulls. These sounds, all very faint and distorted by distance, blended in the echo chamber of the cisterns.

Anna shuddered.

"You're looking at the wrong wall," Sister Elizabeth whispered behind her. Anna turned. On the left wall, near the floor, a two-foot diameter brick pipe descended away from the room.

"This pipe," Sister Elizabeth explained in a low voice, "runs straight out to the beach. There is an iron grate near the end of the pipe to prevent little troublemakers like you from sneaking out. And to keep other things from coming in." She looked at Anna with a gleam in her eye, "Trolls and such. If you should find that the grate is missing or broken, you must come tell me at once. Do you understand?"

Anna looked into the pipe. A spectral, wispy mist hovered around the opening. *It leads to the sea.* The whispering voices of the cisterns felt like a dream language. The susurration of the sea and the crying seagulls spun out of the pipe and into her head.

"Do you understand?" Sister Elizabeth did not raise her voice.

She is afraid, Anna thought. She nodded at the sister, wide-eyed. "Come tell you if the grate is open."

"Your tools are in there." Sister Elizabeth nodded to the burlap bag. "Crawl down the pipe until you reach the blockage. Fill this sack with whatever you find, and drag it back here. While you are doing so, I will fetch a cart to haul the debris up to the dock and dump it."

"You're not staying with me?"

"Ha!" Sister Elizabeth startled herself with the loudness of her laugh. She continued in a quieter voice. "I never thought I'd see the day that you were eager for the comfort of my company."

"It's just…"

"Shut up. The task is before you. It is simple enough." Sister Elizabeth slapped her crop in her palm. The *snap* called to fresh life the welts on Anna's face and forearms.

The nun pulled a pair of gloves, a trowel and a tin miner's hat from the burlap bag. She took the lamp from Anna and secured it in a socket on the helmet, set it on Anna's head and cinched the chinstrap. It was ridiculously large on Anna's small head.

"In you go." Sister Elizabeth waved her crop in the direction of the pipe. "Get on with it!"

Anna knelt and placed her hands on the slimy stone floor. She peered into the pipe. The lamp on her head illuminated only ten or fifteen feet. Mist swirled and churned in the darkness, creating the illusion of movement just beyond the reach of her light. The dank air smelled of rot. The bricks were red, but the crumbling mortar between them had turned a moldy black. Green algae lined the bottom of the pipe.

She placed a hesitant hand on the lip of the pipe and crept forward. There was a rustle and swoosh behind her. *Snap.* Fire flared again across her left thigh.

"Move!" the nun hissed.

Anna screamed and leapt forward. Her helmet struck the top of the pipe and slid off her head. She scrambled into darkness. Her hands slipped in the algae and shot out from under her. She sprawled face-first into the sludge. Her scream, distorted, dismembered, echoed back from the depths of the cistern's labyrinth.

Behind her, Sister Elizabeth laughed hysterically. She paused for a moment to yell, "Boo!" into the tunnel, then burst out laughing again.

"Boo," repeated up and down the pipe, mingling with the nun's mad laughter. It came from ahead, then from behind, then from both at once, before finally fading into the constant background echoes.

"Boo," Sister Elizabeth said again, still chuckling, then, "Don't forget this." She threw the sack into the pipe. It landed across Anna's legs.

Anna tried to turn around for the sack, but the pipe was too narrow. It pinned her shoulders, trapped her hands in front of her.

"Oh, and this…" Sister Elizabeth threw the trowel in at her. It bounced off the top of her head and clattered into the sludge near her hands. "Now stop dawdling. You'll be safe from my crop while you're in the pipe, but unless you intend to sleep down here tonight, I suggest you be quick to your work."

Anna dragged herself forward into the dark. The lamp on her tin hat still burned, but the hat dangled upside down from its chinstrap, shining most of its light underneath and behind her. Her eyes were too filled with tears to see anything, anyway. She inched forward, not daring to breathe until Sister Elizabeth was gone. The door screamed closed. When the bolts slipped into their holes, Anna collapsed again into the algae, sobbing violently, choking on her tears.

Chapter 3

ANNA RECOVERED HERSELF BEFORE SISTER Elizabeth returned. She backed out of the pipe to retrieve the gloves and sack, and to adjust her hat. The water dribbling around the edges of the iron plate formed pools on the floor. She caught her reflection in one of these. *I look like the cover of a Jules Verne story.* She touched the dented metal cap with its glowing yellow eye. In the uncertain mirror of the puddle, the swelling weal on her cheek looked like native war paint.

The *thunk thunk thunk* of a cart rolling down the stairs prompted her to move. She quickly squirmed into the tunnel, keeping her elbows beneath her. The pipe was just wide enough that, if she pressed her back against its top and scraped her elbow against its bottom, she could extend one arm out before her. The cold green sludge soothed the stinging welts on her arms, but it chilled the rest of her body.

She exhaled plumes of fog with each breath. And with each breath, the vapor obscured more of her vision. By the time she heard Sister Elizabeth unbolting the door, she could see no more than two bricks ahead of herself. The mist thickened into a tangible thing, like a cold blanket around her head and chest. The yellow lamp reflected off the vapor, solidifying it. It sucked the energy out of her, cinching around her ribs like a creeping constrictor.

Noises, furtive movement, whispers churned in the fog. A scream echoed, very distant. Was that her own scream, still trapped in this catacomb? The ghost of her own pain entombed forever in this darkness? She trembled at that thought.

But if it wasn't *her* scream, that meant someone else was down here, and *they* were screaming. That thought made her shudder all the way to her bones. She already wore a skin of goose-flesh from the cold, but suddenly her goose pimples were sweating. The wall of yellow-tinted fog before her seemed as solid as the bricks on either side. Anna reached a trembling hand into the mist. The tips of her fingers disappeared behind its curtain.

"Hello?" She whispered. There was silence, as if the mist had consumed her voice completely. Then the fog twitched, something disturbed its even flow. Something moved nearby. Anna snatched her hand back. A distant, terrified voice whispered, "hello?" Another voice, farther away, sounding as if it were below her, "hello?" Then a third "ello?" Then a flurry of fainter and fainter "O?"s.

Only echoes. Only echoes. But she could not move. The fog and the bricks and her fear wound a tight cocoon. The mist drifted this way, slid that way, like a magician's sleight of hand, proving that it hid something by refusing to reveal it. She breathed through her open mouth, to be as quiet as possible, and strained her ears. So many little sounds, elusive noises. What waited for her in the fog?

Then, behind her in the drainage chamber, Sister Elizabeth opened the door. In Anna's stillness, the screech was as loud as a train whistle. She didn't jump or scream this time, but stiffened, arching her back into the top of the pipe. A draft moved through the tunnel, from behind Anna, sucking the mist away from her in a horizontal whirlwind. Sudden vertigo struck her. She felt as if she were falling head first into the pipe – a bottomless pit opening beneath her.

The most disconcerting discovery, as the fog dissipated, was that she *was* alone in the pipe. Nothing waited for her. Her miner's lamp illuminated only the red bricks and green slime.

Anna still trembled, now with relief, and felt near to fainting. She gulped air through her mouth and exhaled slowly through her nose, willing herself not to vomit.

Sister Elizabeth, she told herself, *nothing to fear here but the sister. Which means move, and quickly.* Anna wriggled forward, elbowing her way through small nests of seaweed and bits of driftwood. The pipe's slight downslope sped her progress.

"Anna!' Sister Elizabeth called into the pipe. "Anna, have you reached the iron grate?"

Her voice bounced back, from all sides, above and below. Again, Anna felt disoriented, she had a natural urge to turn toward the voice, but the pipe confined her. She opened her mouth to answer, but a fresh wave of echoes spiraled at her out of the darkness, "Anna?" overlapping "..ate" overlapping "…iron," in waves of copied words.

When the phantom words stilled, Anna answered, in a quiet voice, "I can't see it, but I see the blockage."

Sister Elizabeth grunted, then said, "You fill this cart by noon and you'll get lunch. Otherwise you get nothing. If you continue to dawdle, you'll spend the night down here," she paused to let the echoes die, then added, "and if it rains tonight, the devil may have you. Do you understand?"

"Yes, ma'am."

Sister Elizabeth said nothing more. Her heels clacked on stone as she walked out of the room. As soon as the door shrieked closed, the draft stopped, and the mist began to reassert itself. Anna had seen the blockage, but it was at the very edge of her vision. She determined to reach it before the fog completely blocked it from her view.

On her return trip, crawling backward, she would not be able to see where she was going regardless of light or fog. And that would be fine, she already knew what was behind her. But she was loath to grope blindly into the fog and unknown again.

Within a few minutes, Anna reached a tangled heap of brown kelp. The mass obstructed more than half the diameter of the pipe. She shoveled handfuls of the slick guck into her sack. The mist engulfed her again. Her effort drove the chill from her body, warmed her even, until steam rose off her skin. The mist no longer bothered Anna. She had seen a little way beyond this blockage to another pile of debris a few yards further down the pipe. Nothing lurked close enough to reach through the fog and touch her.

When she had filled her sack, she squirmed and wriggled and inched backward. It seemed like an eternity before she found a means of efficiently backing up a sloping, slippery pipe while dragging a fifty-pound sack of kelp.

The bell tolled ten o'clock as she dragged her sopping sack out of the pipe. A wooden cart waited for her in the drainage chamber. The kelp filled about a third of it. She had two hours to fill the rest. It should be enough time, but time wasn't the only factor. She had already rubbed the skin off her elbows. Her knees were hard with calluses, but she knew they would also be bloody by the end of the day.

Anna looked at her hands, gloved, and her feet, shoed. She quickly stripped the laces out of her shoes and after a few minutes of experimentation, fashioned her laces and gloves into a pair of elbow pads. *That will help*, she thought, *but what else?*

She looked longingly at the door. Either Sister Elizabeth had locked it, or she had intentionally left it unlocked to tempt her. Anna had no intention of trying it. If it had been left unlocked as a trap, she knew she would probably fall for it. The call of the Pacific was even stronger than her loathing for the pipe.

But, there was the peep window. Anna stuck her finger through the little bars in the window and slid the shutter open. *Why would you need a peep window into this room?* To check if the room was flooded, perhaps. *Could there be another reason? Sister Elizabeth made me enter the room first, even after checking the window.*

But Anna abandoned these thoughts as soon as she felt a draft wafting through the little window – a draft that would keep the tunnel clear of fog. She wedged a chunk of debris between the bars to hold it open. Then, taking a deep breath, she plunged back into the pipe.

Anna made three more trips down and back up the pipe without incident. She heaped debris into the cart until it could hold no more. Her impromptu elbow pads held up better than she had hoped and her knees were breaking down about as she had expected. The knees didn't bother her much, though, because she couldn't feel them. Her fingers, too, were numb with cold.

Noon came and went without an appearance from either Sister Elizabeth or lunch. Anna was disappointed but not surprised. The sisters always honored their promises, in their own way, *to the Lord a day is like a thousand years,* and such. Anna knew if she kept working, they would feed her eventually.

When lunch finally arrived, Anna was at the bottom of the pipe. The bell struck one as she shoveled driftwood and fish parts into her sack. Sounds traveled to her down the pipe, the familiar clatter of the door screeching open, an annoyed grunt, then the clank of a metal plate on the stone floor. She held her breath and listened. The door opened again, then slammed. There came a second, smaller slamming noise, the peep window being closed.

She had reached the iron grate, though the last clot of sea junk partially obscured it. Rust had diminished it to a net of lumpy wires, but they appeared to be intact. Her sack wasn't full, and if she filled it, she could nearly call the job done, but hunger was louder than logic. She scrambled out of the pipe, leaving her sack and trowel behind.

Lunch was toast and fish stew, the same as every lunch she had eaten over the past five years, except that today the stew was cold. She consumed it before she knew she had started, and downed the tin cup of water in a single guzzle. Not until it was gone did she realize how thirsty she had been, and still was.

There is plenty of water here, somewhere. This is where all the water comes from, but how do I get it?

On the far wall of the chamber, water glistened around the edges of the iron plate. It dripped from a slimy film of algae and rust that grew around the plate's seams. Rust streaked the lower half of the wall. It bore other marks as well, wear marks, grooves worn into the iron.

It's a drainage control gate for the cisterns, Anna thought, *a flush mechanism.*

A narrow gap ran along the top edge of the plate. Beyond the iron wall lay another chamber, a chamber full of fresh water.

Anna examined the lift chain and the huge gears of the apparatus. A locking lever and ratchet device held the plate in place. A vertical strip of iron teeth ran from floor to ceiling along one side of the plate. A wheel gear engaged these teeth and was in turn engaged by the ratchet lever.

Anna squeezed the ratchet catch and let the locking lever drop one notch. The plate slid down about an inch. She hooked her fingers over the top of the plate, stood on her tippy-toes and peered into the space beyond, a square channel receding into the darkness. Water rippled a few inches below the top edge of the iron plate. She returned to the lever and lowered the plate two clicks more. The gap widened enough for her to reach over and fill her cup.

The water tasted sweet, so sweet she filled and emptied her cup again, and again. The fourth time she dipped into the water, she heard, for the first time in hours, the echoes. She had tuned them out as she worked, but these echoes were clearer, closer even, and very disturbing.

She froze and listened. Myriads of ducts conveyed the noise of machinery and conversation from all quarters of the orphanage to this point. But the conversation she heard now seemed so much more distinct.

Anna wedged her foot into one of the cogs on a large gear wheel and pushed herself up until she could squeeze her head through the opening above the plate. Water filled the room beyond. Anna could not see how far back the cistern went, but she guessed it was vast. Her lamp light did not reach the far wall. Holes riddled the domed ceiling of this room, regular circle or square shaped holes. Many of them dripped water.

The walls of this room, *the cistern* Anna decided, angled outward away from the iron plate. A ledge, maybe eighteen inches wide, ran along the walls, just above the water. Small rectangular holes penetrated the walls just above this ledge. Discoloration surrounding the openings indicated that water often flowed into the cistern through them, though they were dry just now. After a moment, Anna understood. These were the downspouts. These pipes led to the roofs and gutters where rain collected.

And the voices, the echoes through these pipes, must be from someone speaking near one of those downspouts. *Someone on the roof?* But that didn't make sense. Then she remembered Sister Eustace's patio. A grand patio like that would have gutters. Suddenly she realized *if I'm hearing conversations from one of the patios, it must be either Abbess McCain, or one of her proprietresses.*

The voices rose and fell, distance and bizarre acoustics garbled the individual words, but the tone of the conversation was clear: ambition, conspiracy, treachery.

Anna's head was already through the opening and, as Jane frequently pointed out, her head was the thickest part of her. She worked her scrawny chest onto the top of the plate, walking her toes up the cogs of the gear. Then hoisted herself over the lip and slid out onto the narrow ledge.

Anna crept along the edge, worm crawling at first, then carefully, ever so carefully, rising to a hands-and-knees crawl. She put her ear to each of the downspout openings as she came to them. A fat white frog leapt out of the third pipe, squeaking loudly as it flew past her face.

Anna let out half a squeak of her own before clamping one hand over her mouth. The frog splashed into the black water and disappeared. Anna tottered on the ledge, almost falling in herself. Only by flopping flat on her belly did she managed to stay on the ledge.

For several seconds she, lay flat on the stone, her heart slamming against the inside of her ribcage. This is stupid, Anna, get back to where you belong, she thought, and she was right. But just then, voices started up again. Very close now. Intrigue permeated the conversation's tone. Secrets were being passed, big secrets, and Anna was so close. She scooted forward again, just a few feet, to the fourth pipe.

With her ear to the hole, Anna recognized Abbess McCain's voice at once. "Are your sure?"

"No, not entirely," said the second voice, one Anna did not know, "but her story lacks credibility."

"Yes, it does, and so does her *telling* of her story. Sister Dolores does not strike me as either strong-willed or incorrigible."

The other voice laughed. "I can't even call her devious, though she is trying to be such."

"Has she given any indication of her true purpose?" Abbess McCain asked.

"No, but I would speculate that she intends to smuggle someone off the island... Or, perhaps she is trying to make a name for herself as a reformer, a crusader against child labor."

"Hmmm..." McCain paused. Anna pictured her pacing the room, deep in thought. "Has she indicated special interest in any of the children, or any of the newer sisters who have been sent to us?"

The other voice didn't respond immediately, and in the pause, a new noise put Anna's heart in her throat. Sister Elizabeth's keys jangled outside the drainage room door.

Abbess McCain and the other voice may have continued speaking, but Anna heard none of it. Her muscles went as rigid and cold as icicles. She slapped the cover closed on her lamp. Thoughts blew through her mind like flakes in a blizzard.

Will she notice the iron plate is lowered?

No. I only moved it a few inches, and she is a dunce. All of my tools are at the bottom of the pipe. She will assume I'm there as well.

What if she calls to me? Will the echoes fool her?

Probably not.

Anna heard the key turn and the lock click.

If she calls to me, if I have to speak to her, she will know where I am.

And then what?

Only one answer came. *And then she will kill me. That is all.*

I could lie. I could tell her I finished cleaning the pipe and decided to clean in here…

But, that wouldn't work. *And then she will kill me.*

There would not be time for a single word of explanation, not with Sister Elizabeth.

The moment she sees that I am not where she put me, she'll beat me senseless and then drown me, right here in this room. She'll hold my head under water until my eyes roll up and my lips turn blue.

Anna knew exactly what a drowned child looked like. She had seen it before.

She thought of the echoes in the pipe, the ghosts of voices wandering through the dark, lost in the lightless catacombs forever. In the deep pool, she saw – with dreadful clarity – Sister Elizabeth thrusting her head under that black water. She felt the sister's sinewy fingers clutching her hair so she couldn't get away.

Will my ghost be trapped like those echoes?

What a lonely place to haunt.

The drainage chamber door screeched open.

Unless you kill her.

This new thought electrified Anna. *I can't…* But she knew she could. She saw it as clearly as she had seen Sister Elizabeth drowning her. The sister would call for her. Anna would not answer. Sister Elizabeth would shout down the pipe at her, probably throw a pebble down as well. While she was thus engaged, Anna would slip out of the cistern and fully release the ratchet lever. The iron plate would drop to the floor, thousands of gallons of rain would crash into the drainage chamber. Sister Elizabeth, with her head already in the pipe, would be washed away in the deluge, crammed and contorted down the length of the pipe and finally crushed against the grate.

Anna trembled all over with the vision. Adrenaline spiked as her terror gave way to a wild excitement she had never known. The welts on her face and forearms and thigh flared. The knuckle where her pinky should have been throbbed. The black void of grief inside her swelled, swallowing her heart and lungs and guts.

Part of her brain still screamed *I can't kill her.* But that was the little girl part, and Anna was done being a little girl. *I won't die like that. I can't stay here anymore.* It occurred to her that she might also be swept away, but that didn't seem to be of much consequence just now.

She crept to the edge of the gap, staying just out of view. Sister Elizabeth's shoes clacked across the wet floor. Anna waited.

And what will you do once you really are a murderer? The little girl voice asked.

She thought of the warehouse, the dock, and the boat. She thought of the Pacific.

You don't know how to drive a boat. But that didn't seem to be of much consequence, either.

"Anna!" Sister Elizabeth finally called, "Anna, haven't you finished yet?"

Anna poised at the gap.

Please don't, the little girl voice begged.

She visualized the sister bending down to peer into the pipe. The next sound would be the sister calling her name. *I will be swift as an adder.* She hoped the noise of her echoing name would cover any sound of her movement.

"Sister Elizabeth?" A child's voice called out of the drainage pipe. Anna gasped. The voice from the pipe continued, "Sister Elizabeth, I'm nearly finished."

"What is taking so long?" the sister called. "You ought to have been done an hour ago!"

Anna gaped around the inside of the cistern. She held a hand in front of her face and stared at it.

I am here. I am not in the pipe. She clapped the hand over her mouth and thought. *I am not speaking,* as the voice continued.

"There is a branch stuck in the grate, Sister Elizabeth. It's stuck real good, but I almost got it."

That's a boy's voice, Anna realized, *that's a boy's voice, but Sister Elizabeth is too dense to notice.*

"Well, I am much too busy to come checking up on you every ten minutes. If you want to miss dinner, that's just fine by me. I'm sending a troop of boys down to haul this mess out of here. If you are not finished by the time they arrive, you will spend the night in this hole."

"Oh, I'm quite sure I'll be done by then."

"Humph," Sister Elizabeth's shoes clacked away. The door screeched, and the bolts clicked into their holes.

Chapter 4

CURIOSITY HAD DRIVEN ANNA THROUGH the gap to eavesdrop on Abbess McCain. Curiosity had often overpowered her better judgment, and she wore the scars to prove it. But now, with her nerves as tight as piano wire, her wits as frayed as her old shawl, and every ounce of adrenaline spent, curiosity held no power over her.

None at all.

She had no interest in discovering whose voice had answered Sister Elizabeth from the pipe. If she went to her grave without ever knowing, that would be fine with her — so long as it wasn't today.

"I wouldn't really have done it," she said to her reflection in the dark water. Her face peered out of the pool at her. It seemed to float below the surface. In the sallow glow of her miner's lamp, her skin was sickly yellow, it alternately distended and shrunk with the slow ripples.

That's what you would have looked like after she drowned you, her mind replied. *Just like little Ephraim.*

Anna didn't say anything to that. She didn't think anymore, either. She reverted to the quasi-catatonic state that typified the little ones in her care. No questions, no forethought, no introspection, just do the next thing that must be done.

The next thing that must be done was simple. She slid through the gap into the drainage chamber, surprised to see that nothing had changed. Every aspect of the room stood exactly as she had left it. Though she had been in the cistern for mere minutes, Anna felt as if she hadn't been here, in the drainage chamber, for a very long time. Not since she was a little girl.

Memory came to her one bit at a time.

What must I do, now?

Retrieve the trowel and gunnysack.

Where are they?

At the end of the drainage pipe.

Is there a boy in the pipe?

I don't think so.

She bent to the pipe and crawled inside. The echoes and whispers and mist danced around her, but she didn't notice. Over and over in her mind, she saw Sister Elizabeth being crushed and dismembered by the torrent of water, saw her being propelled in a crumpled ball through the narrow pipe. It horrified her now. She was weak and sick with the dread of what she had nearly done. Her body ached in every joint, worse than she could remember ever aching. Her head pounded and her knees bled.

By the time she reached the grate, she was too spent to be startled. The blockage was gone. Her sack, which had been half-full, now lay flat and neatly folded beside her trowel. Anna tried to make sense of what she was seeing. Someone else had to be in the pipe. That was the only possible explanation, a young boy. How was it that neither she nor Sister Elizabeth had seen him?

"He must have come through the grate." Echoes of her whisper hissed through the pipe. "It must not be secure." A glimmer of hope re-ignited the life in her eyes. The mist had condensed heavy around her, and her lamp grew dim. She peered through the fog at the iron bars.

Can I open it and slip away? Could it be that easy?

Wrapping her fingers around the center bar, Anna heaved it forward. It didn't budge. She pulled it toward her with all her remaining strength, but only succeeded in dragging her body forward until her face pressed against the bars.

She coughed a short laugh, then dissolved in sobs, slumping flat against the curved and slimy bottom of the pipe. She lay there crying, weakly thumping the bars with one fist. The echoes rose and fell as the mist thickened.

Then, she heard the whisper.

"Stop that."

Anna snapped her head up so fast she dented her tin helmet on the top of the pipe.

"Stop crying." This whisper was not an echo, and it did not echo. It was crisp and close. Anna could almost feel the breath in her ear.

"Who is there?" she asked.

There was no response for so long Anna began to wonder if she had imagined it.

Then it came again. "You are Anna Dufrense, the little girl with the finger around her neck?"

The whisper was so close, but Anna could get no sense of the speaker, boy? girl? child or adult? She couldn't tell. "Yes…"

"Clever in your thoughts and stupid in your actions."

"Who are you? Where are you?" she asked.

"I'm where you want to be," it said, "outside."

Anna pressed her face against the grate, peering into the swirling fog.

"My name is Joseph, Anna, and I can help you, but you must listen carefully." The whisper now softened, sounding like the boy who had answered Sister Elizabeth. "If you come to me, I will keep you. I promise. Abbess McCain will never find you."

"How?" Anna pleaded, "How can I get out?"

"I left you something, Anna, under the trowel. Hide it in your shoe. Meet me in the factory, five nights hence, behind the main boiler, at ten o'clock."

Anna lifted the trowel. Beneath it lay a long black key. She reached for it gingerly, terrified that it would prove to be as insubstantial as the swirling mist. But when her fingers closed around it, it was cold, and heavy. She stared at it as if it were an enormous diamond or an ingot of gold rather than a simple iron key.

"And Anna," this was the clear, sweet boy voice she had heard earlier, no longer whispering, but further away, "be sure to bring your finger."

Anna looked up from the key. The glow of her dimming lamp seeped into the haze. Beyond the grate, something twinkled. *Eyeshine.* Two large yellow disks pierced the fog, floating in mid-air. Anna's breath caught in her throat. A second later, the eyes turned away and vanished.

Chapter 5

THE REST OF THE EVENING CONCLUDED without further incident. A herd of boys hauled two cartloads of sea junk from the drainage chamber and dumped them on the beach. Normally, Anna would have jealously envied the boys for being allowed outside, even for just a few minutes. This evening, her thoughts were too cluttered to even notice.

Once the boys had left the warehouse, Sister Elizabeth filled a large laundry vat with tepid water and ordered Anna to bathe before going to dinner. "You are filthy!" she exclaimed. "You smell like sewage and seaweed."

Anna tossed her sodden, soiled work dress and under garments into the potato sack. She bathed as quickly as possible and dressed in a clean but equally threadbare uniform.

At dinner, fish stew and toast, Jane teased her about the bright red welt on her cheek and the blood in her hair. She said it served Anna right for playing hooky at the factory. Anna wondered, absently, how she had gotten blood in her hair, but for the most part, she didn't hear much of what Jane said. Jane prattled on between bites of toast, goading her about her missing finger, taunting her about being Abbess McCain's favorite.

"The trowel," Anna interrupted.

"What?" Jane asked, happy to finally get some response from her.

"Sister Elizabeth threw a trowel at my head," Anna said. "That must be where the blood came from."

"I guess that would do it," Jane mused, "but I would have used a brick, considering the thickness of your skull."

Anna smiled, "Yes, you probably would have." She almost added, *I'm going to miss you*, but thought better of it. Jane continued heckling, and Anna, whose toes restlessly curled and uncurled around the key in her shoe, continued ignoring her.

After dinner, Anna walked down the back stairs and into the Great Round Room, struggling not to limp on the lump in her shoe. Her girls followed her through an oak door into the dormitory wing. A corridor stretched out before them, lined with doors on either side. Between the doors, ragged tapestries hung, depicting unicorns and dragons, martyrs in gruesome passion, saints with crooked heads, witches burning at stakes. A single bookcase stood lonely and forgotten half way up the hall.

The bookcase once held secret treasure, back when Anna was a little girl, back when Rebecca had been the head girl and both of them had ten fingers each. Now, only encyclopedias and massive theology tomes burdened its shelves, including several well-worn copies of Malleus Maleficarum. Rebecca had told Anna that Malleus Maleficarum was German for The Witch Hammer. She said it was pretty funny, but Anna refused to touch any of the proper books, just on general principle.

Anna looked back over her shoulder. Two long tapestries hung on either side of the door through which they had just walked. These tapestries covered the wall from the floor to the vaulted ceiling of the twenty-five foot high corridor. Between them, near the ceiling, a circular window opened into Abbess McCain's private office. The Abbess's silhouette darkened the stained glass, her arms folded, her keen eyes peering through the small bit of clear glass at the window's center.

One of the girls bumped into Anna. She realized she had stopped in the middle of the hall. Mary One and Mary Two each took one of

Anna's elbows and pulled her into their dormitory. Behind her, Lizzy whispered to Jane, "What's the matter with her, do you think?"

"That trowel must have knocked the sense out of her," Jane said, adding loudly, "not that she had much to begin with."

All the girls stared at Anna. She thought back over dinner, Jane's rhetorical onslaught had been much more intense than usual, and the girls had been staring at her then as well.

"What?" she asked, after Sister Eustace had counted the girls and locked the arched door behind them. "What is it? Have I grown a tail?"

The little ones giggled.

Jane said, "A tail would suit you, to go along with your pitchfork and horns."

More laughter mixed with gasps.

"Anna!" Lizzy said, "You haven't asked us about the quota!"

Anna looked around the room. The piles of gray blankets were gone. Her cot was bare, no blanket, no pillow, not even the waffle-thin mattress remained. *Laundry day*, she remembered. *Is it* still *laundry day?*

"Well," she asked, "did you make it?"

"We made it!" Lizzy threw her arms in the air. "We did have to, 'call out the reserves.'" She added, with a ridiculously overt wink. "But we made it, with two pairs to spare." She held two fingers out to Anna.

"Sister Eustace promised to run our radiators tonight," Jane said. "We'll see if it does any good."

The girls heaped all the straw into great nests around the two radiators. Anna put her smallest girls closest to the heat, then snuggled all the rest up to them. *We really do look like a litter of rats*, she thought as she curled around Lizzy.

The radiator banged, as if someone had hit it with a mallet. It hummed, then banged again. It hissed, then vibrated, then rattled. It banged five or six more times in quick succession, before settling in to a routine of random clanks and hisses. *That's going to keep me up all night. I just hope Mary Two doesn't pee herself again.*

37

Anna still wore her shoes, hoping they would keep her feet warm and fearing she would lose the key if she took them off. Her toes prodded and caressed the iron. She sank deeper into the straw as the girls nestled together. Her mind flashed the images of the day. Sister Elizabeth dashed to pieces in the pipe, swept away like the refuse in one of those new flushing toilets. Her own drowned face floating lifeless below the surface of the water. The face of her baby brother who drowned all those years ago. The black iron key lying on the burlap sack, hard and heavy and real. And the eyes. Those disembodied yellow disks hovering in the mist and darkness. Those eyes promising to take her away from here, promising to rescue her and protect her and care for her. Those eyes following her down into dreamless sleep, undisturbed by the radiator's racket or the squirming nest of rats.

Chapter 6

LIFE AT THE SAINT FRANCES de Chantal Orphan Asylum was a study in monotony and exhaustion. Days bled into weeks and weeks into months. The routine had become a horrible opiate, hypnotizing the little workers until thoughts were muddled, individual personalities were ground down and nothing was said or done or thought, except for 'the next thing that must be done.'

In this state, months had slipped away without Anna noticing. Seasons had come and gone and come again while she had no sense of their passage. But now, with the key wearing a blister on her sole and a hole in her sock, every hour felt like days. Every cruel word, every lash of the crop seemed an insufferable evil. The five days felt to her like a sentence far greater than the four more years she had been expecting to live in the Asylum.

During dinner, three days after Anna's encounter in the pipe, Lyla announced there had been a death on her hall. Lyla was one of the other head girls. She claimed to be Italian, but Anna had overheard Sister Eustace say that she was half Negro, "which is why they sent her to us rather than to one of the favored institutions. Her white mother is still alive, probably the father, too. But what would they have done with a *thing* like that?"

It didn't matter to Anna what Lyla was. In here, everyone was equally wretched.

"Amy caught cold on the night we had no blankets," Lyla explained. "There was never much to her to begin with, and she wasn't able to eat the next day. Then, she got the pneumonia, I guess, started coughing so much. When we woke this morning, she was gone."

Lyla told the story without emotion, as if she were reporting the number of shoes she had boxed and crated that day. Anna knew the inner distress she felt, and knew the danger of admitting sorrow in a place like this. She had lost more than one little girl in her care, and she had expected to lose more. Maybelle, the mute who had been added to her fold just a few days ago, probably wouldn't last the year. But Anna planned to be long gone before she lost another one.

"They buried her at sea while we were working today," Lyla continued. "She had always wanted to go on the boat. She wanted to see the ocean, again. I guess we all get to ride on that boat at least one more time."

"I saw the ocean," Anna said. "Sister Eustace has a balcony off of her office that overlooks it."

"We all saw the ocean, Anna, when we came here," Jane said.

"But I saw it just three days ago. It was beautiful," Anna said. "When I leave here…"

She stopped. The other girls looked at her with a mix of wonder and disgust. Every child in the building would have sold their soul to escape Saint Frances, but only the little ones, or the perpetually stupid, expressed a hope of ever leaving.

Jane bailed her out, but only after letting her fumble for words and come up short. "She has been behaving very oddly ever since Sister Elizabeth hit her in the head with a shovel."

Lyla nodded, still eyeing Anna. The other girls relaxed a bit.

"It was a trowel," Anna said. "I only meant to say that I would like to swim in the ocean someday."

Cheryl, a redheaded head girl with more pimples than Jane, and fewer teeth, choked on her fish stew. "Anna! That's horrible! Every child that ever died here has been dumped out there."

"Yeah," added Jane, "and all the sisters, too."

"Never mind," Anna mumbled. She spooned chunks of fish out of the thin broth.

"Just think of all those bodies bobbing around down there," Cheryl said.

"Cheryl, please!" Lyla said, her eyes glistening with moisture. "When they go into the water, the Lord takes them," Lyla insisted.

"My parents were buried at sea," Ester, the oldest of the head girls, said, "and the Lord took them. And that is all we will hear of that."

The girls fell silent. Anna wondered if the Lord had taken her baby brother when he went into the water. She thought it was probably different with bathtubs. Would the Lord have taken Sister Elizabeth if Anna had flushed her down the drainage pipe? Would He have taken Anna? She felt the key pressing against the bottom of her foot and decided that didn't matter anymore.

***

The following morning at breakfast, the new sister was among the nuns serving the meal. Anna startled, suddenly remembering Sister Dolores, the spy. So much had happened down in the cisterns, Anna had completely forgotten the conversation she had overheard. *The conversation that almost killed me*, she thought. *The conversation that almost made me a killer.* But, here was Sister Dolores now, who was not what she claimed or appeared to be.

Sister Dolores had the look of a dog who had been beaten its whole life, yet still yearned to please its master. She hopped eagerly to the demands or requests of the other sisters and forced a smile in reply to every comment. As Anna watched her, however, Sister Dolores looked up from the cauldron of porridge she was stirring and locked eyes with Anna. A true smile spread easily and warmly across the sister's narrow lips. Anna felt a sudden embarrassment for staring, as well as some deeper uneasiness.

Sister Dolores straightened her back, still smiling at Anna. She reached into her habit and very deliberately fingered her crucifix. Anna copied her gesture, coming up with her mummified pinky rather than a silver cross. Sister Dolores's smile twisted just a little, taking on a knowing, satisfied appearance. She casually looked away from Anna, back to the cauldron, reacquiring her subservient posture.

She is a spy! What did they think was her purpose here? Did they know? Anna couldn't remember, except that she may have come to rescue someone. Obviously, Sister Dolores knew something about Anna. *Is she here to rescue me? How would she even know me?* Anna couldn't begin to imagine.

"Anna!" Jane snapped.

Anna looked up to see all five of the other head girls staring at her. She glanced around, confused.

"Put that thing away," Jane said. "What has gotten into you?"

Anna was still holding her finger. She stuffed it back into her dress, then bent over her porridge and did not look up again. She spooned the sludge into her mouth and thought about Sister Dolores, the spy.

I have to warn her.

No, stay out of it.

If she is here to rescue me, and they catch her...

You don't need her help, you have the key.

That's right, I am leaving tonight, I can risk warning her. Abbess McCain won't find out until after I am gone.

If you warn her, she will want to know how you found out. If you tell her, she might turn you in.

But if I don't warn her... What if she was the one who left the key?

How could she have done that?

How could anybody? But if she is the one helping me escape, and she gets caught...

The whistle blew, signaling the end of breakfast. Anna surveyed the hall. Hundreds of children shuffled into rows. The racket and clatter of feet and benches and tin utensils filled the vaulted chamber. Most of the sisters collected in the kitchen behind the stone archways separating it from the hall. Sister Dolores dragged a mop bucket across the floor toward the hall's exit.

Anna grabbed Lizzy's sleeve and whispered, "You take the girls to the factory, Lizzy, I'll be right behind you. "

"Anna, no," Lizzy whispered.

"Do it, Lizzy. I promise I will be there in no time." Anna darted off before Lizzy could protest further.

She hurried along the wall, as inconspicuously as possible, toward Sister Dolores. The nun mopped around a section of floor near the corner. She was out of view of the rest of the nuns. Anna had never seen the sisters mop the dining hall. But, then again, she had never lingered in the hall after the whistle.

The key in Anna's shoe had worn the skin away in two places, and she couldn't completely hide her limp as she scurried toward Sister Dolores. When she was close enough to whisper, the nun looked up from her mopping. She looked first puzzled, then annoyed.

"Why aren't you at the factory?" She demanded.

Suddenly, Anna decided this was a bad idea, a very bad idea. She turned for the door.

"Wait a minute. You stand right there. I asked you a question," Sister Dolores said. "Why did you not go to the factory with the other children?"

Anna tried to speak but couldn't think of any words, at least not any words for Sister Dolores. For herself she thought, *stupid, stupid, stupid*…

"You came to tell me something," Sister Dolores said. "What is it?"

Anna's mouth bobbed open and closed like a clubbed salmon. She halfheartedly pointed toward the door. Finally, a thought came to her, from Jane, of all people. *Tell her you get really confused ever since Sister Elizabeth hit you in the head.* She said, "I get…" and abruptly stopped.

Sister Dolores's dull blue irises blurred and suddenly turned black. They faded to purple, then faded back to dull blue. "Tell me the truth."

Without the slightest intention of doing so, Anna said, "Abbess McCain knows you are a spy!" She clapped her hand over her mouth.

"Who told you that?" Sister Dolores whispered, glancing quickly around the hall.

"I..." Anna surveyed the empty room, then studied Sister Dolores's eyes. "I overheard Abbess McCain talking with another sister. I don't know which one. Are you a spy? Are you here to rescue us?" Anna asked, blushing to the roots of her hair.

"Rescue you? Rescue you from what?" She sounded stern, but there was also something playful in her tone.

"Sister Dolores!" Sister Eustace's voice boomed through the dining hall. "What are you doing?"

Sister Dolores's posture slumped back to a cringe.

"Oh, and look here, it's Anna, who wears her shame like a medal!" Sister Eustace continued. "Why are you not at the factory?"

Anna's blush went paper white as she took up her mantra, *stupid, stupid, stupid...*

"Oh, Ma'am," Sister Dolores said, "Anna was only asking if she could have a bandage. Something seems to be wrong with her foot."

Anna's eyes popped and her heart sank. Sister Eustace looked at Anna's shoe. Anna shot a pleading look at the younger nun. Mischief twinkled in Sister Dolores's eyes and the corners of her lips raised. But before Sister Eustace returned her eyes to Sister Dolores, the young nun's face fell back into its desperately eager and subservient mask.

"A bandage? Why would she be asking *you* for a bandage? Are you a nurse, Dolores? Is this the infirmary?"

"No... no, ma'am," Sister Dolores said. "This is the..."

"*I* know this is the dining hall!" Sister Eustace yelled. "Why would this pest, ask *you*, for a bandage?"

"Ma'am, it is for her foot."

"But why *you?*" she demanded, bellowing into Sister Dolores's face. Sister Dolores stared into her eyes, petrified.

"I'll tell you why. This little wretch is playing you for a fool. She thinks you are weak. And do you know why she thinks you are weak? She thinks you are weak because you let her think so. I told you what kind of refuse we house here. These children will walk all over you with their lies and their scams. Worse than niggers and gypsies, all of them! Do not be taken in by her sniveling and her pitiful eyes. I don't know *what* she's up to, but I do know it's no good! If she truly needed a bandage she would have asked *me,* or she would have gone to the infirmary. Are you listening to me, Sister Dolores?"

"Yes, ma'am."

"Where is your crop?"

Sister Dolores drew the leather crop from her habit.

"Have you used it yet?"

"No, ma'am."

"Well then, allow me to show you how it's done." Sister Eustace seized Sister Dolores's left wrist. With the other hand, she snatched the crop, raised it over her head and lashed Sister Dolores's knuckles. She struck so violently that Anna thought the crop would snap in half. Sister Dolores uttered a sobbing gasp. Her knees buckled and her eyes instantly filled with tears.

"Stand up," Sister Eustace spat, "Now, you *know* that I am not weak, don't you?"

"Yes, ma'am," Sister Dolores said in a quavering voice. Sister Eustace held her wrist so tightly that the skin of Sister Dolores's hand had turned white. A red and bright-purple ridge swelled diagonally across the back of Sister Dolores's hand.

"You know that you cannot play *me* for a fool."

"Yes, ma'am," Sister Dolores said, with a little more composure.

"Very good." Sister Eustace smiled warmly and handed the crop back to Sister Dolores. "Now, you teach little Miss Anna the lesson I just taught you."

The servility and pain in Sister Dolores's eyes turned to cruel glee as she shifted her gaze to Anna. She rubbed the leather against her palm, smiled at it, even seemed to be whispering to it.

"Three lashes, Sister Dolores, one for lying about her foot, one for thinking you are a fool. And one for the pain she has caused you," Sister Eustace said. "Anna, hold out your hand."

Anna stretched her hand out. It tingled already in anticipation of pain. *Just focus on my hand and my lies and all my other little sins and forget about my shoe.* She thought, desperately. *I'm a wicked little girl and I don't deserve a bandage. I didn't even ask for a bandage. Lash my knuckles all you want, take another finger if you must, but leave my shoe alone.* She saw the hideous stripe across Sister Dolores's hand and whimpered. She closed her eyes, and her thoughts changed, *this is the last time, this is the last time, this is the last time…*

Sister Dolores's pale, bony fingers curled around her wrist. Anna heard the whistle of the crop slicing through the air, and then a crack like a pistol shot. Her eyes flew open and she gawked at her knuckles with a terror of unbelief. A red welt rose there, but she felt nothing, not the slightest sting. The crop fell again with a gut wrenching snap. And again, no pain accompanied the blow. Anna stared wide-eyed and open-mouthed at Sister Dolores. As the third painless blow echoed through the dining hall, Anna's knees gave out and she flopped to a cross-legged seat on the floor.

Sister Eustace laughed out loud. "My, my, sister, I don't believe I've seen little Anna so surprised in many years." She laughed a bit more then added, "I doubt she will mistake you for weak again."

"No, I don't suppose she will," Sister Dolores mused, watching Anna. The mischief twinkled again in her eyes and, when Sister Eustace turned to walk away, she winked at Anna. "But, I really think you ought to have a look at her foot, ma'am, just to be safe. If it gets infected…"

"Sister Dolores! The last thing in this creation I wish to see is that girl's infected foot," Sister Eustace said without turning. "Especially so soon after eating."

"Yes, ma'am," Sister Dolores called after her.

"March her straight down to the factory, Sister Dolores, and if she asks you for anything, lay a lash across her lips," she said as she strode out of the dining hall.

When they were alone again, Anna looked up at Sister Dolores and marveled, "You're a witch?"

Sister Dolores's eyes changed, her pallid skin darkened to a healthy bronze and her mouse-colored hair turned jet black. "I dabble," she said, smiling.

"You're not a nun, then?" Anna whispered.

"Never was." Sister Dolores's features melted back into their former state.

Anna thought she should be terrified of the witch, but could not summon her fear. Wonder and confusion crowded it out.

"Sister Eustace tells me that you killed your baby brother," Sister Dolores said, "that you drowned him in a bathtub. Is that true?"

"I don't know. I don't remember."

"Hmm. I have to kill my baby brother, and I don't know if I can do it. I was hoping you could advise me."

Confusion and wonder still filled Anna, but the fear finally forced its way through. "I need to go to the factory, ma'am." She pushed herself to her feet with her back against the wall.

"Anna," Sister Dolores placed herself between Anna and her exit, "you know my secret and I," she tapped Anna's shoe with her own, "know yours. Can I trust you to keep my secret?"

"Yes, ma'am."

"Pinky swear?" Sister Dolores held out the little finger of her left hand.

Anna blushed again, hesitantly raising, lowering, then raising again her pinkyless left hand.

Sister Dolores giggled, "Oh, sorry, I forgot."

Anna looked toward the door. The dining hall and the corridor beyond were empty of both person and sound.

"Anna," Sister Dolores said, "I do thank you for telling me. That was a brave and noble act. This house may become a very dangerous place in the next few days. I am not here to rescue anyone, but I will remember what you did, and may repay the favor if a chance presents itself."

The next few days here meant nothing to Anna. She would be long gone by sunrise. Joseph had told her so. "May I go?" Anna asked, "to the factory?"

"Go," Sister Dolores said.

Chapter 7

ANNA ZOMBIED THROUGH THE HOURS of factory work, cutting, stamping, stacking leather soles. The sisters overseeing her conspicuously ignored her worsening limp. Apparently, Sister Eustace had informed her staff of Anna's attempt to fake a foot injury. That was fine by Anna. She had expected to be giddy, restless. The phrase *last day of school* kept coming to her. She had feared her excitement would arouse suspicion, but as it was, she felt too exhausted, too overwhelmed, too uncertain to be giddy.

She had just warned a witch spy that the sadistic nuns were on to her. The witch had to be evil, because she was here to kill her own brother. And she was a witch, which made her evil by default. Now the evil witch had become her... her what? Not her friend, but maybe her ally.

Would that make Anna complicit in the murder of the witch's brother? And what about all the children the sadistic sisters had worked to death? Or neglected to death? If the witch was here to kill Abbess McCain or Sister Eustace, that would be just fine, but she was here for one of the children.

Then a new thought occurred to Anna. *If I leave, who will take care of my girls?* Sister Dolores said that danger approached, who would protect Lilly and the Marys? Her meaner half laughed. *I can't protect them, I can't protect myself.* She looked at the knuckle where her pinky belonged. *I can't protect Sister Dolores's baby brother, whoever he may be. The one person I did protect turned out to be an evil witch.*

She considered her right hand. It should have been throbbing and useless but proved to be whole and unharmed. Anna wondered if being an evil witch was such a bad thing.

Variations of these thoughts occupied her mind from the time she entered the factory until she returned to the dining hall that evening. She caught herself either giggling or weeping or both at random intervals throughout the day.

At dinner, the other head girls whispered about her, but no one spoke to her. Her fears of arousing suspicion seemed silly. If she had gone stark raving mad, no one would have cared. None of the sisters would have shown the slightest interest, as long as she met quota and got her girls out of bed on time.

At nine o'clock, Anna lay on her back, waiting. The giddiness finally came, in waves alternating with dread. The little ones snored little snores. Jane gibbered in her sleep. Anna waited. Wondering what would happen if her collaborator didn't show up. Wondering where they would go from the factory.

Why the factory?
Why not the loading dock?
Or the back entrance to the kitchen?
Where will I sleep tomorrow night?
Will I even be alive tomorrow night?

The bell, in its lonely tower, struck nine thirty. Anna rose. She slipped her pinky out from beneath her pillow and hung it around her neck. Abbess McCain had ordered her to wear it at all times, as a reminder of her sins, but that wasn't why she wore it now. She was going, and she had no intention of leaving a single piece of herself behind.

Anna slipped into her work dress and shawl. For the first time in five days, she pulled her shoes off, hoping to move silently in bare feet. Carrying her shoes and the key, she crept to the old door and leaned her ear against it. Nothing stirred.

She knelt down and peered through the key hole. Across the hall, on a maroon tinted tapestry, a woman martyr writhed in agony of fire. In the corridor, few candles flickered and no one waited.

Anna slid the key into its hole, wincing at the barely audible scraping sound. As she turned it, ever so slowly, she realized that she had never considered the possibility the key might not fit. It would have been a wasted worry. The lock clicked open with no resistance.

"What are you doing?" A high-pitched whisper, so close the lips must have been touching her shoulder.

Anna spun around, choking her scream. Mary Two stood behind her, holding her blanket up to her chin. Straw clung to her hair, smaller bits stuck to the snot trail under her nose.

"Mary!" Anna struggled to keep her voice at the level of a whisper, "go back to bed. This instant."

"You aren't s'posed to be doing that."

"Quiet, Mary, go back to bed." Then she added, "I *am* supposed to be doing this. It's head girl duties."

"Lizzy said we need to keep an eye on you 'cause if you go loopy Sister Eustace won't feed us anymore."

"She...What? No, Mary, you must be quiet," Anna whispered, her nerves jangling like Sister Eustace's key ring. "Lay down now and hush up!"

Mary backed away from her, looking toward the pile of straw. "Lizzy..." Her tentative voice rose, no longer a whisper but not quite the volume of normal speech. She would be yelling soon.

Anna rushed her, clamping her hand over the little girl's mouth. They tumbled together into the straw. Mary tried to thrash free, but Anna wrapped one arm around both of Mary's and used the weight of her body to hold the girl still. Her right hand, over Mary's mouth, pushed her head into the straw. Anna pinched Mary's nose shut with her thumb and forefinger. The panic in the younger girl's eyes burned as bright and feverish as it did in Anna's.

Anna pushed her face to Mary's until their noses touched. She could feel Mary sucking against her palm, desperate for a breath, but Anna held her fast, glaring into her eyes. *You have to be quiet,* screamed through her head. It took all Anna's will not to scream it out loud. Her body trembled all over. She felt the girl under her kicking the straw, felt her chest spasm and hitch for air.

The unlocked door floated open on its silent hinges. Candlelight spilled across Mary's face, revealing her black, terrified eyes and her bluing skin. Anna's own drowned face from the cistern flashed into her mind, and her brother's. Tears burst into Anna's eyes. She released Mary's nose and mouth, wrapping that hand around Mary's head, hugging her to herself.

"I'm sorry, Mary!" She wailed in a strained whisper, kissing her forehead repeatedly.

Mary gulped air in harsh, sobbing gasps. Around them, girls mumbled and murmured, turning in the straw.

"I'm so sorry, Mary, I didn't mean it." Her eyes streamed. "I swear, I didn't mean it." Anna dropped the little girl into the straw and sprinted for the door.

She plunged into the corridor without the key or her shoes. Mary's weeping drifted out behind her, chased her into the hall. It was too late now. Too late to turn back, too late for stealth, too late for a clean get away. She had no plan. She had no clever ideas. She had only one thought, but that thought filled her mind, *behind the boiler at ten o'clock.*

Her bare feet slapped the stone floor as she dashed toward the Great Round Room. Tapestries fluttered on either side, giving life to long dead saints and devils. The cyclopean eye of Abbess McCain's office was dark, no stern silhouette watched from above.

Anna sprinted for the thick shadows surrounding the rotunda's door. Just as she reached them, a stout figure stepped from the gloom. Sister Eustace loomed two feet in front of her. Anna had no time to stop. She plowed straight into the old nun's bulk.

It was like running into a padded tree. Anna bounced back and sat with a thud on the flagstones. She gaped up at Sister Eustace, as powerless to breathe as Mary had been. It felt as if the nun had taken hold of her windpipe and was crushing it. Nothing ran through Anna's head now but a white-hot scream.

Towering over Anna, Sister Eustace appeared to shake with rage. She uttered odd sounds, tinkling sounds like a wind chime. As the blizzard of terror in Anna's mind settled into glittering drifts, she realized it wasn't anger that shook Sister Eustace, it was laughter, a wispy, stifled giggling. The red patches on her cheeks were not from rage but high merriment.

As Anna realized this, Sister Eustace's features changed. Her hair darkened, her skin bronzed. Her form melted away like a candle in a furnace, condensing into the younger, thinner Sister Dolores. She quickly covered her lips with one finger, giggling through it.

Anna slumped sideways and vomited fish stew across the floor.

"Who do you think is going to have to clean that up?" Sister Dolores asked in a laughing whisper. She hooked a hand under Anna's arm and lifted her to her feet. "Come now, Anna, I'm just having a little fun with you. No need for all this excitement."

Anna's legs felt like noodles and her stomach like water. The corridor swayed back and forth as if adrift on the waves.

"Sister Dolores," Anna said in a vacant voice. "What are you doing here?"

"I'm looking for my brother. Have you seen him?"

"I don't think so…"

"What are *you* doing here?"

"I'd rather not say."

"I'm sure not," she chuckled. "But you may want these." Sister Dolores handed Anna her shoes and the key.

Anna stared wide-eyed and wondering.

"Would you also like me to tuck your little ones in and close the door to your hall? Perhaps I should look out for them and keep them from trouble while you're away?"

"Yes, ma'am," Anna stammered.

"Very well, then. You better be off to…" she waved her hand in the air, "…to wherever it is you are going. But may I ask of you one favor?"

"Anything, ma'am."

"If you do see my little brother, Joey, don't tell him I'm looking for him." Sister Dolores walked toward Anna's dormitory, shifting back into her Sister Eustace disguise. "Thanks, dear."

Chapter 8

ANNA BARELY RECOGNIZED THE FACTORY. It was quiet and still and dark. She was a tiny speck of life in its vast and cavernous vault. Far up near the ceiling, the windows were nothing but black rectangles silhouetted against a blacker background.

There was no moon tonight. No candles glimmered here, either. Only the boiler illuminated this space. Its red glow radiated across the floor and fanned upward, highlighting or darkening the paths and obstacles according to its own unreliable intentions.

The machines, great iron and copper beasts, hovered around her. They stood as mechanical behemoths, bodies without animation. Their stillness accentuated her isolation. In the daytime, these brutal engines had taken fingers, crushed limbs, had even eaten whole children. In the daytime, they roared and hissed, they shook and churned. Now, they watched in silence. Anna felt their eyes, and their hunger.

She knew she must hurry, but felt it somehow unwise to run past the sleeping machines. She did not want them to see her fear. To her right stood a machine that stamp-cut patterns from sheets of leather. Last year, Samuel Upton was loading the cutter when his sleeve snagged on the conveyor belt. Anna could still hear his screams as the conveyor pulled him into its maw, and her own screams when the belt dumped what was left of him into a bin on the far side.

Anna hurried past in a stiff walk. A pair of stitching machines loomed to her left. Their frenzies of needles had sampled the finger blood of every girl Anna knew. She wore several needle scars of her own. Two girls, a Beatrice that Anna did not know and a Sally she did know, had both lost lower arms due to infection from the stitchers' bites. The needles now glimmered in the red ember glow of the boiler.

She reached the boiler just as the bell struck the first note of ten. The boiler stood as the god of the steam engines, floor to ceiling, fat as a Buddha, complex and baffling, austere. Heat and hell-colored light radiated from an open grill in its lower front panel. As Anna approached, she saw a small alcove cut into the wall behind the boiler. No light reached that space and she wished she had brought a candle. The bell continued to toll.

"Hello?" she said. "Hello, are you here?"

"Shhhh," came the reply, then the whisper, "Come back here."

Anna looked over her shoulder. The doors back to her hall were miles away, through thick darkness and a forest of steam powered killing machines. Whatever waited beyond the boiler must be better than staying here, better than having her body and mind gnawed down to a raw stump. *Like Jeffery's leg*, she thought.

Jeffery had been one of the head boys, one of the *cute* head boys. He had been trying to clear a jam in the coal pulverizer that fed this boiler. He had kicked the jam loose, but he had kicked a bit too hard. With the blockage cleared, the pulverizer sprung to life again and pulverized his leg. He didn't scream, he just turned white, then chuckled. Anna remembered that chuckle, it was far worse than Samuel Upton's screams. Jeffery was alive when they carried him out of the factory, but Anna never saw him again.

She slipped into the alcove behind the boiler. No one waited there.

"Where are you?"

"I'm down below," the whisper hissed through the broken end of a pipe. "I will tell you how to find me but you must listen carefully, act quickly and ask no questions."

"Tell me what to do."

"There is no way out of The Saint Frances de Chantal Orphan Asylum unless someone lets you out," the voice said. "The key will do nothing for you now. This house was built to be a fortress, and so it is. It has only four entrances and the sisters guard them all. All except the kitchen, but that one has a bell on it, and it is just outside the sister's quarters. You must lure the sisters away."

"Why are they so intent on keeping us here?"

"Oh," purred the whisper, "they don't post a guard on your account. But, I said no questions, time is short. Come to me and you will know everything." The whisper softened. Anna heard in it the voice of the child who spoke to her in the cisterns. "First, on the side of the boiler, there is a crank. Do you see it?"

"Yes."

"Turn it clockwise until it stops."

As Anna turned the crank, she heard coal sliding down a chute into the belly of the boiler.

"Now, there are a series of levers attached to pipes on the opposite side. Some are opened, some are closed. Close them all."

Anna worked her way around the boiler. Its glow darkened with the new influx of coal. She found the levers and closed each of them.

"Just above those levers there is a pressure gauge. Beside it are two copper devices, a valve and a whistle. Do you see them?"

"Yes."

"Smash them flat. I left a mallet for you on the floor, near your feet."

The mallet was heavy. With one stroke, Anna flattened the valve and bent the whistle. With a second stroke, the whistle ceased to be. The boiler groaned. It shuddered as if Anna's pounding had awakened it. She stepped away, suddenly afraid of what she had done.

"I'm not so sure that was a good idea," she said.

"It is a terrible idea. But this is a terrible place. Now listen close and speak no more. Let my words burn into your memory. If you miss one thing, you will be caught, and if you are caught, they will kill you. Listen and remember. We will not speak again until you are free."

Chapter 9

"THIS WILL COST ME ANOTHER finger if your plan doesn't work," Anna whispered into the dark room.

It'll cost you a lot more than that, her other voice said. *If you fail, they will kill you. That's the only thing Joseph told you that you know to be true.*

She found an odd sort of freedom in that thought. *Once they've killed me, there's nothing more they can do. Nothing is off limits now. There is an upper limit on punishment, but the potential for wickedness is infinite.*

Anna had fled the factory after hearing Joseph's instructions. The boiler moaned and growled, its red glow brightening to orange. The stitchers, with their needle teeth, hissed at her as she ran past.

At this hour, the back stairs between the factory and the dining hall had been deserted. Anna slipped through the dining hall and into the kitchen undetected. Joseph had told her to wait here until she heard the signal. *Rest, sleep if you can. Even if you sleep deeply, you will hear the signal. When you hear it, run for the kitchen door. It will be open for you.*

She found the kitchen door. It was nestled deep into a recess in the stone wall. A heavy oak beam barred it, padlocked into iron brackets on either side. Another padlock attached a spring to the door. The spring was fastened to a cable that disappeared into a small hole above the frame.

That cable goes to the bell in the sister's living quarters, she thought.

A round window opened near the door's top. Anna had to stand on tiptoe to see out the small pane. Beyond this door, wide wooden stairs descended to the loading dock. The little steamer bobbed alongside the dock, its lights turned down.

Anna sighed and turned back to the kitchen, hugging herself. Her breath floated in the air before her face. *I'll be needing a coat*, she thought, *if I am to be outside all night. And food.*

Two coats hung by the door, oiled lambskin on the outside, fleecy wool on the inside. Both were too big for her. Anna pulled the smaller of the two from its hook and slipped into it. *I've been swallowed by an inside-out sheep.* It was something Lizzy would have said, and Anna felt an urge to scold the precocious girl. *Well, at least it will keep you warm and dry.*

The kitchen was too big, too open. Anna knew she could not rest here, much less sleep. She surveyed the room a second time and found what she needed. Beyond a long butcher-block counter, a pair of plain doors opened into the pantry.

Anna tiptoed around the counter and crept inside. It was a closet sized space that smelled of coffee and yeast and potatoes. A few loaves of leftover bread filled one shelf. Canned fish lined most of the other shelves. The pantry floor was devoted to sacks of potatoes.

Anna discovered that her inside-out sheep had very deep pockets. She crammed a loaf of bread into one of these. The other she filled with potatoes. Having secured her provisions, she huddled under a pile of empty burlap sacks, listening, thinking, waiting for the signal.

He said it would be loud. If I hear it, won't the sisters hear as well? Will they all be lured away from the exits?

Not exits, Anna, that other voice said, *he didn't say exits, he said* entrances.

But what does that matter? As long as I get out. How does he know they will all be lured away? Will they all need to go check the boiler? That doesn't make sense.

Anna wrangled these thoughts, puzzled over them, all the while listening intently to the sounds in the old stones. She worried that she would miss the signal if she slept, but Joseph told her to sleep if she could. She burrowed deeper into the empty potato sacks and closed her eyes.

You know what you've done, Anna, you are not a little girl anymore, her other voice said.

But she didn't listen. *What does it matter now, as long as I get out.*

She hugged herself and worried and rocked and slept.

***

Anna woke to someone calling her name. It took only a minute for her to remember where she was. The smell of fish and bread and potato dirt filled her nose. She lay still as death and listened. The old stones groaned. They seemed to pulse with anticipation. Pipes overhead vibrated and thrummed.

Then her name again. "Anna Dufresne! Show yourself!"

Not in the kitchen, but close. One of the sisters.

Anna didn't know which, and she didn't care. If one knew she was out, they all knew. A cold sweat broke on her neck and arms. She curled into a ball, trembling, feeling as if she had been punched in the stomach. *I couldn't have missed the signal,* she insisted. *I couldn't have.*

The bell tolled. Anna held her breath. It struck twice, then stilled.

Two in the morning. I've been asleep almost four hours. She stared, wide-eyed, at the dark underside of a potato sack. Her mind groped desperately for a plan or an idea.

What had Joseph *said? Wait for the signal. When I hear the signal, the kitchen door will be open for me. What signal? Is the door open now?*

If I slept through the signal, it should be.

She slipped out from under the burlap and gingerly pushed the pantry door ajar. Through the crack, she could see the recess that housed the kitchen door, but it was shrouded in shadow.

Anna crawled out of the pantry on hands and knees. Her lambskin coat, heavy with stolen food, dragged along the floor under her. Keeping the butcher-block island between herself and the dining hall, Anna worked her way toward the door.

The kitchen brightened a bit, light seeped in from somewhere. Anna could make out the frame of the door, its bar, its locks, its bell wire. Whether she had slept through the signal or not, the kitchen door was still closed, bolted, locked and alarmed.

Then, the dining hall door burst open. Light flooded the kitchen. Anna froze. The long counter stood between her and the dining hall. Whichever sister had entered the kitchen couldn't see Anna yet, but she surely would as soon as she rounded the counter.

"Anna," it was Sister Elizabeth, "if you are in here, you had better show yourself. Right now."

Anna slid to the counter and pressed her back against it. She looked left and then right, searching for anything that might save her. Then she looked straight ahead. Her lungs locked up. The pantry door still stood ajar.

Sister Elizabeth saw it too. "Aha!"

But, that was all she said. At that moment, the floor rose. A slow, powerful heaving of the stones lifted Anna. Sister Elizabeth shrieked, and apparently dropped her candle. Darkness swallowed the kitchen once more.

A noise like nothing Anna had ever heard enveloped her, a deafening, grinding roar. Thunder crushed Anna's eardrums, as if the sound had fingers, and was pushing those fingers into her ears. It came from everywhere. It was inside her, vibrating her organs, rattling her brain. Jittering her teeth. The rising floor wobbled, rippled. Seams popped open between the floor's stones.

Hell colored light, like she had seen in the boiler, bloomed in the windows. Everything in the kitchen suddenly moved, rotated. Only two colors existed, black and orange. Shadows spread outward, drifting in graceful arcs, painted by the fireball erupting into the night sky.

And still the roar escalated. A burning filled Anna's throat. She realized she was screaming. A saucepan bounced off her left shoulder. A heavy skillet hit the floor by her hand. Ladles and kettles and pots rained down around her from the counter top and overhead racks. Any sounds they may have made were swallowed by the terrible pounding thunder.

Potatoes and onions spilled out of the pantry, rolling and wobbling across the floor like drunken marbles. Terrified rats scurried among them, darting this way and that.

The floor stopped rising, ratcheting to a halt, then suddenly dropped. Anna dug at the floor with her fingertips, pressing her face into it. It fell nearly two feet, rippling and rolling like a wave, before settling.

The roar began to subside, taking on a crackling, splintering texture, like an enormous tree toppling. Other noises surfaced in the receding tide of sound. Clashing, jangling, clattering. Beams snapping, doors slamming. The bell, high in its great tower, bonged and clanged and reverberated. And screams. Someone screaming very close to her.

Anna remembered Sister Elizabeth and clapped her hands over her own mouth. The screaming continued. Anna peeped around the counter. Sister Elizabeth lay writhing and shrieking, pinned beneath a fallen oak beam. Anna decided she was thrashing about too much to be seriously injured, but had no interest in finding out for sure.

She turned toward her exit. The door hung ajar, its frame sprung, its oak bar snapped in two. *That was the signal, stupid. Run!*

Chapter 10

ANNA SPRINTED INTO THE NIGHT. She flew through the kitchen door and plummeted into darkness. Her feet continued running, they continued striking the wooden stairs as they ran, but it felt as if she were tumbling into a bottomless abyss. She had been confined within those walls for five years, never once allowed outside. Now, Saint Frances was exploding behind her, the surf of the Pacific crashed just ahead, and a limitless universe of stars spiraled into infinity above. She was free, and it terrified her.

As she ran, the stairs became a boardwalk became a dock, stretching out into the churning Pacific. Anna, dizzy and overwhelmed, trying to see everything at once, failed see how close she was to the edge. Just before the line where sea met shore, she ran right off the side of the dock, dropping, with a muffled thud, onto the soft sand.

She rolled twice, coming to rest alongside a beached rowboat. Overhead, the empty void of night twinkled at her. Stars spun slowly. Anna lay on her back gasping cold salt air until they stilled.

When her breathing slowed and her vertigo calmed, she sat up, facing the sea. Glassy black breakers rolling shoreward reflected the inferno behind her. Blood-red caps of foam rode these waves as they crested.

A high-pitched whining, like steam escaping a damaged pipe, filled Anna's ears. As this whining subsided, the calming hush of waves replaced it. She listened for a breath or two, gathering her wits, then turned to look at what she had done.

The sight took her breath away again.

Fire blazed from a pit where the factory once stood. Great stones and timbers and mangled machinery littered the grounds around The Saint Frances de Chantal Orphan Asylum. A few large pieces had fallen as far away as the upper beach, but the sand near the water was clear of any wreckage. The rubble cast long dancing shadows in the wavering firelight.

The boiler had exploded. It had leveled the back half of Saint Frances's southern wing. Anna sat, mesmerized. It had occurred to her that the boiler might rupture, but she had no idea it would explode so cataclysmically. People must have died.

Lots of people.

Just sisters, she thought.

It was a wicked thought, but she rubbed the knuckle where her pinky used to grow and felt no guilt. *Just sisters, what does it matter now?*

Children began emerging from the broken walls. One or two at first, then in groups, until their shadows crowded out the shadows of the fallen debris. They drifted around the wreckage, awe struck and wondering, looking at the ocean and the stars and the smoldering hulk of the factory. A few, mainly the older boys, pointed south to the forest, but none drifted beyond the bright ring of firelight. Not yet.

Anna looked to the forest, where Joseph told her to hide. It lay two hundred yards down the open beach. Where she lay now, in the shadow of the beached and peeling rowboat, she felt safe. But, the icy sea was rising. When she fell to the sand, the waves were only outlines and highlights. Now she saw each one clearly, and some foam had already reached her. She had read about the tide, how it rises and falls. Her boat would not be beached much longer.

Suddenly, Anna heard screaming. She turned back to where the children had been milling about. Sisters, dozens of them, poured out of the openings in the wall like hornets from a kicked hive, screaming orders at the children. "Get back inside this instant!" "Come back here!" "Don't you run from me!"

Children scattered, some running for the woods, some running back to the dormitories, most running with no idea where they were heading. They ran through the night, busting shins and breaking ankles on the scattered stones. The walls of Saint Frances de Chantal, even when blown to bits, refused to let its children go. The sisters fell upon them, shrieking like banshees.

Anna knew she had to move. The tide, slow and relentless, advanced behind her. Abbess McCain and her minions swarmed the beach in front of her. The orange fireball in the pit etched their shadows across the beach, shrieking and screaming and thrashing and running shadows. *A pagan carnival*, Anna thought.

She looked to the forest, far across the diminishing curve of sand. She had to go, but it was too bright. They would spot her at once if she ran that way. She considered the rowboat, but it was heavy, and she was not. Even if she could manage to get it into the water, *I have no idea how to row a boat. I'd be a sitting duck.*

She surveyed the beach on the other side of the dock. To the north, the soft sand gave way to boulders and a high, craggy outcropping of rock.

That won't work, she thought. *What did Joseph say?*

Wait until the fire dies. Run to the forest beyond the crescent beach.

She huddled against the curve of the rowboat. Waves splashed over her shoes.

I can't wait much longer.

She peeked over the boat. A few of the boys had reached the wood line, but most had been caught. Anna could see them, black silhouettes against the fire. They stood in rows, lining up to be marched back to their rooms. Several children limped or leaned on each other. Three were being carried. One boy still thrashed and kicked in a circle of sisters, but Anna could hear in his cries that he had already accepted defeat.

What will it be like for them tomorrow? She wondered.

You did this to them, the other voice answered.

Before she could consider this, an icy wave sloshed over her legs. She squeaked a startled, "eep!"

I have to move.

"Anna Dufresne!" Abbess McCain's voice boomed across the beach. "I know you did this, you murderer!"

Anna peeked around the end of the rowboat. Abbess McCain stood on a large stone, a black outline with the inferno behind her. She looked like a hole in the fire.

"I know you can hear me. You better hide, you miserable imp!" She held her cupped hands to her mouth, the sleeves of her habit flapped like bat wings. "You better run, Anna! You just see how far you get!"

Another wave sloshed over Anna's legs, rocking the rowboat.

"I will find you, Anna! This is an island, you wretched murdering girl, there is nowhere for you to go! I will find you and cut you down! I will slice off your head and hang it on my wall, you miserable, murdering devil!"

Another sister, Anna guessed it was Sister Eustace by her considerable bulk, took hold of Abbess McCain's elbow, trying to lead her down from the rock. Abbess McCain struck her a backhand blow across the face and the larger nun fell to the sand.

"Anna, you listen to me…"

A rumble erupted from the hole that used to be the factory, followed by a violent hissing rush. The fireball sank into the earth.

"…you better run as fast as your evil little feet will carry you! You better run…"

The hissing flared to a roar as a wall of white steam billowed out of the ruined factory. It glowed orange for a split second, then the fire was gone. The subterranean cisterns had swallowed the inferno. Darkness swallowed the beach.

Anna ran.

Chapter 11

SHE RAN LIKE A GIRL caught between the devil and the deep blue sea, her heavy wet shoes slapping the sand. She hugged the waterline, running as close to the surf as she could. The white lines of foam, all that were visible in the dark, served as her guides. She had seen that no stones or logs littered this stretch of beach, so she dashed blindly toward the forest. Behind her, Abbess McCain ranted on into the night

Never in her life had Anna run like this. Her hair flew in the wind. The wind sang in her ears. She was flying. Her feet slapped the wet sand, but she didn't feel them at all. Nor did she feel her legs, they ran of their own will. The air tasted like it had when she was only a toddler. She remembered a park of green grass and flowers and honeybees. She remembered the swing in the park where her daddy would push her so high.

Tears streamed from both eyes and she relished the way their tracks stung in the icy wind. Her lungs burned, and she relished that as well. Every breath that burned them was *free* air. *I'm coming alive again,* she thought as she flew.

It seemed to take an eternity to reach the trees, but when she did, she barely remembered how she got there. High grass stood between the beach and the wood line. By the time she reached it, her eyes had adjusted to the dark enough for her to see the grass and pick her way through it. Once inside the woods, Anna stopped running and sagged against a tree, panting.

Abbess McCain's voice carried on the night air. She still bellowed, but now her shouts were commands directed at the sisters. Anna couldn't make out the words, but she could guess. Abbess McCain was organizing the search.

Anna looked back to the tower and the pillar of smoke rising from the factory. Dots of light appeared, lanterns or torches. She looked across the gentle curve of the waterline, and that made her smile. The tide was still rising. The first tracks she made on the beach had already washed away. Her last tracks would be underwater long before the sisters could find them.

She turned to the forest. Even with her night-adjusted eyes, she could see nothing. Only a fool would linger here in the open, but blundering through the woods in the dark didn't seem wise either. What had Joseph said to do next?

Keep your back to the tower and the sea within earshot. Work into the forest. Find a crevice or a cavern, somewhere to hide when the moon rises.

Anna ventured into the woods. She walked as the blind walk, groping from tree to tree. The ground was spongy and uneven. Ferns sprung from the forest floor like giant feather dusters, taller than Anna's shoulders. The massive firs and gangly, smooth-barked madronas creaked in the night breeze. Low creeper vines and fallen tree limbs snagged her ankles, but she pushed deeper into the forest.

A few hundred feet beyond the tree line, the ground rose in a low cliff. The rise was only five or six feet high, but it was undercut, forming little caves and overhangs all along its length. A large fir, which once stood atop this bluff, had recently fallen. It now lay at an angle over the cliff face. Anna crawled under its still-green boughs, into the dirt crevice that opened behind it. She wedged herself into the fissure, working her way deeper into the crack until the dirt above her pressed down on her back.

She recited Joseph's instructions. Her lips moved with the words, but she spoke them only inside her head.

Slow your breathing. Still your heart. Wedge deep into the crevice. Cover your lair with fir boughs and pillow your head with lush moss. Do not mind the centipedes or the ants. This is their home. You are their overnight guest. Be soundless as the spider tiptoeing across your cheek. Learn her secret of stealth.

Wait. Breathe. Think. Rest, but do not sleep. Watch the horizon through the cedars and ferns. Watch for the glow of dawn.

And so, she did. Nestled in her hole, Anna waited. The moon rose, full and bright. She could see, through the curtain of dangling roots and the boughs of the fallen tree, moonlight frosting the edge of the wood line. The upper limbs of the trees glowed with silver light. She couldn't see the ocean, but she heard its comforting hush. Night birds called and coyotes yipped.

Then, she heard something else. Two separate sounds, both equally unsettling. In the distance, but closer than she would have liked, voices called, whistles chirped. Abbess McCain's search parties had begun in earnest. Much closer, a twig snapped, and hot breath rasped in a raw throat.

She held her breath, strained her ears, remembering Sister Eustace's words, *the wolves would have eaten you...the wolves or something worse.* And, hadn't Sister Elizabeth told her that something lived down in the drainage pipe? Something that would eat her if the grate was open?

Anna wanted to believe that the sisters had just been toying with her, torturing her emotions. But, something big moved in the trees, picking its way through the underbrush. The thing that moved in the darkness tried to walk quietly, but seemed too eager, too intent on its purpose. Anna tracked its progress by the rustle and crunch of its feet.

The beast came from the beach, directly ahead of her. It wasn't following her trail, she had come to this place on an angle from the beach. *Maybe it is following my scent.*

Anna felt as if she were being choked. Her heart pounded. Her head pounded. She couldn't breathe.

Then, she remembered that she was holding her breath. Opening her mouth, she slowly, silently let the old air out and drew in new.

She no longer heard the thing in the woods. It had stopped. Was it listening for her? Smelling for her?

The other sound came again, sisters calling into the woods, calling to each other. Anna closed her eyes, taking slow, slow breaths, willing herself out of existence, willing herself to be a stone or a log, a lump of clay, just a cold and uninteresting strand in the fabric of the island.

A snatch of something very old came to her, *they will pray for the rocks and the hills to cover them.* Anna prayed that prayer.

One of the search parties stood on the beach at the edge of the woods. They spoke in whispers, Anna couldn't make out the words, but she could tell they were very close. There were three or four of them, and they seemed to be arguing. Agitation, desperation, fatigue colored their whispers, but also a sense of excitement.

They can't have found me, Anna insisted. *I did what Joseph said. I did exactly what he said. They can't have found me. I am a rock. I am a log. I am a lump of clay.*

A whistle sounded on the beach, two short bleats. They were close enough that Jane, if she were here, could have thrown a shoe and hit them. *She probably would, too,* Anna thought. *That whistle was calling for additional sisters. I might as well fight them now, while there is only a few.*

But she held her place. *There is no way they can know I'm here, I am a rock, I am a log…*

The whispering intensified, more sisters voiced opinions, the tone of excitement prevailed. Then, the crashing commenced. The search party left the beach and began breaking through the underbrush and ferns, advancing into the trees. Anna could no longer hear the stealthy thing that had been creeping toward her. Had it slunk off into the deeper forest when the sisters arrived? She began wishing that it had found her rather than the sisters.

The yellow glow of oil lamps replaced the silver moonlight on the boughs beyond Anna's nook. The sisters' tromping feet sounded like the boots of marching soldiers. Their advance was slow but unrelenting.

Sisters of Sorrow

As they came within a few yards of Anna's hole, the woods exploded with sound. Something crashed through bushes and ferns. Branches snapped. Throats screamed. Clothes ripped. For one glorious second, Anna imagined the beast which had been stalking her had turned its fury on the sisters. Then, as the screaming crescendoed, she realized the truth. The stealthy thing wasn't a beast but a boy, just another refugee from Saint Frances. He had left tracks on the beach and the sisters followed him here.

They dragged him through the vines and ferns to the beach, lashing and kicking him as they went. He screamed and thrashed, landing one good kick. A sister cried out in pain. But there were at least six of them by now and his efforts only enraged them further. The nuns were in a fever frenzy, acting out their rage, a gang of unhinged and hysterical women.

Pagan Carnival, Anna thought again. *They are afraid. They have lost control and their world is spinning all catawampus.*

The sisters continued beating on the boy. The sounds carried to Anna from the beach. They beat him until he stopped screaming. They beat him until he stopped moaning. After he stopped breathing, they quit.

All was quiet for a moment. The birds and coyotes had stilled. Waves rolled their soft rush upon the sand.

Eventually, one of the sisters said, "Should we leave him here?"

"No, better bring 'im wit' us," another said, "we'll say we found 'im like that, in the rocks and surf." The others made sounds of agreement. They trudged back down the beach, dragging the boy behind them.

I am a rock. I am a log. I am... Anna's whole body shuddered. Her mouth peeled open involuntarily in a silent wail. She curled into a ball. Uncontrollable sobbing wracked her small frame. She mashed her face into the dirt to stifle her weeping. *You did this* and *it's all my fault* and *I didn't mean it,* chased each other around and around and around inside her head.

She cried like that until her lungs and jaw and throat ached, until mud covered her face from the tears and slobber, until she was just too tired to cry any more. Then, she nearly *was* a lump of clay, staring catatonically at the silver frosted boughs of a dead fir tree.

The moon had moved, its light finding different branches now than when it first rose. Little bugs, and one big spider, crawled over her skin, interested, but not very, in their visitor. *I used to be afraid of spiders*, drifted through Anna's head. She realized it was the first thought she'd had in a very long time, probably over an hour.

Anna had felt like this before, sometimes for months. This was how one survives Saint Frances. Don't think, don't feel, just do the next thing that must be done. Anna had done the next thing that must be done for five years. She never wanted to do it again. Lying there, under the roots of the forest, she remembered the feeling of running on the beach, *flying* on the beach, flying on the swing in the park with the flowers and the honeybees and her mom and her dad and having no next thing that must be done.

She could do the next thing, for just a little bit longer. She *would* do it, to be free. And if it killed her, well, *when I'm dead, there's nothing else they can take away.* And, that is its own kind of freedom. *What does it matter now?*

The next thing, according to Joseph, was to watch for the first light of dawn. *As soon as pink haze cuts the top of the sea from the bottom of the sky, move. Don't walk on the beach or trample a new path. Stick to the deer trails and rabbit trails. Keep the tower to your back and the sea within earshot.*

As the stars faded, Anna felt an uneasy restlessness. It dawned on her that it must be nearly six o'clock, time to rouse the little ones. Time to trade insults with Jane and slap Lizzy for one of her boneheaded insolent remarks. Anna felt her chest tighten, felt like she might fall apart again. But she didn't. She was all out of tears and sobs and emotions of any kind at all for now.

The girls will be safe, she decided. When the other voice in her head tried to tell her how ludicrous that was, she silenced it. *They will be fine. And that is all we will hear of that.*

Sister Dolores had promised to keep them out of trouble. Anna hoped the witch still felt compelled to honor her promise. She hoped Sister Dolores was still alive, for that matter. But, the subject was closed for now. Anna saw the pink line at the bottom of the sky. She moved.

Chapter 12

ANNA HURRIED ALONG DEER TRAILS just inside the wood line. A bank of thick fog had settled over the island. Enough light filtered through the fog for Anna to see a few steps ahead of her, but nothing farther. Massive tree trunks disappeared into the mist above her. Her path wound and turned, sometimes inland, sometimes toward the sea. Joseph had told her to find a rusted windmill to the south, she had to maintain her southward course.

Keep the tower to your back and the sea within earshot.

Well, she thought, *I cannot see the tower through the fog, and the sea is very quiet this morning.* A few times, the path curved too far inland, or emptied onto the sandy beach. When this happened, Anna had to retrace her steps until she found a branch of the trail that paralleled the sea more closely.

In the thick fog, the ocean sounded muffled and dreamlike. Seagulls cried and cackled. Other birds, Anna did not know their names, squawked and croaked and cooed and made all sorts of odd noises. *There must be hundreds of them.* Countless voices came to her out of the fog, sounding like human speech or laughter or screams, all nearby, all unseen.

Anna felt as if things moved in the woods around her. Her eyes fought with the fog and dusky light, trying to make sense of the shadows she passed in the mist. The bird chatter may have masked stealthier sounds. The birds, themselves, seemed to be talking about her. A low murmur, a conspiratorial crooning, lay below their louder babble.

As long as it's not the sisters, she told herself, pushing farther and farther south.

The day brightened, and as it did, the fog thinned. Anna pulled the loaf of bread out of her pocket. Seawater had dampened it when she hid by the boat and she had smashed it flat when she hid under the cliff. It tasted more like a soggy cracker than bread, but Anna was too hungry to care.

She guessed she had been walking for two or three hours when the fog finally lifted. The sun shone brightly and the day warmed. She no longer felt followed or gossiped about by the island's animals. Every few minutes, the ocean would sparkle through gaps in the trees, and it was beautiful. She actually started to feel... good.

Anna inhaled deeply. The air was full of smells – the rich, damp earth, the sweet wild flowers, the tang of fir sap, and the sea. There was no odor of coal smoke or leather or fish stew. She smiled, pulling a potato from her pocket. It was raw, but she had eaten many half-raw potatoes at Saint Frances. *I'll just pretend it's an apple.* She brought it to her lips. Then something moved.

It wasn't her imagination. Something moved quickly through the brush. Anna stopped. She squatted down, trying to be as small as possible. The trail was wide here and there was very little underbrush, nowhere to hide. The moving thing, whatever it was, wasn't a person. Anna could tell by its quick, discreet steps.

It passed by her, just a few feet off the trail, then trotted out onto the path a stone's throw ahead of her. A scruffy looking dog with sharp ears and snout. It stopped and looked back at her. *Not a dog,* she thought, *a coyote.*

The coyote held a large chunk of meat in its mouth. At first, Anna thought it looked like a pale, thin ham. Then she saw the shoe. The coyote turned and loped away down the path, carrying a nun's lower leg in its mouth.

Anna decided not to eat the potato. She didn't feel good anymore.

The woods darkened as a cloud passed over the sun. Anna waited, dropping the potato back into her pocket. The coyote had taken her southbound trail. She wanted to give him plenty of space before following.

She wondered about the sisters. What were they doing now? Last night, at the height of the chaos, they had swarmed the beach and combed the ground around Saint Frances. Then, shortly before dawn, their whistles and calls had ceased. If they had been out this morning, the screech and squabble of the sea birds would have covered the sister's whistles. But now, the birds had quieted. Anna thought she might have heard the sisters once or twice, but if it *was* them, they were far away.

Anna stood and walked south again. The woods and sea remained as charming as they had been earlier, but Anna reminded herself that it was a very dangerous beauty. She would not be safe until she found Joseph.

Her thoughts turned to Joseph and his instructions, then to Abbess McCain and the other sisters. *What are they doing?* As she walked, she tried to piece together the events of the previous night. She knew what *she* had done, but she tried to envision what the sisters saw and how they would have responded.

The boiler had exploded, taking out most of the factory and a large portion of the sister's living quarters. But apparently, many of the sisters were not in their quarters at the time of the explosion. If they had been, they would have all been killed. But they had been out, looking for her. Why? How had they known she escaped? Sister Dolores had promised to cover for her, had the witch been discovered? Had she ratted Anna out? Had Sister Dolores been killed in the explosion?

That thought put a rock in Anna's stomach. She decided to think of something else. The fire. Joseph had told her there would be a fire, he had known. He had also known that the fire would go out. His plan had worked perfectly. The fire's sudden death had given Anna a window of darkness through which she escaped.

What had extinguished the fire? A blaze that intense would take hours to extinguish. It would have taken all the water in the cisterns... Then she got it. The cisterns lay below the factory. The fire, in its intensity, had burned through the floor supports, causing the whole factory to plunge into the cistern.

Joseph had known it would happen. He had also known where the tide would be when the boiler blew and where it would be when the fire died. He had known that if she ran along the waterline, the tide would cover her tracks before the sisters found them. He had known that the moon would not rise until she had found a safe place to hide. He had known that they would stop searching for her as dawn approached.

Why had they stopped searching? *If I was Abbess McCain*, Anna thought. She reflected on what she had seen, the inferno that looked like the gaping maw of hell and Abbess McCain's empty black silhouette standing on the rock, waving her arms and ranting. *If I was Abbess McCain and completely insane with anger*, she revised, *what would I do?*

Then she understood. Rage and frenzy had fueled their search last night. They had run themselves ragged until they tired and calmed enough to think. This was an island, after all. They didn't need to find her tonight. She wasn't going to get very far. The sisters had decided to regroup, probably eat breakfast, tend to their wounded, and organize a planned, systematic search.

Joseph had known that they would do that, too. He had foreseen the lull in the nun storm. *He must have been planning this for months*, she thought. The timing of the tide and the moonrise had been perfect. Anna wondered if Joseph had intentionally clogged the overflow pipe in order to meet her there. *How did he know that they would send* me *down there?* she wondered, *or did it matter that it was me? Was he just looking for any child willing to blow the boiler?*

That thought stopped her in her tracks. She rested against a crumbling tree stump. *Did Joseph trick me into killing all those sisters? Was that his real purpose, to blow up Saint Frances, and I was just the rube that helped him do it?* She thought of all the barred doors, the high, narrow windows, the grate covering the drainage pipe and the peephole in the drainage chamber door. The sisters had definitely been trying to keep *something* out.

But, he knew who I am. He knew my name and he told me to be sure to bring my finger, she thought. *Besides, why would he devise a plan for my escape from the beach if all he wanted was to kill the sisters?*

She started walking again. Ahead of her, the trees thinned, as if there may be a clearing. She decided that Joseph had wanted *her,* specifically, and had intended for her to escape, but he must have known how deadly his plan was. *If he kills so easily, can I trust him?*

The other voice in her mind said, *they're just sisters.*

That still doesn't make it right! I'm not a murderer.

What about your little brother?

She didn't want to think about that, but it reminded her of what Sister Dolores had said. Sister Dolores had come to Saint Frances to kill her own little brother, Joey, Joseph. Had she known what he was going to do? Had she known that Anna was helping him?

What does it matter now? Everyone else was behind her. Only Joseph waited ahead. He had freed her from Abbess McCain and Saint Frances. No one else had ever done her such a kindness. Whatever he may be to the rest of the world, to her he was a friend. *They may call him a murderer, but they called me a murderer, too.* That's why they had sent her to this island in the first place. *Murder to get in, murder to get out.* She smiled her wry smile. *They're just sisters.*

She decided she could live with that, if she had to, though the thought rubbed against her conscience the way the key had worn blisters on her sole. She had several other things to consider. The effect of her actions on the other children, for one. The fact that she really had no idea how her brother had ended up drowned in the bathtub, for another. But, those musings would have to wait. To the north, from the beach, came the shrill voice of a whistle.

Chapter 13

ANNA JOGGED AGAIN. THE WHISTLE had been at a distance, but it meant the sisters had resumed their search. They would be organized now, searching in careful patterns, with the light of day on their side. She needed to reach the safety Joseph had promised, and she needed to reach it soon.

She now ran through a younger section of forest. The trees were short and thin trunked. The underbrush grew thick, with tangles of blackberry vines claiming large clearings. Anna's path lay in a straight line rather than the random turns and gradual curves it followed earlier in the day. Stubs of rotted posts poked out of the ground at regular intervals, perhaps a dilapidated fence line. Joseph had said she would find him at an abandoned farm…

As you near the fallen farmhouse, listen for the creek of the rusted windmill. Make your way toward the sound. As you near it, find the mass of thick brambles. Crawl inside. The thorns will prick you and cut you, but pay them no mind. Abbess McCain will not look for you here.

I can do that, she thought. *I must be getting close.*

The trees gave way to tall, windswept grass. Anna's trail crested a short hill. As she reached the top, she gasped in amazement and fell to her knees. The Pacific Ocean stretched all the way from one side of the horizon to the other, sparkling brilliant blue under a nearly cloudless sky. She had never seen anything like it.

She might have knelt there, staring out at the sea, for the rest of the day, if not for the sounds. A whistle blew, off to her right. Tall grass and a copse of thin alders stood between her and the whistle. She hadn't been seen, but the sisters were very close. She guessed that they were working south along the coast. From her vantage, she had seen the southern end of the island. The nuns would reach it in less than an hour.

Would they then continue around the island on the beach, or would they make their way back to the orphanage through the woods? Anna didn't know. She did know that *somebody* would search the woods, whether it was this group of sisters or another. They may be in the woods already.

As she crouched in the grass considering this, she became aware of another sound, a metallic *clank*. The sound was still a ways off, but it was clear. *Clank*, several seconds of quiet, then *clank*. Anna rose to a crouch and ran, keeping low, toward the noise. Eventually, another noise joined the *clank*, a high-pitched *screee*. Each *screee* started as an imperceptible whine that would grow louder and louder until the *clank* silenced it. Then, the cycle began again.

That must be the windmill.

The trail dropped into a low, overgrown pasture, then topped another rise. Anna saw the ocean again, but this time, she also saw a little steamer, probably the same one she had seen moored to Saint Frances's dock six days ago. The boat cruised slowly south, close to the beach.

Anna ducked and scuttled in a half crawl toward the metallic noise. It sounded very close. The trail dipped again and Anna rose to her full height. The head of the windmill appeared above the tall grass. It stood at the crest of the next rise. *ScreeeeeeeClank... ScreeeeeeeeClank...*

A few yards to the west of the windmill, between it and the west-facing beach, the heap of brambles piled out of a clearing. It was twice as tall as a man, nearly the size of a house.

She ran up the trail to the base of the windmill. From the windmill to the south beach stretched a pasture of short grass. A curve of sand wrapped around the grassland where the south beach became the west beach. The screen of alders still stood between her and the search party to the west, but if they turned inland, she would be standing in plain sight. She sprinted for the brambles.

A rectangle of old bricks surrounded the massive heap of blackberry vines. It had been a house, long ago. Either fire or storm or simple time had taken the wooden structure, leaving only the foundation behind.

Anna searched around the foundation for a way into the tangled thorns and vines. A distant whistle sounded. Anna sighed with relief. It was farther away than she had imagined the search party to be. Then, she realized the whistle had come out of the east, from a second party. The east whistle was answered by a whistle from the west, a very *close* whistle from the west.

A rabbit darted through the grass, nearly hopping right into Anna. It danced away from her at the last minute with a fancy, zigzag hop. Then, it bounced into an opening in the briars. Anna followed.

The rabbit had been plump, and Anna was orphan thin, but it was still a very tight fit. Thorns snagged Anna's coat and shawl, they hooked into the skin on her wrists and neck. The barbs lining the floor of the warren dug into her knees and palms. Above her, vines wove an impenetrable canopy, creating false night within the mass of brambles.

This is worse than the drainage pipe. This tunnel has teeth!

Another whistle cried. She couldn't tell from which direction, but it sounded close. She crawled deeper into the thorns. Something twitched just ahead of her. The rabbit poked its head out of a nook, eyed her with unconcealed astonishment, then disappeared down a hole in the ground.

Yes, I am as crazy as I look.

Anna dragged herself toward the rabbit's hole, now flat on her belly, thorns digging into her scalp and palms and legs. Ancient dust and pollen drifted down out of the canopy. She was shaking vines that hadn't been disturbed in years. When she reached the rabbit hole, it was too small for even her head to enter.

He didn't say go down a rabbit hole, dummy, she scolded herself, *he said lift the iron ring. He said…*

Take care as you crawl, as you approach the entrance. Feel around under the brambles. Feel for the crumbling wooden planks. Do not crawl across them. They will not support even one as small as you. Run your fingers along the edge of the wood. Mind the splinters. You will find an iron ring. Lift it. Lift it only enough to slip inside. Lower yourself through the hole. Test each step before your weight is on it, the bottom is a long way down. It is very dark, but don't worry, they will never find you here.

She searched the ground around her but did not discover any planks. *What if this is the wrong thicket?* she thought. But this had to be right. This was exactly where Joseph said it would be.

Unless he is just using you, said the other voice. *Maybe he wanted you to blow up the factory and then lead the sisters on a chase so that he could sneak into the orphanage while they are away.*

That is stupid, she thought. *People try to sneak out of Saint Frances. Nobody sneaks in.*

Sister Dolores did.

Shut up, she thought and dragged herself further into the brambles. *He wanted me. Specifically me. He knew my name.*

Nun's voices carried on the breeze, too far away to be understood, but still way too close. Anna rummaged under the bed of leaves and dead bramble branches, finding no planks.

Her tunnel had narrowed to an end and she could go no further. She attempted to squirm backward, intending to try a different path, but as she did so, the vines and branches collapsed in on her. She struggled backward, but the harder she pushed, the tighter the brambles held her, the deeper the thorns bit her.

You are in the jaws of the briar monster and it has begun to chew, the other voice said in her head.

Shut up, she screamed back.

Anna's arms ached with effort. Her eyes watered from the dust and her skin stung everywhere from countless punctures and scrapes. She let her head flop forward onto her arms, discovering that her neck ached as well. Come to think of it, her feet, ankles and knees felt used up, too. And she was so tired. *Maybe I'll just sleep here for a little bit,* she thought.

Then she coughed.

The first cough snuck up on her. She hadn't expected it, but now an entire herd of coughs were lining up for their chance to rat her out. The dust and pollen settled over her, thicker than the morning's mist. Anna choked down one cough and stifled a second into her hands.

She didn't hear any chatter from the search party. Had they moved away from her, or had they quieted to listen? Anna imagined them looking at each other, silent, asking with their eyes, "Did you hear that?" "Was that a cough?" "It was just a chipmunk or blue jay." "Sounded like a little girl coughing, to me."

She squinted into the darkness. Thick vines blocked the path ahead and to the left. A gap opened to the right, too narrow for her whole body, but wide enough to slip her arm through. She reached over, trying to feel for the boards beneath the leaves.

But, as her hand passed through the opening, she felt nothing. Nothing at all. Under the groundcover was nothing but thin air.

That's it! she thought. The vines clutched her tightly, much too tightly for any little girl to tear free of their grasp, but Anna did it anyway. The thorns punctured, then scraped, then deeply cut into her skin, but she pushed through. Turning onto her side, folding to an L shape, she coiled into the narrow gap.

As she pushed herself through, the thorns broke off in her skin, and her progress became easier. Her hips slid most of the way through the gap. She balanced on a ledge of some sort at the edge of the hole.

Anna looked around, trying to define the edges of the pit, trying to locate the iron ring. Darkness and dust hid any details. The ground below her was hard and regular, like wood. She lowered her arm, past her elbow, into the hole, but felt nothing below.

The whistle cried again, at a distance, followed by an answering whistle even farther off. *The search parties are moving away*, she thought, and coughed quietly into her hand.

A closer sound drew her attention, a snapping noise below her, then a slow crackling. The ledge on which she lay sagged, slumping toward the pit. Anna stifled a scream and flailed for a handhold. Brittle blackberry vines snapped off in her grasp. Her ledge collapsed, dropping Anna headfirst into the darkness. Her lower legs, still in the clutches of the briar monster, hung up at the crumbling edge of the pit.

She dangled upside down for a moment, too startled and frazzled to think. Then the vines released her. She plummeted. Half a scream escaped her lips before she crashed onto the middle step of a moldering staircase. Rotten wood crumbled under her weight. The entire staircase crashed into the pit with Anna. There was a crack and a flash inside her skull. She stopped thinking then, stopped knowing. When night fell, hours later, Anna still had not stirred.

Chapter 14

ANNA DREAMED. SHE DREAMED OF the day she had arrived at the orphanage. A flat blanket of cloud hung low in the sky. Heavy mist fought light drizzle for ownership of the air. Anna sat at the front of the boat watching The Saint Frances de Chantal Orphan Asylum emerge from the haze, its single tower rising like an enormous headstone.

Then, it *was* a headstone, in her dream – her brother's headstone.

Here lies Ephraim Dufresne

1902 – 1904

Drowned in a bathtub

By his big sister

Beside it stood her mother's headstone.

Here lies Maria Dufresne

1881 – 1904

Opened her veins

In the tub that took her son

Her father didn't have a headstone. He hadn't died.

Anna's grave was unmarked. It was just a pit covered with rotting timbers and wild, ravenous blackberry vines. She saw herself lying at the bottom, legs and arms splayed in all directions, covered in mud and cuts. The ruins of the collapsed staircase littered the floor around her. Something heavy, perhaps a piece of lumber, lay across her chest.

Anna reached into the grave to lift the heavy thing from her chest. The other Anna grabbed her hand and said, "Leave it. That's not for you."

"I want to get it off my chest."

"Do you?" asked the other Anna in the other Anna voice. "Then look at it!"

Suddenly, she did not want to look at it. She didn't want anything to do with it or with the other Anna. She tried to run, but the other Anna refused to let her go.

"Look at it," the other Anna repeated.

She tried not to look, but, as happens in dreams, her head and her eyes ignored her desires. The thing on the other Anna's chest was a door. She recognized the door from a familiar place, long ago. Her hand, of its own accord, took hold of the knob and turned. The door opened. Anna and the other Anna stepped through.

The mirror above the sink reflected two Annas, standing side by side. One was groomed and dressed according to the manner to which she had been born. The other wore a mud crusted drape of unidentifiable cut, her hair, nails, teeth unkempt. She bled from countless scratches.

Tiny six-sided tiles covered the floor and the first three feet of the walls, mainly white, but with a few blue tiles scattered about. Water dripped idly in the sink. Dust motes loitered in a shaft of late morning sunlight that fell through the window. Anna looked at everything except the bathtub.

"You have to look," said the other Anna.

"I already know what is in there."

"You already know, but you do not see."

"I don't *want* to see."

"Yes you do," said the clean Anna in the mirror.

The bathtub moved toward the Annas, walking on its claw feet.

She couldn't run. She couldn't turn away.

The tub stopped when its rim rested against her thighs. The water lay flat and smooth, undisturbed. Beneath its glassy surface, on the bottom, lay her brother – eyes open, lips parted, pale hair adrift, still dressed in his nightshirt. A slab of concrete lay across his body, holding him under.

"Did you do that?" the other Anna asked.

"I don't…"

"You can't lie to me, Anna." The other Anna's eyes did the Sister Dolores thing, shifting black to violet to blue again.

"You're not a witch," Anna said.

"How do you know?"

Anna said nothing.

"Don't lie anymore, Anna. Look."

The tub took another step, shoving her back.

Anna looked at her little brother. He looked back at her. He was talking, under there, talking in his inquisitive, content little voice, though no sounds came forth.

"Did you do that?" the other Anna demanded.

"No," she admitted.

"Then who did?"

Anna whipped her head around and stared wide eyed at the other her. "I… I can't say."

"Where are you supposed to be right now, Anna?"

"I'm supposed to be at school, but I got sent home for punching Harry Resnick."

"You punched Harry because he said your mother was crazy. Is your mother home right now?"

Anna eyed the other Anna warily. In the tub, little Ephraim reached playful fingers up at her.

"If I say momma did it, they'll take her away and lock her up forever," she whispered.

"Did she do it?"

Anna looked into the bathtub. Ephraim was gone. It now cradled her mother's body. The water had turned nearly black with blood.

"She did it, didn't she, Anna?"

Tears streamed over her cheeks. She looked at her other self and nodded.

***

The dreams flowed on, the way dreams do, but the bathtub, and what she saw there, were what she remembered when she opened her eyes.

Her first thought upon waking was that she was in the bathtub, under the slab of concrete. She lay in a few inches of water. Something heavy had fallen across her. Water dripped nearby. She moved a little, but found it was much more comfortable to remain still.

She thought about Ephraim and her mother. She thought about the house where they had lived. How different all that had been, how naïve she had been about the world.

"I didn't kill him," she whispered into the darkness. "I didn't do it. I didn't kill my little brother." Then, when the darkness failed to answer, she said, "My mother killed him."

Overhead, flecks of moonlight winked through small openings in the canopy. Anna could see nothing of her surroundings. The pit smelled like mold and rotten seaweed and dead things.

I don't want to be down another dark hole. I want to see the sun and the ocean. I want to smell the forest.

The night dragged on. Irritable sea birds called now and then. The coyotes yipped and howled nearby. The windmill *screeeeee clank*'d relentlessly. Rabbits scurried through the brambles, marveling at the hole Anna had made in their warren. Somewhere close, water dripped. And dripped. And dripped.

Anna drifted in and out of troubled sleep. Dreams faded into reality faded into dreamless oblivion. She didn't know or care which was which. Her mind and her two voices murmured inarticulate arguments about innocence and guilt and the ramifications thereof.

Had I told the truth, maybe my mother wouldn't have died.
But they would have locked her up.
Maybe papa wouldn't have run off if she was still alive.
And maybe they would have hanged her.

The debate dribbled on and on like the slow, insistent trickle of water, weaving through her dreams and waking.

Then, a new voice, "You have something for me?" It was the dream whisper she had heard in the drainage tunnel.

"I have a potato," Anna murmured, "but it's raw."

"Your finger," the Joseph voice said. "You brought me your finger."

"It's here," she murmured, "but it's too heavy." She lifted her hand out of the water and brought it to her chest. A sloshing sound echoed through the pit, like a wet mop slopping onto a floor. The splashing sounds drew nearer. She could see a form moving toward her. It was either kneeling or very short.

A snake-like appendage slid out of the black, wrapping around the object on Anna's chest. She realized that a wooden beam – not the concrete slab from the bathtub, not her severed finger - had been pinning her to the floor. The snake, or tentacle or whatever it was, hoisted the beam off her chest and dropped it into the shallow water just beyond her. She realized how hard it had been to breathe, how much easier it had become to fill her lungs with its weight gone.

"Let me have it." The voice alternated between a whisper and a child's voice. A hand reached toward her out of the darkness.

She drew the finger from under her dress. It twitched against her palm. She held it out to the dark form. "I don't want it anymore," she said.

The hand plucked the pinky from her, snatching it from its leather thong. She saw the hand clearly now, either by dreamtime magic or a trick of moonlight. The hand was more bone than flesh. The flesh still clinging to it was mottled and sagging. Three of the fingers were missing entirely, having been replaced by two octopus tentacles and a crab leg. The arm which extended the patchwork hand was not a human arm, but in the intense gloom, Anna couldn't make out any details.

Its eyes floated above the other end of the inhuman arm, like twin yellow moons veiled by a scrim of coal smoke. The form behind the eyes appeared shapeless, just a huddled mass, dark and wet, as if it were wrapped in shiny brown seaweed. It loomed over her, watching, contemplating her for several minutes. Anna wished to either wake up or fall asleep, whichever would banish the creature.

The thing turned away from her, slosh-clomping into the further recesses of the pit. A sickly, wan light rose out of a hole in the floor. The thing with her finger hobbled to the hole and crawled headfirst over its edge, disappearing into whatever lay below. As it went, Anna saw its leg, a pale leg wearing bite marks from a coyote, and a nun's black shoe.

Chapter 15

NARROW SHAFTS OF SUNLIGHT STREAMED through rifts in the bramble canopy. Anna opened her eyes and, without sitting or even moving her head, surveyed the room. It had once been a basement. The walls were stone and mortar, as was the floor. Bits of staircase dangled from rotting floor joists overhead. Planks and the remainder of the staircase lay scattered around her. Shallow water covered the floor.

Above, the windmill continued to creak and clank, finches twittered, seagulls cackled and squalled. Down here, water dripped. She did not hear the sister's whistles. It was morning. She was still alive.

Anna felt for her severed pinky. She was not surprised to find it gone. Something had taken it in the night. *Good riddance.* Whatever had taken her finger had also moved the plank off her chest. She inhaled deeply. Her ribs throbbed, but the pain was tolerable.

She sat up, grimacing. Her stiff joints ached.

"Gee whiz, miss," a weak voice drifted out of the corner behind her. "I thought for sure you was dead."

Anna startled and turned to the voice, wincing at the tightness in her neck. A boy, slightly younger than herself, sat slumped, palms up, against the far wall. He wore a heavy wool peacoat bearing the Saint Frances de Chantal emblem. It was identical to the one Anna had worn on her boat ride to the orphanage, all those years ago. *A travelling coat.*

"You ain't dead, right?" he asked.

It was a stupid question, she thought. But looking at the boy, Anna was more than half-surprised that *he* was not dead. *I guess I probably don't look much better.*

"I'm not dead," she said. It came out as a croak. "Not yet, anyway."

"Yeah, me neither." He spoke with a southern draw and twang, though his lethargy muted it.

"Did you lift that plank off of me last night?" Anna asked.

"Miss, I don' know if I can even lift my own bottom off this floor." The boy's pale skin stretched tight over his sunken cheeks and hollow eyes.

"So, you are not Joseph?"

His eyes twitched with startled amusement, then he chuckled weakly. His laugh sounded like the creaking windmill. "No, ma'am, I ain't Joseph, thank the Lord. Name's Donald Lawson." He lifted his hand to his head as if tipping a hat, then let it fall back into his lap. "But you can call me Donny. Pleased to meetcha."

"Anna Dufresne," she replied, smiling in spite of herself, "and the pleasure is mine."

Donny laughed again, a little less horribly this time. "Well, ain't we just the pair."

Anna looked at him, trying to make sense of their predicament.

"You don't happen to have any food, do ya?" Donny asked. "I've been down here almost a week."

"I have a raw potato," she said. "Would you like to share it?"

"That sounds mighty fine."

Anna stood, cautiously. Her knees creaked, her ankles and feet ached, but they held her. She walked across the basement to Donny, stepping over the fallen debris, and sat beside him.

She pulled a large potato out of her coat pocket and handed it to him. "Eat slowly, little bites, and chew it completely before you swallow, otherwise it'll make you sick."

"Yes, mother," Donny said, then nibbled through the skin.

Anna thought about her girls. Were the sisters still feeding them? The kitchen had been in shambles last time she had seen it. The bell had not rung since the explosion. How would they know when to wake for breakfast? The factory had been blown to bits. How would they earn their food?

"Don't call me mother," she said. "Let me have a bite of that."

They passed the potato back and forth for several minutes, consuming half of it. Donny pointed to a rusty can on the opposite side of the basement. "It's full of good water if you're thirsty. I sure could use a drink."

Anna retrieved the can. It was about twice the size of a quart jar. Between the two of them, they drank it all.

"Where does the water come from?" Anna asked, after stowing the remains of the spud (as Donny called it) in her pocket.

"That windmill," he pointed up, some animation returning to his body and voice. "It draws water up from the well. But the pipes are all busted, so the water leaks back down and drips all day an' night. Like to drive me mad when I first got here. I juss put the can under where it drips."

"Not a well," Anna said, "a cistern."

"A what?"

"A cistern, it's like a well, except it collects rain water instead of ground water."

Thinking of the cistern at Saint Frances brought her mind back to Joseph. "Do you know a boy named Joseph? He was supposed to meet me here."

"A *boy* named Joseph?" Donny said raising his eyebrows. "Anna, Joseph ain't a boy."

"What do you mean?"

"Don't know what he is, but he sure ain't no boy. Some kind of ghoul, I reckon," Donny said. "If he told you to come here, it's just so he can eat you."

"That's ridiculous…" she said. The thing from the previous night's dream-laced delirium, the seaweed thing that came for her finger, flashed into her mind. And Joseph's words, *Come to me and I will keep you. Abbess*

McCain will never find you here. "He said he wanted to help me. He gave me a key and told me how to escape," but she was suddenly confused and a little frightened.

"He told you to come here?"

Anna nodded.

"An' now you're trapped in this hole, juss like me," Donny said. "He checks on me when I'm sleeping, when *he thinks* I'm sleeping. He comes to see if I'm dead yet. I seen him a couple times. It was too dark to see much, but I was glad of that. I don't wanna get a good look."

"I saw something last night," Anna said. "I thought it was a dream, you know, because things like that aren't real."

"He's been real every time *I* seen him."

"What makes you think that thing is Joseph?" Anna asked.

"Oh, he talks all the time. Always muttering and whispering. He says his name over and over, like he's trying not to forget."

"But he didn't eat you."

"Not yet, he has to wait until I'm dead." Donny scrunched up his face. "He said he's going to take my parts."

Anna clasped her hand over the leather thong around her neck, the thong that had held her finger.

"Guess he's gonna have to wait a bit longer, now that you showed up," Donny said with forced cheer. "That spud sure hit the spot. I'm feeling better already."

"I'm not," Anna said, dismally. "You really think he wants to eat us?"

"What else is he gonna do with our parts?"

Anna thought of the seaweed thing that had taken her finger, thought of its rotten patchwork hand and the nun's leg on which it stumped away.

She surveyed the basement again, four stone walls, a collapsed staircase, a leaking pipe running up to the windmill, a stone archway leading to an alcove that housed the opening to the cistern.

"He comes out of there?" She pointed to the alcove.

"Uh-huh." Donny nodded. "He always makes this terrible screech juss before he shows up."

"Have you ever gone down there?"

"It's dark down there." He looked at her as if she were insane. "And *he's* down there. No, thank you, ma'am!"

"Did you try shimmying up the windmill pipe?"

"'Course I did. The floorboards up there are solid, can't bust through 'em."

"That figures."

They sat together on the wet floor for a long time, listening to the basement's sounds and looking into the alcove. Anna may have dozed, but she wasn't sure. When Donny spoke again, the dusty shafts of light slanted in a different direction.

"I'm sorry you ended up down here," he said, "but it sure is nice to not be alone, an' to have someone to talk to."

"Believe it or not, this isn't as bad as where I came from."

"I don't believe it," he said with a wan smile. "Would it be okay if I held your hand?" When she didn't answer, he added, "juss so I know you're not afraid?"

She took his hand. It was dry and cold. "Why don't you tell me how you got here?"

Chapter 16

"HA! WHEW. WELL, IT'S QUITE a story," he said. "Momma and papa got sent to prison and none of our kin wanted to take care of me an' my little sis, Maybelle. So, the judge said that we would have to go to a home. Only, none of the homes would take us, on account of what our folks done. So..."

"What did they do?" Anna asked.

Donny ignored her. "So then, this priest comes and tells the judge about a place that will take kids that nobody else wants."

"Saint Frances?" Anna asked.

"Yeah!" Donny's eyes lit up. "You heard of it? I figured that priest just made it up."

"No, it's real, Donny. Why would he make that up?"

"I dunno. I guessed it was just a lie they made up so they could get rid of us. They hauled us all the way across America on a train, put us on a little boat an' throwed us overboard into the ocean."

"They threw you in?"

"Yeah, well, *she* threw me in. Some crazy nun on the boat hauled me up by my collar and britches and pitched me over the side. I figure she done the same to my little sis, too, but I don't know, 'cause I went under right away." Donny looked at her with a strange mix of emotions playing in his eyes. "I'm a real good swimmer, honest, but the waves were so big and I..." he trailed off. It took a minute, but Anna realized he was struggling not to cry.

"You are still alive, Donny, you made it," she said.

He looked at her with a startling fierceness in his eyes. "I got sick. On the boat, 'cause of all the waves. That's why she threw me over. I'd never been on the ocean before and I got sick, an' I couldn't swim with my coat an' shoes on, an' the water was so cold, an' my stomach was all cramped up. An' the waves were so big."

He took a deep breath, hitching a little, then continued.

"I figured I was done for. I bobbed up an' screamed for help once, but I couldn't even see the boat no more. It must'a already been on the other side of one of them big waves. All I seen was the trail of black smoke it puffed out." He looked up through the broken floorboards and bramble canopy. "I knew I was a goner, so I just closed my eyes an' said a little prayer for me an' my sis. A wave washed over me an' pulled me under." He shrugged his shoulders. "That's all I really remember."

"So, you woke up here?" Anna asked.

"Not exactly," he said. He hesitated, studying her expression, then continued. "I think a great fish swallowed me, you know, like in the story of Jonah? But that part might'a just been a dream."

"Probably," Anna said, but she squeezed his hand.

"Well, something *did* grab ahold of me, some sea monster or something. It pulled me down so deep, I thought my head was gonna cave in. The water was all black, but there was these little glowing things floating around. I guess I fainted then." He shot her a furtive glance. "I don't like to say I fainted, but I think I had good right to faint at that point. I think anybody else would'a fainted by then."

"I fainted when I fell through the floorboards," Anna said.

"Yeah, but you're a girl."

Anna snatched her hand away. "So was the nun that tossed your skinny carcass off the boat."

Donny stared at her wide-eyed, looking as if he really might burst into tears. "Oh, Anna, I'm sorry! I didn't mean nothin' by it. It's just boys aren't supposed to faint. It's okay for girls."

"Where I come from, girls who faint get eaten by machines with needle teeth." She offered her hand to him again.

"Oh," he said, cautiously accepting her hand.

"I think I probably would have fainted, too, if I'd been thrown into the sea and pulled down by a sea monster," she said. "What happened next?"

"I woke up down there," he pointed toward the cistern in the alcove at the far side of the basement. "Somebody was draggin' me through a pipe or a tunnel. In the dark, I *thought* it was a somebody, later on I found out it was a some*thing* – that Joseph thing I told you about." Donny shuddered. "At first, I thought he rescued me, an' I was relieved. Then, when I caught a peek at him in the dim light, I knew I'd died an gone to hell. He looked just like the devil – if the devil was made out of dead animals and fish all stitched together.

"I'll tell you another shameful thing," Donny sighed, "when I saw that, I screamed." He shot Anna a mischievous glance. "I screamed like a little girl." Donny gripped her hand more tightly in case she tried to yank it away again.

Instead, she said, "That doesn't offend me, Donald. I am not a little girl."

"No, I suppose you ain't, not if you come from a place where they feed little girls to machines with needle teeth. Where *did* you come from, anyway?"

"I was at the orphanage, at Saint Frances. But finish your story," Anna said. "I need to know about Joseph. He rescued me from that place. He rescued you, too. I thought he was going to meet me here. And help me." Her words trailed off at the end as she stared into the alcove.

"He didn't rescue me, not on purpose, anyway. I don't think he means to help anybody. When I screamed, he screamed back, an' not a scared scream, an angry scream, cussin' an' swearin' – juss like the devil, stompin' up an down… only his feet weren't feet. I don't know what they were, seaweed or octopuses... something wet an' sloppy. I just don't know, but he sure was havin' a fit." Donny shook his head slowly and whistled. "He was madder'n that nun that tossed me out.

"When he finally settled a bit, he said I's s'posed to be dead. Said the only reason he pulled me out was to get my parts before the crabs and dogfish nibbled 'em down to nothin'.

"Then he pulled me up here, into this room an' just plopped me up against the wall. I started sayin', 'please don't kill me,' and he got mad again, cussin' an' such. Then he said, 'I can't kill. I can't kill you.' Just like that, said it twice, then he said, 'You'll die here soon enough, then I'll come get your parts, I'll come get your parts.' Then, he kinda oozed over the side of that well and dropped in. He kept on repeating 'I'll come get your parts,' as he moved away down there.

"I been stuck here ever since. Probably would have died today or tomorrow if you hadn't come along."

"You said he didn't have feet. Are you sure about that?" Anna asked.

Donny gave her a puzzled look. "Yeah, I'm sure. I didn't see much of him, 'cause I was layin' down while he was draggin' me, and it was dark, but I did get a good look at where his feet should have been. He didn't have any. Why do you care about his feet?"

"When I saw him last night, he had a foot, a nun's foot and leg. It was from one of the sister's I k...one of the sisters that died in the explosion."

"What explosion?" Donny asked.

"I don't think he plans on eating us, Donny. I don't think that's what he wants with our parts."

"What do you mean?"

"This was a trap," Anna said, talking out loud but only to herself. "This was a trap, and I walked right into it."

She surveyed the room again. The walls offered no exits, no doors, no windows, not even a wide crack. The rotten staircase never would have held her, even if she hadn't dropped onto it headfirst. Now, two steps dangled from the underside of the decayed floor joists. The remainder of the staircase lay in broken ruin across the basement floor. Only the cistern offered hope of escape.

"What does he want with our parts, Anna?"

She looked back at Donny. "I don't know for sure, but I think he – it, might need...parts, like arms and legs and fingers. He's made out of pieces, lots of pieces of...pieces of *dead* things."

"That's why he wants us dead?" Donny asked.

"But why not just kill us?"

"He said he can't," Donny said.

"But why not?"

Donny shrugged, "Maybe he's a pacifist, like them Amish?"

"I don't think he's Amish," Anna said.

They sat together in the filtered, fractured shafts of light under a ceiling of dry rot and brambles. Anna wondered where her finger was and what exactly it might be doing. She wondered if Joseph laid this trap for her specifically because of her dead finger. She thought about the nun's leg, attached to Joseph, and wondered how many parts she had scattered across the grounds of Saint Frances. *How did Joseph get that leg from the coyote? Did the coyote bring it to him?*

"My sister isn't here." Donny interrupted her musings.

"What?"

"My little sister," he repeated. "She was on the boat. I figured those crazy nuns woulda tossed her off, too. So she couldn't tell what they done, you know? But, she ain't here. Do you think, maybe, they didn't drown her?" His face darkened, "Or, maybe Joseph was too busy with me an' she just sunk."

"Wait a minute, Donny," Anna said. "What'd you say your last name was?"

"Lawson."

"And your little sister, is she a tiny blond girl named Maybelle, who can't speak?"

Donny's eyes popped as big and shiny as brand new silver dollars. "Why yes! Have you seen her? Is she okay?"

"I saw her two days ago, I think it was two. She was fine then."

"Now, hold on. You say she can't speak? We never could get Maybelle to shut up. She ran her mouth as constant as that dripping windmill. Maybe it ain't the same Maybelle."

"No, it must be her. The Maybelle at Saint Frances had a brother named Donald. And you look just like her," Anna said. "Saint Frances is a bad place, Donny. She thinks you're dead. Maybe the shock made her mute."

"Well, then, we gotta go find her," Donny said, struggling to stand.

"Hey, take it easy. Sit down." She restrained him with a hand on his shoulder.

"No, when they took momma away, she told me, come hell or high water, Maybelle and me gotta stick together. I can't never leave her," Donny said. "We gotta go get her."

"We can't just 'go get her,' Donny. Abbess McCain, she runs the place, she has every sister on the island looking for me. They are trying to kill me."

"They already killed me," Donny said with smug contempt, "didn't do too good a job of it, did they?"

"You don't understand. She said she was going to cut off my head and hang it on her wall! She already cut off my finger. Look!"

Donny startled when she thrust her diminished left hand in his face. He took hold of it in his own hand, gawking at the white stub of knuckle where her pinky should have been. After a minute, he looked up into her eyes and said, "My sister is in a place where they cut off little girls' fingers, and you think I oughta leave her there?"

Anna opened her mouth to reply, but didn't know what to say. She pulled her hand away.

"You can't even stand up, Donald," she muttered, after a pause. "You can't get out of this basement, can you?"

Donny glared at her. "I can too stand up," he said. "You're runnin' away from that place, ain't you? You're scared to go back?"

"Of course I'm scared," she said. "The only reason you're not is because you don't know anything about it."

"I know enough," he said, nodding at her left hand. "If your little sister was in a place like that, would you run off an' leave her?" Anna's other hand still rested on his shoulder. He brushed it off and tried to stand.

Anna watched him, letting his words sink in. She thought of Lizzy and Jane and the Marys. She thought of Ephraim.

Donny got his feet under him and pulled himself up the wall until he was standing. "'Cause if you're that kind of coward, I don't need you."

"I'm not a coward, Donny. I…" She thought of several examples of her courage, not the least of which was taking the blame for her brother's murder. "I…" she began, but none of the examples were stories she wanted to tell. "I don't think you should call someone a coward when you don't know what they've done," she said, "or what's been done to them."

"I'm not running out on my sister," he said. The effort to stand took its toll. He trembled now, as if he were very cold. His bravado deflated to petulance. "I'm not leaving her in a place like that."

I'm not a coward, Anna thought, *not a murderer either*. She looked at Donny, shivering in the basement's dusty light, and wondered about Ephraim, *If he was still alive would he have come to save me?*

She remembered Little E, just a toddler, wrapping himself around her leg as she tried to leave for school every day. She remembered him stomping on a roach that had terrified her mother.

"My brother would have come for me," she said.

"'Course he would. That's what brothers do."

"Sit down, Donny, save your strength." She patted the floor beside her. "We need to talk about this."

Chapter 17

"I AM NOT A COWARD. It's just that I don't know what to do. We are on an island, there's nowhere to go." Anna pulled the half-eaten potato out of her pocket.

Donny reluctantly sat down again, a few feet from Anna. "Where were you planning on going when you got out?"

"Here, I guess," she said. "I didn't know where I was going. I just needed to get out. Joseph gave me a key and told me how to escape. He said to come here and he'd keep me safe. I didn't know. I didn't know what he is."

"Well you know now, don't you?" Donny said. "That home can't be as bad as being down here. Maybe them nuns are crazy and mean, but at least they fed you, right? At least they aren't gonna eat you...or chop you up for spare parts."

"It's bad, Donny."

"If it's that bad, I ain't gonna leave Maybelle there."

"Donny, we are stuck in this trap. The only way out is..." Anna nodded toward the opening of the cistern. "You said yourself that you're too scared to go down there."

"I didn't say I was 'scared.' Besides, that was before you told me 'bout Maybelle needing rescued." Donny looked down at his hands. "I might not be so scared if I had someone to go with me."

Anna leaned her head back against the wall, looking up toward the broken floorboards.

"You got out of there, Anna," he persisted. "If you got out, you can help me get Maybelle out."

"It's not that simple, Donny. Everything has changed. I don't know how things are there, now that I left."

"What do you mean?"

Anna sighed. She handed Donny the potato. "Eat this."

Donny looked at the potato but did not take it.

"Donny, if you want to help Maybelle, you need to eat."

He slid across the floor to the wall beside Anna. He accepted the spud and took a bite.

"I escaped by blowing up the factory. Exploded it to smithereens."

Donny choked and spit chunks of half-chewed potato across the dismal basement. "You blew it up?"

"It was kind of an accident...I mean, I didn't really know..." But that was a lie.

You knew it would explode. You knew people would die. The other Anna said in her head. *I thought we decided to stop lying, especially about murder.*

"I blew up the boiler," she tried again, "Joseph told me to. I thought he was helping me. I think some of the nuns may have died, maybe a lot of them."

Donny chomped into the spud, staring at her wide-eyed. Around the mash in his mouth he asked, "How many of 'em did you get?"

"Donny! I didn't want to *get* any of them. I just couldn't stay there any longer. I had to get out. And..." She wiped savagely at the tears on her mud-caked cheeks. "I thought I was a murderer. I thought I had murdered Ephraim – and momma, too – so it didn't matter if I killed some evil sisters. But I didn't kill Little E, I never did," she sniffed, "so I wasn't a murderer after all, but now I am. And all my girls are probably going to die because nobody is going to feed them because of what *I* did, and I think I knew that too when I did it, but I just couldn't stay any longer."

Anna buried her face in her hands and sobbed. Her shoulders bounced up and down as she lowered her head between her knees. "I couldn't stay. I didn't want to leave them like that...but I couldn't do it...I couldn't stay. I killed the sisters and that's going to kill everybody."

Her sobs and gibbering echoed around the small room until the basement reverberated with the sounds of her grief. The torment and anguish of the last five years, pent up behind wall after wall of self-preservation and robotic obedience, poured out of her like puss from an infected wound. Donny, looking as mortified as if he were seeing and attempting to tend to such a wound, awkwardly patted her shoulder.

Anna wept on, barely noticing him. When the patting didn't work, Donny slid up against her and wrapped his arm over her shoulder, making shushing sounds. Other than holding his hand earlier, it was the first time a boy had touched her since her father had handed her over to Abbess McCain, five years ago.

Under any other circumstances she would have pulled away, half embarrassed, half disgusted. But here, in the waterlogged basement, so completely disconnected from familiar experience, Donny's touch imparted an odd, profound comfort. For five years, Anna had starved – starved of food, starved of hope, starved of comfort. However taboo it may have been, Anna leaned into Donny's one-armed hug, crying into her hands until she slept.

***

Late afternoon sun pierced the blackberry vines. Spears of light dappled one basement wall or sparkled off the surface of the water on the floor. A finch perched on the bit of staircase that still dangled from the floor joists, but it flitted away as soon as Anna raised her head. Donny's arm had slid off of her, but they still rested against each other at their shoulders. His head hung down, with his chin on his chest. The last of the potato had rolled out of his hand and bobbed in the stagnant water.

Anna sat up. Donny startled awake, blushing, and sliding away from her.

"Are you okay?" he asked. "I guess I really upset you."

Anna smiled. It was a weary, battered smile, but it warmed her inside and seemed to solidify and call to order the jumbled chaos of emotion in her head. "I have to tell you something..."

"If it's about me putting my arm around you, I juss did that 'cause you were crying so hard. I didn't mean nothing by it."

"No, it's about your sister...and my sisters." Anna swallowed, then continued in a deliberate tone. "I have lived at Saint Frances since I was nine years old. I'll tell you all about it if you like, but the important thing to understand is this, I would rather die right here in this hole than spend another night inside that hell." She wiped a coagulation of tear-mud and snot off her face. "I will *never* return to that. No matter what."

Donny's face hardened and his hands balled into fists, but Anna held up a hand, a wait-a-minute gesture.

"But that's okay," she continued. "I *can't* go back, even if I wanted to. They will kill me the moment they lay eyes on me. So it doesn't matter, don't you see? They can't do any worse than kill me, and I'd die anyway if I stay here."

"So, then, you *will* help me get Maybelle?"

Anna scoffed, and looked away. "I used to be brave." She held out her left hand, as if examining her nails. "I had a friend when I first arrived at Saint Frances, Rebecca Fontan. She was the head girl before me. They cut off her little finger, too." She looked up from her hand to Donny's green eyes. "Do you want to know why?"

"Probably not," Donny said.

"Well, you *need* to know, Donny. If you are asking me to return to Saint Frances, you need to understand what you're asking," Anna said. "And you need to understand what you are getting yourself into."

Donny studied his hands, "Tell me."

"They cut off my finger because I stole a box of books out of Abbess McCain's office. They claimed that they cut off Rebecca's finger because, as the head girl, she was responsible for my actions." Anna stared at Donny, though he still didn't look at her. "The real reason was just sheer meanness. They cut off her finger because she was my friend." After a pause she added, "That's the kind of place you are asking me to return to."

"It doesn't make no sense, though," Donny said. "I mean, they're *nuns*. I ain't Catholic or nothin' but I always thought nuns were s'posed to be good. What's wrong with 'em?"

"Not these nuns, Donny. Why'd they send you and Maybelle here? Because nobody wanted you back home, right? Same with me, everybody knew my name, all across the state. I was the little girl who killed her baby brother. After my mother died, none of the homes would take me. Saint Frances is where they dump the kids nobody ever wants to see again.

"It's also where they dump *nuns* nobody ever wants to see again – the ones that really embarrass the Church. All the sisters of The Saint Frances de Chantal Orphan Asylum have dark secrets. They *are* dark secrets.

"None of them want to be here, but in most cases it was either here or jail, or execution. I know that at least two of the sisters were sent here after they killed someone. They resent the orphans, blame us for their exile, take their anger out on us. And no one checks up on them. Everyone else is happy to forget that any of us exist."

Donny was looking at her now. His jaw clenched, then jutted, then relaxed. His green eyes widened, as if in sudden understanding, then narrowed as if scheming. His lips pursed, then narrowed. Twice he opened his mouth as if to speak, then closed it again, continuing his contemplation.

When he finally did speak, he said, "So, why'd you steal the books?"

Anna laughed, surprised. "I wanted to read them…" she said, "and because I was angry. One of our little girls died from the cold. Two nights earlier, Rebecca had shown me a hidden ladder into Abbess McCain's office. We searched the place for extra blankets, or a coat, anything to keep little Norma alive. I found the books – all dime store novels and penny dreadfuls, books Abbess McCain had confiscated from the disgraced nuns upon their arrival – but we didn't find anything for Norma.

"When she died two nights later," Anna shrugged, "it was kind of like, revenge, rebellion, I guess. I didn't want Saint Frances to win every time. I wanted," Anna paused, "I don't know what I wanted. But swiping those books made sense, at the time.

"It took Abbess McCain three months to realize I stole them." Anna laughed again, but with no humor. "I hid them on the book shelf with all the other books, right on the main corridor. I put the skinny ones inside the fat boring books, and the thick books I shelved spine in, so the nuns wouldn't know what they were."

Donny chuckled, clearly impressed.

"Those were the best three months of my stay here. Not only did I put one over on the sisters – and all the other kids knew it – but we also got to read some of the wickedest stories in print."

Donny chuckled again, "Thought you said the nuns had been reading those books."

"Yeah? I also told you the nuns had dark secrets, right?"

"Who would'a thought," Donny laughed.

"Anyway, somebody finally caught on," Anna said. "I admitted, right away, that I had taken the books. I knew they'd figure it out eventually, and I didn't want anyone else to get in trouble." Anna's spirits had lifted a bit, thinking of Rebecca and their little victory, but the happy part of her story was over.

"I already told you what happened next," she said. There was a sharpness in her voice she hadn't intended. "They cut off my finger, and then they cut off Rebecca's, just for spite. Her hand got infected. Two days later, she was delirious with fever. The day after that, she was dead." Anna sat quiet for a moment.

"I tried not to make any friends after that," she said, the hard edge in her voice gone now. "I think I just gave up, you know? Saint Frances won. Then, when I saw a chance to escape, I ran and didn't look back..."

Anna propped her elbows on her knees and put her head in her hands. The broken floorboards above her reflected in the water around her feet. A slight twitch of one toe destroyed the picture.

After a few moments, Donny spoke. "You said, before, that everybody was gonna die 'cause of what you did. Is that true? Do you think they'll just kill all the kids out of spite?"

"No, not exactly," Anna said. "But I blew up the boiler, and the factory. They won't have any heat. And Abbess McCain won't feed us if we don't work. We can't work if there's no factory. With no food or heat, they won't last long." Anna paused, wringing her hands in her lap. "They already killed one boy, out on the beach." A shudder gripped her. She bit down hard on the inside of her lip, determined not to start crying again. "I don't think they meant to kill him. They didn't mean to kill Rebecca... but she's still dead."

Donny gingerly lifted his arm, intending to comfort her as he had before, but Anna pushed it away. She shoved herself to her feet and paced across the basement's puddled floor, running one hand through her hair.

"I put one over on them *this time*, didn't I?" Anna said. "A real whopper."

Donny eyed her, nodding.

"Somehow, they knew it was me. Abbess McCain accused me by name," Anna said. "She's got to be mad as the devil. She's going to want revenge. And if she can't find me, she'll take it out on my girls."

"That's why we need to get 'em!" Donny said.

Anna groaned. She dug both hands into her hair. "It's a *fortress*, Donny! Stone walls, iron bars on all the doors, nuns guarding all the entrances…"

"But you got out," Donny pleaded. "Anna, I can't leave Maybelle in that place. I just can't. There's gotta be a way. If you blew it up, maybe it's easier to get in now, especially if you killed a bunch of the nuns."

Anna winced. She stopped pacing and dropped her hands to her sides. "I didn't mean to kill them. Please don't bring it up again."

"Sorry."

"There may be someone who could help us, if I can find a way to contact her," Anna said. She suddenly felt very tired again. "Sister Dolores…"

"One of the nuns!" Donny exclaimed.

"No, well yes, but not really. She snuck in to Saint Frances, pretending to be a nun."

"Why?"

"To…" *kill her brother,* Anna thought. "To… I, um, I don't really know. Maybe she's there to rescue someone?"

Donny eyed her, suspiciously.

"Sister Dolores might help us," Anna said more resolutely this time. "And, maybe you're right. If the explosion did enough damage, we may find a way in."

"'Course we will!" Donny said, beaming at her with his obnoxiously infectious smile.

"Stop that," Anna said, turning her attention to the rim of the cistern in its dark alcove. "This is not something to be happy about." She felt a wave of some indescribable emotion wash over her. It was the way she had felt the moment before she confessed to stealing the books. "Smiles like that don't last very long were we're going."

Chapter 18

THEY STOOD AT THE ROCK-RIMMED edge of the cistern, peering into the blackness below. The basement's ambient light revealed the first four rungs set into the cistern's wall. Darkness hid whatever lay beyond.

"Do you think, maybe, we should wait 'til morning?" Donny asked.

"If we are going to do this, we are going to do it now," Anna said. "It won't be any brighter down there whether the sun is rising or setting."

Donny worked his way around the cistern, toward the rungs, until he stood at the back of the alcove. "Do you have any more food? Maybe we should eat first."

"We can eat as we go, Donny," Anna rummaged in her pockets. "But if we start thinking up reasons to wait, we'll never go down that hole."

She found two more potatoes, and, at the bottom of her deepest pocket, the iron key. She handed a potato to Donny, but didn't look away from the key. There was something off about it. How did she have the key? She had dropped it during her flight from the dormitory. It had been in the straw beside Mary Two.

Donny crunched a bite out of his spud and made an "mmm, mmm," sound.

"Sister Dolores gave me this key," Anna said, wondering.

Donny tongued the potato chunk into his cheek, "Thought you said Joseph gave you the key."

"He did, but I lost that one, dropped it in the straw when I fled the dormitory hall…" Anna said. "Then, I met Sister Dolores… and she returned it to me, but I don't know how she got it."

Donny swallowed his bite of spud. "What's it open?"

"Joseph's key unlocked my dormitory. I think this is the same key, but I don't know. It *feels* different."

"Can I see it?" Donny held out his hand.

Anna passed it to him.

No sunlight reached the back of the alcove, where Donny stood. As he grasped the key and drew it into the pool of shadow, it began to glow. Donny gasped and yanked his hand away, dropping the key. It struck the rim of the cistern with a *ping*, then splashed into a puddle on the floor. Dim light filled the alcove, rippling across the ceiling.

"How'd you do that?" Anna whispered.

Donny backed into the wall and edged away from the key. "*I* didn't do it," he whispered.

The glow began to flicker and dim.

"Grab it, Donny! Before you lose it."

He looked at her, doubtfully.

"It won't bite you. I've been carrying it around for two days." Anna started working her way around the cistern.

Donny pulled the key out of the puddle with his thumb and forefinger. At his touch, it resumed glowing. "Why's it *doing* that?"

"Maybe Sister Dolores bewitched it."

"She's a *witch*?" Donny exclaimed. "The only friend you have, the one that's supposed to help us, is a witch?"

"She dabbles," Anna said.

"Dabbles in what?"

"I don't know, Donny! I don't know if Sister Dolores is a witch. I don't know what she is. I do know she helped me get away. She promised to look out for my girls," Anna said. "And apparently, she has given us a light when we needed one."

Donny held the key out to Anna. "Witches are evil."

"It was your idea to go back. I told you it's a bad place. There are some very scary people where we're going. A lot scarier than Sister Dolores." Anna did not take the key. "And Joseph is waiting somewhere between here and there."

Donny's eyes popped at the mention of Joseph, but then he jutted his lower jaw and said, "I am going to get my sister." He dangled the key over the cistern and looked down. A moth fluttered up out of the depths, but all else was still. "And you're gonna get your girls."

Holding the key aloft, he offered his other hand to Anna and nodded at the iron rungs.

"You want me to go first?" she asked.

"Well, I'll go first, if you want, but...well, I mean, I'm not too scared or nothing. It's just..." Donny blushed. He looked at Anna, then into the hole, then back at Anna.

"What?" Anna demanded. "You are the one who wanted to go."

"Yeah, we're both going, but," he motioned at the rungs, "it's a ladder...and you're wearing a dress..."

Anna's cheeks burned as bright as the boiler. She shot Donny a look that could have melted iron. "Give me the key."

He lowered it into her palm. "I just..."

She brushed away the hand he had offered and climbed over the stone rim of the cistern. Pebbles and dust tumbled off the edge and dropped into darkness. Seconds later, an echo of hollow *plip*'s rose from below. Donny raised questioning eyebrows. She glared at him, but when he offered his hand a second time, she took it.

Anna lowered one foot toward the first rung, scraping the toe of her shoe down the stone wall. Once she found it, she swung her other foot over the edge and down to the second rung. Donny held her left hand tightly. Her right arm was wrapped over the rim, with the key in her right hand. Her knees trembled. Her hands felt as if they could, at any minute, lose their ability to hang on. She clung to Donny's hand so hard it must have hurt him, but his grip didn't falter and she was very glad he was there.

When she had descended to the fourth rung, she could no longer reach Donny or the rim of the cistern. She found that she could not hold onto the key and a rung with the same hand. Hooking the rung with her elbow while holding the key in her palm worked, at first, but then she wasn't able to unhook her elbow once she had stepped down to a lower rung.

Donny saw her dilemma. "Hold it in your teeth. You know, like how a pirate holds his dagger."

She thought about saying that she had never seen a pirate hold a dagger in his teeth, but held her tongue. She wanted to tie it to the string that had held her pinky, but that would require climbing back out.

If I climb out of this hole, I may not have the courage or energy to try it again.

She clamped the key between her front teeth, more like a thermometer than a dagger, and decided that having a key in her mouth was a pretty good excuse not to talk to Donny, at least for a little while.

With both hands firmly grasping rungs, Anna grew more at ease climbing down. The rungs attached to the wall at regular intervals, allowing her to find them easily with her feet. The glowing key illuminated the stones directly in front of her, but the darkness around her seemed deeper by contrast. She couldn't see her feet at all.

"I'm coming down, right behind you," Donny whispered.

Anna grunted, "Mm-hmm."

"Look down, so you don't get any dirt in your eyes."

"Mm-hmm."

She heard him slide over the edge above her. Small pebbles tapped her arms and the top of her head. She tried to whisper, "be careful," at him, but it came out as muffled "s" sounds. *He's probably figured out to be careful without me saying so.* Still, the idea of Donny falling past her or – God forbid – on top of her, sent a chill through her.

"Don't worry," he called down in a loud whisper. "I can see your hands. I ain't gonna step on 'em." Now that he was fully inside the cistern, the echoes of his whispers slithered back out of the darkness like a knot of phantom serpents.

Anna tried to shush him, but that came out sounding snake-like as well. Donny seemed to get it, anyway, and did not attempt to speak again.

The wall they descended remained vertical, but below the fourth rung, the walls to their back and sides curved out and away. The cistern opened into a half-dome shaped room, about twenty feet across. Anna stopped to examine the space. Both feet on the same rung, she gripped a rung tightly with one hand, with the other she drew the key from her teeth and held it out.

Just as she began to get a sense of the size and nature of the room, the rung under her feet broke loose. Anna screamed, and dropped, swinging into the wall. Her hand on the rung held, but just barely. She grasped desperately at the wall with her other hand, her feet dangling and clattering against the stone.

Above the echo of her scream, which pounded and resonated through the room, she heard a watery *PLOINK*, and the room darkened. *The key!* Her free hand found a rung. She looked down. Where her feet hung, a chunk of stone had broken loose from the wall, about three feet below that, black water rippled away into the unseen depths of the cistern. Beneath the surface, maybe ten feet down, glimmered the key, its unnatural glow flickering and beginning to dim.

Chapter 19

"DONNY, THE KEY!" ANNA CRIED, trying to yell and whisper at the same time. Her feet scrabbled against the crumbling stone.

Before she could say more, there came a clumsy *flutter* and *whoosh* from above — beside — then below her, as Donny plummeted past. He struck the surface of the water with a loud *slap*, and a long-echoing splash.

Anna bit back another scream, focusing her attention on trying to regain her footing. The rung below the one that had dropped her looked as if it might fall out at any moment, even if she did not step on it. She pulled herself up by her arms, walking her toes up the wall until they reached the next rung.

Below, the key's glow dwindled. Darkness crawled out of the deeper reaches of the cistern, closing in from all sides around the small light. Anna strained to see Donny under the water. Ripples rolled over the surface, lapped against the stones, then slid back the way they had come. The waves distorted Anna's view. She could make out a dark form backlit by the key. Or was it two dark forms? The masses dove toward the bottom, swimming down toward the glow. In the rippling dim light, the silhouettes and shadows merged and separated and merged again. Arms, legs, tentacles — Anna couldn't tell.

The forms wavered and shifted. Anna needed to scan the room, find the drainage pipe, before the dim glow vanished completely, but she could not drag her eyes away from the dying light and the shadow she hoped was Donny.

Anna had been holding her breath since Donny had dived past her. A hungry ache gnawed her lungs. She let the stale air out and inhaled. *How long can he stay down there,* she wondered, *I'm going after him...*

Then the light vanished.

Blackness rushed in from all sides, so fast and solid it seemed to physically strike her. An airy fluttering noise chased itself around the semi-circular room, the echoes of her last gasp.

She strained her ears, longing for any hint as to where Donny might be, terrified of what else she might hear. She peered down, praying for just a little glimpse of light. But the harder she stared into the tarry blackness, the darker it grew. It pressed against her as if it was dirt, and she was buried in it.

"Donny?" a pleading whisper.

The echoes taunted her, "Neeee...neee...nee..."

A terrible idea bloomed in her mind. *Just go back up. There's light up there. Donny's dead. You can't help him. You can't save your girls. Just go back up, where you are supposed to be.*

Above her, a hair-thin crescent of light broke the intense darkness. The cistern's rim glowed like the corona of an eclipsed moon. *Maybe there's another way out up there. Maybe we missed something.*

"I'm *not* going back up," she said. But she couldn't stay put, either. Think. The pipe must be close to the surface of the water...

Go back up.

No! I'll swim around the edge. I'll feel for the pipe.

Donny's dead. Drowned just like Ephraim. You're going to be swimming with his corpse.

Shut up!

What if you bump into it? What if it grabs your ankle and pulls you down?

"Donny?" She yelled into the black.

The echoes thundered back at her, deafening. Anna buried her face against her hands where they clung to the iron bar. If he is dead... "I'll get Maybelle for you, Donny. I'll try, at least."

Anna lowered herself, extending her arms and letting her feet slip off the last solid rung. She took two deep breaths, holding the third and prepared to drop.

Suddenly, the room filled with light. Anna looked back, over her shoulder, and down. An unearthly bluish luminosity radiated out of the water. A black silhouette raced toward the surface, swimming straight at her.

In her head, Anna was screaming, *It's Donny! He has the key!* But her feet kicked and scrabbled and her hands clawed desperately for a higher rung.

Donny burst through the surface, gasping and splashing, the key glowing in his hand. "I got it! I got it!"

The overlapping echoes of the splashing and yelling built upon each other until it was too overpowering to hear anything – so Donny probably didn't hear Anna screaming curses at him. She decided to throw a potato at his stupid, laughing head. But, as she reached into her pocket with one hand, she lost her grip with the other, and fell.

Chapter 20

ANNA SPLASHED TO THE SURFACE and grabbed onto a nub of stone on the wall. The echoes quieted. Donny dogpaddled toward her, holding the key over his head. Its light reflected off the water, sending shimmering ripples across the curved stone ceiling.

"You okay, Anna? You look kinda ruffled."

"That was a damn stupid thing to do, Donald Lawson!" Anna sputtered, her head just barely above the water. "I thought you drowned."

"I nearly did drowned. The light went out 'fore I got to it. Took a while to find in the dark." Donny looked past Anna to the broken iron rungs. "Guess we're not going back up that way."

Anna wanted to slap Donny, or continue yelling at him, but she couldn't reach him without letting go of the rock, and she couldn't think of anything else to say. Also, she didn't want to consider what would have happened if he *hadn't* retrieved the key. So she said nothing, turning away, instead, to the remains of the ladder.

The rungs below the water line, and the next three above it, had rusted away completely, leaving only orange stains in the rock wall. Rust had gnawed so deeply into the next two rungs that they surely could not have supported either Anna or Donny. Above these, a hole gaped in the stones where her rung, and the rocks surrounding it, had broken loose.

"We're certainly *not* going back that way," she said. "If we wanted to be up there, why'd we climb down in the first place?"

"I just mean I sure hope we can find that drainage pipe, else we're gonna be stuck down here," Donny said. "You sound kinda upset. Are you sure you're okay?"

"Yes, Donny, I'm fine. Let's just find the pipe, no more talking for a bit, okay?"

The flat wall that held the ladder extended away from her about ten feet in either direction, with no visible openings. The key's glow did not penetrate into the darkness where the half-domed ceiling curved down to meet the water.

Anna pulled herself along the wall, rock by rock. Donny followed, swimming, holding the key aloft. The sounds of their progress fluttered around the confined space, returning to them as whispers and secretive movement.

At the corner where the flat wall met the curved dome, just above the water line, they found two openings. Red brick pipes with black-molded mortar, and greenish algae glazing their curved bottoms. Both pipes smelled like rainwater and old wood and wet stone, not like salt water or seaweed.

"Which one is it?" Donny whispered.

"Neither goes to the ocean. Look," Anna pointed into one of the pipes, "it slants up, not down... maybe something else drains into here."

"If it goes up, maybe we can get out faster that way."

"When Joseph brought you here, do you remember which pipe he used?"

"No, I was in a tunnel, then I was up there in the basement," Donny said. "I don't remember this room at all."

Anna looked around the cistern, marking their position in relation to the ladder. "The alcove, for the cistern, it was on the east wall of the basement, I think..."

"Right," said Donny. "In the afternoon, the sunlight almost reached it."

121

"Okay, so that means this wall, the one we climbed down, is the east side, so these pipes are running..."

"North and north-east," Donny whispered, excitedly, then paused and added, "So, what does that mean?"

"It means, they go farther inland, away from the sea. The drainage pipe to the ocean should be on the opposite side." Anna considered for a moment, then said, "I think we should go that way. These pipes, I don't know, they could put us anywhere. It could take forever to find our way back to your sister. If we go to the ocean, we can just follow the beach around."

Without further conversation, Anna pulled herself along the curved wall. Donny followed close behind her, forcing back the shadows with the glowing key. Slick black algae coated the rocks. Twice, Anna lost her grip and bobbed under the dark water. She wasn't a great swimmer, and her clunky leather shoes didn't help, but she managed to regain the surface and her hold on the wall without assistance from Donny. Donny, on the other hand, seemed to be half fish, able to swim along beside her while holding the key above his head. He was really starting to annoy her.

"This might be it," Anna said as she reached the opposite corner. An iron grate, severely rusted, hung halfway open just above the waterline. It was round with vertical bars and a hinge on one side. Opposite the hinge, a clasp provided a means to lock the grate, though the lock was gone. The hinge appeared to be rusted in place, but when Anna squeezed herself between the grate and the wall, the grate swung open with a sickening screech.

Anna froze. The screech continued for what seemed like several minutes after the grate stopped moving.

"That's the screaming I told you about," Donny whispered. In the dim light, it was hard to be sure, but Anna thought he looked very pale. "I thought it was Joseph. He always showed up just after I heard that noise."

"That means we're going the right way," Anna said. "If this is how he comes and goes, then it must lead out. Come on, this time, you're going first."

***

Donny scrambled out of the water and into the pipe, holding the key out in front of him. As he did, the cistern fell once again into complete darkness. Anna quickly followed. Donny's body nearly filled the diameter of the pipe, and blocked out most of the light. All Anna could see was the silhouette of Donny's backside, and the dim halo around it, as the key's light reflected off the walls of the pipe. Under other circumstances, this would have been a funny sight.

A halo around his bottom, if Jane or Lizzy were here, I'm sure they'd have something to say about that.

But the girls were not here, and Anna needed to stay mad at Donny as long as possible. It was the only way not to be terrified. She decided his hallowed butt wasn't funny at all.

At first, Donny hobbled forward like a three-legged dog. It was going to take forever to get through the tunnel that way. Anna handed him the leather thong that had held her finger. "Tie the key on that and sling it around your neck. It'll free up your hand and keep you from dropping it."

"I wasn't the one who dropped it," Donny said, but he did as she suggested.

When they had crawled another ten feet, Donny said, "It's getting kinda hard to see. It's all foggy up here."

"Just keep going, Donny. The fog will clear once we get out."

"'Get out,' yeah. That'll be somethin', huh? To be out in the fresh air again?" He started shuffling forward a little faster. "How far do you think it is?"

123

"Shh. Keep it down. I don't know how far it is. Could be a really long way."

"'Cause I think I see light up ahead."

Anna's heart froze. "Donny!" she gasped in a harsh whisper. "Donny, stop! Cover the key!"

Donny did and the tunnel collapsed into blackness. "What's wrong?" he whispered.

"It's night out there." She moved forward, as close to him as she could get, and tried to see around him. "There shouldn't be any light ahead."

Donny whispered, "I don' see it no more."

"Shh." Anna strained her ears. The ubiquitous echoes flittered up and down the pipe. As the ghosts of their voices died away, a new noise emerged. From deep in the tunnel came the sound of wet, furtive, movement.

In a voice, so low it seemed to come from inside Anna's head, Donny said, "It sounds like somebody's moppin' the floor down there." He opened his hand just a little, releasing a thin shaft of light from the key.

Over Donny's shoulder, deep in the mist-shrouded tunnel, Anna saw it. Eye shine.

Chapter 21

"IT'S JOSEPH," SHE WHISPERED.

The moment the words left her lips, the formerly secretive sloshing sounds amplified to a frenetic, sloppy splashing.

Donny scuttled backward into Anna so hard that he crammed himself between her and the pipe wall, wedging them in place. Anna tried to back up, but Donny's frantic scrambling pinned her to the wall. She couldn't tell him to wait for her to get out of his way, her own panic trapped the words in her throat.

Her hand ended up on the back of his thigh. So, she pinched, severely. Donny squealed in pain and terror. His hands slipped out from under him on the slimy algae, and he fell forward. Anna managed to scramble back before he got up and pinned her to the wall again.

Within a half a second, Donny was back up on all fours. He and Anna scampered and scuttled madly backward down the pipe as Joseph's glowing eyes sloshed toward them. Anna felt the wet skin peeling off her knees, and twice slammed her head into the top of the pipe, but barely noticed either. The eyes racing toward them were her only concern.

Anna's knees went over the end of the pipe before she realized she had reached it. The lower half of her body dropped. Her stomach hit the pipe's edge, knocking the wind out of her. Momentum carried her the rest of the way out. The cistern's black water pulled her under.

She struggled back to the surface, gasping for breath. Donny shot out of the pipe, splashing under the water beside her. Anna stared, wide eyed, at the gaping mouth of the pipe. Joseph was coming. She looked across the cistern toward the broken ladder, then to the other pipes. Darkness hid her escapes, but she already knew they were too far away.

Close the grate! she thought, just as Donny bobbed up out of the water.

"The grate!" he yelled, already paddling back toward it.

Anna grabbed the bottom arc of its iron rim and flung it closed. The screech of its hinge reverberated through the cistern. Corroded iron slammed against stone with a loud, dead, *Clank!* Donny pulled himself half out of the water, fighting to pin the clasp.

"Hold it closed! He's coming!" Donny yelled.

"There's nothing to push against!" Anna yelled back. She held onto an iron bar with one hand, the hinge with the other, and sought somewhere to anchor her feet.

Donny held the clasp against its hook on the wall. "I'm going to tie it closed with the leather cord you gave me."

As he reached for the key, a black tentacle shot through the grate and wrapped around Donny. It yanked him back, slamming him against the iron bars. He bleated a strangled, miserable yelp. The rusted bar Anna had been holding snapped off in her hand with the force of the impact. The tentacle crushed Donny against the grate, bending the bars inward.

A terrible, guttural churning filled the cistern. The noise became words, roaring and infuriated, "You're supposed to be dead!"

Then the face appeared. A stark, terrifying image. From the nose up, a human skull, wrapped in a yellow parchment of skin. Luminous silver fish eyes, larger than Anna's fists, protruded from its sockets. Below the eyes, starting where the nose hole should have been, the mouth of some horrible predatory fish. Row after row of twisted needle-sharp teeth.

"Anna!" Donny choked, reaching for her.

She was already swimming away, the voice in her head screaming at her to flee. *He can't catch both of you. You have to get away. You can't die like this, not after all you've been through! You don't know Donny. You don't owe him anything. Just go! GO!*

"Anna!" Donny cried again.

She turned. The Joseph thing pushed its teeth through the iron bars until they scraped Donny's ear.

"She won't help you," its horrible voice whispered. "She only cares about herself. Little Anna killed twelve holy nuns just so she wouldn't have to make shoes anymore."

Anna swam back toward Donny, the other Anna ranting in her head. *It's a trap, he's luring you back...*

Shut UP!

As clear and as vivid as if she were real, Other Anna bobbed out of the water in front of Anna, blocking her path. *Get away, while you can,* the spectral Other Anna said in a menacing stern voice. *Do not go back for the boy!* Anna slammed the iron bar into Other Anna's head and the vision splattered to dark water. She lunged toward Donny, grasping the grate's hinge.

With its foremost teeth, the Joseph thing bit down on the top of Donny's ear. Donny started to scream, but the patchwork hand reached through the bars and clamped over his mouth. The tentacle pinned Donny's arms at his sides. He thrashed wildly with his feet, but could not break free.

"Little Anna drowned her own baby brother in a bathtub because he was a snotty little brat. She won't help you."

"He wasn't a brat!" Anna screamed and plunged the iron bar through the tentacle. She ripped it out, preparing to strike again.

Joseph thrust his other hand through the grate, grabbing her wrist with crushing strength. It lifted her all the way out of the water. She dangled against the grate, staring into its dead empty eye.

"Why'd you come back, Anna?" it croaked at her. "You knew better, didn't you?"

"You were supposed to be my friend," she said, surprised by how betrayed she felt.

"Your friend?" the thing asked. "I've been back to the castle, little Anna. All of your friends are dying because of you. It's so cold. So, so cold. And they have nothing to eat. I think being your friend is a very bad idea. What do *you* think, Donald?" The Joseph thing removed its hand from Donny's mouth.

Donny gasped, "Anna, the key!"

Anna looked down. Her free hand hung within inches of the glowing key. She snatched it off its cord and jammed it through the bars, driving the enchanted relic into Joseph's silver eye.

Lightning erupted inside the thing's skull, flashing in one eye socket and out the other. Joseph screamed, releasing Anna's wrist. She dropped into the water and sank.

As she thrashed below the surface, strong fingers wrapped around her wrist again and hoisted her upward. Anna reared back to strike again, but as she came out of the water, it was Donny who held her.

"Easy, there, Anna," he said.

The Joseph-thing flailed and writhed in the pipe, screaming, wailing, sounding exactly like a six-year-old child throwing a temper tantrum.

"Quick," Donny said, "give me that iron bar."

Anna, dazed, offered it to him. Donny crammed the rusted bar through the clasp and the latch. The Joseph thing continued to scream, but had stopped crying. The pain was gone from his wailing, replaced by rage. A tentacle lashed out of the darkness, striking the grate. Two iron bars bent outward.

"C'mon, Anna!" Donny dragged her away across the cistern. Seconds later, Anna began swimming with him toward the far corner.

Donny splashed through the darkness toward the two pipes. Anna fought to keep up. She wasn't able to hold the key above the surface as Donny had. It dipped in and out of the water as she swam. The cistern alternated between flashes of dim light and complete blackness. Darkness hid the walls.

Just as she was beginning to fear they were swimming in circles, Donny asked, "Which one?"

There was only a vague suggestion of Donny's outline ahead of her. Beyond him, two black circles defined the openings of the pipes. The cistern was much darker than it had been. Behind them, Joseph slammed against the iron grate, screeching and roaring.

"Just pick one," she said.

"Hold the key up so I can see."

"I *am* holding it up," Anna said.

"I think you broke it," Donny whispered.

The part of the key that had penetrated Joseph's eye no longer glowed. It was just dead black iron. The rest of the key flickered and blinked in spasms, dimming.

A metallic screech reverberated across the cistern, followed by a splash. Anna guessed that Joseph had torn off one of the bars and flung it at them.

"Get in the left tunnel," she said. "Go!"

Donny scrambled out of the water. Anna tossed him the key and followed. This time, as they scampered through the tunnel, his butt had no halo. No light at all reached Anna.

***

They crawled frantically at first, but as time passed, the savage noises from the cistern died away. The sharpness of their terror gave way to fatigue and they slowed, plodding through the darkness. Anna lost track of time. She felt as if she had been crawling for days, or maybe it was weeks. She couldn't be sure. By the time Donny found the end of the tunnel, they both trembled with exhaustion. Anna's bleeding knees ached, her neck and shoulders burned. Her eyes felt hollowed out from staring so long into blackness.

"Where are we?" she whispered.

"I think it's another cistern," he said, "only this one's empty...and it stinks."

Donny fidgeted and squirmed at the mouth of the pipe, trying to get his feet around in front of himself. The narrowness of the pipe constrained him. After nearly wedging himself stuck crosswise, he gave up.

"I can't turn around. Gonna have to go head first," he said. "I don't think it's a very long drop...I hope not. Hold my feet."

Anna felt around in the dark until she found his ankles. "I'll try to hang on, but if you fall, I won't be able to hold you."

Donny didn't reply, and Anna couldn't see what he was doing. She felt him lie flat then inch forward. "I'm just gonna slide out, nice and slow." Donny's upper body dropped out of the way. The top of the pipe shimmered dimly, reflecting the key's glow. Suddenly, Donny lurched forward. It felt as if something yanked him out of Anna's grasp. She heard a thump and a muffled clatter. Then a groan.

"It's a longer drop than I thought."

"Are you okay?"

"I'm fine. It's just my head," he replied. "Ease yourself over the edge. I'll try to catch you."

Anna moved forward to the rim of the pipe. The key illuminated Donny, below her, but little of the space around him, just the stone wall below the pipe and a bit of dry floor. The top of Donny's head, sporting a fresh abrasion from his fall, reached almost to the bottom of the pipe.

Anna lowered her belly to the floor and wriggled forward until her shoulders were clear of the opening. She reached down to Donny, who took hold of her under the arms and pulled her forward. She carefully eased herself out, trying to fall as softly as possible. Leaning heavily on

Donny, she curled one leg out of the pipe, hoping to catch herself on it when she dropped.

It might have worked, except Donny, walking backward while looking up at her and supporting her weight, tripped over something in the gloom. He fell back with a wet *splat,* and she tumbled out on top of him. He grunted, the impact knocking the breath out of him. The reek that immediately followed took what was left of Anna's breath away.

The stench of rot was so intense she could taste it. Donny tried to push her off, but his efforts seemed weak. Anna rolled to the side, her stomach clenching. If there had been any food in her, she would surely have vomited. Donny retched behind her. Anna staggered to her feet, grabbed Donny's arm and dragged him away from the horrid smell.

When the room stopped spinning and her equilibrium returned, she saw what had tripped Donny. A fat, speckled harbor seal lay sprawled across the stone floor. Its head and one of its flippers were missing.

"Joseph do that?" Donny choked.

"It didn't do that to itself," Anna nodded.

Donny took her hand and pulled her away from the dead beast. They worked their way around the curved wall. The key had dimmed even more since they fled the flooded cistern. It now only illuminated a few feet on either side. At one point, they found a crack in the stones, running up the wall and as far as they could see across the floor.

"Explains why there's no water here," Donny muttered.

"If this *is* another cistern, there should be a house above us, right? Or at least a basement?"

"Hope so," Donny said.

It scared Anna how tired he sounded. "Are you doing okay, Donny? Is your ear okay?"

"Yeah..." he said, trailing off. He took a few steps before adding, "I'm glad you came back for me."

131

Anna felt herself blushing all over, and was glad for the deep gloom. The knowledge that she might not have gone back for Donny filled her with intense shame.

"Sorry I almost didn't," she said, squeezing his hand.

"Almost never accounts for nothin'," Donny said.

Anna was still trying to figure out what that was supposed to mean when Donny said, "Hey! Here we go."

He held the key close to the wall. Iron rungs set into the stones led up to...well, she couldn't see where they led, but wherever they went, *It's got to be better than here.*

Chapter 22

THIS TIME, IT TURNED OUT Anna was right. At the top of the ladder, the key's failing light revealed a tiny room, just barely big enough to house the cistern's opening, three stone walls and a low ceiling. The fourth wall was wooden and held a short door. The reek of the dead seal permeated their clothes and nostrils, but it was better up here.

"This is just like the cistern alcove in the other basement," Anna whispered. "Except this one has a door." She reached for the latch.

Donny stopped her with a hand on her arm. "What if someone's out there?" he whispered.

Anna covered the key with her hand. In the pitch-black silence, they strained their ears, listening. Nothing stirred beyond the door. Nothing moved below in the cistern. Several minutes passed.

Finally, Anna whispered, "Let's go. Let's find the stairs and get out of here."

She turned the latch and eased the door open. Donny put his face up to the crack and peered through.

"Give me the key," he whispered.

She handed it to him, and he slipped it through the crack, staring into the opening. Then he drew back, looking up at Anna.

"What?" she whispered. "What do you see?"

"I think it's preserves." His voice seemed to tremble.

"What?"

"You look," he said. "I might be seeing things."

Anna cautiously pushed the door outward and slid the flickering key through the crack. As her face neared the opening, a new smell overpowered the stench of rotting seal, still an odor of decay, but this smelled more like vinegar and compost. Shelves lined the wall beyond the alcove. Broken glass jars slumped on the shelves and littered the stone floor.

"I can't see much..." she said, "looks like it used to be preserves, maybe not anymore."

She opened the door wider and crept through. Glass clinked and snapped underfoot. Wind sighed through the ruined house above. Silver moonbeams spotlighted patches of basement, accentuating the blackness of the places it didn't touch.

To her left, crude shelves lined the wall. Directly in front of the door stood a heavy oak hutch, the kind of thing Anna's mom had used to display her fine china, though this hutch was bare except for cobwebs and dust.

Thick posts on either side of the hutch supported the beams overhead. At the opposite end of the basement, across from the alcove, the support posts had collapsed. Floor joists and floorboards hung down, almost touching the basement floor.

"What do you think?" Donny asked.

"I can't see any stairs. We might be able to climb up that." She pointed to the sagging floor.

"No, I meant the preserves." He stood behind her squinting at the glittering shelves.

"I don't think they are preserved, Donny, can't you smell it?"

"Let me see the key."

Anna looked to the moonlit opening above the sagging floor, then back into the dark cistern alcove. "Make it quick."

Donny snatched the key and ran it along the lower shelf. Anna stuck close to his little circle of light as he moved away from the alcove door. He searched the bottom shelf all the way to the far wall. Most of the glass jars had either fallen off the shelf or had ruptured from their contents fermenting. He found a few jars intact, but whatever produce these once contained had now become an unappetizing black sludge.

Donny started working his way back toward the alcove, searching the second shelf. Anna wanted to grab him by the scruff of his neck and drag him out of the basement. The moonlight and wind reminded her of her frantic dash for freedom, the night she escaped Saint Frances. She wanted out, out of the darkness and stench and echoes and stale air and the soaking wetness. *Freedom is right there!* her mind insisted, *grab that little snot and drag him out of here!*

But, he needed to eat. *She* needed to eat. Especially if they were going to rescue her girls and Donny's sister. "Hurry it up, Donny," she said, hearing the strain in her voice.

"Hey! Look!" he said, loud enough to make Anna jump. Her heart spiked so hard she saw flashes.

Anna wheeled around to face him, feeling dizzy and a little faint. She intended to scold him – harshly. But, when she saw what he held, she forgot all about the moonlight and wind, at least for the moment.

Strawberry jam, half a quart, still sealed. She hadn't eaten today, hadn't had anything other than fish stew, toast and porridge for five years. Anna slumped against the shelves, staring at Donny's treasure.

If you eat that, it's probably going to kill you, the other Anna stated flatly.

That's the best way to die I've discovered yet, she answered.

Donny popped the lid off the jar. When he saw the crazy way she eyed his jam, he said, "Easy now, Anna, small bites, chew it completely, otherwise you'll get sick." He stuck two fingers into the jar and scooped a huge red glob into his mouth.

"Shut up, mom," she said. "Give me some of that, or next time, I won't come back for you."

"That's not something to joke about," he said, handing her the jar, but he was grinning.

Anna crammed a glob of jam into her mouth. She had intended to say she wasn't joking, but the sweet intensity of the strawberries obliterated every other thought from her mind.

She slid from her slump to a sitting position on the floor. Broken glass poked her bottom, but she barely noticed. It was as if the last five years of summers had been distilled into that single bite of strawberry jam.

Judging by the dilapidated state of the house, the berries had probably grown many summers before Anna had even been born. Whoever had put up these berries was probably long dead, but, *God bless you!* she thought, *God bless you, whoever's aunt or grandma you were.*

Then the sugar high hit. Her stomach twitched and tightened, but didn't quite cramp. Her head buzzed and her body tingled all over. Donny reached to take back the jar and Anna threw her arms around him in a ridiculous bear hug. Donny startled, then shoved her back, coming away with the jam.

"Geez, Anna!" he said, stumbling back. "I swear, if you try to kiss me, I'm not gonna give you any more jam." He sounded as scared as he had ever been.

Anna giggled. She sounded foolish, was *acting* foolish, but she didn't care. Something about the supreme decadence of that much sugar, of that much pure summer joy. She remembered what it felt like to be just a child – not an orphan, not a worker, not a head girl – to be somebody's daughter, somebody's niece.

"I'm not going to kiss you, I promise." She laughed again at the comically worried expression he wore. "Help me up. Let's see what else we can find."

Donny offered his hand, making sure he stayed far enough away that she wouldn't try another surprise hug. She didn't. Together they scoured the remaining shelves. After a few minutes, Donny relaxed again, cheered by the sugar and Anna's lightened mood. They passed the jam jar back and forth, as they searched, until it was empty.

"Do you think we should have saved some for later?" he asked.

"Of course," she replied, giggling.

Donny started giggling, too. "We'll save the next one we find."

***

They found one more jar of jam, not strawberry, something dark like grape or blackberry. Donny wouldn't let Anna open it to find out.

"This'll be to celebrate, once we get my sister," he said, then reconsidered. "Or for extra energy if we really get in a fix."

"We *are* in a fix," she said, still giggling. "You've never been in a fix like this in your whole life."

"Well, it could be worse."

"Donny!" she laughed. "How could it possibly be worse?"

"It'd be worse if we were completely out of jam," he said and stuffed the jar into his coat's oversized pocket.

"I guess that's true," she said.

"'Sides, you're gonna get sick if you eat any more right now."

"Why would I get sick?" she asked.

"When was the last time you ate jam?"

"When I was nine, before I came here."

"'Fore you were old enough to remember how sick you get if all you eat is sweets," Donny said.

"You're cute when you try to talk like your dad," she laughed, but she did begin to notice that her giddy lightheadedness wasn't as pleasant as it had been a few minutes ago. It had taken on more of a dizzy feel. Her stomach felt...*squishy*, and her tongue and the roof of her mouth felt chapped.

Donny scowled at her and turned back to the shelves. Anna decided to help him search, and she decided not to eat any more jam, at least for now. The next two shelves held nothing useful except a can of sardines, which they gobbled nearly as quickly as they had eaten the jam.

The real prize awaited them on the top shelf. They almost missed it because the shelf hung six inches above their heads. Neither could see what it held, even on tiptoe. Donny tried to climb up the lower shelves, but the first one he put his weight on snapped in half, dumping glass across the floor. They both winced at the clatter, suddenly remembering that they were being hunted.

"That's enough, Donny," Anna said. "We really need to go, now."

"There's something up there..."

"I don't want to be down here any longer," she said. "We have a chance, right now. We need to go while we still can."

"Come here, let me boost you up," Donny said. "Grab the case up there, then we'll split."

Anna looked at the moonlight frosting the far wall of the basement, looked at Donny, then back to the moonlight.

"C'mon, hurry up," he said. "I don't wanna be down here either."

Anna returned to where he waited. He made a stirrup with his hands and she stepped into it. She held onto the shelves for balance as he hoisted her up. On the top shelf sat a rat-gnawed leather case. It was roughly a cube, about one foot on each side. Anna grabbed the handle, but it snapped off as soon as she tried to lift it. She wrapped her arm around the case and stepped down.

"Was there anything else up there?" he asked.

"Just some hand tools, a hammer and a saw...no food."

"What's in there?"

"I don't know," Anna said.

She set the case on the floor, flipped open the brass latch and lifted the lid. When she let the lid fall open, the hinges broke off and the lid dropped to the floor. Inside, crumbling red velvet lined the box. Something brass glimmered in the velvet nest. It stared at them with a single glassy eye.

"What is it?" she asked.

"Looks like one of them pagan idols they keep digging up down in the Amazon," Donny said.

But, as he held the key closer, they both cried at once, "It's a lamp!"

CHAPTER 23

ALONG WITH THE LAMP, THE case held a striker and a waxed cardboard tube of carbide crystals. Anna and Donny managed to wring enough water from their wet clothes to activate the crystals – Donny tried spitting on them but found he was running low on spit. Anna refrained from spitting – and within a minute, the lamp blazed.

The darkness disintegrated like funeral crepe in a firestorm. Both children shielded their eyes against the sudden brightness, then laughed with delight.

"Wow!" Donny said.

"You should have found that first," Anna said, "would have made the rest of the search a lot faster."

"You didn't want me searching at all, remember?" Donny shone the light across the shelves.

"I just wanted to get out of here, that's all," she said. "And I still do. But I am very glad you found a lamp."

"And the jam?"

"Yes, Donny, and the jam, and those horrible little fish. Now let's go."

Donny stuffed the tube of carbide crystals and the striker into his pockets. He moved toward the drooping floor and the patches of moonlight. "When we get to the orphanage, I'm gonna tell your friends that you ate fish heads," he teased.

"I'm going to tell your sister that you peed your pants when Joseph grabbed you," Anna replied, moving quickly toward their intended exit.

"I did not!" Donny blurted, racing after her with the lamp.

Beyond the sagging floor joists, the rock wall of the foundation had crumbled in a 'U' shape. The fallen stones formed a natural ramp out of the basement. Anna easily clambered over the rocks into the star spangled, moonlit night. The wind lifted her hair and blew through her soggy, tattered dress. Moon-frosted pine boughs danced and swayed in the restless night air.

Anna held her arms out, looking up, wanting to scream for joy, wanting to wrap her arms around the night and embrace it. Donny was running up the rocks behind her, bellowing that she better not tell his sister lies about him. It felt so good to be out of the pits and pipes that she really did think about kissing him...at least it would shut him up. But, on second thought, that wouldn't work, her lips were smiling so hard she'd never be able to pucker.

"Anna, I did not..." Donny began, then sucked in a gasp so hard his ribs popped.

She snapped her eyes from the heavens to Donny, "What..."

He stood frozen behind her. Terror gripped his face. He held the lamp at eye level. Slowly, very slowly, he extended his other hand toward her, motioning with his fingers for her to come to him. Anna turned and faced forward, to the ground this time instead of the sky. Surrounding the sagging house, six pairs of yellow eyes glimmered. Half a dozen wolves stood within twenty feet of the foundation. Saliva dribbled from their open jaws. Lamp light glinted off their wicked fangs.

Anna lifted a hand toward Donny, stepping backward. Her foot missed its mark by several inches and she would have tumbled all the way to the basement floor if Donny hadn't caught her. They stumbled together back down the broken foundation and scuttled across the floor to the far corner.

As they reached the back wall of the basement, one of the wolves padded down the broken foundation, hackles bristling, shoulders rolling as it walked. The beast stopped halfway down the stones. It lowered its head to stare at them below the sagging floor, tongue lolling to the side, panting, watching.

"In there," Anna breathed, pointing to the alcove door.

Donny inched along the wall until his back was against the door. Anna crept with him. She grabbed something off the floor, whatever she could find, to throw if the wolves advanced. With his back to the door and one hand shining the lamp at the wolves, Donny cranked the door's latch with his other hand. He stepped forward, pulling the door open about a foot. "Go!" he whispered.

Anna slipped into the alcove. Donny followed, keeping the light on the wolves until he shut the door behind him.

"They were waiting for us," Donny said, bewildered. "How'd they know?"

"I didn't even see them," Anna said, slumping against the back wall of the alcove. "If they had wanted to eat us..." Anna silenced mid-sentence, then whispered, "Donny, cover the lamp!"

He flipped the cover over the lamp's lens, expecting darkness. No such luck. From below, buttery yellow light shone out of the cistern.

Donny and Anna crept to its edge and peered in. From this vantage, they saw most of the floor – and wished they hadn't. Lamp's, like the one Donny now held, illuminated the space. The dismembered harbor seal lay where they had seen it. What they hadn't seen before, in the dark, was the macabre menagerie that surrounded it.

Bodies, and parts of bodies, littered the cistern's floor – seals, deer, most of a shark, an octopus, the hind legs of a bear.

And people.

The boy Anna had seen beaten to death on the beach lay beside several dead nuns. One of these was Sister Evangeline, the Woodpecker, her frizzy red hair and sharp nose were unmistakable. Anna didn't recognize the other sisters. Most, like the seal, were partially dismembered, their features obscured.

"Donny," Anna whispered, "Donny!"

The boy stared into the pit, not acknowledging her.

"Donny, look at me!" She reached across and shoved his shoulder.

He raised his head, eyes huge, "Anna..."

"Shh!" She whispered. It felt like the sardines were swimming through the strawberry jam in her gut, trying to find their way back up her throat. Donny looked as if he felt the same.

"What..." Donny started.

A sound below them cut him off, a familiar gurgling voice. "No need to whisper, I know you are there. Know where you are."

The Joseph-thing pulled itself into view. "We all know just where you are."

It was even more horrible now, with the light revealing exactly what it was. Human arms attached to a deer's torso. Tentacles dangled from below each arm. It had human legs, apparently from the nuns, that sprouted out of its back and faced the wrong direction. A porpoise tail was sewn to the thing's hips, where its legs should have gone. Several seams were stitched closed with leather shoelaces from the factory. At other places, gobs of glistening kelp held the unnatural connections together.

"And we will keep you, me and my island, me and my dogs, just like I promised, and Abbess McCain will never find you." It turned its face up toward Anna and Donny. The eyes were gone, only burned black sockets regarded them.

Then it hobbled, on its backward feet, out of their view. "I have more eyes, more eyes. More eyes, little Anna, I have more eyes and hands and fingers and lots of fingers, lots of little parts. Lots of little...I'll take *your* parts, too."

There was a meaty thump below, then a dragging sound.

"I have to thank you for all these parts. Never had so many parts, good fresh parts. I can make lots of things. I made this one for *you*." It reemerged into Anna's field of view, now walking on all fours, using its tail as a fifth leg and dragging something with its tentacles. "I made this one for you, and you, so I can hold you both and swim you both."

Donny made a thin keening sound as the Joseph-thing dragged a new abomination into view. Its bottom half had been a harbor seal, once. This was sewn to a nun's torso. The nun's breasts had been replaced by a second set of arms. A third pair of arms protruded from her back. A coyote's head lolled above this hexagon of arms.

"I don't need to swim here," Joseph said, "but this one has eyes, nice *yellow* eyes. This one has good eyes so I can see, so I can see how to fix the eyes you burned. How did you burn my eyes? I don't know. I think you had help..."

The Joseph-thing dropped the horrible six-armed mermaid at his backward feet and stood erect. As he continued talking, he worked his finger into a hole in his own chest.

Anna became aware of an uncomfortable pressure around her ribs, then realized that she and Donny had their arms around each other, nearly squeezing the life out of each other.

Joseph worked his entire hand into the hole in his chest, then began pressing his other hand in as well. "You two wait right there while I change." It gurgled something that must have been laughter. "While I change. I'll only be a minute. Then I can fix my eyes. And when I have new eyes, I'll come get you, and get you and put you back where you belong."

With his second hand now fully inside his chest cavity, the Joseph-thing squatted backward on his knees, and pulled outward on his ribs. He uttered a sobbing groan. His ribcage split along a seam in its breastbone and popped open like the jaws of a bear trap. Then, something fell out, something like a Thanksgiving turkey, if the turkey had been coated in black blood. After a second, Anna recognized it for what it was — the ribs, spine, and one upper arm bone of a small child. The rest of the Joseph thing, the backward-legged porpoise-tailed monstrosity, collapsed in a heap, lifeless.

Anna whispered into Donny's ear, "We have to go!"

"I know," he whispered back, squeezing her tighter.

Below them, the remains of the child that had fallen out of the Joseph thing squirmed and dragged itself onto the body of the six-armed mermaid. At least it had stopped talking.

"We have to go down...get past it...We have to get back to the..." Anna broke off. There was no way she could climb down into the cistern with that thing. "I'd rather be eaten by the wolves."

"Me, too," Donny whispered. "Do you think maybe they are friendly wolves? Maybe your witch friend sent them?"

"No."

"Me neither."

A horrible, wet slurping sound echoed out of the cistern. It reminded Anna of the time Lizzy had made an improvised straw from a piece of shoe leather and tried to suck porridge through it. At that memory, Anna giggled, on the verge of a laughing fit.

"Don't crack up on me now, Anna," Donny took her hand, "I'll get us out of here." His attempt at bravery made him sound even more terrified. It helped Anna quell the giggles.

She peered into the cistern again. Joseph's mermaid lay on its back, alive now. A wide incision ran up the center of its sternum. Anna could see the tiny child's ribs squirming inside the chest of the patchwork mermaid. The creature twitched and jerked in grotesque spasms. When these passed, it snatched up a length of leather shoelace and stitched closed the incision on its sternum.

"It's inside that thing," Donny whispered. "If it gets us, it's gonna make *us* into monsters, too."

"It won't get us." Anna tugged Donny away from the cistern toward the door. "We're going to be eaten by wolves, remember."

"Right." Donny said, seeming to relax.

"Flip that cover off the lamp," Anna said.

She turned the handle and eased the door open. Donny shone the lamp into the basement. The wolf had not moved. It perched halfway down the crumbling foundation wall. When the light hit it, it growled and curled its upper lip, revealing fangs.

"You can eat the jam. Before we get eaten. If you want," Donny said. "Sorry I didn't let you earlier."

"I'm not very hungry anymore," Anna said. "Maybe we could throw it to the wolves? Distract them?"

"I don't think jam will distract them," Donny said.

Anna looked at her hand. She still held the glass jar she had snatched up earlier. Rotten goop sloshed within it. "What about rotten preserves? If they eat the rotten food and get sick, maybe they'll leave us alone."

"Maybe. Do you think the key might scare 'em off?" Donny fished it out of his pocket. It didn't glow. Not even kind of.

"Well, you could try it." Anna gave him a half-hearted grin.

"It's better than throwing rotten food at them," Donny said but stuffed the key back into his pocket. When he pulled his hand out again, he held the waxed paper tube from the lantern case. He eyed it, speculatively, then a radiant smile beamed across his face.

Chapter 24

"PAPA TAUGHT ME THIS," DONNY said, bubbling. "Said he'd skin me alive if he ever caught me doin' it."

Joseph's voice drifted up from the cistern, muttering to himself. "...eyes, eyes, who has some pretty eyes for Joseph..." Other noises drifted up as well, the mermaid thing dragging itself around, parts being shuffled and tossed. "...fishy eyes, girly eyes...Irish eyes a' smiling...too many spleens! Too many *spleens*!" A wet splatting noise. "...eye of deer, eye of dog, eye of...eye...of...Margaret!"

"I promise not to tell your papa," Anna said. "Whatever you're doing, please hurry."

"Hold this," he gave her the lamp. "Keep that light on the wolf, tell me if he moves. We're going out there with him."

Anna went through the door first, out of the alcove and into the basement. Donny slid through after her and pushed the door closed. The wolf stepped further down the crumbling wall, almost to the floor. A second wolf worked its way down as well, snarling and yapping. The second was bigger than the first, at least twice as large as Anna herself.

Donny fumbled around on the floor with a Mason jar and a splintered board. It looked like he was trying to build something.

"Donny?"

"Just hold 'em back! Just for a minute!" He used a nail in the board to pop a hole through the lid of a jar. "You're gonna love this!"

"Hold them back with what?" she nearly shrieked at him. Anna wound up and flung the rotten preserves at the closest wolf. The jar struck the wolf's shoulder with a hollow thump. The wolf yelped and stepped back as the preserves bounced off and shattered across the floor. The second wolf leapt over him, roaring, landing squarely on the floor less than ten feet from Anna.

"Donny!"

Something flashed beside her. "Look!" Donny said. He stood, holding two Mason jars, each with a two-inch flame jetting through holes in the lids.

"We already have a lamp..." Anna said, groping for another weapon.

Donny flung the first jar at the giant wolf's feet. It exploded like a flashbulb, bright as lightning, with the crack of a rifle shot. Tiny bits of glass peppered Anna and skittered across the basement. The wolves howled, bolting topside. The big wolf turned tail so fast his back legs skidded out behind him as he scampered out of the basement.

Beyond the alcove door, Joseph shrieked.

Donny threw his second bomb at the big wolf's hindquarters just as it cleared the foundation. Anna turned away, covering her face with her arm. The second report was not as loud, probably because most of the blast was above ground, and less glass hit her. But the wolf howled and yelped as it fled into the night.

"Yeah!" Donny shouted, throwing his arms up in a V.

"Ha, ha!" Anna cried. She hugged Donny without intending to do so, and he hugged her back. They danced in a circle for about a second. Then, they heard Joseph.

Beyond the alcove door, Joseph bellowed in rage. He was coming for them. Whether he had replaced the eyes and returned to his other body or whether he still inhabited the six-armed mermaid, Anna didn't know. And she didn't want to find out. She crammed a broken piece of shelf under the alcove door like a doorstop.

"Let's go, Donny! Quick this time."

"Grab the lantern," Donny said. He stuffed a jar into each of his two coat pockets. Then he leaped up and wrapped his fingers over the top of the tall oak hutch. He swung his legs out away from the cabinet.

"What are you doing?" Anna yelled.

"Just go, I'm right behind you!"

Joseph slammed into the door from the cistern side. It opened about two inches before catching on Anna's doorstop.

Donny swung his feet away from the hutch. It rocked onto its front feet, balanced briefly, then slammed back into its upright position.

"Hurry!" Anna yelled, "The wolves are coming back!"

The smaller of the two wolves stood just outside the foundation, peering in at them. Anna hucked a jar at it. She missed by several feet, splattering the wall with rotten green beans, but the wolf bolted as soon as she began her throw.

Joseph hit the door again with a sick meaty thud. It shuddered, sliding open another inch. One rusted screw popped out of the hinge and bounced away. A black tentacle slithered through the gap, groping around the opening.

Anna leapt up beside Donny, latching onto the hutch's top. "Together!"

As soon as they started to swing out, the hutch's right front leg snapped off. The heavy cabinet lurched forward and sideways at the same time. It began to topple, but instead of falling against the door, it crashed into one of the support posts, resting against it at an angle.

Donny, surprised by the hutch's diagonal motion, also slammed into the post. Anna missed it, backpedaled two steps, tripped over her feet, fell on her back, and rolled against the alcove door. The hutch had pinned the tail of Donny's coat to the post. He dangled by it like a marionette.

Anna staggered to her feet. Joseph's tentacle lashed out at her, but missed. Some other appendage slammed into Joseph's side of the door. Anna ran to Donny. The hutch's corner had snagged the post, but only by a few inches. If she and Donny could dislodge it, they could still trap Joseph in the cistern.

"Help me shove this!" she shouted.

Donny stood, dazed but conscious, and tugged at his coat. It started to rip. "I'm hung up."

"Never mind that! Push!" Anna yelled.

Joseph slammed into the door. Donny startled and snapped to. He and Anna slammed into the hutch. It refused to budge, was wedged in place. A hand shot through the alcove door, fingers searching the gap, trying to pry it open. Anna and Donny slammed the hutch again. This time, though the hutch didn't move, the post did. It gave out a creek, like an old rocking chair, and began to crackle.

Overhead, the ruined house groaned. The post tilted, slowly, like a falling tree. The crackling intensified as floor joists splintered, popping like pine knots in a bonfire. The other support post snapped in half.

Donny slammed the cabinet again, determined to topple it. Anna hooked her arm around his midsection and hauled him toward the broken foundation wall. She screamed at him, but the roar of the collapsing structure was so loud neither of them heard what she said.

Anna ripped him away as violently as her tired, battered body could. The back half of Donny's coat, still snagged between the hutch and the post, finally ripped free. She half stumbled, half sprinted toward their escape.

One breath later, Anna no longer needed to pull Donny. Both ran as if the devil was on their tail. They bounded up and over the rocks, into the moonlit forest. The dilapidated house collapsed in on its self, crashing into the basement. A plume of dust belched out of the pit, chasing them into the woods.

Anna grabbed Donny's hand and sprinted through the trees, not looking back. The lamp swung back and forth in her other hand, illuminating the next tree, the next blackberry patch, but nothing beyond. Branches thrashed their faces. Brambles tore at their ankles. Neither slowed them in the least.

Anna ran until her lungs burned and her throat felt chafed. Donny began to feel like an anchor she was dragging through the woods. But still, she ran on.

Donny's legs eventually gave out. He fell while still trying to run, and Anna actually did drag him about four strides before she collapsed as well. Donny got up on hands and knees, wheezing, and pointed to a fallen tree. He and Anna crawled to it, resting their backs against its thick trunk. They sat for several minutes, panting, sucking in the night air.

When he could talk, Donny said, "The wolves..."

"I know," Anna said.

"They're followin'..." He pulled a jar from the pocket of his shredded coat.

"I know, Donny." She laid her head back against the tree, looking up at the low-slung cedar branches.

He nudged her leg with the jar. Black orbs bobbed in thick brown liquid. "Take this," he wheezed, "In case... they come..."

Anna laughed, coughed, and laughed again. She took Donny's hand, instead of the jar, and squeezed it. "They won't be coming close, Donny." She laughed again. "I think those wolves will," *cough* "...they'll be telling their grand-babies about you, Donny."

He coughed a single laugh, then asked, "Joseph?"

"I hope to heaven he's..." *wheeze* "...squashed flat as a bug under that house."

"You sure he didn't get out?"

"I still can't believe *we* got out," she said. "Didn't you see the whole thing was coming down on you?"

"Yeah, I saw it." He flapped his hand in an *aw shucks* gesture. "I seen worse."

Anna rolled her head to the side and looked at him, grinning. "In the mirror?"

Confusion flitted across his face for the briefest moment, then he got it. He turned to her, trying hard to look angry but unable to hide his smile. "You oughta see yourself! I don't know which you got more, mud or blood, but there ain't a clean patch of skin on ya!"

"Shh!" she giggled, and coughed.

"Shh, yourself," he said, grinning. "When you say your prayers tonight, thank the Good Lord you ain't got a mirror!"

*If you mention my complexion one more time...*Anna thought of Jane and sobered immediately. The weight of the night settled on her. She felt a chill and her skin prickled. They slumped together, shoulder to shoulder, head to head, backs to the fallen tree, looking up at the brightening sky.

"You know I have a nick name, Donny?" she asked.

Donny heard the change in her voice. The levity left him, "What is it?"

"My friends call me Pinky." She held up her three-fingered hand.

"That's awful," Donny said.

"I know." She quickly looked away and swiped a tear. "I miss them." Her voice cracked.

Donny squeezed her hand, but said nothing.

"We just whipped a wolf pack and a..." She looked back to Donny, questioning. "We whipped a wolf pack and a lunatic's nightmare. You and me." She laughed again. To her ears, it sounded a little bit sad and a little bit savage. "We are going to get my girls and your Maybelle. If Abbess McCain and her crazy nuns try to stop us..."

"Lord have mercy on their souls?" Donny finished for her.

"Lord have mercy on their souls," Anna repeated. She let her eyelids droop until they closed.

Overhead, night was the color of a purple bruise, except in the east, where a pink line cut the sea from the sky.

Part 2:

Return from Darkness

Chapter 1

ANNA SLEPT UNTIL LATE MORNING, undisturbed. When she awoke, the sky hung low with soggy clouds. Forest birds twittered in the trees around her, but there was no rush of waves nor the squabble and chatter of ocean birds. Daylight felt funny on her eyes, almost hurt them. She was thankful for the cloud cover.

She took in a deep lungful of the cold, humid air. Donny startled awake. He looked anxiously side-to-side, saw Anna, and relaxed.

"G' morning," he said, settling back against the tree.

"Morning," Anna said. "Or afternoon. The sun was coming up as we were falling asleep. I don't know how long we've been here."

Donny looked up at the sky. "Can't tell where the sun is."

"Yeah, that's a problem," Anna said. "I can't tell what time it is and I can't tell which way is north."

"Well, it's an island, right?" Donny said. "If we just walk in one direction, we'll find the beach. The beach will take us to Maybelle."

"It is an island, but I have no idea how big an island it is. It could take days to find the beach, even longer to get back to Saint Frances – and I don't think we have that much time."

"Will the sun come out later?"

"I don't think so. We get these kind of clouds often. Usually, it's overcast like this for days without a break."

Donny sighed. "What are we gonna do?"

Anna took another deep breath – the air smelled absolutely wonderful – and smiled. She stretched her legs, then her arms, and stood up. "Come on, Donny." She offered him her hand and pulled him to his feet.

As he stood, his eyes brightened. "I got an idea. What if you hide an' I start makin' a bunch of noise? Those sisters that are searchin' for you will find me. Then you can juss follow our trail."

"Donny," Anna looked at the ground, chuckled, looked back at Donny and shook her head. "The last boy they found out here while looking for me, they killed him on the spot. That was him back there in Joseph's cistern."

"I don't wanna end up down there again," he said.

"Look, we'll walk...that direction. It's clear for a ways. As we go, we'll adjust our course so that we're always going downhill. I think that should be the quickest way to the beach."

Donny smiled. "I like that plan better." He retrieved the Mason jars from the ground, dumped their rotten contents and handed them to Anna. "Can you put these in your pockets? Mine are full."

Anna slipped them into her coat, without asking why. The front of Donny's coat bulged with the jam and a few other things he'd picked up. The back of his coat was gone, probably still snagged on the corner of the hutch. He held the lamp and an alder pole walking stick.

Anna looked at Donny's face, for the first time seeing him in full daylight. *He's only a child, for Pete's sake!* And a battered child at that. The top of his ear was shredded and crusted-over where Joseph had bit him. A red-black scab topped the purple lump on his forehead. Dark half-moons cradled both eyes.

He caught her staring. "What are you smiling about?"

"I'm glad I met you, Donny Lawson," she said.

"I'm glad I met you, too," he looked at the ground, grinning, "Pinky."

Anna saw him blush, even through the caked dirt on his face. She gave his shoulder a friendly shove and started walking. Donny followed.

They walked in silence for over an hour, listening to the forest, smelling the sweet air. The ancient cedar and fir trees eventually gave way to smaller alders and white-barked birches. As the trees thinned, the ground to their left fell away at a shallow angle. They turned downhill and walked on. Impassable blackberry patches and devil's club swamps forced them to backtrack uphill a few times, but soon the smell of salt air mingled with the other forest scents.

As they walked, Anna ran her fingers through her hair, picking out leaves and twigs. She also dislodged several shards of glass. She picked more bits of glass from cuts on her hands and forearms. Donny had been right about her skin, not a clean patch on it. *I'm going to need some ointment.*

"Donny," she said, "how'd you make those jars explode?"

"It's the Union Carbide crystals, from the lamp. Mix 'em with water an' they make gas," he said, smiling. "In the lamp, it burns real bright, a bit at a time. But, when it's in a jar an you bust the jar, it burns all at once. Boom!"

"Wow. That's really something," she said. "Do you have any crystals left?"

"Yeah, I got a few. Are those wolves still followin' us?"

"I've seen one. He pops his head out now and then, but I don't think he'll give us any more trouble."

"He's just keeping track of us, huh?"

"Yeah, I guess."

"Do you hear that?" Donny stopped in his tracks, cocking an ear. "I think I hear waves."

Anna stood still, held her breath and listened. Ahead of them, in the distance, foamy surf rolled and crashed over a pebbly beach. She smiled, even as her heart raced and her chest tightened.

The trees thinned and the underbrush thickened as they drew nearer to the sea. Giant ferns, salmon berry bushes, stinging nettles, skunk cabbages choked access between the woods and the beach.

Donny and Anna spent nearly an hour pushing through the final two hundred yards of brush.

When they reached the shore, the ocean spread out before them, restless and immense, the color of milky jade. Under a sagging gray sky, the sea undulated, whipped frothy by a steady wind. Vertigo overtook Anna. She grabbed Donny's arm and sat them both down on a beached log. Donny sat with her in silence, watching the waves roll in. Mist and icy drizzle hid the horizon, but even so, the vista astounded Anna.

"I always wanted to see the ocean again," she said, finally. "I'd like, just once, to see it on a clear day, when I'm not hunted, or starving."

"That's not too much to ask," Donny said.

"It goes on forever, you know. Goes to every place in the world. If we had a boat, it would take us anywhere."

"And without a boat," Donny said, "it won't let us go anywhere."

"We could swim."

Donny eyed her. "You'd freeze solid before you got past the breakers."

"Not today, Donny," Anna said. "Someday, though. When we leave here, someday I want to swim in the ocean."

"The ocean is warm where I come from. Maybe you can come," Donny said, "after we leave here."

Anna stood, bracing against the chill wind. "I feel better now, just needed to catch my breath."

"Yeah," Donny said, "me too. Which way is it?"

"I think it's that way." Anna pointed to the right. "I'm guessing that both of the farm houses were on the same side of the island, since they both used the same drain for their cisterns."

"Makes sense to me," Donny said.

"Well, I ran down the beach and turned left into the forest, so if we leave the forest and turn right at the beach, it should take us back," she said, "as long as we're still on the same side."

"Whether we're on the same side or not, if it's an island, either way will get us there."

"True enough, but this way might get us there *today*," Anna said.

Pebbles and sand crunched under their feet as they walked. The low clouds spit thin icy rain, which the wind drove at them sideways. Anna could not see more than a few hundred yards through the rain, but she knew this was not the beach she had ran across the night she escaped. That one had been smooth sand. Rocks and driftwood logs littered this one.

"Do you think we should walk in the woods," Donny asked, "in case they are still searchin' for you?"

"We'll make better time out here. Just keep your ears open for their whistles."

As the afternoon dragged on, they heard no whistles, only the relentless wind, the churning sea and lonesome seagulls' cries. Constant spears of icy rain pelted Anna's left side. Her head ached from the cold. The frigid wind drove the feeling from her left hand and the left side of her face. Her other hand, holding Donny's, stayed warm. The back of Donny's shredded coat fluttered and flapped. Beneath it, the rain plastered his white shirt to his back.

Anna began to believe that they had gone the wrong way. Her fatigue and hunger and apprehension, along with the element's incessant lashing, made every hour feel like five. Then, she heard a new sound, a familiar chugging to her left.

Anna tugged Donny's arm and dragged him, running, into the wood line. They hunkered behind the trunk of a gnarled pine, scanning the ocean. The icy rain stabbed at their cheeks and eyes. It acted as a gray curtain, obscuring the source of the chugging, but Donny recognized it at once.

"It's the boat," he said, "the one they threw me out of. Do you think they're searchin' for you?"

"No, they're too far off shore," she said. "Why would they be out in this weather?"

"You wanna flag 'em down and ask?"

She flashed him a reproving glare. He looked as miserable as she felt. His lips trembled, a ghastly pale purple. The bruised knot against his wet white forehead looked like a green-purple yolk on a fried egg.

The chugging grew louder, passing their location, and continuing north. At its closest point, its green bow light and the faint outline of the little steamer's cabin materialized out of the fog. Then it passed and the misty, brittle rain swallowed it once more.

"Guess that means we're prob'ly headed the right way," Donny said, trying to sound chipper.

"Guess so."

"Does it seem darker to you?"

"It's just because we're in the woods," she assured him.

The woods were very dark indeed. She had hoped to reach her girls before nightfall. But now, the rain had washed all the courage out of her. *What are you thinking? By the time you get there, you'll both be dead of pneumonia. You don't even have a plan, do you?*

A scruffy black crow cawed at them from a branch above their heads, then launched, flying for shelter deeper in the woods. Fat, cold baubles of rain, released by the crow's departure, splattered on and around the two orphans.

"Donny..." she started.

"I'm goin', Anna. It's the only thing to do." He forced the words out, mumbling through numb lips.

She heard desperation in his voice. He was trying to persuade himself as much as he was trying to convince her. She might even be able to talk him out of this insane rescue mission. But if she did, he would hate her for the rest of his life. You *would hate you for the rest of your life*, her other voice said, as bitter as it had ever been, *not that the rest of your life will be very long.*

"I'm going, too," she said. "You can't stop me."

The corners of his purple lips twitched slightly up, gratitude filling his eyes.

"We're both going." She wrapped her arm around his shoulder. He relaxed into her embrace. "But we can't go like this. This rain will kill us before we even get there. We are going to curl up in a dry spot, eat some jam, rest for a spell. Maybe the weather will dry up a bit."

He resisted, at first, tried to pull away, but she held him tight and, a moment later, he complied. They trudged into the forest along a game trail, trembling and huddled together. *Don't go too far in*, she warned herself, *keep the sea within earshot…*

And, suddenly she recognized the trail. Just ahead of them, a low cliff rose about four feet from the forest floor. The bluff created a slight overhang, a wall of dirt and roots and rocks shaped like a cresting wave. Over this cliff, a large fir tree had toppled, forming a perfect natural shelter.

"Come on, I know this place!" She pulled Donny faster.

He stumbled forward, startled by her sudden enthusiasm.

"This is where I hid on the night I escaped! This means we're very, very close." She pushed aside the boughs of the fallen fir and pulled Donny into the den beneath. "We'll be dry and warm in here."

"We shouldn't leave Maybelle…" he trailed off, mumbling. Then, "Amma? I think I might have hydrophobia…or hyperthermia…the one where you get too cold to think."

"Maybe it's hypochondria. The doc said that's what my mom had," Anna said. "Actually, I have no idea what any of those words mean, but if there's a condition where a body gets too cold to think, you probably got it."

Anna squeezed into the crevice with Donny. Sheltered from the rain and the cutting wind, she felt warmer already. She also felt a guilty reprieve from the daunting task ahead.

"Open that jar of jam," she said. "We'll save some for your sister, I promise, but we need to eat."

Donny fumbled around his pocket. His hand flopped like wet spaghetti. After what seemed like a ridiculously long time, and by using both hands, he managed to produce the jam.

"Yer gonna hava opennit," he mumbled. He tried to hand her the jar but dropped it into her lap instead.

"Are you okay, Donny?" The crevice under the fir tree had grown very dark. She could barely see his face.

"I'm not cold anymore, just sleepy," he said. Only, it came out *I'mot cole amymore jusssleepy*

He is going to die, the other Anna said. *Just like Madeline…and Erma…and Alice. No food and no blankets gets you dead little girls and boys.*

"Donny! No sleeping, not yet. You have to eat first." She cranked on the lid of the Mason jar. It stuck tight, then slowly turned with a gritty grinding sound.

"Spud?" he mumbled.

Anna smelled the jam. Sweet, mouth-achingly tart blackberries, a hundred summers old but still wonderful. Her belly cramped at the aroma. "No, Donny, this is better. Just eat a bit. Then you can sleep."

Donny replied with an inarticulate grunt.

Anna scooped a glob of jam with her fingers, *good thing it's too dark to see how grimy those fingers are*, and pushed it into Donny's half open mouth.

He smacked his lips, mumbling, and swallowed. Anna repeated the process twice more, taking small bites herself while he swallowed his. On the fourth attempt, the jam slipped out of his lips and plopped to the ground. He'd had all he was going to have. *Either it's enough…or it isn't.*

Through the boughs, Anna saw night had fallen. Wind rustled the trees overhead. She could not be sure whether the rain still fell, but assumed it did. The temperature inside their shelter was much warmer than outside, but she was still chilly. *If I'm cold, it's not warm enough for him to recover.*

"I need you to live, Donny."

His lips moved but no sound came. A terrible déjà vu took her, remembering her brother's mumbling, soundless lips from her dream.

"I don't want to go back in there by myself."

No response.

"I don't know if I can."

She put her hand on his chest. It was cold and, for a moment, motionless. Then, his ribs slowly expanded. A moment later, they shrunk back as he exhaled.

"I'd rather die here with you than go back in there alone."

She took off her heavy coat, intending to drape it over both of them. A metallic *clink* caught her attention. In the darkness, a straight silver edge gleamed. Anna reached down and felt the lamp.

It gets hot. When it's lit, it's too hot to touch.

She rummaged in Donny's coat pocket for the crystals. A steady trickle of runoff just at the edge of her shelter provided the water. When she hit the striker, the lamp popped like a flashbulb and went out. On her second attempt, it lit. She closed the cover, wrapped it in her shawl and cradled it in Donny's arms on his lap.

Then she snuggled up to him as tight as she could and draped her coat over them both.

She closed her eyes and prayed. In five years with the nuns, she had only prayed twice. Both times, it had been here, under this tree. On the night of her escape, she prayed that the rocks and hills would cover her. That prayer had been answered. Tonight, she prayed many things, but most especially, she prayed that, one way or the other, this would be her last night on the island.

Chapter 2

ANNA DREAMT SHE RETURNED TO The Saint Frances de Chantal Orphan Asylum. She stood before the door to her dormitory. Her girls were dead. All of them. Just like Donny.

No food and no blankets gets you dead little girls and boys.

If a child will not work, neither let him eat.

Being Anna's friend is a bad idea.

She didn't want to see them dead, but could not turn away. Her hand, of its own accord, inserted the key into its hole. Anna begged not to see her girls dead, but the key turned and the door swung open. She willed her eyes to close, but they would not.

Beyond the door they lay, still as stone, arranged on the bare floor in two neat rows, oldest to youngest. Their black leather shoes glimmered in the pale light, all else was dull gray.

Anna woke with a start. White fog had replaced the previous day's wind and rain. Eerie silence floated on the fog, giving the morning an unreal, dream-like cast. Gull cries penetrated the unnatural hush, but their distant, ethereal quality reinforced the surreal atmosphere.

Anna held as still as the morning, listening. Nothing stirred beyond the fallen fir. Nothing stirred beneath it, either. She felt detached from her body. Her body and Donny's and the coat and the dirt and the tree were a single lump of matter.

She wondered if they had died during the night. The thought was a relief.

Then Donny snored.

Anna breathed again. *I'm not done yet.* With an intentional effort, she twitched the fingers on the hand she'd curled around Donny's shoulder. They were still her fingers, life still coursed through them.

She squeezed his shoulder, flexed her arm, hugging him. "Donny, you still with me?"

He snorted, then looked up at her, questioning. Some color had returned to his face. The bags under his eyes were only half as horrible as they had been the night before. The eyes themselves, though confused, sparkled with life.

"Hi, Anna," he said. "Where are we?"

"Don't you remember?" she asked. "We are very close. Nothing but a fifteen minute walk from here, I think. How are you feeling?"

"I can walk fifteen minutes," he said, smiling.

"Donny, you nearly died last night, from the cold."

"Well, I don't remember that," he said. "And I feel fine now 'cept for a crick in my neck."

Anna sighed. "We have to do this today. I don't think we can survive another night out here."

"Well, of course we're gonna do it today. Why wouldn't we?"

"Because they'll kill me as soon as they see me."

"So let's make sure they don't see you," Donny said.

Anna squeezed his shoulder again. "Right."

They collected their meager supplies and slipped out from under the overhang. White mist softened everything but hid nothing. Tree trunks stood in stark contrast, black against the white fog. The lush ferns and moss glistened with dew. Beyond the trees, the sea churned, still agitated from last night's wind.

Anna and Donny picked their way through the underbrush to the edge of the wood line. A crescent of smooth sand curled away from them in its graceful arc. Anna smiled, in spite of her dread, remembering her midnight flight across this beach.

I've never been so alive, she thought.

You've never been so close to dead, the other Anna said.

She decided both voices spoke true.

At the far end of the beach, The Saint Frances de Chantal Orphan Asylum waited. Through the fog, it appeared as an ominous, indistinct black mass. Its tower still stood, but beyond that detail, Anna could not determine how much of the structure remained. Nor could she determine if any sisters guarded it.

"That's where we're going," she said.

"That's it, huh? Not much to look at, is it?"

"You'll see," she said, stepping out of the forest. "Let's stay right up against the trees until we get close, then we'll duck back into the woods."

Donny followed her onto the sand. Reefs of driftwood logs lined the boundary between beach and forest. The two worked their way through this maze toward their objective. It took twice as long as Anna had guessed to cover the distance, but they would not be seen among the tangle of logs.

Anna chose not to look at the tower as they approached. By focusing on the next few feet of their journey, she could keep her mind off their destination – in the same way that, when she was in the factory, doing the next thing that must be done helped her block out the suffering of her maimed and dying friends.

As they approached the edge of Saint France's grounds, they slipped back into the trees. Anna heard a low whistle behind her.

"Holy geez, Anna! You did *that?*" Donny whispered.

She looked up at the ruin of the factory and gasped.

The dormitory wing and rotunda stood, as they always had, but nothing remained of the factory except a scorched black wall and a gaping pit. A spider's web of cracks crept up the height of the tower. It seemed more like a column of loose stones than a bell tower. Again, Anna thought of it as a grave marker. It conveyed the sense that no one had lived here for centuries. A forgotten ruin, lost to memory, condemned to oblivion.

All its windows were as dark as Joseph's empty eye sockets. In the early morning fog and the eerie silence, it would be easy to believe she looked upon the ruins of an ancient castle – the kind of castle where evil sorcerers had once conjured plagues and curses.

"Good Lord," Donny whispered. "I think it's the sisters that oughta be scared of you. Not the other way 'round."

Anna stared, open-mouthed, at the black hulk that had been her prison for nearly half her life. To her left, the indomitable Pacific rumbled. Before her stood the carcass of a stone demon that had devoured so many children. She suddenly felt very fragile and small. A creeping terror chilled her from her marrow outward. *I killed it. How long did it stand, just beyond the reach of the sea? How many children has it eaten? How many childhoods has it claimed? And I killed it!*

"Anna?" Donny asked. "Are you okay?"

"Just..." she held her palm up to Donny. "I didn't know...I...What if that was the wrong choice?"

"What?"

"All these years, Donny, the ocean is right here, but not even the ocean could...break it down...couldn't overcome...I'm not the ocean..."

"You're not making any sense, Anna."

"I...I can't *un*do it, if it's wrong, I can't *fix* it!" she said, "Little girls shouldn't be *able* to do something like that!"

"Anna, you ain't no little girl, remember?"

"But I *want* to be! Don't you see? I want to get to be a child. Just for once. I don't want *this*," she thrust a hand at the ruined tower. "I don't want to be responsible for this! Or for you, or your sister, or all those girls!"

Anna turned away from the ruins and sat on the damp earth, gazing back into the forest. *I want someone to be responsible for me.*

The other voice said, *then you should have stayed inside.*

Anna vowed to herself, if she ever found that other Anna, she would drown her in a bathtub. For now, she planted her face in her hands and wept.

"Somebody had to do it." Donny put his hand on her back and said, with simple sincerity, "I'll be responsible. Thank you for helping me get this far, Anna." He patted her shoulder. "I have to go get Maybelle now."

She snatched his hand as he began to move away.

"Wait, Donny..." She sniffed, wiped her eyes, and stood.

He looked at her, questioning.

Anna shrugged and forced a smile. "I didn't say I wasn't going."

Donny smiled back at her. "Uh...you have a booger hanging out of your nose." He dug a filthy hanky out of his back pocket and handed it to her.

"Thanks, Donny," she said with a weak smile.

Chapter 3

"SO, HOW DO WE GET in?" Donny asked.

"I left through that door." Anna pointed to the kitchen entrance on its patio above the main loading dock. "It sprung open after the blast. Looks like they fixed it, though."

"I don't know, Anna, the place looks deserted. What if everybody juss up an' left?"

"We saw that boat yesterday. Remember?" Anna pointed to the little steamer bobbing alongside the dock.

"I don't recall much of yesterday, really, but if you saw a boat, I believe you."

Anna looked him over, wondering just how much more they could endure. She again wondered if they had died in the night and were now just ghosts searching for a hell to haunt. She reached over and pinched Donny's arm.

He slapped her hand away and glared at her. "If you think you're dreamin, you're supposed to pinch *yourself*."

"Sorry."

Anna and Donny turned back to the orphanage. Thick planks barricaded the kitchen door. A Celtic cross hung from the center plank. The double doors in the front of the rotunda had also been boarded over with heavy planks and sealed with a large cross, as had the loading bay door.

"Looks like they're tryin' to keep the devil out," Donny said.

"Maybe they are. When I lived here, the sisters were always very careful to keep all the doors locked up tight. I used to think it was to keep us in, but maybe they were trying to keep Joseph out."

"You think they knew about Joseph?"

"I don't know. I never knew about him until he slipped me the key...even then, I really didn't know about him..." Anna said.

"You think that key will get us back in?"

"Not if all the doors are nailed shut. Besides, it only works on the interior doors."

"Well, there you go," Donny said, smiling. "We'll use it on the exterior doors that *used* to be interior doors." He pointed to a door in the charred wall that had separated the factory from the rest of the south wing.

Anna rubbed the key and considered. "That might work. We'd have to run all the way across the grounds, out in the open, and there's probably going to be a lot of rubble blocking our path once we get close."

"Let's not," Donny said, his voice suddenly ice.

Anna looked back at him, about to ask *why not*. Then she saw what he had seen, not at the ruined factory, but on the beach – foot prints, animal and human. And hand prints. And tentacle prints, as if a single file parade had marched up out of the sea, across the beach, directly toward the burned-out shell of the factory.

"You think that's from Joseph?" Anna whispered.

"What else could have left that track?" Donny asked.

As if in answer, the two children heard a metallic *clank* from the pit beneath the factory. A moment later, they heard another sound, like stones sliding against each other, then plunking into a puddle. In the fog, and at this distance, it was hard to be certain, but Anna thought she saw movement among the fallen stones and timbers of the factory.

"What's he doin' here, Anna?" Donny asked.

"What are you asking me for?" Anna replied. "I think he's been trying to get in there for a very long time, but I don't know why. Besides, that's not what matters. What matters is staying away from him and finding a way in. If he's busy here, that's good. My girls lived at the other end of the building. Let's work around to the other side. They must have at least one working door."

Saint Frances's lawn wrapped around its ancient stones in a semi-circle, as if some great leviathan had risen up from the sea and taken a bite out of the forest. The fog thickened with the brightening morning. Anna and Donny crept along in the ferns and underbrush, just at the edge of the open ground.

"We're gonna have to get closer," Donny said. "I can't see nothin' through this fog."

Anna reluctantly agreed. "If we must leave the cover of the woods, we might as well run right up to the base of the wall. Less chance someone will see us from a window."

They stole across the lawn as silent as shadows. When they reached the foundation stones, Anna pressed her back to the wall, closed her eyes, and listened. Distant, eerie gull cries, the hush of the surf, Donny's rapid breathing beside her. Nothing else disturbed the stillness.

Anna opened her eyes, and her heart sank.

"Donny!" she whispered. "Look."

The dew soaked grass of Saint Frances de Chantal's lawn glimmered in the mist. Its frosting of tiny droplets coated the grounds with perfect uniformity – except for a green line cut directly from the woods to the wall, a trail of footprints left by two little lost orphans. It stood out like a beacon.

"Well," Donny said, "we'd better not be here if someone looks out the window."

He took her hand and dragged her with him. They jogged along the back of the wing that had housed Anna and her girls. She could see the windows, nearly thirty feet above them, but had no idea which ones opened into her old hall.

The wing stretched over two-hundred feet away from its connection to the rotunda. They made their way along its base. Two sets of stairs led down to doors below ground level. The first of these doors was boarded up and sealed with a cross, like the others they had seen. The second door also appeared secure, though no cross hung there.

"You think they ran out of crosses?" Donny asked.

"Someone took it down, look."

Several feet from the descending stairs, a cross lay in the grass. A short trail through the dew led up to the cross, as if someone had tossed it from the stairwell.

Donny hurried down the stairs.

"Look," he called up to Anna, "this board is loose."

Nails squealed as Donny yanked a plank off the entrance. It set Anna's teeth on edge and her spine tingled. She looked left and right down the length of the wall. Nothing but grass, stone, and fog. "Be careful, Donny," she whispered.

"I got it open, c'mon," Donny said. "It wasn't locked."

Anna surveyed the yard again, then scrambled down the stairs.

"This isn't right," she said. "Why would they barricade all the other doors but leave this one unlocked? What if it's a trap?"

The door stood open about three inches. Donny had pulled off the bottom board, but several others still obscured the doorway.

"Look, we'll leave the rest of the boards up. We'll crawl in under 'em, and close the door behind us. They'll never know we were here." He started into the opening.

Anna grabbed him and whispered, "But what if they're waiting for us, just inside the door?"

"We were looking for an opening," Donny gestured to the door. "We found an opening. It's the best we could have hoped for. I'll go in first, since they're not lookin' to kill me. If it's safe, you follow."

Anna sighed. "Right."

Donny eased the door open another few inches. The rusty hinges protested, but not loudly. He crawled under the lowest board into the dark interior. Anna waited in the stairwell with her back pressed to the wall.

The heavy mist condensed into drizzle. Curls of fog hovered over the lawn, drifting this way and that. Dark shapes floated with the fog at the edge of the forest. The *tick* and *patter* of drizzle played with her ears, distorting the silence. She could no longer tell if what she heard was distant seagull chatter or crying children.

She dropped to her knees, squirming under the board and through the door.

Chapter 4

DONNY'S LAMP REVEALED A COMPLICATION of pipes spreading across the ceiling. Jumbled crates surrounded Anna and Donny, stretching out, maze like, into the dark basement. The air was redolent of rat droppings and damp dust.

"How do we get upstairs from here?" Donny asked.

"I've never been down here," she said. "I guess we should...Shh, listen."

Donny flipped the cover closed on his lamp. From deep in the recesses of the basement, heavy shoes *clomped* on wooden stairs, and voices quietly conversed. Lamp light glimmered off ceiling pipes.

Anna grabbed Donny's elbow and pulled him away from the door. They nestled under a tarp between two crates. She strained her ears, picking up pieces of the conspiratorial murmurs.

"...this is insane. Why are we still here..."

"...hold it steady...can't see..."

"This one is still locked."

"Sisters!" Anna whispered to Donny, "I can't tell which ones."

"Does it matter?" he whispered back.

The voices drew closer. "How much longer are we going to do this? We can't stay here forever."

"You want to leave? Get on the next boat. Where are you going to go? The Church doesn't want you, anymore. I doubt anybody does. You stay with us until the job is done, maybe we'll take you in."

"That's Sister Eustace," Anna whispered.

Donny lifted the edge of the tarp and peeked out. Lamp glow highlighted the ridges of the cobblestone floor. The sisters were less than fifty feet away. Donny started to slip out from under the tarp. Anna grabbed him and pulled him back.

"Gotta lock the door," he whispered.

"They're too close," she whispered back, tightening her grip.

"I can make it..."

Anna wrapped her arm around behind his head and clapped her hand over his mouth. "Hush!" she hissed directly into his ear.

The space beyond the tarp brightened as the sisters approached. When they reached the door, they stopped. Under the hem of the canvas, within spitting distance of her nook, Anna saw their black leather shoes and white stockings. Beside one pair of those shoes hung the rusty head of an ax.

The sisters had stopped talking. She and Donny had stopped breathing. Anna's heart thumped so loudly the sisters must have heard it as well. Some crazy part of her wanted to charge out from between the crates and attack. *I can wrest that ax away if I startle them ferociously enough.*

And then what? the other Anna asked, sounding amused. *Chop them up like kindling? Trade their parts with Joseph for another key, or can of sardines?*

She shuddered. The images – and the stench – from Joseph's lair welled up in her mind, like bile in the throat. Donny tightened his grip on her hand, either from his own fear or from sensing hers. Muted daylight overpowered the lamp as the sisters opened the door. One began muttering in Latin. Her rapid, frantic voice trembled. Rosary beads rattled.

"Stop that!" Sister Eustace hissed. "Look, the boards are still in place. He's not here."

The other sister stammered, then asked, "But, who would unlock..."

"Lucifer's *whore*," Eustace spat. "Who do you think?"

The other sister gasped at the vulgarity.

"Oh, grow up, Evelyn!" Sister Eustace slammed the door and threw the bolt. "You're in the real world now — and demons are afoot. Soon you will witness far greater evil than a foul tongue."

"Sister Eustace..."

"I told you, call me Betsy. We aren't sisters anymore."

Evelyn tried again, meekly, "Betsy, what about the cross?"

The two women began moving farther down the corridor, toward the next door.

"The cross doesn't appear to be doing much good. It certainly didn't keep *your* demons away, did it?" Betsy chuckled. "And point that thing at the floor. You're making me nervous."

Sister Betsy Eustace's thick calves strode away with the ax bobbing along beside them. Bobbing along beside Evelyn's calves were the blunt, brutal barrels of a side-by-side scattergun.

Betsy's voice trailed behind her, "But don't you worry, child. The rest of the men arrive tomorrow. We'll scour this rock, end to end, until we find those witches — and their little pet. We're going to warm them up real good, so hell won't be too much of a shock for them."

Chapter 5

WHEN SHE COULD NO LONGER SEE the gleam of Eustace's lamp, Anna moved her hand away from Donny's mouth.

"What is going on?" she whispered.

"Sounds like they think you're a witch."

"Yeah, I got that part, Donny."

"Can't say that I blame 'em...er...I mean..." Donny stammered, "I'm not sayin' *I* think you're a witch...what I mean is... "

"I'm not a witch."

"I *know* you're not a witch. All's I'm sayin' is if they got a witch problem *and* a demon problem, an' then you come along an' blast the whole place to damnation, well, they're gonna think you're in cahoots with the witches and demons..."

"I'm not in cahoots, Donny," Anna said. "Did you see that ax?"

"Yeah. And I saw the shotgun. Sounds like things might be getting real bad around here, real fast. I reckon we need to get what we came for an' get gone, lickety split."

"Lickety split," Anna agreed.

The two crawled out from under the canvas, looking down the corridor after the women. The only visible light leaked in through a crack under the locked door. Betsy and Evelyn were no longer in evidence.

"They came from this direction," Anna whispered and pulled Donny down the corridor. Several yards ahead, muted daylight leaked in around the frame of another door. "I heard them checking a door just after they came down the stairs," she said, pointing to the patch of light. "The stairway should be just ahead."

They covered the distance noiselessly, and did not see or hear any other patrols. Directly across from the door, a set of oak steps wound around a massive stone pillar. Enough light seeped under the door that Anna and Donny found it with little difficulty.

They felt their way up the dark spiral. At the top of the stairs, another heavy door waited, leaking daylight onto the upper landing. Anna laid her ear against the old wood and listened. Donny knelt and peered through the keyhole. A tiny spear of light sparkled his green iris.

"What do you see?" she whispered.

"A golden unicorn," he replied, perplexed, "sewed into a purple curtain."

"Tapestry," Anna said, smiling.

"What?"

"Not a curtain, a tapestry, a wall decoration."

"Ain't much of a decoration, kinda ratty."

"Yeah, well, it's all we had. More importantly, it tells me where we are," she said. "Out this door, to the right, is the Great Round Room. To the left, three doors down, is where they kept Maybelle and my girls."

Donny reached over and squeezed her hand. "Listen. Go on back down a couple steps, keep an ear out for that gal with the ax. I'll open this door an' see if the coast is clear..."

"We should go together..."

"We're *gonna* go together, long as no one's wait'n on the other side of this door, right?" he whispered. "But let me check first. That way, if I do get nabbed, you can still go fetch my sister an' your girls. 'Sides, sounds like they don't just wanna kill you. Plain ol' dead ain't good enough for the likes of you."

"I don't know," Anna sighed. "If you do get caught...you could tell them you saw Sister Eustace in the basement and she said to come up here –, tell them you've been lost since the explosion."

Anna chewed her lip, thoughts racing. *Eustace and that other nun will probably be back soon. Is this door locked? Is someone waiting to open the door for them? Did they lock it from this side when they went down? If Donny gets caught, his cover story would only save him until Eustace returns.*

"Donny," she whispered. "Do you have enough carbide crystals for another bomb?"

"Well," he started, "not sure that's such a good idea. Everyone'll hear an' come runnin'."

"If you get caught, it's all over," she said. "I'm not going to leave you, Donny. It won't take long for them to figure out that you were helping me."

"Anna..."

"Hush your mouth and listen to me," she said as harshly as her whisper allowed. "You saw what those sisters were carrying. They mean to kill me and Joseph – I guess Sister Dolores is the witch they're after – they mean to burn us at the stake if they get the chance. That's what you do with witches, right?"

"I guess, but..." Donny said.

"If they catch you, they'll do the same to you, because now *you're* in cahoots. I can't let that happen. I won't. I told you before, and I meant it with everything that's in me, I will die before I ever let them catch me. If they are waiting for us out there, well, we have to fight. We have to fight until they let us go or kill us. That's all there is to it. Do you understand?"

Donny nodded, green eyes sparkling with awe.

"Now, if we go out there and hit them with one of your bombs, they are going to think its devil magic, and they'll either run away to get help, or they'll shoot us dead on the spot. Either way, we win. If I'm dead, they won't have any reason to harm the girls, right? Worst outcome of that plan, all of us still get free of this place."

"Ho-lee Geez, Anna," Donny whispered.

"Come on, Donny, we don't have any time, Sister Eustace..."

Donny hushed her with his finger on her lips. "Yeah, Anna, I know," he whispered. "I'll make some bombs, but, well, you gotta go down the stairs a ways, so you can't see me."

"What? Why?"

"Well, uh, I, uh have enough crystals, an I got two jars...but uh, I don't got any water...I'll have to, um..."

"You know what," Anna interrupted, "I'll go down a few steps and keep an ear out for Sister Eustace while you get those bombs ready."

"Good idea."

Five steps down took Anna around the curve of the spiral staircase and put the stone pillar between her and Donny. She listened intently to the dark basement, hoping only for silence, but she heard more of the bomb making process than she wished. Bits of conversation drifted up from the darkness below. They were still too distant to discern what was being said, but Anna clearly recognized the tone and timbre of Sister Eustace's smug prattle. Then, there was a pop and a flash of light behind her.

"Anna," Donny whispered, "all ready."

Anna returned to the door. The two remaining Mason jars sat on the floor. Twin tongues of fire hovered over their lids.

"They're still a ways away but they're coming," she whispered. "Here's plan A, if it's clear out there — we run down the corridor to my dormitory, and pray to God your sister is still there. Once we get inside, close the door and hide. There's lots of hay to burrow under. After ten minutes, Eustace should be out of the basement. We'll take the girls and leave the same way we got in. We'll hide in the woods until late at night, then we'll sneak onto the boat. In the morning, when they try to take the boat out, there will be enough of us to overpower the pilot. We'll make her take us to the mainland.

"Plan B, if they are waiting for us out there," she said, "we fight to the death. I'll take the bombs, you take the key. Stab for the eyes. It'll all be over in a few minutes."

Donny whistled low through his teeth, shaking his head. "Anna, I swear, if I hadn't seen you cryin', I guess I'd swear you were an angel. An' not one of them angels that sang for Jesus, I mean one of those Old Testament Angels that visited vengeance on the wicked."

"Are you still glad you met me?" she asked.

"I'll tell you in a few minutes." For once, Donny wasn't smiling.

Chapter 6

ANNA RAISED A MASON JAR overhead, at the ready. Donny twisted the key. The lock clicked. The door swung silently inward. Anna held her breath, nerves humming. Donny withdrew the key, gripping it like a knife. The hinges squealed as the door opened farther. Donny stopped it with his foot. He craned his neck through the gap, scanning the corridor in both directions.

"It's clear," he whispered.

"Go," she said.

Donny stepped into the hall, held the door as Anna slipped through, then locked it behind them.

"Don't shake them up too much," he said, nodding at the jars.

"Come on," Anna urged, jogging toward her old dormitory.

Donny ran alongside her to the right, key in hand. To her left, the dormitory doors were spaced along the wall at fifty-foot intervals. Anna knew every tile in this floor, every threadbare tapestry, every crack in the ceiling plaster. During her stay here, Anna had never noticed the odor, but she recognized it now, the smell of tears and desperation. It was all familiar, but different. She no longer belonged to this place. She was no longer *part* of it.

They ran past the second door. Anna turned to Donny and smiled. He looked back at her, favoring her with a rakish grin. Beyond Donny, something sprang out of an adjoining hallway. Something gnarly and nasty. It, *she*, seized Donny from behind, clamping gnarled hands over his shoulders.

"I got you, you wretched!" the woman cackled, digging sharp fingers under his collarbones. Then she shrieked, "Lucile! I fetched you a devil!"

Anna skidded to a stop, turning back toward Donny. The thing that had grabbed him looked like an animated, bowlegged scarecrow, only uglier. She was bone thin and knobby all over. A profusion of gray-black dreadlocks sprang out of her head and were only partially corralled by a filthy red bandana. Her eyes, and her six remaining teeth, were yellow and crooked. Her right ear hung an inch lower than her left. She wore a heavy cross around her neck, a quiver of stakes on her back, and a pair of flintlock pistols on her belt.

"An' don't you be tryin' to run off, neither, faery child," she said to Anna. "I got my irons loaded with *silver*, if you take my meanin'!" She nodded at the pistols in her belt, then screamed, "*Lucile*! I gots two of 'em!"

Heavy footsteps thundered toward them from the adjoining hall, presumably Lucile, whoever that was. Anna stood frozen, back pressed against the wall, Mason jars in limp hands. Donny, stone rigid at first, now wriggled and squirmed against the woman's iron-hard hands.

"Let's have a looksee..." The scarecrow lady spun Donny around, his back to Anna, his face to the woman.

Lucile rounded the corner from the hall at a full run. Anna choked on her scream. The woman's frizzy red hair and sharp nose were unmistakable, Sister Evangeline, *the Woodpecker*, whose dead body lay in Joseph's cistern. Anna was so startled she almost didn't notice the ax, and by the time she did see it, it was too late.

Lucile's eyes (Sister Evangeline's eyes) bored into Anna as she ran past the paralyzed orphan. Surprise and recognition gleamed in those eyes. Then, a wickedly playful grin spread across the dead nun's lips. Lucile sprinted at Donny, dropping the ax into a lavish windup.

"Hold him tight, Hattie!" she bellowed at the scarecrow lady. "Judgment's a'comin'!"

Hattie's jaw dropped. Her eyes dilated in simultaneous terror and exultation, as she saw what Lucile intended to do with that ax. Horrible sounds bubbled out of her – giddy, hungry, yearning laughter. She dug her skeletal fingers into Donny's shoulders and thrust him out to arm's length.

Anna's hands felt like stone. The jars felt like lead anchors. She screamed, "No!" And kept on screaming for the eternity that it took to hurl the bomb at the ax-wielding nun. The jar tumbled end over end in the air, fire flaring through the hole in its lid.

Lucile's ax traveled through the bottom of its arc and soared upward, over her head. Her charge brought her between Anna and Donny, and as the ax passed its apex, Anna saw nothing but Lucile's back and her horrible orange mane.

The ax plummeted, gleaming. The Mason jar bomb finally struck Lucile square in the back – and bounced off, unbroken. There was an explosion, however, an explosion of bright red blood, spraying the ceiling and walls on both sides of the hall. The ax splitting through skull – all the way to spine – made a crackling, wet *thwock*, like a watermelon dropped from a rooftop.

Anna's scream turned to a wail.

The Mason jar hit the floor and exploded.

Lucile, Donny, and Hattie tumbled forward, propelled by the blast, landing in a heap. The concussion knocked Anna back against the wall. Glass bees stung the exposed skin of her face, hands and legs. She tried to yell for Donny, but her voice sounded muffled, as if her ears were packed with cotton.

Anna staggered. Her feet didn't want to stay under her. She groped her way along the wall toward the pile of bodies. New trickles of blood sprang from her scarred and battered shins. Blood glistened everywhere – all over her, on the back of Lucile's calves, speckling the walls and ceiling, spreading in a pool across the floor.

One of Anna's ears popped. Her hearing in that ear returned, and she heard a muffled crying – or laughing – she couldn't tell which.

Lucile stirred, rising slightly, and rolled off the body pile. Anna tried to make her feet work, intending to rush the nun, fight to the death as she had promised Donny. But at the thought of Donny, and the vivid echo of that sickening *Thwock*, Anna's knees buckled. She grabbed for the wall and sat down hard.

Lucile was laughing, trying to stifle it, trying to stop it, but laughing all the same. She sat up, covering her mouth with her hand, chortling through her blood-wet fingers.

Fire surged through Anna, burning high in her cheeks. She set her teeth and raised the second Mason bomb.

Then, Donny rolled off Hattie and sat up, looking bewildered.

Lucile held her hand up, "Wait, Anna," she said between giggles, "Anna, it's me."

It happened in the eyes first. Lucile's emerald irises dimmed, fading to black, then flared purple. Her red hair darkened to the oily black of crow feathers. Her milky skin bronzed. Lucile's pointy features melted away, revealing Dolores.

"You should have seen your face!" Dolores cried. "Oh, Anna! It was priceless!"

Anna looked to Donny. He sat on the floor, poking at his ears as if trying to rid them of water. Blood coated his face, and the front of his shirt, but it wasn't *his* blood.

The room rotated sideways, like a capsizing ship. Between Donny and Dolores lay the scarecrow woman, Hattie, feet splayed, ax handle protruding from a wet mass that had once been her face. As Anna began to understand what had happened, the floor struck her in the side of her head.

***

"Don't worry, Anna," Donny's voice floated to her. "I won't let them feed you to the needle machine."

"What?" she said.

"You fainted," he said.

"Did not," she mumbled, letting Donny help her to her feet.

"Do you know that crazy lady?" he whispered into her ear.

"That's Dolores," she said, "the witch I told you about."

"I was afraid you might say that."

"Hurry up, you two lovebirds," Dolores called. "We've got to hide this corpse. Quick."

Anna and Donny eyed the witch.

"Come on, come on! We're in this together," she said. "I'll explain everything as soon as we clean up this mess."

The ax now lay at the base of the wall. Dolores had placed a black cloth over Hattie's ruined face.

"I think we'll drag her...down there," Dolores said slowly, coming to the decision as she spoke it. "Yes, to that door you came through. We'll toss her down the stairs."

"Sister Eustace is down there." The words wandered out of Anna's mouth as if lost.

"I know!" Dolores clapped her hands. "Won't it be a hoot? She'll probably wet herself when she sees this. Hee, hee! But, we haven't much time. Now, stop gawking and help me. You two grab that arm."

Anna moved toward the body, then hesitated. Donny lifted the left arm and shot her a cock-eyed grimace. She stepped forward and grasped the limp arm. Loose skin seemed to slide independent of the stringy, lifeless tissue beneath. Anna's stomach turned.

"Heave ho!" Dolores called, taking hold of the right arm. Together they dragged the corpse to the basement stairs, painting a trail of blood behind them. When they reached the door, Dolores dug a key out of Hattie's pocket and unlocked it.

The door swung inward, squealing. Dolores helped them drag the body to the edge of the stairs. "Oh, I almost forgot, grab those pistols," she said, nodding at Hattie's belt. "They may come in handy."

Suddenly, from below but very close, Sister Eustace called up. "Hello? Who is that on the stairs?"

"It's just me..." Dolores shouted, shoving the children back into the hall. "Dolores the *witch*!"

With that, she rolled Hattie's corpse down the stairs, and tossed the remaining Mason bomb after it. She slammed and locked the door, just as the bomb exploded. Evelyn screamed.

Dolores dropped a bar into brackets across the door. "Well," she said, brushing her hands together, "that ought to keep them busy for a while."

Chapter 7

"ANNA! *I AM SO GLAD* you came back!" Dolores said, as if just now noticing Anna. She clasped her hands together under her chin and beamed an exultant smile. "And who is your little friend? But wait, let's not chat here. Come with me."

The bloody witch grabbed Anna's hand in hers, then took Donny's in her other hand, and marched them down the hall. When they reached the archway through which Hattie had appeared, Dolores peered around the corner, then proceeded toward the third door on the left, Anna's old dormitory.

The ringing in Anna's other ear finally stopped. She looked over at Donny, then up at Dolores, then back to Donny. His eyes were as wide as she'd ever seen them. He stared straight ahead and walked as stiffly as if he had been a wooden marionette. *He's terrified of her...I guess I am, too.*

"You put an ax in that woman's head," Anna said, talking more to herself than Dolores. Vocalizing what she had seen helped solidify the memory into reality.

"I have been wanting to put an ax in that bitch's head for fifteen years," Dolores said. "She shot my mother in the back with one of her ridiculous pistols. This seemed as good a time as any. Don't you think?"

Anna didn't know what to think. Everything other than the last five minutes had left her mind completely. She had forgotten about Joseph and Maybelle and her girls. Images repeated over and over in her mind, like voices from a broken phonograph. Hattie's crooked, cackling face – the dead woodpecker swinging her ax like she was splitting a log –

Donny's terrified eyes – the Mason jar suspended in midair, tumbling impotently – the explosion of blood when the ax struck.

"Anna," Dolores now knelt in front of her, looking directly into her eyes. The nun, or witch, or whatever she was, no longer sounded flippant or jovial. She spoke in a tone so grave and full of compassion it made Anna want to cry.

"Anna, I know everything – almost everything – that is in your heart. I lived here. I escaped. I left everyone behind." Dolores held Anna's hand in both of hers. "I am not as nutty as I seem, my happy potion makes me a little foolish at times. But, there's too much sorrow here, too much sorrow for this heart. Not everybody gets to live, Anna. Just come with me. You'll see, I'll tell you everything. Okay?"

She realized why Dolores was addressing her this way. Anna had stopped, just feet from the dorm room door. This is where she had stood in her dream, knowing what waited beyond the door, unable to stop her hand from rising to the latch, unable to turn away from the carnage within.

Not everyone gets to live.

Now, the exact opposite occurred. She did not know what lay beyond the door. Nor could she make her hand reach for the latch.

I don't want to know. If I don't open the door, I can keep on believing, pretending, they are alive.

Donny stood behind Dolores. His look of terror softened to worry as he alternately eyed the hallway or watched Dolores and Anna. He asked softly, "Anna, is this the door?"

They are gone, she lied to herself, *they all left, to another orphanage*. She nodded – granting affirmation to Donny and acquiescence to Dolores.

Donny didn't hesitate. Anna suddenly loved that about him. He slipped the blackened key into the keyhole and lifted the latch. The oak door swung silently into a silent room. Foul air wafted out, carrying the faint but undeniable odor of death.

Donny was through the door in an instant. Before Anna could protest, Dolores dragged her in as well, and locked the door behind them.

Gray light from the overcast sky percolated through high windows. The chandeliers did not burn. Stillness permeated the room, as if in this space, God Himself held His breath.

The two iron cots, along with all the straw, had been pushed to the far end of the room in a great heap. Anna started toward the heap but stopped in her tracks. Her heart leapt so hard it felt as if she had been struck in the chest. Two small girls lay side by side against one wall. Dark splotches mottled their gray skin. A torn patch of blanket lay across their faces.

Anna moved toward the bodies but Dolores restrained her, pulling her instead toward the heap of straw.

"I have to see..." she started.

Then a shrill voice screamed, "Anna!" and the pile of straw exploded. Six girls – Lizzy and Jane at the lead – ran to her, crying and laughing and yelling her name. They crowded around her hugging and babbling until the whole mess collapsed in a dog pile of giggles and shrieks and tears.

Chapter 8

DOLORES ALLOWED ABOUT THIRTY SECONDS of the frantic reunion before commanding, "Hush!" Silence retook the room. Anna looked from face to face, trying desperately to account for all her girls. Gaunt faces stared back, dark-eyed and hollow-cheeked. But, their lips were drawn in unrepressed smiles and their wet eyes gleamed with joy.

Maybelle was not among them. Anna glanced back over her shoulder to the dead girls. "Where's Donny? Where's Maybelle?" she asked.

"Who's Donny?" asked Jane.

"Here," Donny said in a choked voice. He knelt in the pile of straw, tears streaming down his cheeks.

The girls helped Anna to her feet, their eyes never leaving her for a moment. Awe and admiration shone in those eyes, and it scared Anna. Even worse, she saw hope in those eyes. She tried not to think about that as she made her way to Donny.

He knelt beside Maybelle in the deep nest of straw, holding her limp hand. Tears glistened in his eyes and at the corners of his broad smile. Anna could see that he was trying to talk, but no words came. Maybelle stared up at him, whispering, smiling.

"We almost lost that one two nights ago," Lizzy whispered. "It's been real bad, Anna."

"Anna," Dolores tapped her shoulder, "I was about to smuggle in some food when you two showed up. If you promise to keep them quiet, I'll try to fetch the basket before Sister Eustace finds her way back to us."

Anna nodded, unable to speak.

***

"I was pretty mad at you," Jane admitted, looking at her hands as she spoke. The girls sat in a rough circle in the straw nest. "At first I wanted to kill you. How could you just leave us like that?"

"I just...just had to..." Anna started.

"No, Anna," Jane cut her off, "I know. We've been talking about it, all of us. There's been nothing else to do. We all agree we'd have done the same thing, every single one of us."

The other girls nodded and murmured agreement.

"But none of us would'a come back," Lizzy said. "Sister Dolores said you might come back for us, but we all agreed that if any one of us ever got outta here, we'd have just kept right on running."

"Lizzy, Jane..." The guilt in Lizzy's voice broke Anna's heart.

"But now, everybody got to go free, did you know that?" Jane asked, her eyes dancing with light.

"What do you mean, 'free'?" asked Anna.

"The Church condemned this institution. They condemned the whole damned island," Jane said. "A delegation from the Seattle Diocese came out to inspect the damage. They said you wrecked this place real good, too good to be fixed. They also said that the living conditions here are deplorable and an embarrassment to the Church."

"They up an kicked Abbess McCain right out of the Church," Lizzy said. "And Sister Eustace and a bunch of others!"

"So all the children got to leave," Jane continued. "There's a new program going. Instead of keeping all the orphans cooped up in factories, now they're sending us out to the farms, almost like getting adopted. You still have to work for your meals, but at least you're with a family, and you get to see the outside sometimes."

"But Abbess McCain kept you here?" Anna asked. "Because of me."

"Sister Eustace said they would let us go as soon as they found you," Lizzy said. "Told us everyone is concerned for your welfare, but we know she's a liar."

"They've kept us locked in this room since you blew up the factory," Jane said. "They haven't fed us since then. And there's been no heat."

"Abbess McCain hid us when the delegation was here. I think she told them that all the children had already been sent away," Lizzy said. "She means to leave us here to die. Noel and Mary Two..." Lizzy choked on her words, pointing toward the bodies by the door. "No one would have ever known if you hadn't come back."

"Mary Two?" Anna asked, her voice breaking. She tried to rise, to move toward the shrouded bodies, but Jane and Lizzy both held her.

"She's gone, Anna," Jane said, in tones kinder than Anna had ever heard from Jane. "We tried to keep her warm, but..."

Mary Two's bare ankle rested against the cold stone floor. Her tiny hands lay folded on her chest.

"I almost killed her the night I left," Anna said. "I didn't mean it, Mary, honest I didn't."

"She knows," Lizzy whispered, "we talked, me and Mary, before she...you know, before, and she understands. She wasn't mad at you or nothing."

"But I guess I really did kill her," Anna continued. "If I hadn't..."

"No," Jane said, anger replacing the kindness in her voice. "Abbess McCain did this. She could have sent us off with the others, but she left us here. Mary's death, Noel's death, Abbess McCain is guilty of both." After a pause, Jane continued. "We all would have died already, if not for

Dolores. She snuck in here a few nights ago to bring us food and blankets."

"And water," Lizzy added.

"Yeah," Jane continued. "Sister Eustace wouldn't even bring us water, and they took all our blankets, too. If we'd had blankets the first night, maybe Noel..." Jane didn't finish, and all the girls fell quiet for a time.

Eventually, Anna broke the silence, "Did Dolores tell you why Abbess McCain kept you?"

"Of course not!" Dolores said, slipping through the door. "They've had enough on their minds without having to worry about demons and witches and such." She carried a basket full of food. "Eat up, girls...and Donny, is it? Eat up. This could be your last supper."

Chapter 9

"DOLORES," ANNA ASKED, "WHAT IS going on?"

"Well, why don't you nestle in with your sisters, and...uh," she paused, studying Donny, "...and Donny. Donny, where did you come from, anyway?"

"Nun tossed me off a boat," Donny said through a mouthful of potatoes. "Joseph drug me up a pipe an' dumped me in a cellar. Said he wanted my parts."

"Ooh, that's wonderful." Dolores's eyes lit up when he mentioned Joseph. "I want to hear all about that, as soon as you're finished eating. But," she turned her attention to Anna, "as I was saying, nestle down my little chickadees, eat your food, and I will tell you a tale."

The potatoes Dolores brought were cold, but they were cooked. She also had two loaves of bread and a large jug of water. The girls devoured the feast as daintily as any pack of starved orphans can, and they passed the jug around until they drank it dry.

Maybelle, who had been drifting in and out of consciousness, made a miraculous recovery as soon as Donny showed her the jam. She half sat, half lounged against him while he fed her bits of jam-smeared bread. He crammed potatoes into his own mouth with the other hand.

"Donny," Maybelle said after her fourth morsel, "Mamma said you cain't never leave me. Daddy's gonna skin your hide when he finds out you left me. Just 'cause they're in prison don't mean you don't have to mind 'em."

"Hush up an' eat, chipmunk," Donny replied, not unkindly.

Once it was clear she wasn't going to die for lack of jam, Donny began to offer the jar around the circle of girls. After the third girl tasted the rare treat, Donny realized they were all staring at him with unabashed adoration. He stuffed the jar into Jane's hands and told her to finish distributing it. Then he nestled back into the straw, trying to hide behind his little sister.

Anna ate without taking her eyes off Dolores. Finally, she said, "Dolores, tell me what is happening here."

"I will have some questions for you, as well, young lady. Many questions. But for now, eat, and rest and I will tell you a story. We have at least an hour before Sister Eustace finds her way out of that basement. And I doubt McCain will be bold enough to send any more patrols today." Dolores smiled, "No, not today she won't."

"Sister Eustace said men are coming tomorrow," Donny said.

"Oh, yes, Hessians I should think, mercenaries, fanatics, restless adventure-seeking rakes," Dolores said. "All from McCain's secret order. They've got their little hearts set on capturing a witch. It should be a barrel of fun – but not for them, not now that I've found you two."

"Found us?" Anna demanded. "We don't have anything to do with this! I don't know you! We just want off this island! Whatever bad blood runs between you and Abbess McCain, I want no part of it."

"I'm very sorry, Anna," Dolores said, "but if I am not mistaken, Joey offered you something – a key, perhaps. And you accepted it?"

Anna said nothing. The truth was plain enough.

Dolores smiled on her, very warmly. "You are right in the middle of this, Anna. As I told you on our first meeting, you are a brave and noble spirit, which is probably why Joseph trusted you...also because you are a little unhinged upstairs." Dolores tapped Anna's head. "I suppose I owe you a complete explanation." She turned to the other girls. "Jane, I have some gauze and ointment in my basket, oh, and some tweezers. Would you be so kind as to help Anna pick the glass out of her shins, and dress her wounds?"

Jane jumped to the task.

"Donny, do you have any wounds that need attention?"

"No, ma'am," he said, crouching lower behind Maybelle. "I'm just fine."

"Very well," Dolores sat on the iron cot. "Where shall we begin?" She crossed one leg over the other and started picking glass from the back of her calf. "I told you that Hattie shot my mother, fifteen years ago. She did so because my mother was a witch..."

The girls gasped and murmured and fidgeted in the straw, moving closer to Anna.

"Oh yes, little ones, mama was a witch. I, in case you are wondering, am not. My mother's coven kicked me out, believe it or not. Seems I broke the rules. Anyhow, no need to fear me, I'm not a witch.

"Now, that's not to say I don't know a trick or two." She held up a bloody glass shard between thumb and forefinger. When she released it, instead of dropping, the glass floated in midair. The girls gasped with delight and awe. "And speaking of tricks, Anna, that exploding preserves gag is pretty nifty, you'll have to teach me that one."

"Actually, that was Donny's idea," Anna said.

"It's not a trick, it's a bomb," Donny said, peeking out from behind his little sister.

"Well, trick, bomb, whatever," Dolores said. "As I was saying, that lovely creature you met in the hall, Hattie – she's a witch-hunter...well, she *was* a witch-hunter. I don't suppose she's much of anything now." Dolores grinned and stifled a giggle.

"Abbess McCain heads the order of witch-hunters to which Hattie belonged. When I was a child, she and Hattie and two others, snuck into my home and shot my parents while they slept. And burned the house down."

The little circle of orphans murmured and hmm'ed appreciatively. In an orphanage, the story of the demise of one's parents is the proper way to begin any introduction.

"My brother, Joey, and I woke when we heard the gunshots. We jumped out the bedroom window and ran for the woods. I don't know if Hattie and McCain intended to kill us, but they knew we were there and they certainly did nothing to save us." She stopped picking glass from her leg and quieted for a moment, apparently distracted by dust motes floating on the air.

When she spoke again, a darker breath colored her voice. "They sent us here, Joey and I. Somehow, the county learned we were witch kids. It just would not do to have the children of witches mingling with the poor, unfortunate orphans of good Christian folk. This place, The Saint Frances de Chantal Orphan Asylum, is where they hide the horrible and misbegotten. It is a place for children who wouldn't be accepted anywhere else.

"The fair people of the Church withhold charity from any institution housing children such as you. They may even have shown up with pitchforks and torches. And, no one in their right mind would ever adopt a child who had been living among children of witches, whores and thieves. So, this place was established, and all the vile orphans of the world – like my brother and I, like all of you – were shipped away and hidden here." Dolores made a sweeping gesture, as if displaying merchandise in a showroom.

"Unfortunately for little Joey and I, Saint Franny's also became a dumping ground for the most nefarious nuns. The Church holds the concept of forgiveness in very high regard. It holds its own reputation even more dearly. So, when a nun disgraces the Church in splendid and spectacular ways, or if she is likely to do so, rather than defrocking her and risking a scandal, the Church allows the sister to maintain her vows, but exiles her to this rock." Dolores returned her attention, and her tweezers, to the glass in her calf, but proceeded with her tale.

"The Church discovered that McCain and her cohorts had murdered my parents. But, because they had committed their heinous sins as an act of faith, and because the Church still considers witchcraft a graver transgression than murder, rather than turning McCain over to the authorities, the bishop exiled her."

"Lucky us," Lizzy muttered.

Anna hissed a shush as her.

Dolores snapped her eyes to Lizzy. "Lucky indeed, little chickadee. Lucky you are here now rather than then." She grinned a mad grin. "McCain has mellowed over the years."

A rare sobriety washed over Lizzy's countenance.

Dolores stared at her for a moment longer, then continued. "So, just after Joey and I arrived, Sister McCain and her merry band of witch-hunting nuns also took up residence here. When McCain saw me, she realized what a 'splendid opportunity God had granted her.' He had 'turned her personal tragedy into a pathway to even greater glory', and all that malarkey. The Church was sending her every witch orphan in the country. We were, in her mind, a veritable treasure trove of information.

"She still had contacts in the Order of Inquisitors, that's the name of their little club, by the by, the ones who are coming to kill us tomorrow." She held up a bit of glass, cocked her head with a fake, plastered smile, then flicked the glass away.

"McCain established a network of Inquisitor sympathizers inside Saint Franny's, then went to work interrogating any orphans who may have had witch parents. Starting with me and Joey.

"Joey was only six. He didn't know anything that would interest McCain, but she found him very useful, none the less. She, um...she knew I wasn't going to talk. Not easily, anyway, so...so she tortured Joey while interrogating me..." Dolores giggled, then drew a flask from under her habit and took a long drink. She breathed deep, then hit the flask once more.

"It's an elixir," she said, answering the orphans' quizzical looks. "It makes a mournful heart happy..." Dolores dropped her eyes to the flask and made a sound that was either a scoff or a sob. "...the same way that rose petals make an outhouse smell lovely."

"But, this is important for you to understand, so I must tell it," Dolores continued. "I was eleven then. I knew much. About my mother's craft, about her friends and the tracts they haunted. If I talked, mother's friends would die. I could not do that. And, I confess, I took great pleasure in infuriating McCain." Dolores snorted. "It was my little revenge.

"I underestimated McCain's resolve, and her cruelty. In the end, she got nothing from me, not a word...well, not a word I can repeat in mixed company." Dolores gave Donny a suspicious eye. "She got nothing from me, but from little Joey, she took a hand. Hacked it off with a meat cleaver. Right in front of me."

Anna had to look away. She examined her own hand, recalling the terror of the day she lost her pinky. McCain lecturing, waving the knife, accusing. McCain laying the blade across Anna's wrist. *Do you know, little Anna, what the Arabs do with a thief?* Anna nodded, she had read about it in one of the stolen books. McCain pressing the cold edge into Anna's wrist, increasing pressure bit by bit until a tiny trickle of blood seeped from beneath the blade. *But we are a civilized country, Anna, a Christian country. We are not that cruel here...* McCain moving the cleaver toward Anna's little finger. She knew what happened next, but the details had been swallowed by pain.

Anna felt Dolores staring at her, knowing her thoughts. When she looked up, Dolores continued. "I had a week, McCain said, to remember all the names I knew, because as soon as Joey was out of the infirmary, we were to start the interrogations all over again.

"Joey never made it out of the infirmary." She swallowed and her throat clicked. The flask trembled in her white-knuckle grasp. "His stump took infection. By the second night, he was delirious with fever. The sisters wouldn't let me see him. Of course they wouldn't, you know how this place is. But, as I told you, I had learned much from my mother.

"I made use of this simple glamour," Dolores's face changed to Eustace, then to McCain, then back to herself, "and sneaked into Joey's room. As soon as I saw him, I knew. His skin had gone milk white. He was covered in sweat and trembling all over. I felt the heat of his fever from across the room. I knew he was dying.

"I couldn't let that happen. So, I did the only thing I knew to do. I cast a spell." Dolores's lips trembled and her voice hushed as she spoke the word *spell*.

"It was an incantation from mother's forbidden book. I, um, found it, one day, about a year before my parents were murdered. The spell, that is, an interesting incantation, a fascinating little string of words. I had to have that spell, but I knew I'd likely never see it again, so I did exactly as you would have done." She stared at Anna.

"You memorized it." The words turned Anna's insides cold as she spoke them.

"Exactly!" Dolores smiled a real smile this time. "I memorized it. Something about those words, I felt like I needed them. The spell was old and its language unclear, to me at least, but it sounded as if it prevented death. I thought it was a spell of blessing. You see, I didn't know. It is important for you to understand that." She brushed the hair away from her face, drew out the flask, grimaced at it, and stowed it again.

"I was caught in the wheels of a machine much larger than myself. Sometimes there is no solution, Anna, sometimes there is no right decision. You just choose the least horrible option. I thought that is what I was doing." Dolores shook her head, stared down at her hands in her lap.

"Never!" she shouted, startling everyone. "Never perform an incantation you don't fully understand. Never. Never. Nev – I knew this. I know it even better now. But, but I couldn't let Joey die. I had to..." She trailed off, then drew a long, ragged breath. "It did not heal Joey, this old spell of mine. It didn't prevent his body from dying. It bound his spirit to his body. When Joey died the following day, his spirit did not find Summerland. When they cast his poor little body into the sea, all of his awareness and his will went with it."

Dolores snatched up her flask and guzzled, and shuddered. She looked at Anna, then to each of the other children, searching their eyes for understanding or accusation. "Being alive is good," she said at last, "and being dead isn't really that bad, but dying – dying is horrible. It's intended to be quick, an instant for some, a few minutes in the worst cases. But Joey has been dying, piece-by-piece, for eleven years. And I did that to him.

"But, you must understand, I didn't know. I just believed my spell had failed. I believed Joey had died. The following morning, I used the glamour to get onto that little boat that goes to the mainland. I ran and didn't look back. I tried to find my mother's friends, but they had disappeared." Dolores shook her head with a wry grin. "Turns out, they have a spy inside the Seattle Diocese who told them what McCain was up to. They were long gone before McCain even started her interrogations. It took me most of a decade to track them down.

"Once I finally found them, I explained how I had tried to save Joey. They had heard, from their spy, of a strange devil haunting Saint Franny's. It first appeared shortly after Joey's death. I understood, then, what I had done, and so did my mother's coven. They were quite appalled, as you might imagine. In fact, they cast me out." She spread her arms, the gesture a cross between presenting herself for inspection and a shrug of indifference.

"So now you know." She took a deep breath and sat back. "I am here to undo the evil I have done. My mother's coven has sent a ship for me. They have promised to come for me, to take me back, as soon as I have righted my wrongs."

"You've come to kill your little brother," Anna said.

"I've come to kill my little brother," Dolores confirmed.

Chapter 10

"I INTEND TO FREE HIS spirit," Dolores said, "so that his soul can at last find the peace of Summerland...since I cannot return life to his body."

"Which body?" Donny asked. "He's got at least five."

"Five bodies?" Dolores asked.

All the girls turned to Donny. Donny turned red, but continued. "He collects dead things an' sews 'em together to make new bodies. One of 'em is a six armed mermaid with a wolf's head."

Dolores and the girls looked to Anna, incredulous.

"I saw the mermaid," Anna said, nodding, "and the other things."

"That's why he kept me, for my parts. But he said he couldn't take 'em 'til I was dead," Donny said. "He got pretty mad when I didn't die."

"Why would he want to sew up a bunch of dead bodies?" asked Lizzy.

"He gets inside 'em an' they come to life," Donny said. He no longer blushed and there was a hint of the devil in his eyes. Also, he had covered Maybelle's ears. "He wears 'em like a monster suit. One of 'em has two shark heads and crab claws for fingers."

"That's quite enough, Donny, thank you," Dolores said.

"He needed new eyeballs, so he used an antler to cut eyes out of a dead nun..."

"Donny!" Dolores snapped.

"Why did he need new eyeballs?" Lizzy asked.

"Lizzy!" Jane and Anna said at the same time.

"'Cause Anna gouged the old ones out with this key." Donny held up the blackened key.

The girls gasped and murmured, looking from the key to Anna and back to Donny.

"Yes," Anna said, doing her best to sound exasperated. "Donny got himself caught and I had to go back and rescue him." She glared at Donny with what she hoped was a knock-it-off look.

"You stabbed a monster in the eye?" Mary One gaped at Anna.

"He's not a monster, he's my brother!" Dolores said.

"You should'a seen it!" Donny said. "Miss Dolores put some magic in that key. It blew the monster's eyes clean out of his head. Boy was he steamed!"

"It did?" asked Dolores.

"Sure did. Just 'bout emptied his skull, I reckon," Donny beamed. "You could'a looked in one eye an' seen out the other."

"No, *you* couldn't," Anna said. "You couldn't see anything because it was pitch black and you were under water."

The girls clamored. "You blew his brains out with a magic key?" "You fought the monster in the dark?" "Underwater?" "How is it still alive?"

"He just crawled out of the old monster suit," Donny answered, "an' slipped into a new one. I guess he's pretty hard to kill, 'cause later on we dropped a house on him, but that didn't kill him either."

This set off a new round of questions and chatter. *It's amazing what a little potato and jam can do,* Anna thought, *and a little hope.* She looked apologetically at Dolores, but the fake nun seemed as enraptured with Donny's tale as the rest of his audience.

"...The savage wolves had us cornered in the cellar an' Joseph was comin' up outa the well, looking like something so disturbin' he could'a scared your worst nightmare. Anna fought off the wolves, held 'em at bay with rotten green beans and stuff while I knocked out the pillars of the house, kinda like Sampson in the Bible. Only, the house didn't land on me like it did on Sampson 'cause Anna pulled me out," his voice quieted a little, "just in the nick of time. The whole house came crashin' down like Satan gettin kicked out'a heaven. Must'a squashed the monster flat. But the wolves were still comin' for us, they were his wolves, see..."

"Where is this house?" Dolores interrupted.

"I could take you there, but he's not there anymore," Anna said. "We saw him here, this morning."

The girls hushed and turned wide eyes on Anna.

"That's wonderful!" Dolores said, clapping her hands. "Tell me where you saw him."

"He was crawling through the rubble, where the factory used to be."

"Well, it's about time he showed up," Dolores said. "I was expecting him days ago. I guess you two slowed him down a bit."

"It was you who unlocked the door for him?" Donny asked.

"Yes, of course. He wants his hand back. When he comes for it, we'll be ready." Dolores said. She practically glowed with delight.

"What do you mean, 'we'?" Jane spoke up in her most authoritative head girl voice. "Anna might have made some deal with the devil to get out of here, but I certainly did not!"

"He's not the devil, he's my brother," Dolores nearly shouted.

"Why does he want his hand back?" Donny asked. "He's already got a whole pile of hands."

"Abbess McCain kept the hand?" Lizzy asked.

"Why were the wolves helping him?" Anna asked.

That seemed to catch Dolores's attention. She raised her hands and hushed the girls. "That is a very interesting question." To Donny, she said, "You stop agitating these girls, young man, or I will turn you into a toad." To Anna she said, "Did you see him when he was not wearing one of these 'monster suits'?"

Anna nodded.

"Well?" Dolores asked, "What did you see?"

Anna looked at the seven faces staring back at her. Maybelle slept, leaning against Donny, but the others were enraptured. How could she tell Dolores what she had seen without further inflaming the rampant imaginings of her roommates? She considered the tiny torso, the remains of a six-year-old child.

"He must have been insane with terror," Anna said gently. "I...I can't even begin to imagine. How long? How long do you think he was down there? Before he...revived, became aware again?"

"What did you see?" Dolores repeated, her shell of frivolity cracking.

"There isn't very much of him left," Anna said in a low, flat voice. "Just ribs, and half of one arm. It's like he has fallen apart. The rest, it's just gone."

Dolores stared into Anna's eyes, silent and motionless. The other children sat as still as death. Dolores's features waivered, like a summer mirage. Drops of wetness appeared on her lap. *She is falling apart, too. She's crying, balling her eyes out, but using the glamour to hide it from the girls, or from me.*

Anna took Dolores's hands. They trembled in her grasp. "You and me, Dolores," she said in a near whisper. "We are in this together, remember. You and me, true sisters. You know everything that is in my heart, because we are the same."

Dolores's face shimmered again, revealing the tears. The woman's body shook with sobs. "The sisterhood of sorrow," she said.

"All these years," Anna said, "I believed that I had killed my brother. I let momma say I did it because I wanted her to be okay. I think daddy knew it was a lie all along, but he wanted her to be okay, too. Then, when she wasn't okay, he blamed me. As if I should have killed Ephraim, so that it wouldn't have been momma. Nothing I could have done would have saved him. And what I did trying to save momma just made everything so much worse."

"Wait, Anna," Dolores said. She released Anna's hands and straightened her spine. "Quiet. We've travelled similar paths, you and I, but do not try to get close to me. You don't want me as a sister. I have only one thing left to do in this life, and it will cost me my life. I must die for Joey to die...and Joey must die. I have to do that for him, it's all I have left to give him. But I do not wish to hurt you, Anna. These are your sisters," she gestured to the silent, awestruck girls, "care for them. Do not bond with me. I hope to be dead before sunset."

Dolores wiped her eyes and hardened her face. "All of Joey is alive. Not just the monster suits, not just the thing that you saw crawl out of the suit. All of the bits of his little body still carry his soul – his will and consciousness – with them. That's why I asked you what you saw, that's the only reason.

"You asked why the wolves were helping him. At some point, those wolves must have ingested part of his body, if I understand the spell correctly. The coyotes and the crows, as well. He is in them. He does not control them, not completely, but is able to influence them. The wolves attacked you because Joey directed them to do so. But they ran away because their instincts were stronger than his influence. Also, Joey knows what those animals know. The island, too, I imagine. Particles of little Joey scattered by the tide and surf, carried away by crabs and seagulls..."

"That's how he knew about the moon and tide," Anna said. "On the night I escaped, Joseph knew just how everything would be. He knew how to make me disappear into the island."

Dolores smiled. "He is the island, and the sea around it. For eleven years, he has been becoming this place – and losing himself to it. He influences everything of which he has become a part, but those things influence him as well. The thinner he is spread, the less himself he will be. When he dies, if his soul finds its way to Summerland, he will have peace. But, if he is scattered to the four winds, he may never find it. I have to free him while he is still aware of who he is, and what he is."

"And to release him from your spell, you have to die?" Anna asked.

"Someone has to die," Dolores said, "and it should be me. My mother's craft, its power is drawn from balance. As he is now, Joey can neither kill nor be killed. But if he takes a life, the magic that binds his soul to his carnal relic will begin to unravel. The curse will slowly drain away and he will be free."

"Well, shucks," Donny said, "just turn him loose on this McCain you keep talking about. He could rip her to shreds and solve two problems at once."

"He could kill her," Dolores said, "but he won't. He could have killed you, but he didn't. Evidently, he understands the limitations of his power. I think McCain understands as well. She is well studied in the ways of the witch.

"I believe McCain has known about Joseph for quite some time. That is why she keeps his hand in her office, to torment him, to draw him. All these years, she has kept this place sealed up, taunting him. Joseph wanted you," Dolores nodded at Anna, "to blow up the factory for several reasons, but mainly so he could retrieve his hand.

"McCain knows she can't keep him out anymore, and knows he can't kill her. So, now she has summoned her army of witch-hunters to help her capture Joseph and burn him at the stake."

"But that won't kill him?" Donny asked.

"No," Dolores said, "He would be reduced to vapor and ash, but he would not die. His soul would be doomed to eternal limbo, never knowing the peace of death." Dolores paused, the unreliable glimmer stole across her eyes. She looked up at Anna. "This is the other half of McCain's devious little scheme, she expects you and me to try to rescue Joey once she catches him. She used your girls as bait to bring you here. She'll use Joey to catch the two of us, so we can all burn together."

"But, if she wants to catch Joey, why do they keep lockin' all the doors?" Donny asked.

"Because they are cowards," Dolores said, "a bunch of old women terrified of a little boy who has been dead longer than he was alive." She laughed aloud, then added, "They don't want to let him in until they have more troops. A few of the mercenaries arrived early this morning, and some of McCain's long-time cohorts. They have barricaded themselves in the rotunda, waiting for the rest of their reinforcements. The only reason you saw Hattie and I in the corridor is *somebody*," Dolores winked, "keeps unlocking the doors. McCain has been sending out patrols to find the creep and to re-lock the doors.

"However, after Eustace's little adventure this morning, I'm guessing she will discontinue the patrols and focus her efforts on securing the rotunda, until Thaddeus Everstout arrives. I expect his boat to set sail from Seattle this evening or early tomorrow morning. I have to finish this before then."

"What about us?" Jane asked. "What happens to us after you and your little devil-monster brother kill each other?"

"Well, I don't know, Jane," Dolores said in a perky voice. "I owed Anna a favor. She asked me to look after you while she was gone. I did. Now she's back, and I have other responsibilities. I guess you'll just have to grow up and fend for yourself."

"Dolores," Anna said, "none of this is their fault. They shouldn't suffer for what I did, or for what you and Joseph have done."

"No, they shouldn't." Dolores raised her eyebrows at Anna. "Nor should McCain have killed my brother. Nor should I have cursed him with eternal life. Nor should Eve have eaten the apple. Take it up with God. There's nothing I can do about it."

"But, you're responsible," Donny said. "Anna never would have blown up the factory if..."

"Anna blew up the factory because she chose to do so. And she chose to run off and leave every one of you to pay for what she had done," Dolores said, staring down at the ring of girls. "Well, everyone but you, Donny. If she didn't blow up the factory, you would have died where Joey stowed you. It was not I who put you in this peril."

"I am not a witch. I'm not a fairy godmother either. Maybe I would help you if I could, but there is nothing more I can do for you.

"Anna, I already told you I'm not here to rescue anyone. Sometimes there are no solutions. Sometimes there is only bad or worse. Not everybody gets to live. I have taken care of your sisters, as I told you I would. Now I must go take care of my brother."

Dolores stood awkwardly, brushing straw from her habit. She looked weary and subdued, but, as she turned and walked toward the hall, her face was a mask of stoic resolve.

"You have to stop her!" Jane whispered at Anna, "We need her help." The other girls, several crying, crowded around Anna, clamoring in whispers. "Don't let her go!" "You can't just let her leave." "Make her change her mind." "Bring her back." "She has to save us!"

Anna questioned Donny with her eyes.

Donny shrugged.

Anna jumped up and sprinted after Dolores, catching her just as she reached the door. "Please, Dolores, can't you stay for just a moment longer?"

"No, Anna!" Dolores's voice cracked.

"At least tell me your plan. We can help you, we can help each other."

"I can't ask you to help me. I will not be the source of any more misery. I refuse to be responsible for any more death."

"You know we are all going to die here. How can we possibly hope to escape without help? They are going to burn me alive, because of you and Joseph."

"Because of McCain!" Dolores said.

"Please, Dolores, let us help you defeat her. We have nothing to lose."

"Defeat?" Dolores scoffed. "I don't care about defeating McCain. She is of no concern to me. This is about me and Joey, and nothing else." She drew a key out of her pocket and inserted it into the keyhole.

"I have to defeat her." Anna grabbed the fake nun's wrist. "You are bound to a task, you must free your brother. I accept that. I am bound to a task, as well. I must free these girls. The only way for me to do that is by defeating McCain."

"Let go of me, Anna. I don't want to hurt you."

The bones in Dolores's wrist vibrated, Anna's palm and fingers tingled. Goose pimples sprung up her arm. She held fast. "Tell me your plan, Dolores. At least do that for me. Or tell me when you hope to face Joey. If we both move at the same time..."

The tingling had engulfed Anna's entire hand and now worked its way up her arm. Her palm felt as if she held a ball of buzzing needles rather than Dolores's wrist.

Dolores finished for Anna. "McCain will be distracted by one of us, and the other might have a better chance." She sighed and looked at the ceiling.

Anna nodded, releasing Dolores. Iridescent lines, like gossamer spider silk, shimmered between Anna's palm and Dolores's wrist, faded, then vanished. "What are you doing?"

"I am loosing the floodgates of heaven," Dolores said. "I'm opening the fountains of the great deep. I'm calling up a storm, Anna, one like you've never seen before.

"Joey still fears letting go of this life, as awful as it is. He knows that killing will break the spell, so, he will not kill me. Even if he thinks I am McCain. Even if I have his hand right there and refuse to give it to him, he won't do it.

"Joey has become one with this island and its creatures and the sea around it. I will whip the sea into a fury. I will terrify the animals and shake this house to its foundation. I will stir the sea until it matches the rage that has consumed my little brother.

"The violence of the storm and the violence of his passion will fuel each other until Joey can no longer control his impulses. Then, I will present myself to him as McCain and taunt him with his hand and he will strike. We will die together, and we will be free."

The room darkened and wind whistled around the frames of the windows. Dolores opened the door and stepped into the hall. "I wish you all the best, Anna, I really do. You won't need to worry about McCain tonight. She will be very busy with the storm. Captain Everstout and his minions will drown in the sea if they try to cross over to the island tonight. If you do manage to get out of here, take your girls inland. You don't want to be anywhere near the beach while Joey and I still live."

"Why didn't you tell me this before?" Anna asked.

"Because I didn't think of it until just now." She pulled the flask out of her habit and took a sip. Mischief replaced the melancholy in her eyes and she smiled broadly. "Sitting with the girls in there, it was just too much like my life when I lived here. It makes me too sad. Here, take some of this, it really helps." She thrust the flask toward Anna.

"I think I better not," Anna said.

Dolores put on a mock pout and pocketed the flask. "Well, maybe you'll take this instead?" She drew the blackened key out of her pocket. "I don't think it has any magic left, but it might still open a few doors for you. Oh, and this might be fun, too." She offered one of Hattie's flintlock pistols. "But watch out, it's got a hair trigger."

As Anna reached for the key, a bright blue spark arced across the gap between the girl and the woman, stinging Anna's fingers.

Dolores belted out a peel of surprised laughter. "Oooh, it's going to be a hell of a storm! Hee hee, sorry about your fingers." She grabbed the lip of Anna's pocket and dropped the gun and key into it.

"I don't know how to work a gun," Anna said, rubbing her fingers and stepping away from the electric fake nun.

"Oh, I bet that Donny boy knows his way around a gun," Dolores said. "He's quite the little swashbuckler, isn't he? And a looker, too, if you ignore the dirt and scabs. I imagine he cleans up real nice." Dolores flashed a conspiratorial wink. "Be nice to that one, if you know what I mean."

"He's a bit too young for me," Anna said, "and a bit too annoying." Feeling the key and gun in her pocket, she said, "Thank you, Dolores..."

"Well, it's your loss." Dolores shook her head. "If you don't snatch him up, one of those other girls will. But, such is life. Anyway, I have to go now. Good luck to you, little Anna, it has been fun knowing you. I'm off to kill my brother."

Dolores spun and strode down the hall. Her form changed, stretching taller, broadening, shrinking, wavering – and she mumbled as she went. "Now, who should I be? Tabitha is dead, but Eustace knows it. Agatha...no, she's still alive," shaking her head and counting off names on her fingers. "Wilma might work, but she's just so pudgy..."

Chapter 11

AS SOON AS ANNA RETURNED alone, the girls erupted in clamoring questions. They sounded like the cacophonous arguing sea birds she'd encountered near the beach. Jane and Lizzy jumped up out of the straw and rushed toward Anna. The others followed.

"Quiet!" Anna said, holding her hands up. "Keep it down. One at a time."

"Anna! What are you thinking?" Jane grabbed Anna by her shawl. The older girl's eyes flashed fever-bright, her voice cracked with desperation. "You can't just let her go. We need help. McCain is going to let us die in here and it's your fault. You have to go get that crazy witch nun and make her help us!"

Several girls echoed Jane. Lizzy grabbed Jane and pulled her away from Anna. Jane tried to twist out of Lizzy's grip while maintaining her hold on Anna. She accidently elbowed Lizzy in the chin, knocking her into Mary One. Anna, grasping Jane's wrists, looked to Donny, who still sat in the straw with a happily snoozing Maybelle. He cocked an eyebrow and shrugged.

Jane started shaking Anna. "What are we going to do, Anna? She can't just leave us..."

Anna had read several stories in which the hero slapped a woman who had gone hysterical. Jane was edging toward hysterical, but Anna didn't know if that would work in real life, and Jane was much bigger than Anna. And she could hit, really hard.

Just as Anna decided it would be a bad idea to slap Jane, Lizzy bounced up from the side and tackled the larger girl into the straw. The collision knocked Anna backward onto her bottom. Mary One sprang to her feet and rushed Jane as well. Joan, who was one of Jane's girls, leapt into the brawl.

Outside, and far away, thunder growled in the darkening sky, unnoticed to all but Anna. She looked at Jane and the girls scrapping in the straw, the hunger and dread from the last week turning them feral. She wanted to scream at them to stop, but felt too exhausted to raise her voice.

In another story Anna read, a barkeeper stopped a brawl by firing a gun at the ceiling. Anna pulled the flintlock out of her pocket. It was a dainty gun, almost ornamental, and fit easily in her hand. She pointed it in the air. Donny was shaking his head "no" and calling out to her, but she pulled the trigger anyway.

Nothing happened.

Now, Donny rushed to her. Maybelle, behind him, stared bleary-eyed at the chaos. Donny took Anna's free hand and helped her to her feet, then pointed to the large hammer on the side of the gun.

"Ya' gotta cock it first, silly. An' you only git one shot, so don't waste it," he said. "Here, watch this." He cupped his hands around his mouth and yelled, *"Its Abbess McCain!"*

The girls froze, snapping their attention to the door. Seeing no one, they looked back to Donny and Anna. Anna still held the gun above her head and the girls, who had not seen it before, were awe struck.

"Lizzy!" Anna said, "put my girls in order. Jane, put your girl in order. Dolores *is* helping us. I have a way out of here, a plan. But you have to get ahold of yourselves, we are not *savages*."

Silence fell over the room as the girls stared back at her. Some appeared shamed, some confused, some cautiously hopeful.

Then, Lizzy burst out in cackling laughter. "Savages!" She tumbled out of the girl pile and rolled up onto her elbows. "You are the most savage looking thing I think I ever saw!"

The littlest girls, Lilly and Norma, giggled first. Then the next oldest, and soon, the whole pile relaxed into tentative snickering. Jane tried valiantly to stay angry, Anna watched her struggle against the giggles, but in the end, even Jane smirked.

"Anna, put that gun down," she said, choking back a laugh, "you look absurd."

***

"There's a storm coming," Anna said, once she and Jane had collected all of their girls in the straw. The room had darkened to almost twilight. "A big storm. If you listen, you can hear the thunder already. The men that were coming to help McCain, they won't make it here tonight. Dolores said if they try, they'll all drown in the sea."

"I hope they try," Lizzy said.

Anna ignored the impulse to scold her. "Dolores is going to find Joseph. She'll be looking for him near the factory. She's not coming back from that meeting. Whatever happens down there will cause quite a ruckus. Between that and the storm, we should be able to sneak out without getting caught. Donny and I know how to get out through the basement. We'll shelter in the woods until the storm passes."

"Then what?" Jane asked. "We'll still be stuck on the island. Where are we supposed to go? Who will feed us? I'm telling you, Anna, you need to make Dolores help us."

"How?" Anna said. "She's got her mind set. She won't listen to me. Besides, she's crazy and drunk and we don't need her."

"I think we do need her," Jane said. "She's the only reason any of us are still alive. You ran off and left us, and we got blamed for it. The only thing that saved us was Dolores. She told Sister Eustace that you escaped. She said that I reported you."

"That's how they knew to come looking for me..." Anna said.

"We would have all got the lash if we didn't tell," Lizzy said. "But Dolores gave you a two hour head start. That should have been plenty of time."

"That doesn't matter now," Jane said. "The point is she saved us, not just then, either. We'd have froze to death and starved without her. We can't just let Dolores die...because then we'll die."

"Jane, I'm sorry I left like that, I had to, and you know it. But I'm here now. I got out, we can all get out."

"What do you think, Donny?" Lizzy asked.

Donny blushed as all eyes turned to him, then shrugged. "I think Dolores gots bats in her belfry, just as likely to do one thing as another. But she knows how to handle an ax, and that could come in handy."

"Why are you asking *him*?" Jane asked, eyeing Lizzy.

"An ax?" Lizzy asked, ignoring Jane.

"Donny!" Anna snapped. "No more of your gruesome stories. Not now. We've got to settle this." To Jane she said, "Dolores isn't coming back. I wish, with all my heart, that she would, but she won't. We have to make do without her. When the storm gets fierce, we head for the basement, then to the woods. There's a rowboat on the beach, a big one. Before first light, if the sea has calmed, we will take the boat to the mainland."

The room lit, briefly, as lightning fell somewhere over the churning ocean.

"And if it hasn't calmed?" Jane asked.

"We hide and wait. I know a couple places on the island. Donny and I found a few shelters. We can camp out for a day, even two if necessary. When the sea is calm, we'll go."

"And you don't think they'll come looking for us in the woods?" Jane asked.

"Didn't work out too good for 'em last time they tried that," Donny said.

Lizzy giggled.

"This place is falling apart, Jane," Anna said. "If you could have seen it from the outside..."

"I saw it," Joan said, "the night of the explosion. I got out, just for a few minutes. I thought the tower was going to topple. You surely did a number on this place, Anna."

"When that boiler went up..." Mary One said, "well, we didn't know it was the boiler. I couldn't think of anything that could have made a sound like that. Mary Two said she thought God had stomped on us. That's what it felt like."

"What I'm trying to tell you," Anna continued, "is that McCain and her helpers, they can't stay here forever. This place isn't safe to live in. The only reason they are still here is because McCain is obsessed with catching Dolores and Joseph..."

"And you," Donny put in.

Anna scowled at him, but continued her thought. "Once Joseph and Dolores are dead, McCain will abandon the island. She'll have no reason to stay."

Jane opened her mouth to speak, but Anna held up her hand and said, "Jane, I just told you what I'm going to do, me and my girls..."

"And me," Donny said.

"And me," Lizzy said.

"If you want to do something else," Anna continued, "if you have a different idea, you and Joan can do that. But I'm not arguing about it anymore." Anna stood. "Have Donny tell you a story or something, I'm taking a nap. Wake me when the storm hits." She walked out of the circle.

"What?" Donny said. "Anna, I don't know no stories."

Anna kicked at the straw, fluffing up a thick pile in the corner.

"Tell 'em 'bout the time daddy shot the neighbor's piglets 'cause they got into his whisky mash," Maybelle said.

"Well, you kinda jus' told 'em the whole story, sis."

"Bet Donny would have told it better," Lizzy said.

Jane scoffed. Her heels clicked away to the other side of the dormitory. Thunder grumbled like an irritable giant whose sleep had been disturbed. Anna snuggled into her straw nest, oddly comforted by the familiarity of this bed, draped the heavy coat over her face and closed her eyes.

She dozed to the sound of Donny's voice, "...glowing key...somethin' swimmin' aroun' down there with us...eyes like headlamps on a carriage..."

Chapter 12

...CHINESE MONKEY ON A BICYCLE... Anna awoke. She hadn't slept long, half an hour maybe, but outside, the sky was black as night. Lightning flashed as she surveyed the room. Someone had taken a candle down from the chandelier. It's flame danced in the storm driven draft. Donny and the seven girls sat around the candle on the floor.

For a wonder, Donny was not talking. Lizzy was telling him about the needle machines, her dark eyes wide and sparkling in the candlelight. Wind whistled around the frames of the windows and fat rain tapped randomly at the panes. Thunder, still muted by several seconds distance, rumbled through the hall, seeming to seep up through the floor.

"Hey, look," Lilly said, "Anna's up."

"What time do you think it is?" Anna said, to no one in particular.

Jane laughed out loud.

"The bell hasn't rung since you blew the place up, Anna," Lizzy said. "Could be 'bout any time." It seemed to Anna that Lizzy had picked up a bit of Alabama drawl.

"Early afternoon, I'd reckon," Donny said. "Kinda hard to tell time with no sun, though."

"Is it almost time to go, Anna?" Lilly asked, turning her six-year-old doe eyes up at Anna. Her innocent trust hurt Anna's heart.

Lightning flashed again. Hard, sporadic rain rattled out drumrolls on the windows. Anna counted forty-five seconds between the flash and the *boom*. The thunder rolled out across the hall, taking its time.

"Not yet, Lilly. We have to wait until the storm gets here. You should rest, nap if you can. It could be a few hours yet," Anna said, then looked to the rest of the girls. "All of you need to rest up. Once we leave here, you may not get a good rest for a few days."

"Anna!" Lizzy said. "We've been trapped in here for five days. All we've done is rest, and sleep, and fret. We're ready to go. Now."

"Yeah," Jane said. "Let's get, before the storm really hits. Dolores says McCain and her crew are battened down under the tower..."

"No," Anna said. "You wanted Dolores's help? Well this is it. She told us to stay put until the storm really got going, so that's what we're going to do. McCain could have guards at the exits, I don't know."

"And the Joseph-thing is out there," Donny added.

Lizzy, Mary One and Lilly gasped at the mention of the Joseph-thing. Jane's attempt to look unaffected failed. Anna guessed Donny had remembered a few stories to tell after all. She felt a shiver run up her own spine at the thought of bumping into the Joseph-Thing in the woods after dark.

"Right, Joseph," Anna said. "Jane, you do not want to meet Joseph out there, not on a night like this. When the storm is at its peak, Dolores will be with Joseph. All the witch-hunters will be hiding in the rotunda. They'll be too busy to worry about us. Until then, we wait."

Jane muttered an inarticulate grumble. The only word Anna made out was "Pinky." Joan put a hand on her arm and whispered, but Jane shoved her away. She walked to the bare cot and sat, facing away from the others. Joan turned to Anna, shrugged, and mouthed "Sorry."

***

Anna joined the others in the circle. The candle flame quivered, trailing thin, oily smoke. Restless air sucked and tugged at their windows, sometimes whistling, sometimes rattling. Rain pattered in inconsistent spats. Something outside howled.

"What's the biggest storm y'all have had here?" Donny asked.

"We get wind storms often," Anna said.

"But not a lot of lightning," Lizzy said. "It's really, really dark out there." She paused, tugging on her bangs. "We got snow once."

"Never had a cyclone?" Donny asked.

"What's a cy-clone?" Lizzy asked, wide-eyed.

"That's God's eraser!" Maybelle said. "Cyclone'll wash a whole city right off the earth."

"I believe you mean 'hurricane'," Jane said, from her cot. "I've read about hurricanes, big storms they have over on the east coast. You don't need to fret about hurricanes – or cyclones. We don't have either here."

"We'll see about that," Donny said.

"We saw a cyclone once," Maybelle said. "We was in Texas! But not on the beach, and that's good 'cause all the water came up out of the ocean and it washed away a whole city. And all the people, too. And the dogs and horses and boats. And some cows. The sea just took 'em..."

A *thump* interrupted her. Something large and dark hit one of the windows, hard enough to crack it. The girls jumped. Shrill wind strained through the crack with a reedy whine.

"What was that?" someone asked.

Again, a howl rose from the grounds outside. Followed by another.

"It's the wolves," Donny said. "Joseph's wolves."

"Do you think they've come for you, Donny?" Lizzy whispered.

"Oh, for Pete's sake, Lizzy!" Jane said.

"How could a wolf hit the window?" Anna asked.

A high-pitched yipping accompanied the howls. The keening hiss around the window rose and fell with the swelling gusts. As the orphans looked to the windows, lightening blazed, stamping the storm-rent sky, and all it contained, into their retinas. It took a couple of seconds for the image to register in the children's minds. When it did, several girls spoke at once, but a simultaneous detonation of thunder drowned out their voices.

Birds, Joseph's birds.

"That one was close," Donny yelled.

221

"What?" Anna said.

"That lightning strike..."

"Did you see the birds?" Anna asked. Another large bird struck a window.

"'Course I saw 'em," Donny said. "Think we ought to let 'em in?"

"Are you insane?" Jane shrieked. "Why would..."

Another volley of thunder devoured her words. In its power, the windowpanes rattled.

"They're here to help Joseph," Anna said.

"They'll be gettin' in whether we let 'em or not!" Donny yelled, as a third bird crashed into a narrow glass pane.

"But Joseph is a monster," yelled Jane.

"Yeah, a monster who hates Abbess McCain," Anna said. "The more help he gets, the less we need to worry about her."

Thunder rumbled in a constant drone, much of it came from distant arms of the storm, but closer blasts cracked with mounting frequency. The windows flickered as lightning dropped near and far. Another noise arose out of the storm, a tone, or a note, low but melodic, almost like singing. Anna couldn't identify the sound, but it was familiar, something she knew on a subconscious level.

"Any way to reach those windows?" Donny asked.

"Yeah," Anna said, "just have to stack the cots. Do you hear that hum?"

"What hum...oh, yeah, what is it?"

"Don't know," Anna said. "Lizzy, show Donny how to stack the cots, like when I tried to go out the window."

Lizzy nodded, not bothering to try to talk over the storm's clamor. She jumped to the task, pointing and motioning instructions to Donny. They placed one cot directly under a window, then stood the other cot vertically on top of the first.

"Jane," Anna said, tossing her the key. "Get the door open."

Jane caught the key, and scowled at Anna. "Can we go now?" she yelled.

"Soon," Anna yelled back. "Just get that door open so the birds can get to McCain."

"You are crazy, Anna!" Jane yelled, but she ran across the hall to the door.

Donny climbed onto the lower cot. "Hold it steady," he said to Lizzy and Anna.

"I'll hold you," Lizzy said.

He climbed the slats of the upright cot as if it were a ladder. Rain battered the windows relentlessly, now accompanied by chunks of ice. The hail rapped against the panes like Gatling gun chatter. Banshee wind wailed through the cracked pane and around the frames of the other windows. The stones of Saint Frances vibrated with the past and present peals of thunder, and always below and among everything, that constant familiar hum.

Donny reached the window and peered over its sill. He whistled through his teeth. "Ho-ly Geez! Anna, get up here, you gotta see this."

Anna grabbed Mary One and told her to steady the cot. Then she climbed up beside Donny. The cot's iron slats creaked as she climbed, and it tottered, but didn't topple. When she reached the sill and looked out, Anna gasped.

A maelstrom of seagulls and hawks and crows churned above and around the window. Beyond them, the constant lightning illuminated the grounds of Saint Frances de Chantal in fluctuating blue and purple brilliance. Black figures, statuesque in their stillness, surrounded the orphanage. Wolves, coyotes, a large bear, and myriads of raccoons stood as expectant sentinels. Their shadows danced around them on the lawn as liquid fire dropped close and far and close again.

"You wanna let them in, too?" Donny asked.

"No."

As they watched, lightning lanced a tree at the edge of the wood line, blasting it to kindling and splinters. Its thunder drove a shockwave across the grounds and through the stone walls. Anna felt it in her chest and in her palms where they contacted the wall. The iron cot buzzed like a snare drum. The lightening branched out four more bolts, striking again and again and again while thunder continued to pound.

As the detonations settled back into the baseline rumble, Anna heard the voices below, "Hurry back down!" "What do you see?" "Can we go now?"

"Let's get this open and get out of here," Anna said.

"Will the wolves let us pass?" Donny asked, "When we run for the woods?"

"I don't know...I don't think they have any interest in us."

"I sure hope not." Donny pried at the latch and for a moment, it held fast. A fourth bird slammed into the window just to Donny's right. He startled, jerking the latch, and it popped open. A hail-laden gust flung the window inward. It struck Donny across the forehead, knocking him off the cot, then slammed into the stone wall. Its glass shattered and cascaded down mixed with rain and hailstones. Donny dropped onto the springy slats of the lower cot.

The upper cot, unbalanced by Donny's fall, toppled sideways, dumping Anna into a thin bed of straw. The static air inside suddenly equalized with the torrent outside. Anna's ears popped and her lungs seized up as if invisible spirits had sucked all the breath out of her.

Wind screamed through the empty window frame, extinguishing the candles and whipping the loose straw into flurries and dervishes. Blue and silver and electric-purple shafts of light strobed through the bank of windows, replacing the candle's warm glow. Through this frenetic light, borne on the wind, hundreds of birds poured into the room.

Anna sat up, looking for the door. Flurries of loose straw flew away from her as Jane dragged the big door inward. The gale sucked the circling birds and swirling straw devils out into the corridor. Through the empty window, wind roared like a waterfall, competing for volume with the thunder. The stones and floorboards shuddered under the weight of the storm.

Anna tried to call for Donny, but the storm ate her words. She scanned the room, finally finding him in a cluster of girls. Mary One and Lilly sat on either side, appearing to prop him up. Maybelle held his right hand and Lizzy knelt by his left side, dabbing blood off his forehead. A new knot rose above his right eye, to match the purple goose egg growing above his left.

Looks like he's growing a pair of horns, Anna thought.

Horns will suit him nicely, the other Anna responded.

Donny saw her looking at him, must have guessed she was worried, and flashed her a broad grin and an "A-Okay" hand sign. She rolled her eyes and rose unsteadily to her feet. Eyeball sized hailstones shot through the window, clanging off the iron cot and scattering across the floor.

Anna heard screaming above the cacophony. She whirled this way and that, scanning the room. The girls around Donny had helped him to his feet. They were up and moving toward the door.

Who is screaming, is someone screaming for me?

She looked to the wall where Noel and Mary Two lay. The scrap of blanket that had served as their shroud was gone, taken by the wind. Little drifts of straw collected around them before swirling up in whirlwinds and blowing away. The jittery, stark light revealed their sunken eyes, their purple lips and the first hints of corruption marring their pale cheeks.

"Were you screaming for me?" she asked.

Mary Two turned her head toward Anna. Her eyelids opened, showing pits full of nothing but lightning and chaos. Her lips parted. She did not scream, but spoke a single word, clear over the tumult. "Run."

Anna staggered away from the wall and looked to the door. Jane, Joan and Donny strained against the wind, trying to hold the door open. She took two steps forward. A window at the far end of the hall exploded inward in a shower of glass, hail and rain. Anna's ears popped again and her equilibrium wobbled. She sprinted toward Donny.

By the time she reached him, four more windows had blown out. Lizzy and Donny grabbed her and dragged her through the door while Jane held it. A softball-sized chunk of ice skittered through the door with her.

Anna stole a last glance back at Noel and Mary Two, just as the wind ripped the door from Jane's fingers. The two dead waifs lay at perfect peace under the blaze and rumble of chaotic destruction. In that moment, Anna envied them.

Chapter 13

NO EXTERIOR WINDOWS OPENED FROM the corridor. The storm continued to rage – wind whistled through the keyholes and hissed under the doors, hail hammered the roof, thunder continued its assault – but it was quieter here. And darker. Up and down the corridor, from under the doors, dim fans of filtered lightning washed across the floor, but these illuminated little.

"You okay, Anna?" Donny asked, taking hold of her by her shoulders.

"I think so, got a little dizzy there," she said. "I think I might be seeing things."

"How's your head?" Lizzy asked. "You took a pretty good knock when you fell off the cot."

Anna put her hand to the back of her skull. She had been unaware of the pain there until Lizzy mentioned it. Her hand came back bloody. "Let's just get out of here. I can't do this much longer." She looked to Jane. "Where did the birds go?"

"They went straight for Abbess McCain." Jane pointed down the long corridor toward the rotunda. "Can we please go now, Anna?"

"Is everyone here?" Anna asked.

"We got everybody," Lizzy said. "I counted heads while you were lollygagging."

"Donny, we're going to need light in the basement," Anna said. "Do you still have your lamp? Can you get it working?"

"I think so," Donny said. "Anna, it's quieter out here. I hear that hum you was askin' about. What is that?"

Anna listened. "I know that sound, that voice...What is it?" Above and around and throughout the storm's drumfire, a clear, constant note rang.

"It's the bell," said Mary One. "Just ringing one long hour. It just keeps going and going."

"Yes, that's it," Anna said. "The bell, sounding out no time and every time...Maybe the end of time."

"No, Anna," Donny said. He grabbed her by the shoulders and gave her a gentle shake. "It's 'cause of the thunder and the hail, makin' it ring like that. It don't mean nothin' – 'cept that this storm's a doozy. C'mon, Pinky, get yourself together an' let's get moving. Okay? Everybody's counting on you."

Anna surveyed the half ring of girls standing around her, their eyes begging her for salvation. She thought of Noel and Mary Two sleeping so peacefully, no matter what McCain or Joseph or the storm threatened. She listened to the clear, ancient voice of the bell resonating through the stones and bones of The Saint Frances de Chantal Orphan Asylum.

She leaned into Donny until he had to wrap an arm around her shoulders to hold her up. "It means something," she said to him, then raised her voice so all the girls could hear. "It means everything. The bell tells us when to sleep, it tells us when to eat, when to pray, when to work, when to rest. What do you think it's telling us now? How does it sound to you? Tired? Dead? Terrified?"

The girls stared at Anna, wide-eyed. In the dim, uncertain light, Anna couldn't know for sure what those expressions held, but she could guess.

Donny whispered "Anna?" into her ear, his voice thick with worry.

"This is its last song. You will never hear it again after today." Anna leaned heavier on Donny. Her words seemed spoken through her rather than by her, perhaps the other Anna had taken over. "That's what it's telling us. It's saying 'good-bye,' because in a very little while, that bell will cease to be, along with everything here.

"We will be leaving, running outside through this storm. We must make it to the shelter of the forest. We must all stay together. Once we get outside, you will be terrified. Outside, the lightning is brighter. The thunder is louder. You will see shapes moving around you, they may look like animals or monsters, but it's just the storm. If the hail hits you, it will hurt. The wind and rain will thrash you. But no matter what happens, we must stay together. We must reach the forest. Together.

"Do not turn back to this place. There is no shelter here. There is only death here. That is what the bell is telling you."

The girls nodded their solemnest nods.

"Get your lantern going, Donny. Let's do this."

Anna took a deep breath and stood on her own again. She heard the pop and flash of the striker on Donny's lantern. A pale yellow glow softened the glare and shadow of storm light. The little party crowded around the lantern — as if they had been moths rather than orphan girls — and together crept down the corridor toward their escape.

Two doors down, Hattie's blood spread out before them, a red-carpet-welcome to the basement door.

Chapter 14

"THIS AIN'T GONNA WORK," DONNY said.

Anna stood on the step beside him, watching the swirling mass of black water at their feet. Six steps above them, the girls huddled on the landing, inside the basement door. The twist of the spiral staircase put them just out of sight and earshot.

"Can your girls swim?" Donny asked.

"I don't know," Anna said. "I don't think *I* can swim through that."

The water eddied and spun, thick with the smell of sea and decay. Rats floated among the crates and bundles that bobbed into view, then disappeared again into the dark basement. Anna calculated the depth by gauging the gap between the ceiling and the water's surface.

"Maybe we can wade through it...if we hold tight to the little ones," she said.

"It's rising too fast. If it ain't over your head already, it will be by the time you convince all them girls to jump in."

A rat fighting against the current hooked his claw on the step just below them. After a brief struggle, it dragged itself onto the stair and began to scamper up. Anna stomped on its head.

"Anna!" Donny said.

"It would have scared the girls," she replied, without looking up. The rat's hind leg jittered. Its tail coiled and uncoiled stupidly. Anna kicked it back into the flooding basement. "I'm taking them out of here, Donny. Every last one of them."

"I know, Anna. I know you will, but this ain't the way. We gotta find another exit. How'd you get out the first time?"

Rising water lapped over the edge of their stair step, rinsing a smear of rat blood off Anna's shoe.

"The kitchen," she said. "But we'll have to go straight through Abbess McCain to get there."

Below them, the rat's crushed body pirouetted in a slow eddy before drifting into dark oblivion under Saint Frances de Chantal. Donny watched it disappear, then looked up at Anna. "Makes me real glad I'm not Abbess McCain."

Chapter 15

"BASEMENT'S FLOODED. WE HAVE TO go out the kitchen," Anna told the girls at the top of the stairs. She waited for objections. No one spoke, so she continued. "You all know how to get there, but Abbess McCain is camped out in the Great Round Room. We'll have to get up on the balcony, creep around the back of the rotunda and drop down into the factory wing without being seen or heard. From there, it should be easy."

"I thought you blew up the factory," Mary One said.

"We're not going into the factory, just over to that wing," Anna said. "The kitchen is a wreck, but it's still there."

"And you think you can sneak all nine of us right under McCain's nose without any of her mercenaries seeing us?" Jane asked.

"You got a better plan?" Donny said, stepping toward her.

Anna put a hand on his arm and said, "I don't know, Jane. It's a lousy idea, but it's the only one we've got – other than stay here and die."

"All their offices are up there, on the balcony level, McCain's, Eustace's, Martha's..." Jane said.

"Martha is dead," Anna said. "Dolores said they'll be below, trying to keep Joseph out until reinforcements arrive. If they are up there, well, we might have to fight. But, Dolores will likely be giving them a fair piece of trouble herself, just for the devilry of it. McCain will have a lot on her mind this evening, and the storm will cover any noise we make."

"We're going to *fight?*" Jane rolled her eyes and flopped her arms in the air. "Fight, Anna? Have you seen yourself? You can't hardly keep your feet under you. And your boy, here, appears he couldn't stand up to a nasty look."

"I've stood up to plenty of nasty looks from you already," Donny said.

"Nasty looks are the only kind of looks Jane's got," said Lizzy.

Donny snickered. Jane balled both fists. Anna stepped between them. She kept her eyes on Jane but said, "Careful, Lizzy, Jane's got a right hook like a mule kick." To Jane she said, "I have never, in my life, ever heard you scared of a fight, Jane."

"*Anna!*" Jane nearly cried, "They have *guns*! And axes! There's one guy I saw out there – he's an ogre, I tell you, at least seven feet tall. One of his legs is as big around as my whole body, and I only come up to his belt buckle. He's got a *sword*, Anna, a sword taller than this door. How are we supposed to fight against that?"

"I've got a gun," Donny said flatly. "There's an ax up in the hall, if you want it." He paused, then added, "Swords are over rated."

"Jane," Anna reached out and took both her hands, "Dolores said..."

"I know what Dolores said. I was there, remember?"

"We can't..." Anna tried.

"We can't stay here," Jane said. "We can't go through the basement because of the water. I get it, Anna, I do. We have to go through the kitchen, and to do that we have to get past McCain. I understand.

"This is what *you* need to understand," Jane continued. "Dolores is insane. She's unreliable at best. McCain is also insane, and so are all her henchfolk. If we go for the kitchen and McCain finds us, she will kill us. We are *not* strong enough to fight her." She glared at Donny. "Even if we do have *one* gun and *one* ax."

Jane's words settled into the muffled background rumble of the storm, and sank into the hearts of the little party of orphans. Dark water churned, only four steps below them now. Darker thoughts swirled in

Anna's mind, circling this central vortex — *They can only kill you once. After that, they can never hurt you again.*

Anna squeezed Jane's hands. "Last time, you were going to freeze to death if I didn't save you. This time, it's ogres with claymores. I'm taking us out of here, Jane. After tonight, one way or the other, we will be free of this place, forever."

Jane stepped back from Anna as understanding dawned in the older girl's eyes, but did not release her hands.

"Will you come with me?" Anna asked.

Jane sighed, looked at the other girls, then answered, "Yes, Pinky, I'm coming with you."

Chapter 16

DONNY DREW THE FLINTLOCK AS they re-entered the corridor. He extinguished his lantern and handed it to Lizzy. Storm light and memory were sufficient for Anna to guide her party toward the center of Saint Frances de Chantal.

She picked up the ax as they passed it. Hattie's blood, sticky and dark, covered its head and most of its handle. The girls huddled close behind her. Jane guarded the rear of their pack, wielding a long sickle of window glass with a scrap of blanket serving as its handle.

Stealth seemed irrelevant. The storm's violent bombardment raged against the roof. The stone walls shuddered, as if the island itself were being shaken by the storm. The constant rumble of thunder and the bell's eerie wail covered any sound the orphans may have made. But Anna could not make herself hurry along the hall. The storm's erratic, wavering light sent shadows jumping and dancing on all sides. In Anna's eyes, every one of these shadows was McCain, or Joseph, or Hattie – her face split in half, coming to reclaim her ax.

Something jumped at Anna from her left. She swung, eliciting shrieks from several girls. The ax sliced straight through the menacing shadow, glanced off the wall in a flash of orange sparks, and splintered into a wooden bench. The blow sent a shock of pain through Anna's wrists and elbows, nearly jarring the ax from her hands.

Donny said something that the pounding storm obscured. His tone was cautious, patronizing. Anna gave him a miserable, irritated glare and yanked the ax free from the bench. After that, the girls spread out, at least far enough that Anna wouldn't decapitate one of them in the event of another false alarm.

The shadows continued to leap, but Anna did not swing again. Not until a real pair of claws sprung at her out of the darkness.

The thing screamed as it attacked, dropping from the ceiling in a flurry of beak and talons and feathers. The girls screamed with it. Anna fell to the floor, flailing her ax. The bird, Anna realized it was a seagull, flapped and squawked in circles around the children, bumped the ceiling, collided with the wall, then settled awkwardly on a wall sconce.

Anna lay on the floor, panting. Agitated birds murmured and cooed above the din of the storm. The air smelled of sulfur smoke, and blood. The corridor was darker here. They had passed the final set of doors. All the light came from behind them, ahead lay only darkness...and apparently, several birds.

"Donny," Anna said, not bothering to whisper, "Light your lantern. This is the end of the hall. There's no one here."

Anna stood in the darkness. She planted her feet, tightening her fingers around the ax, preparing for whatever Donny's lamp may reveal. Her hands ached from death-gripping the handle, but when the darkness melted, she would be ready.

The darkness held. She heard talking behind her, loud whispering. A second later, she understood the reason for the delay. Donny was teaching Lizzy how to work the lamp.

"Donny!" she said, turning on them.

The lamp flashed to life, blazing a hole in Anna's vision, just to the left of center.

"Oops, sorry Anna," Lizzy said, redirecting the light away from Anna's face. Then she gasped, "Holy moly!"

Anna turned. Birds, thirty to forty of them, roosted everywhere, seagulls, crows, cormorants, a bald eagle, a couple of owls. They sat on the chandelier, on wall sconces, on benches, on railings. They waddled and stalked, patrolling back and forth across the hall, murmuring and bickering and squawking.

Several more lay dead, scattered around the floor. As the lantern's glow stabilized and Anna's vision cleared, she also saw blood – more blood than the dead birds provided – splattered on the floor, sprayed on the walls.

"What is this, Anna?" Donny asked.

"This is the end of the hall," she replied. "Those stairs," she pointed to four wide steps descending to a pair of oak doors, "lead to the Great Round Room, the rotunda at the center of Saint Frances. That's where McCain and all her goons are holed up. These birds were looking for McCain. I guess this is as close as they got."

"I smell gun powder," Donny said. "I think somebody was shootin' these birds." He kicked at a limp seagull on the floor. Its beak opened slowly, bubbling blood out its nose holes. "Not too long ago, either."

"Lizzy," Anna said, "Bring the light over here, shine it down the stairs. I think someone's down there."

Lizzy's approach agitated the birds. Their murmurs took on a tone of warning. The eagle spread his wings and cawed a low, ratcheting caw. Lizzy slowed. This hall, which had always seemed enormous, now felt crowded and tense.

"Jane, keep the girls back," Anna said. "Donny, come with me."

She and Donny moved to Lizzy's side. The three of them crept toward the stairwell. As the lamp penetrated deeper into that recess, they saw a figure slumped against the double doors at the bottom of the stairs. In the gloom, they were unable to discern any details of the figure except that it moved wrong – twitchy, slight movements, inhuman gestures.

Donny took two careful steps to the right. He held his flintlock in both hands, thumbing back the hammer. Anna stepped away from Lizzy, two steps to the left, and raised her ax. The three inched forward, the lamp revealing more details with each step.

Light gleamed off the toes of black patent leather shoes. It glinted, in two parallel lines, along the twin barrels of a blood-streaked shotgun. It glowed in the brass of several spent shotgun shells. It scintillated among the black feathers of crows that swarmed over the body, like ants on a bit of fallen food.

The rest of the figure sparkled red in the dark basin of the stairwell. The oak doors behind it were splatter-painted crimson. Blood and bird droppings marred the body. Its head hung down, chin to chest. So much of its face had been pecked off that Anna could not tell if it had been a sister or one of the off-island recruits. A large crow perched half on the shoulder, half on the chest, craning his beak around and up, prospecting in the figure's empty eye socket.

"It's dead," Donny whispered.

As soon as Donny spoke, the large crow flicked his head around, gore flying from his beak, and stared at Donny. The black feathers along its neck and head ruffled. Then it shrieked a long angry squawk, *caa- aaa- aaa- ca- ca- ca - ca- ca- aaaeeee.* The other crows stopped pecking and cocked their heads toward Donny. They, too, began to croon low, hateful caws.

"Careful, Donny!" Lizzy whined, retreating in comically stealthy steps.

Donny froze. The birds around and behind them stirred, their chatter turning ominous. He glanced over at Lizzy, then followed her lead. Anna, also, backpedalled as smoothly and inoffensively as she could.

"Anna!" Jane said in a half shout, half whisper.

"Shh!" Anna hissed back at her. "Dim the light, Lizzy."

Donny and Anna returned to either side of Lizzy and together the three of them retreated to Jane and the girls. The birds continued to fuss and squabble, but Anna saw the big crow turn its attention back to mining the dead witch-hunter's eye socket.

"Did you see that?" Lizzy gasped as they rejoined Jane's group. "They're eating that person, the birds are! Do you think they killed him?"

"Hush, Lizzy!" Anna said. "Everybody, quiet."

"What's going on up there, Anna?" Jane whispered.

"We can't get through this way. McCain must have posted a guard at the door," Anna said. "It looks like Joseph's birds killed the guard..."

"It's horrible," Lizzy whispered, wide-eyed. "You should see it! The birds ate his..."

Anna clapped a hand over her mouth. "I don't think the birds will let us near the stairs."

"If it wasn't for those birds," Jane said, "the guards would have got us."

Anna nodded.

"And McCain is just beyond those doors?" Jane asked.

Anna nodded again.

"What did you think was going to happen if we did get through those doors?" Jane demanded.

"I had hoped that Joseph would be in there by now. We could have crept up the grand staircase to the balcony without being seen," she sighed. "But, I think if he were in there, we would know."

"Could be just 'bout anything goin' on in there," Donny said. "Can't hear nothing over this storm. What now, Anna?"

"There is another way." She pointed up. "The window." High above, near the peak of the cathedral ceiling, the stained glass eye stared down at them. "It opens into McCain's office. From there, we get out onto the balcony. We'll be able to see what's going on, and we'll be able to get to the kitchen from there."

"That window is twenty feet up," Jane said.

"We climb up the tapestry," Anna said with a wicked grin. "It's easy. I've done it lots of times."

Lizzy giggled.

Jane said, "Anna!"

"Where do you think the books came from?" Anna said. "It's easy, really. There's actually a ladder cut into the stones behind the tapestry. Rebecca showed me years ago. We might have to help Lilly and Maybelle, but the rest of you should be fine."

Jane opened her mouth to object, closed it, shook her head, then looked back the way they had come. After a second, she turned back to Anna. "How do you know she's not up there watching us right now?"

"If she knew I was here, she'd come out and get me, birds or no birds. Besides, see how the lamp-glow backlights the window? If anyone *was* up there, we'd see her shadow." Anna flashed her tired, cunning grin again. "That's how I always knew whether she was watching us or not."

Jane snorted a humorless laugh. "Okay, Anna, okay. You want to go first?"

Chapter 17

ANNA SHED HER HEAVY LAMBSKIN coat and scrambled up the wall. It was almost as easy as she had promised it would be. The circular stained glass window rattled in its frame, buzzing with the storm's fury. Anna pushed on its lower rim. The bottom of the window swung inward, pivoting on two pins. She peered over the sill into McCain's office.

No one waited inside. A kerosene lamp burned low on McCain's expansive desk. Its flame stuttered and wavered. Heavy soot coated the hurricane glass chimney. Oily smoke wafted out the top, only to be dispersed by the restless air. Papers fluttered.

Behind the desk, French doors opened onto an exterior patio. Wooden double doors at the other end of the office lead onto the balcony above the rotunda. Both sets of doors were closed, but the wind slammed them back and forth in their frames.

Anna slipped under the window. Once in the office, she propped it open, then called down to Donny. "All clear. Bring them up."

Donny climbed the stone ladder with Maybelle hanging off his back. Anna worried when she saw what they were up to, but by the third rung, it was clear they had performed similar stunts before. When they reached the window, Anna pulled Maybelle through.

"Goin' back for the other one, "Donny said, "Lilly." He scampered back down.

Mary, Lizzy, Joan, Norma and Jane made their way up and in while Donny showed Lilly how to piggyback. Once Jane was through the window, they started up. Lilly wrapped her arms around his neck so tight that if she had been any stronger she would have strangled him. By the time he managed to get her safely into the office, his face was purple.

The children looked around the office. Anna had been here before – on several occasions – but most of the others had not. Before recent events, McCain's office had held an aura of terror and mystery. This late afternoon, in the grip of the storm's fury, the room was as dark and oppressive as an ogre's grotto. The weight of the storm pressed down on them as if they were miles below the sea rather than thirty feet above it.

In the corridor, there had been no exterior walls, no windows. Layers of stone had muted the thunder. Now, all that separated the children from nature's rage was a set of glass doors, and the boards McCain had nailed across them. Hail rattled off these boards, occasionally slipping between the cracks to strike glass. Wind shook the doors, demanding entrance. Anna's ears pressurized, then popped, then pressurized again.

"This isn't good," Donny yelled. Anna barely heard him above the thunder and howling wind. "Anna, come look at this!"

Donny stood at the glass doors. McCain's view overlooked the ocean, but it should also have shown a broad stretch of lawn and several acres of beach. What Anna saw when she peered out beside Donny was only ocean, bathed in blue-purple storm light. It moved like a living thing, writhing and undulating. Breakers mounted and raced toward Saint Frances, white foam riding their peaks until the impatient wind whipped it away. The beach was gone. The waves exploded in spray across what had once been the lawn.

"Has it come all the way up to the foundation?" Anna asked.

"What?" Donny shouted.

Anna repeated herself.

"I can't tell, can't see that far down," Donny shouted, "but I think it's gonna if it hasn't yet."

"We need to be to the woods before that happens," Anna yelled.

Donny nodded. "I guess Dolores wasn't kidding about gettin' Joseph riled up."

Anna turned back to her girls. Maybelle, Lilly and Norma held hands over their ears and sheer misery in their eyes. Lizzy, Jane, Joan and Mary didn't look much better. Anna's gut hurt. *It's just a little longer, girls, just a few more minutes and we're free.*

One way or the other? Her other voice asked.

One way or the other, she confirmed.

Anna grabbed Donny around the neck and pulled him close enough to talk into his ear. "I'm going to open that door just a crack, so I can see into the rotunda, see if the balcony is clear. I want you beside me. If there is a guard out there, shoot him. The storm will cover the shot...I think."

Donny nodded and turned her head so he could speak into her ear. "Give Jane your ax, she can stand on your other side...in case there's two guards."

Anna nodded. She gestured to Jane, handed her the ax, and pulled her toward the door. Halfway there, Mary One ran up, grabbed her wrist and said something that was lost in the din. She repeated it twice while pointing. Anna still did not hear what she said, but followed Mary's finger to McCain's desk.

Papers ruffled and flipped in the drafts. Several candles, melted into abstract paraffin gargoyles, stood amid the papers, their wicks extinguished. The kerosene lamp struggled to remain aglow. Anna thought Mary One wanted her to douse that flame, to prevent it from being seen when she opened the door. *Good thinking.*

As she reached across the desk, a gust rearranged the papers, unveiling an odd brown lump. It looked like a gnarled root ball from a sapling. Then, she saw the nails, fingernails.

Anna's heart leapt into her throat. Joey's shriveled fingers, curled into a loose fist, looked so much like her own pinky had. The candles, five of them, surrounded the hand. Heavy threads strung between the candles formed a five-pointed star. Three blackened needles protruded from Joey's palm.

McCain has been tormenting him. She's been taunting him, calling him...I hope she's not disappointed.

Anna reached across the desk. *Don't touch it!* one of her voices gasped. Anna obeyed, grasping a needle, instead, and yanking it free. As she took hold of a second needle, the hand twitched. Anna flinched away, yanking the needle as she did so. She withdrew her hand rather than pulling needle number three.

Joey's fist tightened on the table, flecks of dried skin crackling. The index finger straightened until it pointed directly at Anna. Then, it began curling and straightening in a come-hither gesture. Anna stumbled away from the desk.

Donny grabbed her upper arm. She turned on him, eyes wide, questioning. His eyes were bigger than hers. He nodded. *Yeah, I saw it.* Then gestured to the door. In her ear he said, "I've had enough fun for one afternoon, Anna. We need to go."

Anna spun and headed for the door. Donny and Jane raced forward with her. Lizzy huddled with the rest of the girls behind McCain's desk. Anna knelt down in front of the doors. She turned the handle and eased one door inward, peeking through the narrow gap. Nothing waited for her but the railing. She opened the door wide enough to poke her head out and looked each way. The balcony curved away from her on either side. Still, she saw none of McCain's goons.

Anna crawled out onto the balcony. She stayed Donny with her hand, but he ignored her and followed. Here, the calamity of sound reached an ear hammering crescendo. The bell hung directly above them in its tower, singing and singing and singing its single ceaseless note. Gale force wind screamed through the open bell tower. Anna *felt* the thunder more than heard it.

From the room below came new noises, not borne of the storm. In the rotunda, someone bellowed directives. The words were indiscernible, but the cadence and tone were that of an officer giving orders. There was another noise as well, a terrible thudding sound, something heavy slamming itself against something solid.

Anna raised her head, just high enough to see over the railing. To her right, the balcony swept halfway around the inside of the rotunda before dropping into a curved staircase that terminated near the front entrance. Beyond the entrance, another swooping flight of stairs rose back up from the main floor to the balcony. To the left, the balcony circled all the way around the rotunda until it met with the second staircase. Several doors lined the outer wall, most were offices similar to McCain's. Directly across the rotunda stood the door to the dining hall and kitchen. Boards had been nailed across it.

Anna turned to Donny, intending to point out the barricaded door. To her horror, he was leaning over the railing, staring down into the room below. She snatched him by his shirt collar and yanked him down. *They'll see you, stupid!* But it was no use trying to yell over the bedlam.

When he looked up at her, his eyes were wide with worry, or fear, or something. Anna didn't care which, whatever was going on below didn't concern her now. *Just get to that door and we're home free.* She pointed across the opening to the boarded up door. Donny glanced that way, saw what she meant, and nodded. Uncertainty showed on his face. She pointed again, more emphatically this time.

Donny nodded again. He motioned her back to McCain's office and crawled that way. Anna watched him, wondering. Below, the crashing and shouting ebbed slightly, quieted just enough to admit another sound, chanting. Multiple voices recited verses, prayers or spells or something.

Anna rose up again, intending to look over the rail to the room below. Donny grabbed her from behind. She spun around, startled. Donny shook his head emphatically *No!* and pulled her toward McCain's office. She let him take her.

Chapter 18

"WHAT'S GOING ON DOWN THERE?" Anna yelled into Donny's ear once they were back inside McCain's office.

"You don't want to know," he yelled back. "Just keep your mind on your business. Right now your business is getting Maybelle and your girls to the woods."

"I know what my business is, Donny, I don't need you to tell me."

Donny gave her a grim grin. "I think Joseph is about to bust through those doors down there."

"Yeah, I figured that. What else?" she asked, studying him.

"Nothin' else," he shrugged, then changed the subject. "Ya' think we can pry those boards off the door with Jane's ax?"

Anna nodded. She motioned for Jane to bring the other girls to them. When the group had huddled around Anna and Donny, Anna spoke. "We can see the service door from here. It's on the opposite side of the Great Round Room. If we stay on hands and knees around the balcony, we can make it there without being seen. Just follow us, stay low. Stick to the wall, do not go anywhere near the railing. Got it?"

The girls nodded, faces pale, eyes empty.

"It's too loud out there to talk, so don't try. The door is nailed shut, it'll take a few minutes to pry the boards off. Just sit against the wall until it's open. After that, we're free and clear. There shouldn't be any guards beyond a boarded up door. We'll just run through the kitchen, out the door onto the patio and down the stairs to the dock. Once we get there, it's a quick walk across the lawn and into the woods. You all are doing so good. Just keep it up a few more minutes and this will all be over. Can you do that?"

Again, the girls nodded. Anna recognized their blank expressions and their unquestioning acceptance of ridiculous commands. Abbess McCain's zombies had become Anna's zombies. A troop of broken orphans, shell shocked into doing the next thing that must be done. The only difference was that this time, the next thing that must be done involved sneaking through a storm while being chased by ax wielding nuns and a Joseph-Thing. These girls had faced the stampers and needle machines on a daily basis, this wasn't much worse.

She raised her eyebrows at Donny, then glanced from him to Lizzy to Jane. Donny put a hand on her shoulder and squeezed. Jane smiled weakly and gave her a light punch on the other shoulder. "We got it, Pinky."

Lizzy squeezed Donny's shoulder – at which Jane rolled her eyes. Anna put her arms around the three of them and pulled them into a huddle hug. Joan, Norma, Mary, and Maybelle joined the huddle. Lilly somehow squirmed her way into the middle. They hugged that way for only a moment, then Donny cleared his throat and pulled away toward the door.

One by one, Anna's orphans crept onto the balcony. The ceiling over them bowled upward. A circle, ten feet across, opened at the middle of the dome. The bell hung in its tower, another thirty feet above this oculus. Rain and a few chunks of hail poured through the open bell tower, dropping into the center of the room below. Mist and fine drizzle, floating on restless air, dampened everything.

They circumnavigated the rotunda without incident. Jane, who still held the ax, made short work of the boards. The nails screeched as she yanked them, but it was barely audible over the cacophony. Below, Joseph continued to hammer the doors, someone barked orders at short intervals, and the chanting prattled on.

Anna herded her girls through the door, still on all fours. If someone below looked up and saw the open door, the jig would be up. Anna held her breath and urged her little band to hurry. Jane, with her ax, went first. Donny brought up the rear, his flintlock in one hand and Maybelle's hand in the other.

Once everyone was through, Anna glanced back to ensure they were not followed. No one approached from either direction. She took a deep breath and crawled away from the wall to the railing, again checking both sides before peering over.

Donny grabbed her ankle. She knew it was him before turning back to see. He shook his head and tried to pull her away from the railing, his eyes frantic. She yanked her foot away, but his grip was solid. She tried again, nearly losing a shoe, but managed to slip out of his grasp. Before he could grab her again, she frog-hopped away from him and pulled herself up to the rail. Below, the Great Round Room looked like all the acts of a three-ring circus performing at once in a single ring. Sister Eustace played ringleader, directing the chaos through a cone shaped bullhorn.

Half a dozen men hammered beams and braces against the main entrance. One of them was the giant Jane had described. An enormous sword hung in a scabbard on his back. Three of Joseph's seagulls had apparently made it into the rotunda before McCain's goons sealed the rest out. The birds flapped above the men at the door, pecking and pooping and screeching at them. A little man with a big broom kept the seagulls at bay while the others worked against Joseph's relentless pounding.

Two priests screamed a Latin chant at the door, flailing their arms to emphasize important passages of their litany. A woman dressed like a gypsy, maybe Hattie's sister, swayed and clapped her hands in time with the priest's recitations, throwing her hands in the air and shouting "Hallelujah!" at the really good parts.

Rain and hail poured through the opening to the bell tower. It fell in a circular curtain, forming a hollow, pillar-shaped waterfall. The deluge cascaded around a pair of men. The two stood across from each other pumping up and down on a giant lever. It looked like a railway handcar, but the levered mechanism did not move. After a minute, Anna realized it was a bilge pump. The two worked feverishly against the torrent from above.

A pack of sad, saggy-faced hounds bayed and brayed. Some hunkered under the flights of stairs, others raced around and around the rotunda.

A team of women, some could have been nuns, others certainly never had been, formed what looked like a bucket brigade, only instead of passing buckets of water, they handed chairs and stools and other bits of furniture down the line. The last woman in this line, Sister Elizabeth, hucked the wooden brick-a-brack onto a growing heap, just outside the splash of the rainwater.

Another group of witch-hunters pitchforked straw onto the heap. At the center of the growing pile stood a twelve-foot tall crucifix. Anna thought she had seen it before, maybe among the debris that littered the beach on the night she escaped. One of the crucifix's arms had broken off, giving it the appearance of a signpost missing its sign.

Abbess McCain presided as the calm at the center of the storm. She sat in a high-backed oak chair, cool and serene in the midst of chaos. A contented smirk curled one side of her lip. Around her, soldiers and misfits and ex-nuns scampered and thrashed, holding their world together. Sister Eustace barked orders through the bullhorn, firing off directives as steadily as the late-afternoon sky fired lightning bolts.

Seeing McCain, Anna finally understood. She saw what Donny hadn't wanted her to see. The reason for McCain's peace of mind sat facing her in a second oak chair. Dolores. Coarse rope bound her wrists to the chair's arms. Another length at her waist bound her to the chair's back. A belt strapped Dolores's head to the chair. It had been run through her mouth and synched tight so that it doubled as a gag. A blindfold hid Dolores's eyes. Blood ran freely down her left leg.

Anna felt Donny slide up behind her. He clamped his hands on both of her shoulders and pulled her away from the rail. Her head spun as she fell against him. Both of her voices clamored circular arguments that neither of them believed. Donny dragged her through the door and eased it closed, though he could have slammed it and no one would have noticed.

Anna heard Donny say, "Here, you take her."

She felt someone else grab her arms.

Jane's voice said, "What's wrong with her?"

She felt herself being jostled through the dark kitchen.

"Nothin's wrong, just keep her movin. Which way's the door to the patio?"

"Follow the lightning..." Lizzy's voice.

"Donny," Anna said.

"Jus' keep walkin', Anna."

"Donny, wait..."

"No. Anna. Whatever it is you're thinkin, we ain't doin' it."

"They're going to burn her alive," Anna said, "We can't let them..."

"We can't stop 'em neither! We can sneak past that mob, but ain't no way we can jump right in the middle of 'em and snatch their witch away! Don't you know that's exactly what McCain's hopin' you'll do?"

"I won't leave her to burn. I can't."

"Anna, she came here to die. Said so herself!"

"No, Donny, she came here to *rescue* her *little brother*. She was willing to die to save him. That's not the same as getting burned alive for no good reason!"

"Are *you* willing to get burned alive for no good reason? 'Cause that's sure as hell what's gonna happen if you go back there!"

Anna dug her heels into the floor and grabbed the edge of a doorframe, bringing the party to a halt.

Donny grabbed her arm. "You made me a promise, Anna, an' I'm holdin' you to it."

"I helped you get Maybelle! Just follow Jane, you'll all be out of this place in three minutes. Besides, I'm the one that saved you, remember, not the other way around. I don't owe you anything, but I do owe Dolores."

Anna saw Donny blush bright red. He let go of her arm. "Anna, please, come with us to the woods. Let's take Maybelle to safety, and your girls. Once everybody's safe, you and I'll come back together. We're a team, Anna."

"There's no time, Donny. You saw how fast they're working. They want to make sure to get her burnt before Joseph breaks through..." Something flashed inside her head, crisp as a lightning bolt. "I got it! I know how to save her without getting caught! Listen, get those girls out of here. If there is a cross on the kitchen door, get rid of it. I will be right behind you!"

An explosion at the far end of the kitchen rocked the entire structure. Electricity arced along the ceiling and down one wall, setting one of the tattered tapestries ablaze. A slab of charred plaster dropped from the ceiling and shattered across the floor. Lilly screamed.

"I found it!" Lizzy yelled, "I found the door! Hurry up before we get blown to smithereens!"

"Anna..." Donny started.

Jane, who had been holding Anna's other arm, released her and stepped between them. To Donny she said, "Dolores saved us from starving to death." She turned to Anna, "Can you get her out without getting caught?"

Anna nodded.

Jane embraced her and pecked her on the cheek. "Then go do it." She shoved Anna toward the rotunda. Anna staggered backward, amazed. Jane yelled, "Go!" then grabbed Donny's arm and dragged him in the other direction. Donny struggled against her, but Jane stood at least a foot taller than he, and outweighed him by thirty pounds. Anna lifted a hand to him, then turned and fled back onto the balcony.

Chapter 19

JOSEPH'S HAND RESPONDED TO ANNA'S presence the minute she slipped into Abbess McCain's office. That terrified Anna, but also gave her hope. Dolores had said that every piece of him retained his will and his awareness. If he could see through the eyes of a bird that had pecked his flesh, or pecked the flesh of some other dead thing that had once eaten him, then Anna suspected she could communicate to him through his hand.

Another explosion shook the orphanage, an electric missile slammed through the office next to McCain's. The bolt struck an exterior patio just beyond the glass doors, blowing it clean off the old stones. Electric fingers danced across the interior walls, like cracks through shattering glass, humming and sputtering. Then, as quickly as they had appeared, they were gone, leaving behind an acrid, nostril-burning stench.

Anna screamed *eeeeeeee!* in her head and scooped Joseph's hand off the desk. It immediately grasped hers, firm but gentle. Anna didn't flinch. She grabbed the third needle and yanked it out of his palm.

"Joseph," she yelled at the mummified hand, "I can let you in. I'll show you how. But you have to promise not to hurt my friends. Tell your animals to let my friends get to the woods safely! Can you hear me? Do you understand?"

Joseph's fingers twitched, squeezing her hand twice. Did that mean he had heard? Or maybe electrical storms summoned by a witch made dead hands twitch. That explanation was just as reasonable as the other.

Anna tried to think, tried to calculate how much time had elapsed since she left Donny and the girls. She clearly remembered Jane dragging Donny away from her. He had tears in his eyes. She had waved at him and run for the balcony. Had she sprinted or crawled around the rotunda? She couldn't remember. Nor could she know whether Donny had resigned to leave her and escape with his sister or if he continued to struggle.

The tumult made it impossible to think. She did not want her girls meeting Joseph on the storm-thrashed beach, or in the crumbling kitchen. She wanted them all the way deep in the forest before Joseph was anywhere near this place. But, Anna had long ago given up on getting what she wanted. What she needed was Joseph inside the orphanage. And she needed it now.

"The kitchen!" she screamed at the hand. "My friends are clearing a path for you through the kitchen. Use the entrance above the dock, the one you led me out. Come now. Come take your hand. Leave my friends alone!"

The hand spasmed, dry skin crinkling and flaking. Anna placed it back on McCain's desk, but it would not release her hand. Anna yelled, "Let go!" and tried to shake it off, but the hand clung to her. *Fine! I'll be seeing you soon enough, I suspect.* She headed for the door with Joseph's hand clutching hers.

On the balcony again, Anna looked down at the circus. It had changed. Its tone no longer frantic preparation but foreboding anticipation, like the moment between the spark of the fuse and the roar of the cannon. Anna held her breath.

The pounding at the door had stopped. In its absence, despite the storm's rage, the room felt still. The men who had been barricading the door now stood back, weapons drawn. Joseph's seagulls perched on the balcony's railing near the top of the stairs. The broom man stared at the door, having forgotten them.

The chanting priests and their harpy had silenced. They huddled together, looking from Dolores to the door, then back to Dolores. All three held revolvers. The harpy couldn't seem to stop playing with hers, thumbing the hammer and spinning the cylinder.

Sister Eustace stood silent on her chair, her bullhorn at her side. The hounds were gone, perhaps they knew enough to hide. The pillar of rain still fell from the bell tower and the bell continued to sing. In the office next to McCain's, where the lightning had struck, fire crackled. A hole gaped where its glass doors had been. Wind howled through the office, stirring the rotunda's already restless air.

Hurry up, Joseph, Anna thought, looking across to the other door. She would need to move fast when he arrived. He would either charge down the staircase closest to that door – or just jump over the railing and attack from above. Anna would race down the other stairs at that moment and free Dolores.

How long could Joseph last against McCain's goons? Anna had counted about twenty of them. She guessed it depended on which body Joseph chose to wear. When she had blown out his eyes with the magic key, he had been angry, and hurt, but it hadn't stopped him from throwing a screaming fit. It really hadn't slowed him down much at all, come to think of it. If Joseph could keep McCain busy for just a couple minutes, Anna knew she could get Dolores free and back up the stairs.

What if she won't go with you? that other voice asked. *She's here to kill Joey, remember? She has to die to do that.*"

Then I'll let her kill him, if that's what she wants, but I won't let her burn. Even still, Anna wondered. Dolores had planned a one-on-one confrontation with Joseph. She had intended to trick Joseph into attacking her. Now, no trick was needed. McCain was here. His hand was here. Dolores's storm had to be wreaking havoc with Joseph's mind. Maybe, just maybe she could break Joseph's curse *and* get Dolores out alive.

Anna looked to Dolores. The woman sat motionless, but rigid. All her muscles strained against the ropes. The only movement Anna detected was Dolores's nostrils flaring. A black blindfold covered her eyes and the belt gag cut into the corners of her mouth, dripping blood-tinged foam.

Across from her sat the abbess. Having been still in the chaos, McCain now stirred in the stillness. She rose to her feet and surveyed the room. One by one, her minions noticed her movement and fixed their eyes on her, awaiting commands.

Having captured everyone's attention, McCain took a long, meaningful look around the rotunda, taking measure of their preparations. Her eyes lingered longest on the fortified entrance, then finally fell upon the post of the broken crucifix and the heap of straw and furniture surrounding it.

She cocked her head to Sister Eustace and said, in a voice that sounded like a whisper but carried to every ear in the room, "Roast the witch."

Chapter 20

EUSTACE LEAPT ONTO HER CHAIR and bellowed through the bullhorn, "Roast the witch!"

The circus sprang to life. The chanting chorus stowed their revolvers and took up a new mantra. Some of the men who had been guarding the door rushed over and lifted Dolores, with her chair, and carried her to the pyre. Several women from the furniture brigade scurried off out of view.

Anna held Joseph's hand up and yelled at it, "You have to hurry!" It continued to wriggle and twitch. But, if it was trying to communicate in that manner, Anna could make no sense of it.

The wind whipped through the office to Anna's left, more violently with every passing minute. It flapped the witch-hunters' clothing and whipped up tiny waves on the growing puddles of rainwater. Even the heavy wall tapestries swayed and rippled.

The men struggled to hoist Dolores to the top of the pyre. The heap settled and shifted under them as they climbed it. A burly, red-faced man's foot broke through the woven cane seat of an old chair. As he fell, the chair's arm punched him in the crotch. He dropped his corner of Dolores's chair, curled up in a ball and, after a moment, vomited. Dolores and her chair lurched to the side and rolled on top of the stricken martyr.

More goons rushed over to rescue their wounded brother and finish tying Dolores to the stake. The furniture brigade women who had run off returned, rolling two steel drums. The drums were white with red letters, "kerosene."

Anna squeezed Joseph's hand in both of her own. *Hurry! Hurry! Hurry!* He was no longer pounding on the main door. He had stopped as soon as Anna had spoken to his hand. *He has to have heard me*, she repeated over and over to herself, between bouts of *Hurry! Hurry! Hurry!*

McCain spoke low. Eustace echoed her words through the bullhorn, "Get him out of there! Secure her to the stake! Do it now! Stop dawdling! I want her lit before that beast comes back."

Dolores had not moved, she sat perfectly rigid, her mouth pulled into a toothy sneer by the belt. Her legs and feet were not tied, but they did not move either. Blood dripped steadily from the toe of her left shoe.

Anna fixated on the blood. In her mind, she saw the crimson beads rising on Sally's hand from the needle monster's bite, saw the bright blood running from the stump of Jeffery's leg after its trip through the pulverizer, saw the red pools spreading under the stamping machine while it cut Samuel Upton to shoe leather. She felt the crisp skin of Joseph's hand, exactly as the skin of her own finger had felt. She saw the blood that had poured from Rebecca's finger, imagined the blood that had gushed from Joseph's wrist. She felt her own blood coursing through her veins, felt it begin to boil.

Commotion below called her attention. The furniture brigade tipped the kerosene barrels up on end and worked at peeling open the lids. Another from that squad ran up with four metal pails.

"I want her lit before the beast returns!" Eustace repeated.

Fire flared inside Anna's brain. Her cheeks burned, her teeth clenched. "I'll light you, you nasty, horrible wench!" Anna hissed through grinding teeth. Joseph's hand clamped hard around hers as she said it, but she barely noticed. The nub of her pinky knuckle throbbed. The week old welts on her face and forearms stung as if they had just been applied. And all the other wounds, to her body and to her soul, revived, cried out, demanded she do something to stop the pain. "I'll light you up real good. You just see if I don't!"

She eased away from the rail and scuttled back into McCain's office. The kerosene lamp still burned on the desk. Its reservoir was nearly full, plenty of fuel to light Eustace *and* McCain, if her aim was good. She snatched up the lamp.

Don't you dare! the other Anna said. *You've been through too much to end it like this. If you throw that lamp, you'll only get one or two of them. The rest will find you and kill you.* The voice was authoritative, the head girl voice, but not nearly as self-assured as it usually sounded. *You know they will!*

I won't let them burn Dolores, Anna replied. *I'll wait as long as I can for Joseph, but I won't let them burn Dolores.*

You don't owe her anything! You are even!

She is one of us, one of the sisters of sorrow. I will not let her burn!

Before the other Anna could answer, McCain's office began to rumble. It was a sound below the torrential pounding of the storm. Not even quite a sound, but a vibration in the very stones of the old orphanage. It was rising in volume and intensity, like a freight train barreling through a tunnel, straight toward her.

She stood stock still, listening. The rumble began from the direction of her old dormitory hall. It rolled toward the center of Saint Frances, toward the main entrance. At first, the storm's rage buried it, but within a few seconds, the new rumble was the loudest sound in the sonic menagerie.

With the oil lamp in her left hand and Joseph in her right, Anna ran out onto the balcony. Not until she stood at the rail looking down did she think about stealth. It would have been a wasted worry. No one looked her way. All eyes were on the door.

The rumble had a rolling quality to it, like the kerosene drum being rolled across the stone floor, only much, much louder – maybe the way the drum would have sounded to a bug about to be flattened by it. Anna felt it through the soles of her feet, the whole structure resounded with it, swayed with it, even. She had to place her hands on the rail so as not to lose her balance.

Then it crescendoed, a horrific, thunderous smashing against the main entrance. The huge oak doors buckled inward. Water exploded between the threshold and the bottom of the door, gushed through the crack between the two doors. The crashing wave would probably have torn the doors from their hinges if they had not been reinforced. After a moment that seemed to stretch on forever, the wave receded.

"Secure that door!" Eustace boomed. "Get this bitch burnt!"

Salt water washed across the floor, swirling with the rainwater. Tufts of foam floated atop the rising pools, driven by the wind like tiny clipper ships. Two of Sister Elizabeth's women rushed up the heap to help secure Dolores in place. The rest joined the men at the door, replacing braces that the wave had dislodged and hammering new braces and beams in place. Sister Elizabeth finished prying the lids off the kerosene drums and drew out a bucket of the oil.

Before the others had even finished tying Dolores to the post, Sister Elizabeth sloshed the bucket of kerosene onto the base of the pile. She scooped up another bucket full and splashed it onto the pyre as well, soaking one man's leg in the process. The other witch-hunters scattered off the pile.

McCain, who had moved to stand facing Dolores, grabbed a severe, scrawny woman and said something to her. The scrawny woman climbed back up the pyre, dodging Elizabeth's third bucket of kerosene, and swiped off Dolores's blindfold. Only the whites of her eyes showed.

The scrawny woman and Evelyn, who had been with Eustace in the basement earlier that day, joined Elizabeth. They each grabbed a bucket and went to work dousing Dolores and the pyre. The yellow fuel oil ran over Dolores's head and body, dripped from her hands, mingled with the blood from her leg. Dolores did not react. *She may be suffering some sort of apoplexy*, Anna thought, *Which may be a mercy, if I'm not able to rescue her.*

"I will *not* let her burn," Anna reproved herself.

The water now stood nearly ankle deep, despite the crazed efforts of the two men running the bilge pump. It was whipped foamy by the wind and the splashing about of McCain's witch-hunters. A greasy, shimmery oil slick spread away from Dolores's kerosene drenched pile.

"Hurrrrrry Joseph!" Anna said out loud, bouncing, almost hopping up and down. "I can't wait any longer!" She lifted the glass lamp, preparing to throw, then paused, no longer confident in her plan. With the wind, the water, and Dolores already soaked in kerosene, Anna realized it could go very wrong.

The rolling rumble began again. Another wave raced toward the door, crashing against the dormitory wing on its way to them. With Dolores now staked and oiled, most of the goons turned their attention to barricading the door.

Anna turned the lamp's wick all the way down until the light blinked out. She raised it over her head, *Hurry! Hurry! Hurry!* A flame flashed orange below as Elizabeth ran a flaming torch to McCain. The fire flapped and sputtered in the gale, sending up complex black smoke signals. Somewhere nearby, another lightning bolt struck the building. Anna felt the electricity in her teeth. In the cataclysm of sound, she thought her ears had begun to bleed.

McCain, standing ankle deep in storm surge at the base of the pyre, stared into Dolores's vacant white eyes. She took the torch from Elizabeth and thrust it skyward. "In the name of His Holiness Pope Innocent the..." The rolling wave crashed into the main door, spraying the room with seawater, drowning out the rest of McCain's speech.

Anna looked to the door, praying to see Joseph. The door had withstood this second wave. One of the oak beams that lay across it had splintered, and the top right hinge had broken free, but the doors stood.

She looked back to the torch. It still burned. McCain continued bellowing her benediction through the cacophony. Her voice ringing with hatred and disgust as she reached her concluding climax, "...and send you to your lover, the devil, in a manner worthy of your wickedness!"

McCain marched forward, aiming to thrust her torch directly under Dolores's chair. Anna squeezed Joseph's hand and shot a glance, in hope beyond hope, at the kitchen door. It remained closed. *I will not let her burn.* Anna hurled the kerosene lamp.

The lamp's hurricane chimney detached from the base as it tumbled through the air. As soon as it left her fingers, Anna knew she had missed, had thrown it too far in front of McCain. Both of her voices screamed at her to run for the kitchen. She might still have a chance. But, she was unable to tear her eyes away from McCain and the lamp. Her feet felt welded to the floor.

The glass chimney entered McCain's peripheral vision. She snapped her head up, catching Anna with her eyes – eyes that burned with hatred, determination, and fear. McCain dove forward with her torch, intent on her purpose.

Her sudden forward motion put her in the path of the lamp's heavy base. It slammed into McCain's outstretched right arm, just above the wrist. The torch splashed into the water and hissed out in a puff of steam. The glass chimney splashed down beside it.

McCain spun around, the fire in her eyes hotter than the torch had ever been. She hugged her injured arm to her body, but flung her left arm toward the balcony. "Up there!" she screamed. "It's Anna! Kill her!"

Chapter 21

ANNA STUMBLED BACKWARD, AWAY FROM the rail. Thunder rang out, this time from *inside* the rotunda. Bullets slammed into the rail and the wall behind her. Ricochets whined. Splinters and plaster dust filled the air.

She dove to the floor.

Her head reeled.

The kitchen!

Anna bounced up and sprinted in a crouch toward her exit, hugging the wall. Bullets riddled the wall above her head. Bright red droplets flew from her fingertips as she pumped her arms, and a hot tingly sensation spread somewhere along her right side.

Anna rounded the last stretch of balcony approaching her door. A third wave rolled along the wall, on its collision course with the main entrance. *It can't take much more of that. I can draw them away, maybe long enough for the sea to break through. Long enough for Joseph to...*

Two men topped the stairs just ahead of her, the sword-wielding giant and a very plain looking man with a club. The service door stood halfway between her and the men. The plain man yelled down to the others, "Hold fire! Hold Fire! She's just a little girl for Christ's sake."

The guns silenced.

"I bring her down." The giant's voice was higher than Anna would have expected. In his native tongue, he probably would be pleasant to listen to, but speaking English, his thick German accent sounded like fingernails on slate. "We burn her with other one."

Anna saw caution below their bravado. They believed her to be dangerous, maybe not as dangerous as Dolores or Joseph, but a threat nonetheless. Anna had no intention of disabusing them of that notion. She drew the key out of her pocket, hoping it would glow, even just a little.

The giant grinned. He held his claymore before him in a two handed grip and said—something, his accent too thick to decipher. His intent was clear enough, though. He was up for a showdown.

The plain man put his hand on the giant's arm, staying him. His other hand extended his club toward Anna, defensively. He favored her with a gentle smile, and wicked eyes.

"Now Anna," he said, almost cooing. "Let's not do anything rash..."

Below, in the rotunda, McCain bellowed, "Get me another torch!"

Anna shot a glance over the rail. Elizabeth ran out of one of the lower offices with a blazing torch in one hand and a long wooden stake in the other.

The plain man edged closer. Anna snapped her eyes back at him, and waved the key in a figure eight. "Stand where you are!" she said in the best adventure-hero voice she could muster.

He stopped moving, but continued talking. "Let's keep a cool head, shall we, little one?"

Magic words, Anna thought.

I don't know any, she answered herself.

They don't know that, make some up!

"Maybe we can help each other out a little bit, hmm?" Plain Man said.

"Ominous glominortious..." Anna intoned. That stopped him long enough for her to steal a quick look back the way she had come. The balcony was clear all the way back to McCain's office, but two more of McCain's goons stood at the top of the other stairs.

"EASY NOW!" Plain Man shouted. He covered his fear with anger, but somehow managed to maintain his gentle smile. "There's nowhere for you to go, little one, but you don't have to burn. Maybe we can – can *cut a deal,* as they say..."

Anna looked down. McCain met Elizabeth by the barrel of kerosene. Elizabeth handed her the torch, then dipped her stake into the oil. She withdrew it and touched it to McCain's fire, creating a second torch. Anna saw McCain nod toward Dolores. Elizabeth beamed.

"Malleus metus mortios..." Anna chanted, tiptoeing backward.

"She is liar," the giant chuckled, lowering his sword and stepping forward.

"Let's give her one last chance," Plain Man said. He again held the giant's arm. "Anna, we really need to find the demon..."

"No demon," the giant said. "We take girl." He sheathed his sword. His muscles flexed, preparing to lunge.

Anna wheeled around and sprinted.

Then, the plain man screamed.

Anna heard splintering wood and steel on stone. The giant cried out, first in terror, then in righteous indignation.

Anna stopped and turned. What she saw made no sense, not at first.

Plain Man was flying.

He was parallel with the floor, four feet above it and coming straight at her. She threw herself out of the way, colliding with the wall. He slammed into the railing, fell to the balcony floor and remained motionless, his club still in his grip.

Anna looked for the giant. What she saw instead was a writhing mass of gray-green tentacles – with several human legs and arms, mottled and livid, and at least two huge wolf heads – flailing in a fury to match the storm's.

The giant's sword flashed. It severed a tentacle and a forearm. Then it was sailing, end over end, through the open rotunda. A second later, the giant was also end over end, rolling down the staircase. McCain's goons who had been advancing on Anna dove out of his way as he tumbled past.

It's Joseph! a voice screamed in Anna's head. She stood, mesmerized by the horror of it, of him. His misbegotten construction of human and animal limbs defied reason. It hurt Anna's brain to look at it, to attempt to understand what it was.

The voice persisted, *It's Joseph! It's Joseph! This is what you've been waiting for!*

"Dolores," Anna said out loud. She exhaled the breath she didn't know she had been holding, and dragged her eyes away from the Joseph-Monster.

Below, Joseph's appearance had affected the others as it had Anna. Most stood agape, or fumbled with their weapons. Elizabeth and McCain stood exactly where Anna had last seen them. Each held a glowing torch, each held their mouths open and eyes wide.

Move now! The voice screamed in her head. *This is your chance. Move! Move!*

Anna could almost see those exact same thoughts blooming in McCain's eyes. The head witch-hunter reached over and shook Elizabeth by the shoulder, yelling into her face. Another wave slammed into the front entrance. Salt water sprayed through the seams and cracks around the door.

"Victory is within our grasp!" McCain's voice carried above the chaos. "Now, we have them all. Do them to their death!"

Gunfire erupted, less ferociously than when they had fired at Anna. That first volley had depleted their ammunition. Now, after the first few rounds, the goon's guns ran dry. Men and women with axes, harpoons and swords charged forward while those with guns reloaded.

"We are not afraid of you, Joseph," McCain shouted, her torch raised high. "We know who you are. Do you remember the last time you saw me, you little crybaby? You wailed until your face was nothing but tears and snot. You peed in your little britches, Joseph. Do you remember?"

Anna swept the balcony with her eyes. Joseph was halfway down the stairs. McCain's goons surrounded him, shooting, stabbing, hacking. None of them looked her way. They probably didn't even remember she existed.

The door to the kitchen hung wide and unguarded. Between her and it lay Plain Man, unconscious but breathing. His hand rested on the club. The remainder of the balcony and the other staircase were deserted.

Anna looked at the door leading to the kitchen. It called to her. Her right arm and armpit were wet. Bright red blood dripped from the fingers of her right hand. She was suddenly overcome by a vivid memory, almost a waking dream, of lying in the cool, comforting quiet under a fir tree, the night she and Donny finally broke free from the underground. The roar of the storm and of the raging battle faded out. She lay on the soft bed of fir needles and loam. She was free from Saint Frances. The air was sweet. The moon was full. The hush of the ocean lulled her to sleep.

She squeezed Donny's hand. Joseph's hand crunched in her grip, then squeezed back. Anna gasped, opened her eyes. The cataclysmic, thunderous roar crashed back into her ears. There was pain, now. It felt as if someone had hammered nails into her back and right shoulder. She was slouched against the wall staring at her escape.

Go, her voices told her. *You've done what you can. Your friends need you. They're waiting for you. Go.* Anna staggered to her feet. She stepped toward the door, then looked down.

McCain ranted on while her minions battled Joseph, "You little pants-wetting crybaby. No one is afraid of you! Now, you will watch me burn your sister. And when we're done cutting you to pieces, we'll burn you, too!"

"No," Anna heard herself say. The throbbing in her pinky knuckle outweighed the nails in her back. Her hand was on the doorframe. Plain Man's club was at her feet. She picked it up and raised it above her head, fixing her eyes on McCain. Anna's daddy once won a doll at the carnival, testing his strength with a sledgehammer. Anna swung her club in the same manner, starting from the small of her back, up over her head, then down so hard that her feet actually left the floor. Halfway through its downward arc, she released it, flinging it at McCain.

The club pin-wheeled through the air, Anna's aim perfect. It would have clobbered McCain square on the head, except – as Anna realized only after releasing the club – McCain had been staring straight at her through her entire wind up. As soon as Anna released the club, McCain dove out of its path. Elizabeth, alerted by McCain's reaction, dodged as well, but not as effectively.

The club caught Elizabeth on the hip, a glancing blow. She stumbled sideways, tripped over her own feet in the rising water, and collided with the kerosene barrels. Elizabeth, her torch, and the barrels toppled. Kerosene gushed, spreading like a yellow tide across the top of the swirling seawater. Then ignited.

Elizabeth ignited as well. Her lips pealed open in a scream. Butter-colored flames spread away from her torch in a relentless wave, a medieval army marching across undefended lands. Elizabeth tried to stand, but could find no traction in the oil and water slurry. She thrashed and screamed and rolled. The water around her and under the burning kerosene boiled, hissing and spitting, sending up thick steam to mix with the wafting black smoke.

By the time she managed to get her feet under her and stand, blazing kerosene coated her. She flailed and staggered. Her shrieking rivaled the howling of the wind, but only for a few minutes. As her screams died away, she crumpled into the spreading lake of fire.

Chapter 22

IN HER HASTE TO AVOID Anna's club, McCain had not fallen, but she had lost her torch. The abbess turned in a rough circle, stumbled backward in the deepening water, astonished at Elizabeth's hideous demise. She began shifting her gaze back to Anna when a small woman, the female third of the chanting group, crashed into the water near her feet. McCain turned wild eyes to Joseph.

The Joseph-Monster rampaged through his attackers. The sight of him was as bewildering, as horrifying, as watching Elizabeth burn. From above, he resembled an octopus of human arms — or maybe a centipede — he had way more than eight arms. And tentacles, and bony, spear-like appendages that Anna had not seen on any natural animal.

His skin, in its various piebald and mottled hues, rippled with the impacts of bullets. He bristled with harpoons, which had no effect on him whatsoever. He ripped one of these harpoons out of his neck and drove it, handle first, into the gut of an attacker. The unlucky witch-hunter doubled over in a fetal curl and collapsed into the murky water, disabled but alive.

They can't kill him! Anna wondered. *They can't kill him unless* he *kills. They're wasting their strength against already-dead flesh.*

Bodies littered the stairs and floor around Joseph — broken legs, crushed or severed arms, shattered jaws, but all were still breathing. Some writhed or groped, others panted. The lucky ones had been rendered unconscious.

Anna looked down at Plain Man. He groaned, then rolled his head up to meet her eyes. The terror on his face hurt some tender part deep inside Anna. Then he reached for her ankle.

Anna screamed and kicked him in the nose. She had no thought of doing so, and had no chance to stop, or even slow her foot. The scream came out of her with every ounce of her strength, as did the kick. His body jolted with the impact. Blood sprayed up her shin. He would not reach for her again.

Another monstrous wave thundered against the entrance, drawing Anna's attention back to the room below. The floodwater now stood deep enough for waves to travel across its surface. Untold gallons of kerosene rode the waves in oily rainbows. The lake of fire spread slowly, like a blooming yellow poppy, away from Elizabeth's scorched corpse. The wind played with the flames, here driving them back upon their origin, there pushing them onward across more of the shallow sea. It was only a matter of time before the flames reached Dolores.

Anna sprinted toward McCain's office and the stairs that lay just beyond it. The other stairs lay closer but were cluttered with broken bodies, and Joseph raged on near their base. The farther stairs offered a surer route to Dolores.

Anna ran. Her head spun, slowly. Her scalp and neck prickled, her fingertips tingled. Even her missing pinky tingled. Tiny white and black specks obscured her vision. Her legs seemed a little too long, too gangly. She slowed to a jog, panting.

A chunk of the rail just ahead of her exploded to splinters. The bullet that had torn it ricocheted straight up in a screaming whine. Anna staggered to a stop and looked over the rail. McCain stood below. She still hugged her wounded right arm to her body. With her left hand, she struggled to cock the lever action rifle.

Beyond her, Joseph battled on. He had fewer appendages than the last time Anna had seen him. Arms and tentacles bobbed in the murky water around him, most of them still squirming. One of his wolf heads lolled to the side, only half attached to his torso. Several of the witch-hunters he had wounded fought on, driven either by fear or fanaticism. The giant had risen and was back in the battle, though he now wielded an oak beam rather than his sword.

Joseph kept them at bay, snapping his canine fangs, lashing out with his boney spears. Anna now recognized the spears for what they were, sharpened whale ribs. Burning kerosene clung to one of his tentacles, a flaming whip which he used to great effect.

Burning kerosene washed onto the lower fringe of Dolores's pyre. The straw lit, but was immediately extinguished by an unoiled wave. Seconds later, another patch of straw lit.

I have to go, now! Anna thought.

You'll pass out if you run any more. McCain will shoot you if you get close.

She looked to McCain. McCain had seen her looking at Dolores, had read her thoughts. The abbess gave up trying to cock her rifle. Instead, she sloshed over to the burning kerosene, thrust the butt of her rifle into the fire and drew it out, an impromptu torch. She challenged Anna with a sneer, then slowly turned toward Dolores and the pile of kindling beneath her.

Anna desperately searched the balcony around her, but found nothing to throw. *I'll never reach her in time.*

She screamed "Joseph!"

He squeezed her hand.

Anna saw that his hand still clung to hers. A thought entered her mind, cruel and dark. She screamed Joseph's name again, but this time directed her voice at McCain.

McCain turned to her with a wicked grin. As she did, Anna flung Joseph's hand at her. McCain sidestepped the hand and it splashed down beside her shin. She looked at it for a moment, confused. It was just a wrinkly brown mass floating in the greenish bilge.

Then the hand grabbed the fringe of McCain's habit, and she recognized what it was. McCain screamed and thrashed at the hand with her burning rifle.

Anna wanted to see what would happen next, but there was no time. She started moving again, toward the stairs, pulling herself along the rail with her left hand. The stairway seemed farther away than it had been the last time she looked.

Something had changed below. The sounds were different. She couldn't place it at first, and it didn't matter, anyway. Right now, the only important thing was to get Dolores off that heap before fire fully engulfed it.

Anna reached the stairs at a slow jog. Her head was light, but manageably so. As she headed down the stairs, she saw what had changed. Joseph was winning. Less than ten of McCain's finest still stood against him.

Two steps down the stairs she saw why. Joseph thrust one of those whalebone spears through the giant's chest, impaling him. Then he drove another spear into the giant's temple. The huge German twitched, still standing, until Joseph yanked the spears out, dropping him into the swill.

Joseph is killing. Anna put it together as she ran down the last of the stairs, what she had already known on some level the instant she decided to throw his hand to McCain. Anna had undone him, pushed Joseph past the point of reason. It was almost exactly as Dolores had planned – whip up an unearthly storm to agitate all the flora and fauna connected to Joseph, then appear as McCain, withholding his hand from him.

Dolores said the magic would begin to unravel if Joseph killed, and when it had unraveled, he would die. *How long will that take?* Anna didn't know. *Hopefully a really long time, but I'm not taking any chances.* She hurried off the last step, plunging almost up to her knees in the filthy, oily water.

Fire licked at the straw and broken furniture. Billows of flame rode the waves half way across the room before flapping out in a hiss of steam. Flames caught along one side of the heap, climbing out of the reach of the lapping water. Anna scanned the room for McCain, then started toward the pyre.

An iron hand clamped over her right shoulder. Her wound there, nearly forgotten, flared to new life, sending a series of flashes across her vision, lightning inside her head. Her knees buckled and she fell forward, would have gone face first into the water if not for the hand on her shoulder.

So intense was the pain, Anna almost did not notice the pistol barrel pressed against the side of her head. Then, the hammer clicked back. Anna tried to turn, but the cold steel dug into her temple. A raspy male voice barked in her ear. "Oh, no you don't! Don't you look at me, don't speak a word."

Chapter 23

THE MAN HAULED ANNA UP out of the water by her shoulder. She wailed, an involuntary cry of pain that dwindled to a sob.

"You're my ticket out of here," he rasped into her ear. "I didn't bargain for any of this. You people are deeply cracked." He dragged her backward into a recess below the staircase.

"We're just gonna sit here and watch the show. Both sides seem to want you. God only knows why. Don't look like there's much left of you." He coughed a harsh laugh, the stubble around his lips scratching her ear. "But, no matter. We'll sit back an' see who wins. I'll trade you for a ride off this god forsaken rock."

Anna's vision blurred, her legs wobbled. *I must stay awake. I must not faint. Breathe, breathe, think, breathe and think…*

The chaos outside continued to intensify. Rumbling detonations chased each other across the storm swept sky. The column of rain falling from the bell tower scintillated with the reflected lightning, making it look like a solid pillar of light. The wailing bell and the screaming wind fought to be heard over the thunderclaps.

Fire now had a firm grasp on Dolores's pyre. Reddish flames licked at the damp straw. Thick black smoke rolled upward as flames contended with the mix of kerosene and seawater. Moisture slowed its progress for now, but the higher the flames climbed, the farther from the water, the faster they would move. Dolores, herself, still held that awful rigid pose, fingers curled to claws, back arched against the chair, eyes rolled into her head.

I have to reach her. I have to get away from this man. But the mercenary clamped down on her shoulder the second she twitched. Anna whimpered. Her knees failed and she slouched against her captor. He wrapped his other arm around her waist and hoisted her up.

"Where you going? Huh?" he asked. "Go out there and you'll be dead in four steps. I'm a trained killer an' I sure as hell ain't goin' out there. Best you just stay here with me a while." He tugged at the collar of her dress, then yanked it down on the right side. The coarse fabric across her back ripped. "Damn," he chuckled, "looks like you already got a back full of buckshot. Bet that smarts like hell, huh? I'm surprised you're still on your feet."

Anna was surprised as well. Her breath came in quick little gasps. Her heart throbbed in her temples, behind her eyes, in her shoulder. She decided that, for the moment, maybe she didn't really need to be on her feet. She slouched against the mercenary, letting him support her full weight.

He didn't seem to notice at all. He poked at her shoulder. An agonizing *zing* burst from the spot, pain welling up in her shoulder and radiating outward, white hot wires running down her arm, down her legs, all the way to her toes.

She screamed and lurched into the mercenary. He was a solid stack of muscle and withstood her lunge as easily as if he had been a stone pillar. The strength drained out of Anna. She wrapped her arms around his waist for support.

"Whoa, take it easy," he said. "You lucked out, girly. Have a look." He extended his hand in front of her face. Her blood covered his outstretched index finger. On the pad of that finger rested a flat silver disk. It looked like a bloody button.

"Just a ricochet, if that had hit you square, it wouldn't have flattened out," he said. "And it woulda sunk a lot deeper. You got five or six more. Want me to dig 'em out for you?"

"No," Anna whimpered. "Please, no."

Fresh flurries of pain washed across her back and shoulder, radiating from the wound. She clung to his heavy belt. One of his hands was wrapped around her waist, the other still held the bit of buckshot before her face.

"Well, okay then," he chuckled. "Stop wriggling. Let's just see how this plays out. I've always wanted to see a witch burn." He paused, then added, "Stand up."

Anna tried to pull herself up, clinging to his belt. A thought was forming in her mind...

Something about the belt.

Something about his hands.

And the throbbing in her temple.

Her temple, where he had pressed the gun.

His hands, one around her waist, the other in front of her face. No gun in either.

He must have holstered it.

It's on his belt. It's got to be.

She found it as soon as the thought materialized, a mass of steel and leather on his hip. Anna wrapped her fingers around the handle as gingerly as she could.

"Stand up, I said!" He flicked the flattened pellet into the water, grabbed her with both hands and jerked her upright. Anna held tight to the pistol. As he pulled her to her feet, it slipped smoothly from its holster and dropped, the weight of it nearly yanking her arm out of its socket. The mercenary failed to notice, the roughness of his motion covering the smoothness of hers.

"Now stand still and watch the show," he rasped. "It's about to get good."

His pistol dangled between them. The mercenary gazed out of their nook, enraptured by the chaos in the rotunda. Anna forced herself to slow her breathing. She fidgeted her fingers and thumb against the revolver as she had seen the singing trio do with their guns.

Thumb the hammer, pull the trigger. Anna had never fired a weapon, never even held one before today. A western novel had been among the books she stole from McCain's office, a gunfighter story. The hero, Tumbleweed Tom, thumbed the hammer and pulled the trigger, and the bad guys dropped. Sometimes, Tom would *fan* the hammer, if he had to drop lots of bad guys. Anna had no idea how to fan a hammer, but she had seen the chanting woman thumbing the hammer of her revolver and guessed she could manage that.

Pulling the trigger shouldn't be too hard either, just a gentle squeeze according to Tumbleweed. The difficulty would be aiming the gun. Even lifting it seemed near impossible at the moment. She knew bullets had lead in them, but it felt to her as if the whole gun was made of the stuff. And the mercenary held her firm with both hands. He would break her in half before she escaped his grasp.

Just wait, Anna. Just hold steady. Move when the time is right.

She stared out into the rotunda. Joseph had moved away from the stairs, heading for McCain. He was slowing down, weakening. The magic truly was draining away. The head that had been hanging earlier was now gone. *It's probably bobbing just below the surface of the water, snapping at any ankle within striking distance.*

He continued to fight, but less ferociously. The goons assembled against him also appeared severely worn. Perhaps half a dozen remained. They retreated in a formation, a kind of defensive array, around McCain. Rather than killing Joseph, their purpose now seemed to be the safety of their mistress.

Heavy smoke billowed up from the pyre. The restless air pulled it this way and that, sometimes veiling Dolores, sometimes revealing her. The flames had not yet reached her, but sweat rolled down her red, rigid face. Fire crawled slowly over the kindling. The base of the heap smoldered as the water boiled and steamed. Smog hung in a low curtain around the rotunda.

Movement on the balcony caught Anna's attention. She snapped her head up to see Donny standing at the rail by the door to the kitchen. His eyes flicked this way and that, half glazed in astonishment, searching the battlefield below him. Searching for her.

"Friend of yours?" the mercenary asked. He sounded amused.

Anna nodded. Hot tears sprung at the corners of her eyes. Her two voices simultaneously cried, *Run away, stupid boy!* and, *Donny, help me!*

Donny cupped his hands around his mouth and shouted into the rotunda. Anna couldn't hear him over the roar, but she knew he was yelling her name, over and over.

"Bold little bastard, ain't he?" the mercenary said.

Anna felt a slight twinge of hope, might have even smiled if she had any smile left.

"Ain't that Hattie McLane's flintlock he's got shoved down his britches?"

"It isn't Hattie's anymore," Anna said, feeling a little bit of steel returning to her nerve.

The mercenary laughed out loud. Then hammered the back of her head with his palm. "I told you not to talk."

Anna's knees buckled, but the man caught her and held her up. "If you're gonna talk tough, little lady, then you sure as hell can stand on your own two feet. Besides, I think you might wanna watch this. Looks like your little buddy's 'bout to get himself killed."

Anna looked to the empty balcony where Donny had been, then frantically scanned the rest of the upper level without seeing him. She spotted him on the stairs, picking his way through the fallen witch-hunters. He grabbed a large knife someone had dropped, then continued his descent, eyes focused on Dolores.

"Why, he's a regular swashbuckler," the man laughed. "What do you suppose he thinks he'll do with that knife?"

"Look, mister, that door he came through, that'll take you out of here," Anna said. "You said you wanted out. That's the way, right there, and nobody's close enough to stop you. Let's make a run for it."

"Shut up," he said in a low, flat voice, grinding his hard thumb into the wound on her shoulder. "I told you, I wanna watch the witch burn."

Anna writhed under his thumb, gritting her teeth, trying not to scream. A cold sort of numbness crept down the length of her arm. Her muscles there went slack. She feared she would drop the revolver if he pressed much longer. When he finally did relieve the pressure, he left his thumb on the spot, an implied threat. Anna decided that if she was to have any use of the gun, she needed to do it now.

Tumbleweed Tom popped into her mind again. He'd had a fat sidekick, a character whose only purpose was comic relief. Anna couldn't remember his name, but she did remember his limp. Much fun was made of the fat sidekick because he had shot himself in the foot.

It's already aimed at his foot. If I shoot his foot, I bet he'll let go. Then I can aim it at his head if he still comes after me. She pressed the pad of her thumb against the hammer's ridged spur and applied pressure. The hammer didn't budge.

"Aw, hell!" the man said. "What's he want with her?"

Anna looked up. Donny splashed across the room toward Dolores. A thickening haze of steam and sooty smoke rose from the pyre, swirled in the restless air. Donny reached the heap in a few wet bounds. He circled it, frantically searching for a clear path to Dolores. Something tripped him. He pitched forward, stumbling over some submerged object. Anna feared it was Joseph's other head.

Instead, when Donny rose, he held one of the buckets Elizabeth had used to douse Dolores. He stuffed the knife into his waistband, opposite the pistol, and used both hands to slosh a bucketful of water onto the fire. Impenetrable white steam engulfed him. He disappeared into it. A second later, another plume of steam billowed up from where Donny had been standing.

"God damn him!" the mercenary muttered.

Anna pressed harder on the hammer, squeezing her fingers and thumb together with all her might. The hammer rocked back just a hair, its spring incredibly tight. She pressed harder until the spur dug into her thumb, pressed harder until it felt like it was going to tear the skin off. Still, the hammer barely moved.

"Seize that child!" McCain shrieked from the other side of the room. "Make him stop!"

Her goons ignored the order, instead maintaining their defensive circle around McCain. Joseph stood between them and Dolores. His left side drooped. Several of his remaining limbs dangled limply. But each time one of the witch-hunters advanced on him, he effectively beat them back or struck them down.

Anna looked back to the burning heap. Flames leapt up one side, finally reaching the drier tinder. Donny stood on the other side, enveloped in smoke, having cleared a path through the flames. He fumbled with the gag, the leather belt that held Dolores's head to the chair. After a moment of working ineffectively at the buckle, he drew his knife and cut the belt away.

As soon as the gag was gone, Donny yelled into Dolores's face. Anna heard him this time. "Where's Anna?"

Dolores's mouth moved, but she did not answer Donny. Her lips raced, chanting.

Donny shoved her shoulder, shook her chair, and yelled again, "Dolores, where is Anna?"

"Ain't that sweet? He's coming to find you," said the mercenary. "Better hope he doesn't, for his sake."

Smoke and haze clung to the air, so heavy now that Anna could no longer see to the balcony, or the other side of the room. Screams came to her from the area where she had last seen Joseph, but the veil of smog concealed him and the witch-hunters.

Anna tugged at the hammer. She felt the trigger slide backward under her finger when the hammer moved.

It's a double action! another little tidbit from Tumbleweed Tom. *The trigger will cock the hammer, but you have to pull it really hard.*

She slipped her middle finger into the trigger guard along with her index finger and squeezed, squeezed, pressing the hammer with her thumb.

Up on the pile, Donny sawed at Dolores's ropes. She was moving now, rocking forward and back in quick, jerky spasms. Her head nodded with her chant, flipping her hair back and forth. Donny hopped this way and that as he hacked at the ropes, trying to keep the flames off his feet. Whenever his footwork brought him face to face with Dolores, he screamed, "Where is Anna?"

Anna squeezed the trigger while wrenching the hammer with her thumb. The revolver was huge, a big gun for a big man, and its springs proved too tight for Anna's small hand. Try as she might, the hammer would not cock.

Shadows moved through the haze, moving toward Donny.

Anna grunted with exertion, aiming the pistol where she hoped the mercenary's foot would be. Her arm trembled, her hand, and the gun in it, shook.

"Hold still and be quiet!" the mercenary growled into her ear. His voice was ice. "What are you..." Then he yelled a word Anna had never heard, and lunged for the revolver. Anna tried to spin away from him. The revolver came up, just enough for her to get her other hand on it, get one more finger on the trigger.

The gun roared. The concussion of its deafening blast threw the revolver out of her hands, tearing skin from fingers. It flew past her, dangerously close to her face, skipped off the wall behind her and disappeared into the swirling water.

The mercenary howled. Anna couldn't hear it, but saw it in his contorted face. His left knee, the one closest to her, bent inward, toward his right knee, in a way that no knee should ever bend. The sight of it made Anna's stomach jump up and swirl like the water around her. As he toppled over his ruined leg, Anna saw that the bullet had also torn a hole through his right calf.

In the small space under the stairs, the gun's blast felt like someone had clapped their hands hard over both of her ears. The din of the storm and the bell and the waves at the door was gone. A squealing whine took its place, it slipped back and forth inside her head, from ear to ear, like marbles on the deck of a storm tossed dinghy.

The mercenary writhed and splashed in the nook. Anna staggered away from him, her stomach lurching. The whole room seemed to roll. Four steps from the nook, Anna fell sideways into the water.

Chapter 24

ANNA ROLLED OVER AND SAT up. The huge oak doors buckled inward, admitting a spray of storm surge. Foaming swill burst over the tops of the doors as well as through the crack between them. Beams and braces splintered. The hinges of both doors had detached and now flapped uselessly from the jambs. A few meager beams were all that remained of the reinforcements, were all that held out the sea.

The floating fire had nearly burned itself out. Only a few patches of the kerosene still burned atop the water. But the pyre blazed. Donny hacked furiously at the ropes on Dolores's wrists. Fire licked at his pant leg, caught. He slapped it out, then went back to work on Dolores.

Anna struggled to her feet. The ringing in her head felt like fluid. She moved through the water, fighting for balance with each step. Her sight constricted, narrowed. She saw only Donny and Dolores and the fire. Her peripheral vision faded to black, she waded, as it were, through a tunnel.

As she neared, her shin barked against Donny's pail. Anna scooped it up and flung water at the fire. The squealing in her head faded to a loud hum, allowing a few other sounds through. Donny screamed her name. Anna threw another bucket of water toward the sound of his voice. Steam obscured her vision, revealing only shadows against a wavering yellow glow.

"Get Dolores down from there!" Her voice sounded hollow and weird. "I'll keep the fire off you, just get her down."

Donny burst from the mist. He jumped out of the steam and threw his arms around her and cried, "Anna!"

She hugged him back, at first just to keep from collapsing under him, but once her arms were around him, she couldn't let go. She felt his courage. She felt hope. Donny had not been injured. He still had energy, still had fight left in him. His presence here meant that her girls were safe. It meant she had won. She had saved them, her sisters of sorrow.

Only one sister remained to be saved. A subtle confidence invigorated Anna. With Donny here, they could rescue Dolores and get out alive.

She released him. "Donny, cut her down. Hurry, we need to go!"

He stepped back from her. "You got it!" he said, turning and leaping two bounding steps back to the pyre. His eyes were burned red, but his smile was radiant. "Already cut all the ropes, just gotta drag her down. Throw some water up."

Anna remembered telling Donny *smiles like that don't last long where we're going,* and regretted it. A grin formed on her lips, in spite of herself. She grabbed the bucket and stooped to fill it. A shadow loomed out of the thick haze behind Donny, something bulky and tall.

Anna screamed, "Donny!"

Donny twisted to look at her, turning his back to the advancing shadow. Sister Eustace materialized out of the gloom, just over his shoulder. For an instant, Anna saw both of their faces at once, Donny's innocent, honest concern – Eustace's unbridled malicious rage. Then, an ax handle whistled through the mist. Eustace swung like Roger Conner swinging for the bleachers.

The handle shattered across the back of Donny's head with a sick splintering crack. Donny's head snapped forward. He dropped, as lifeless as a stringless marionette, landing on the edge of the heap.

Anna's mind went blank. Someone screamed Donny's name, but she had no idea who it was. The floor fell out from under her and, though she continued to stand, she plummeted in place. That cold numbness she had felt in her arm now oozed up from inside her, spreading through her body the way the kerosene had spread across the surface of the water. Bile climbed her throat, she may even have vomited, as if the coldness inside pushed everything else out.

Donny lay on the heap, one eye half open, a trickle of blood running from his ear. Eustace advanced toward her, but Anna could not pull her eyes from Donny. *Please don't be dead, please don't be dead, please don't be dead...* His eyelid moved, just a twitch, just a languid blink.

Eustace held the fractured ax handle up before her, examining it. It was too short now to make a good club, but the broken end terminated in a vicious spike. Eustace eyed Anna across the tip of her weapon and grinned. Rationality was gone from her eyes, only madness dwelt there now.

Anna staggered backward trying to think. *If I can find the revolver*, but even as this thought occurred she rejected it. Eustace paced her, leering, deliberating as to exactly where to impale Anna on the splintered handle. Anna's dress hung loose on the right side where the mercenary had ripped it. Her right hip pocket now dangled to her knee. Something was in there, something hard and heavy. It thumped against her knee as she back peddled.

She jammed her hand into the pocket and drew out the key. If Eustace saw it, she made no reaction. Anna thrust the key at Eustace, trying to remember the way the key had felt in her hand when she stabbed Joseph in the eye, that crazy wave of terror for Donny and rage against whoever harmed her friend. She tried to evoke those emotions, but she was so tired, so spent. The only thing she felt now was a cold blackness, as if her heart and lungs had been replaced with the stagnant water from Joseph's cistern.

Eustace closed the gap between them. She lowered the ax handle, preparing for an underhanded, stabbing thrust. Her eyes burned into Anna's midsection. Anna could feel the spot on her belly where Eustace intended to strike.

She pointed the key at Eustace's chest. It did nothing. It was just a blackened piece of dead metal.

Eustace stepped forward, drawing the handle back in a low arc. With her next step, she would swing it up and drive it through Anna's liver. Anna thrust the key forward again, knowing it could not stop her attacker.

Bright red blood bloomed across the white breast of Eustace's habit. She continued moving toward Anna, but her feet had stopped. Anna just barely had time to roll to one side before the enormous, dead, ex-nun splatted into the murky water where Anna had just been standing.

Something began to unravel inside Anna's head. She stared at Sister Eustace, dumbfounded. The woman bobbed face down, just below the surface. Blood seeped from a hole in her back, rising and drifting like smoke from a dying fire. *Fire*, and *dying* resonated through Anna's mind, they meant something, something important, but she couldn't quite catch their significance.

Anna realized that she had no idea where she was, that she didn't want to know where she was. Just some odd room full of smoke and water and thunder. There was a dead nun at her feet, and that was good, but she really didn't wish to know why.

I'm in the drainage room, under the factory. I just released the floodgates and drowned Sister Elizabeth.

But that wasn't right. This nun was much bigger than Sister Elizabeth. And the factory was...gone.

Why is it raining inside?

Then a voice brought her back, a tiny, desperate, voice crying, "Donny, wake up! Wake up!"

"Maybelle?" Anna said.

The little girl lay across her brother's fallen body, stroking his face with her left hand. She looked as out of place in this gloomy hell as would a rainbow or a bouquet of white lilies. In her right hand was Hattie's flintlock.

"Maybelle?" Anna said again. "What are you doing here?"

"Momma said Donny can't never leave me!" Maybelle cried, her words tumbling out of her like lost marbles. "She said just 'cause she's in prison don't mean we don't have to mind her, and she told Donny he always has to stay with me, and I *told* him that, but he tried to leave me in the woods, but we gotta do what momma said, so I came with him so he won't get in trouble, I followed him, only he don't know it."

Anna's mind reeled, trying to make sense of Maybelle's story, trying to maintain her own fragile grasp on reality. She could feel the gaps in her thoughts, as if her mind had simply chosen to discard bits of information, pieces of memory it found distasteful.

But she *needed* those bits and pieces. A voice in her head told her so. She managed, "And you shot the nun?"

"She hurt Donny!" Maybelle wailed, "and now he won't wake up!" Then she screamed, with startling ferocity at Eustace's corpse, "You don't hurt my brother!"

Anna looked at Donny again. It hit her like a punch in the gut. It was impossible to even hope he was still alive. The wood his face rested against pushed it askew. His jaw hung open like the mouth of a dead fish. None of Donny's life shown in his half-opened eye.

Seeing him that way destabilized her. For as long as she could remember, she had been walking a tightrope between what was real and what she needed to believe to survive. The bubble of blood forming at Donny's nostril, inflating, bursting – that stupid, vacant stare of one-half eye – they rocked her tightrope, and now she would fall.

Her mind begged her to fall on the side of fantasy, to just forget again, about Donny, about her little brother, to forget about ever wanting to see the ocean, forget about the chaos around her. If she was just standing alone in a room of smoke and water, that would be good. Her body just cold, dark water. Her mind just thin, white smoke.

And why not, what does it matter now?

Reality, the other side of her tightrope, had only one argument in its favor. The iron key Anna still held in her hand. It anchored her to the here and now, and try as she might, it refused to let her slip away.

She had been given this key twice. Both times, upon receiving it, the key had unlocked her secret reserves of hope. Both times, she had been elated, overwhelmed by joy or relief. And the key had brought her to this place.

Joseph had given her the key. He was here somewhere. And Dolores, that silly, lunatic nun – no, fake nun – or witch or whatever she was, she had also given Anna this key. Whatever happened to her?

You know damn well what happened to her.

Anna grasped the key so hard that her nails dug into her palm. Reality crashed over her like a six-foot wall of surf. Dolores's words, from so many lifetimes ago, spoke calmly inside her head, guiding her return to the present, *That was a brave and noble thing you did.*

Maybelle stared up at Anna, her head on Donny's chest, her eyes huge and streaming. Anna wanted to tell her that Donny would be okay, but that was fantasy, so she said nothing. Instead, Anna looked up the pile to where the witch burned.

The buckets of water she threw had slowed the fire, had most certainly prolonged Dolores's life, but the fire had reached her at last. Flames clung to her shoes, crawled up one stocking, licked at the fringes of her dress. Dolores was oblivious. She sat rigid and strained, chanting endlessly.

She is in the storm.

Donny had told her he cut all the ropes. She hoped that was true, Donny's knife had disappeared under the swill after Eustace hit him. Anna inhaled deeply. Smoke burned her throat. She held the breath and climbed to the top of the pyre. She hooked her arms under Dolores's from behind, clasping her hands together across Dolores's chest, and dragged her backward down the pile.

Dolores's feet continued to burn. She chanted on in hoarse whispers. Anna's torn dress slipped off her shoulder. Flames licked at its tattered hem and caught. Her bullet wounds screamed with the exertion. Anna knew these things, accepted them as reality. She also accepted the reality that she could do nothing about any of it just now.

When they reached the water at the bottom of the pyre, the flames on Dolores's feet hissed out. Dragging her down the steep pile had been difficult. Anna doubted she would be able to drag her up the flight of stairs.

No, the other Anna's voice was grim, *if we are going to be accepting reality now, it is impossible for you to move Dolores to the balcony, let alone drag her all the way through the kitchen, down another flight of stairs, and across the grounds to the woods. That isn't going to happen, no matter how bad you want it.*

"Dolores! Snap out of it!" Anna yelled, to no effect. Anna shook the woman violently. Dolores slumped into the rising water. Anna lifted her shoulders and propped her against the heap. "Please, Dolores, I can't carry you. Please wake up!"

Anna looked to the nook where the mercenary had held her. Flames and lightning illuminated the room, but the smoke grew denser with each passing minute. Anna could not see whether he still lurked there. She scanned the room and saw that the other staircase had a similar nook beneath it.

She placed her hand on Maybelle's shoulder. "Maybelle, honey, we need to hide, okay? I'll bring Donny with us, then I'll come back for Dolores. We're going to hide under those stairs. Do you think you can get yourself over there?"

"Only if you bring Donny," she whimpered.

"I will, I promise." Anna stepped toward Donny.

Dolores's hand shot out, quick as a striking adder, and grabbed Anna's wrist. Anna yelped and jerked away but Dolores held fast. Her grip became painfully tight.

"I'll come back for you..." Anna started.

Dolores pulled Anna to her knees beside her. The witch's chanting quickened, intensified. Her lips flew, her head bobbed.

"Dolores, you're hurting me. We must leave, please..."

"Anna!" Abbess McCain's voice, sweet as poisoned honey, drifted through the haze. "There you are. We've been looking all over for you."

Chapter 25

ANNA PEERED THROUGH THE SMOG, searching for her tormentor.

"I see you've ruined our witch roast, you little bitch," Abbess McCain said. "I think your murderous mother drowned the wrong child. In fact, she said so herself, your father told me..."

Shadows moved, just beyond the bell tower's column of water. Anna couldn't tell how many people were there. More than just McCain. The shadows moved calmly, without rush or alarm. Anna understood that the battle was over.

"Are you aware, Anna, that your father knew who drowned little Ephraim?" McCain continued. "He knew all along that you were innocent. He let you take the blame because he loved your mother," she paused, "but he never really loved you. He told me so."

Anna felt Maybelle cowering behind her, wedged between Anna and the pyre. Hattie's flintlock was in Anna's hand, she didn't know how it got there. Anna pulled the hammer back, as Donny had shown her. *This one has a hair trigger.* She aimed toward the approaching shadows and touched the trigger. Its hammer fell with a dead *clack*. Donny had also said, *you only get one shot.*

McCain's shadow became her form as she stepped into the pillar of rain. Two other witch-hunters accompanied her, one on each side. Bright white light surrounded McCain, the lightning blazing through the open bell tower carried down to her along skeins of rain, drawing a shaft of splendid radiance.

Abbess McCain basked in it.

"Look what I have here, Anna." She hoisted a large, hairy mass. "It's Joseph's head. You have no idea how long I've wanted Joseph's head. Imagine my delight when he showed up with not just one head, but two!"

McCain lifted a second hairy mass. Anna saw them clearly now in the sparkling pillar of rain. Neither head snapped. Joseph was completely dead. Anna's lip curled in a bitter smile.

"Oh, and speaking of heads," McCain continued, "I made you a promise, Anna, do you remember? I told you I would hang *your* head on my wall. And I believe in keeping promises."

Dolores's chant changed. She spoke different words now, and she spoke louder. The smoke had seared her throat, Anna could hear it in her harsh rasp, but Dolores forced the words out, rocking forward and back in the water.

"Perhaps you would be so kind as to ask your witch friend to cast her clever spell on you, so that your head remains alive after I cut it off. I would so *love* to hang a living Anna head in my new office," McCain laughed, then added, "Of course, I would have to sew your mouth shut. Heaven knows what a pain it is to listen to you talk."

The room darkened. It took Anna a minute to realize why. The room quieted as well. For the first time in hours, the lightning ceased and the sky silenced. Without the thunder's agitation, the bell's incessant single note dwindled.

Other sounds emerged that had been hidden in the thunder's roar – the splashing of rain, the crackle of the fire, the moans of broken witch-hunters. Anna held her breath. Maybelle grabbed Anna's hand. Even McCain stopped her taunting.

Then the sky broke. A concussion shook the room, as fierce and bone jarring as the boiler explosion. A rapier of silver sky fire exploded into the top of the tower. The light from the blast filled the tower, flared down the shaft of rain like God's own search light. The bell wailed, not its single steady note, but a discordant and unmelodious warble, growing louder by the second.

Then they saw it, the bell, plummeting from above the domed ceiling, rocketing downward in the shaft of light, a four-ton cannon ball. It blasted straight through the floor as if the floor had been made of tissue paper rather than stone. A great geyser from the cistern below the floor exploded upward, a column of old rain sheathed inside the new. It hung in the air longer than Anna thought possible, then splashed back down into the gaping hole left by the bell's passage.

Only after the geyser settled did it occur to Anna that Abbess McCain had been standing in the center of that shaft of light.

Her two remaining goons stood awe-struck. Water ran past their feet, draining into the hole. Anna's weary mind thought it looked like the world's largest flush toilet. She giggled, but stopped as soon as she heard herself. To her own ears, it sounded insane.

Large stones fell from the ruined tower, each throwing up huge geysers of their own. The goons, now only shadows in the fog, turned and ran for the double doors. Yet another wave rolled along the outer wall, rushing toward the main entrance. A fleeting desire to warn McCain's henchmen crossed Anna's mind. This time when she giggled, she didn't stop herself.

The wave slammed into the doors, finally destroying the last of the bracing. Water rushed across the floor, sweeping away all in its path. The hole in the floor swallowed much of the wave, along with the two goons. They joined their mistress in the cavernous cisterns below The Saint Frances de Chantal Orphan Asylum.

Anna's knees gave out. She flopped on her butt beside Dolores. The woman had stopped chanting, she no longer held Anna's arm. Her eyes were closed and her features relaxed. Lightning resumed in the sky. The storm continued, but its ferocity had diminished.

Waves rolled through the arch where the front entrance had been. They looked like a giant tongue licking out of a stone mouth. After the third wave, the cistern had swallowed all of the sea it could hold.

Pity there's no one left to clean the pipe. It was the first thought Anna had had in several minutes.

Stones from the crumbling tower continued to follow the bell into the abyss. Anna wondered how much of the structure would remain when the sun rose tomorrow. It suddenly struck her as fantastical that the sun would ever rise, or that she would be there to see it if it did.

The water had risen nearly to Anna's chest. It should have been freezing, but it seemed just fine to her. The cartilage in her knees and ankles, the shredded skin on her arms, her pellet peppered back – they had all finally stopped hurting. Her tattered nerves, having fulfilled their sacred duty to report injuries, had at last turned down the lights and called it a night.

A melancholy calm settled over her, contentment. She had gotten almost everything she had wanted, and that was good, good enough. Standing up again seemed like the most ridiculous idea she had ever had, a monumental undertaking. Anna feared that even if she could stand, doing so would reignite her several injuries.

"I would have liked to have run on the beach again," she said, to no one in particular. "With the sun sparkling off the surf."

"And the wind in your hair," Dolores said, her voice like sandpaper.

Anna rolled her head toward Dolores. She said, "Hi," because she could think of nothing else to say. She was afraid Dolores might try to make her move. "Can I just stay here for a while?"

Dolores smiled a sweet, weary smile. "I'll let you stay, if you let me stay."

Ocean water lapped against Anna's chest. It rose with each new wave that rolled through the doors.

"But," Dolores said, "I think Maybelle should join the other girls."

"Is she really here?" Anna asked. She rolled her head the other direction.

Maybelle lay across Donny's body, her face buried in his chest, sobbing. They were mostly out of the water, part way up the soaking heap of tinder. The ocean had extinguished the fire. The pile smoldered on, but the flames were gone.

"Maybelle," Anna said.

"I don't want to leave Donny..." Maybelle whimpered. "Mamma said I have to stay with Donny..."

"Maybelle, I'll stay with Donny," Anna said. She tried to use her gentle but firm head girl voice. "Mind me now, Maybelle. You have to do what the head girl tells you, just like I was your mother. Do you remember when they told you that?"

Maybelle looked up at her, a long string of snot dangling from her nose and utter misery pouring from her eyes. Slowly, she nodded.

"Now, I am telling you exactly what your mother would tell you if she were here," Anna said. "You need to go back to Jane and Lizzy. You found your way here. You can find your way back."

"And you're going to stay with Donny?"

"Yes, Maybelle, I promise."

"Somebody has to hold his hand," Maybelle said, choking, "'cause he's hurt and somebody..."

"I'll hold his hand, Maybelle." Anna reached to where Donny lay. Her shoulder screamed and she winced, but once she found his hand and rested her arm against the wet straw, the pain subsided.

"Can she come with me?" Maybelle asked, looking to Dolores.

"I can't walk right now, honey," Dolores said, "my feet hurt too bad."

"Go on Maybelle," Anna said. "You go as fast as you can, no dawdling now. Mind me."

"Yes, Miss," Maybelle said. She slipped off the heap and waded in the direction of the stairway, like a white ghost drifting across the surface of the water.

Anna looked over to Dolores. The witch's eyes were closed, she breathed peacefully. "You did it, Dolores, you freed Joey." Anna took her hand under the water and squeezed it. "That was a brave and noble thing."

Dolores squeezed back.

At the top of the stairs, Maybelle stopped and looked down at them.

"Go on, Maybelle," Anna called up to her. "Tell Jane that Anna's swimming in the ocean." She looked back to Dolores and murmured, "I always wanted to swim in the ocean."

Dolores whispered, "It's a fine thing to do."

Anna closed her eyes, holding Donny by one hand and Dolores by the other, the best two friends she had ever had. The ocean lifted her. And she swam. And it was, indeed, a fine thing.

Sisters of Sorrow

Chapter 26

ANNA ROSE FROM THE DEAD the following morning, much to her dismay. Intense pain wracked her body. Every limb felt like wood, and her joints were full of gravel. Her throat burned and her lungs ached each time she inhaled. When she tried to open her lips, they stuck together. Her tongue clung to the roof of her mouth.

She wondered if McCain had made good on her threat to sew her mouth closed. *Maybe I'm still dead and she...* But no, McCain was gone, buried beneath the bell and all the stones of the tower that once held it.

Anna pealed her tongue from the roof of her mouth. It came away like the skin from a green banana. She poked at her sealed lips, prying them apart with her tongue. A little cry escaped as her lips parted.

It occurred to her that she was no longer inside the rotunda. The ground beneath her was soft, almost spongy. The air smelled sweet, fir trees and wildflowers. *Summerland?* She squeezed her hands, but they were empty. Knuckles popped. Pain flared along one of the fingers, a souvenir from the mercenary's revolver.

If this were Summerland, Donny and Dolores would be with me...and it wouldn't hurt so bad.

Air moved across her face, ocean air. She heard whispering. Anna let her eyes slide open, just a slit. They stung. Crusty bits of matter glued her lashes together. As her lids parted, gentle light seeped in, a blue green blur. As they opened further, the blur resolved into azure patches of sky and verdant sprays of maple leaves and fir boughs.

"Donny?" she said, her throat so dry she expected to exhale dust.

"Shh...He's right here." It sounded like Jane, but Anna had never heard Jane speak so gently. Anna's ears still were not right, one popped when she moved her jaw, the other rang softly. Maybe that explained hearing sweetness in Jane's voice.

"Where is 'here'?" Anna croaked.

"We're in the woods behind Saint Franny's, the place Donny showed us," Jane said. "He said you hid here before you came back for us."

"You came..." Anna's parched throat seized up.

Someone placed wet fingers on her mouth. Cool water drizzled across her lips. It rolled over her tongue, soothing and hydrating her mouth.

She tried again, "You came back for me?"

"Maybelle told us you killed all the bad guys but you needed help." This was Lizzy's voice.

"Actually," Jane said, "Maybelle told us that Donny needed help. Lizzy, here, insisted we come looking for him." A snide tinge colored Jane's voice when she said "Lizzy." It sounded more like the Jane Anna remembered.

"Yeah, and it's a good thing we did, too," Lizzy said. "Y'all were hung up on that big pile of wood, but the water had almost covered it by the time we got there. Then, late last night, the whole place just fell over. Scared the pee out of me."

"Lizzy!" Jane said.

"Well it did! Anyway, you would have been squished flat if you stayed in there."

"What about Dolores?" Anna asked.

Jane let out a long, ragged sigh.

"Jane?" Anna asked again, trying to prop herself up on her elbows.

"No, no, Anna, lie down," Jane said. "Dolores is right here. We brought her out, too."

Anna relaxed, settling back into a bed of fir boughs. Then realized what she hadn't asked. She turned her head, crackling her spine as she did, and looked Jane in the eyes. "Is she alive?"

"I don't know. I think so...I guess," Jane said. "She's been catatonic since we found her. Stopped breathing for a while, we thought she died. Sometimes she goes a long time without taking a breath. She's been shot in the leg. And her feet..." Jane sighed again. "I can't bring myself to look at her feet, Anna. I almost would think it a mercy if she doesn't wake up."

"I tried, Jane," Anna said, weakly, and closed her eyes.

"Oh, Anna!" Jane sobbed. "It was sheer lunacy for you to believe you could escape that place, let alone bring us all safely out. Never in life would I have believed it."

Anna opened her eyes and looked at Jane. Tears streamed down the older girls cheeks. Clean pink lines through the grime on her face and her swollen red eyes told Anna Jane had been crying for some time.

Jane sobbed again, looking out toward the ocean. She took Anna's hand in her own, squeezed it gently. "I promise I'll never call you Pinky again," she said, forcing a laugh through her tears.

"I like it when you call me Pinky." Anna smiled. "I always have. Didn't you know that?" She did her best to put a mischievous twinkle in her eye.

Jane sobbed a laugh. She looked as if she wanted to say more, hesitated, then brought Anna's hand to her lips and kissed it.

A moment passed. Then Anna said, "I'd like to see Donny. Can you help me up?"

Jane inhaled sharply. "Uh, I don't think that's a good idea right now. Mmm. You need to rest."

The cold blackness seeped back into Anna's chest. "Jane, don't lie to me. Is he here or not."

"Yes, yes, Anna, he's right here," Jane sighed.

"Is he okay?"

Jane was silent long enough for Anna to know the answer. Really, Anna had known the answer already, from the moment Eustace brained him with the ax handle.

"No," Jane said. "He's not."

Anna sat up, shoved Jane's arm away when the older girl tried to stop her. Her head spun. Black spots clouded her vision. She waited, took three slow breaths. The dizziness passed.

Donny lay next to her on a bed of fir boughs. Maybelle slept snuggled up to his side. Two purple lumps stood out against the pale skin of his forehead. Anna didn't want to think about the lump on the back of his head. His face had a deathly pallor, like it did on the morning of the sleet storm on the beach, was that two days ago? Anna couldn't remember. It felt like forever. His mouth hung slightly open, as did his eyes. Dried crusts of blood ringed his nostrils and ears.

Jane wrapped her arm around Anna's shoulder, being careful of the injury there. Anna allowed Jane to pull her close. The cold blackness in her chest was gone, but nothing took its place. She was just empty.

"Why'd you let him come back?" Anna mumbled. "Why couldn't he have just..."

"Shh..." Jane said, laying her head against Anna's.

"He's not dead," Lizzy said. "He might get better, you know, if we can get him to a doctor."

"Lizzy," Jane said, trying to keep her voice steady. "Go fetch more water."

Lizzy stood slowly, watching Donny, then wandered off in the direction of the beach.

"You should have just left us there, Jane," Anna said, slumping into her.

"Oh, Anna, please don't say that."

"Just help me over there, beside him."

Anna rolled onto her hands and knees, then crawled the short distance to Donny. When she reached him, she lay down on the boughs and took his hand.

"I'm sorry, Donny," she said. "Are you still glad you met me?"

Tears rolled down her cheeks, dripped off the tip of her nose. Donny's eyes did not blink, his lips did not twitch. His hand remained cold and lifeless in hers.

"I'm glad I met you, Donny," she said, "very glad I met you."

She lay there watching him as the dapple of sun and shadow moved across his pale face. Now and then, one of the girls would sneak up to check on her, then tiptoe away. Somebody brought her water once. She slipped in and out of sleep. In her dreams, Donny would wake up, stretch, and ask her why everyone was crying. Or, she would dream of water, constantly dripping somewhere dark and buried, sounds that would echo into eternity yet never be heard.

When the six-foot tall woman in a high-collared white silk dress poked her with a parasol, Anna thought it was just a new dream. Then she heard Jane yell, "Stop that!" in that good old Jane tone of voice that meant someone was about to get clobbered. "Get away from her!"

"What is your name, child?" the woman asked.

Anna's face was hot and damp, her eyes had crusted over again. She blinked, trying to understand what she saw. The woman wore an ornate white hat. Her hair was black as crow feathers and her eyes were lavender.

"I...My name's Anna, ma'am."

The woman smiled, but only with her teeth. "And you are the girl who did that?" She thrust her parasol toward the beach.

Anna sat up and looked toward the beach. Agony in her shoulder confirmed that this was no dream. Ferns and low brush blocked most of her view. She saw only patches of sand and sky. After a moment of craning her head this way and that, she asked, in a sleep-groggy voice, "Did what?"

"Oh, for heaven's sake, child, stand up," the woman said.

"No." Jane stepped between the woman and Anna. "She's been shot. She needs a doctor. What is the matter with you?"

"Sarah," said the woman.

A second woman, an exact twin of the first, stepped into Anna's view. She took Jane by the shoulder and whispered something into her ear. Jane's face went blank. She turned and walked a few paces away, then sat down hard on the forest floor.

The first woman offered Anna her hand. "Stand up, if you would please."

Anna took her hand and rose. Her knee popped. The ground seemed to tilt under her feet, like a listing ship. The dizziness rushed back over her, filling her head with prickles and her eyes with black spots. Her stomach lurched. She realized that she was falling over, felt as if she sailed downward, like the plummeting bell.

Strong hands grabbed her by the arms and held her up. Whoever had grabbed her must be holding her in the air, she could not feel her feet touch the ground at all. After several breaths, feeling returned. The prickly sensation, like a sleeping leg waking, rushed through her head. The wobbly ground settled. Strength returned to her feet, at least enough to stand up by.

The woman looked at her impatiently, her hands clasped at her waist. It must be the other one, Sarah, who held her up.

"That!" the woman said, "Are you the Anna who did *that*?" She pointed through the trees, across an open field, to an enormous pile of old stones, the ruins of some ancient fortress.

Part of Anna knew immediately that it was the remains of The Saint Frances de Chantal Orphan Asylum. Yet, most of her mind didn't recognize it at all. The waves had carried an entire coastline of sand up onto the plain upon which the orphanage had stood. Black stones jutted out of the sand like teeth from a discarded jawbone.

Half the rotunda still stood, where it connected to the dormitory wing. One side of the grand staircase swept up its concave wall, reaching into clear blue sky. Two triangular stubs of wall from the dormitory wing supported the curved wall like buttresses. Sand had completely filled the hole in the floor. Anna did not recognize any other feature of what had once been her home.

"Good Lord, child. I haven't got all day," the woman said.

"Uh, I blew up the factory," Anna said. "I didn't make the storm, though..."

"Of course not," the woman said, "but you helped Dolores, yes? And you let Joseph into the fortress, yes?"

Anna nodded her head to both questions.

"Very well. I suppose I should introduce myself. My name is Matilda. This is Sarah. We have come to collect our sister." Matilda nodded toward Dolores. "We will be out of your hair shortly. But first, I need a little bit more information regarding last night's events."

"You are from Dolores's coven?" Anna asked.

"No. We are from her *mother's* coven. Dolores has never been one of us. She was disallowed for weaving magic she had no business knowing," Matilda said. "However, she was given a second chance, an opportunity to right her wrongs, and it seems she may have done so. I told her we would come for her once Joseph's soul had been released."

Anna started to sag again, the dizziness returning. "Ma'am, I don't think I can stand any longer."

"Sarah," Matilda said.

One of the hands holding her released. The other hand continued to support her without wavering. The woman holding her, Sarah, tugged at the flap of dress covering Anna's shoulder. Then, she gave it a firm yank, ripping the dress all the way down Anna's back.

Something sharp pricked into her skin, just under her shoulder blade, a bright, precise pain. As soon as she began to react, a bit of lead popped out of her back. The relief was so palpable that Anna couldn't wait for Sarah to start on the next piece.

In a moment, Sarah had removed all the pellets. Again, the pinprick pain returned as she stitched little X's over each wound, seven in all. The thread slid under her skin. It made her teeth grind, but was in no way as horrible as the mercenary's calloused thumb digging in the punctures.

Sarah finished by sewing three stitches across the ripped dress so it hung, more or less, as it should. It wasn't until she finished that Anna noted she had done it all one handed, and with no instruments.

Anna started to ask how she had managed it, but before she could, Matilda said, "Drink this," handing her a small vile. Anna did, without question. It tasted like a mix of strawberries and copper.

"Now, that should keep you on your feet until our business is concluded," Matilda said.

"Thank you," Anna said. The copper strawberry syrup felt like lead in her stomach, but the dizziness faded and her energy was returning.

"You are welcome. Now I will need you to come back to the ruins with me, for just a moment, and explain how all this came about."

"Okay," Anna said, then, "No. Wait a minute." Walking back to the ruins felt…easy, reasonable. But wasn't there something important here. She tried to remember. Her thoughts in that direction oozed, like syrup. "Can you help…" What's his name? "Donny. Can you help Donny?" then, "You need to help Donny. I can't leave him."

"The boy?" Matilda said, either shocked or amused, as if Anna was joking. Then she saw Anna's reaction and said flatly, "No. We cannot help the boy."

Something sick and sweet in her head said *of course we can't help the boy*. It was neither of her voices. Anna shoved the thought aside. "There must be something that can be done for him."

"Do you have a shovel?" Matilda asked, raising an eyebrow.

"What?"

"A shovel. The boy's brain has been swelling ever since he was struck. If you start digging now, you should have a nice grave ready for him by the time he needs it."

Anna groaned and slumped again, intending to lay back beside Donny, but Sarah held her fast. The new stitches in her back pulled, as if someone was using her back as a dartboard.

"Anna," Matilda said, "I really do not have time for this. Come with us now and answer our questions. You will have plenty of time to mourn the boy once we have gone."

"Okay," the copper strawberry voice said, "but..." *Why?* Anna thought, *Why should I help you?* It seemed like too much trouble to ask. She looked around the little clearing, trying to remember something. The syrup was gumming up her mind. Lizzy, Mary, and Joan sat on a log watching. Maybelle lay beside Donny. Then she saw Jane, sitting blank-faced on the ground.

Forming the demand in her mind took a great deal of concentration, but once she had the words, they came easily enough. "Fix her," Anna said. "Whatever you did, undo it."

Matilda said, "Jane."

Immediately, the girl stood. Her sense returned, and her anger. "Anna..."

"It's okay, Jane, I have to go talk to these ladies," Anna said. "I'm feeling better. I'll be right back. Stay with Donny."

"Anna," Jane said, but as her cheeks flared, she changed her focus to Matilda, "You're a witch? Good for you. But you don't scare me..."

"Jane," Anna said.

"Shut up, Anna," Jane said, without looking at her, "I'm talking to the witch. I saw what they did to your *sister* last night. Tied her to a pole and lit her on fire. She would have died if Anna hadn't gone back and saved her..."

"Yes, yes, we know all that," Matilda snapped. "So what."

"So, I know how to kill a witch, that's what," Jane said. "Keep that in mind, *Matilda*. You bring Anna back unharmed."

Matilda raised an eyebrow and slowly lifted her chin, as if considering how to respond. Finally, she said, "I have no intention of harming her." Then she turned and said to Anna, "But I have no time for any more delays. Shall we?"

Anna smiled at Jane, then followed Matilda and Sarah out of the forest.

Chapter 27

THE STONES OF THE SAINT Frances de Chantal Orphan Asylum littered the beach, as if they had always been there. Beyond the scattered bits of the old fortress, the Pacific rose and fell in gentle swells, like the breathing of some giant sleeping beast. Sunlight flared off its surface, startlingly bright, its glare nearly hiding the ship bobbing at anchor. The clipper's hull and sails were white, almost silver. It shimmered like a mirage, folding in and out of the sunlight.

A radiant white dinghy rested on the beach, bearing no insignia, no markings of any kind. It occurred to Anna, then, to look for the little steamer she had intended to hijack for their escape. As soon as she thought it, she knew the steamer was gone. Nothing remained of the dock where it had been moored. Not even a single piling jutted from the deceptively calm water. Maybe it had washed inland and was scuttled somewhere in the woods. But, judging by the ruins of the orphanage, it was much more likely that the boat had been torn to bits and buried at sea.

"Are you absolutely sure no one is left in there?" Matilda's voice interrupted her thoughts.

"Who?" Anna asked. "The people that tried to burn Dolores?"

"Yes, to whom else could I possibly be referring?"

Anna thought of Noel and Mary Two. It hurt her brain to respond smartly, but she did anyway. "My girls. Two of them died before we left. Why do you care about McCain's people? I thought this was about Joseph."

"This is about a lot of things. And you will do well to mind your manners," Matilda said. "Did any of the witch-hunters survive?"

"Some were still alive when I..." *Died*, is what she thought. "When I fainted."

Matilda flashed a grave look at Sarah.

"They were hurt real bad, though."

"Sarah, check for survivors," Matilda said. Sarah glared at her and stood where she was – just long enough for Anna to wonder whether she would obey – then she turned and headed for what remained of the rotunda.

To Anna, Matilda said, "You would be amazed what one may recover from."

"Will Dolores recover?" Anna asked.

"Oh, yes, I am sure she will be just fine. She put so much of herself into that storm. I am really quite impressed, but it will take several hours for her to return to herself."

"Jane said she was shot in the leg."

"Oh, that is nothing," Matilda said. "The burns, though, the burns may give us some trouble. Fire can be...difficult for us." Matilda paused just a tick, then continued. "Enough about Dolores. Tell me about Abbess McCain. Is she one who may have survived?"

"No," Anna said. "She did not survive."

Somewhere within the ruins, a pistol cracked. Anna whipped her head around, but saw nothing. Matilda pretended not to notice.

"There is a man named Theodor Stevens," Matilda asked, "do you know if he was here? Do you know if he survived?"

Anna, still looking toward the ruins said, "Uh, there were a lot of people here, a lot of men, but I never saw them before last night...I never heard any names."

"Look at me when I speak to you, Anna. This man, right here," Matilda held out a large, sepia photograph, "Theodor Stevens, did you see him?"

Anna turned slowly back to Matilda, intending to ask about the gunshot, but when she saw the photo, she forgot all about Sarah and the ruins. "Yeah, I saw that man. I, uh...I mean, he tried to grab me. I kicked him in the teeth."

Matilda smiled, "You kicked Theodor Stevens in the teeth. You are sure it was him?"

"Yes, ma'am."

"So he was alive the last time you saw him? Can you tell me where that was?"

"There used to be a balcony there." Anna pointed into space, past the end of the hanging staircase. "That's where he was."

"Hmm," Matilda nodded. "And what about this person?" She flipped the photo over. Its back was the same as its front, except the photo now showed one of the men who had been working the pump.

"Yes, he was here, he fought with Joseph. I don't think he lived."

"Very good, and this person?" Matilda flipped the photo again, this time it showed a picture of a man Anna had not seen.

"I don't recognize him, but I didn't see everybody's face."

"Hmm," Matilda flipped the photo again, "and this person?"

The card now showed a picture of Sister Eustace. Anna's world shifted slightly. Eustace's face from the previous night, rising out of the fog behind Donny, flashed through her head. The echo of the ax handle cracking across Donny's skull reverberated in her mind. Anna stood stunned for a moment. At the edges of her vision, the world drifted, rotated.

"Well, yes or no?" Matilda demanded.

Anna blinked. They had been walking as Matilda showed her the photographs, Anna hadn't noticed until just now. They now stood where the main entrance had been. Before them, only a few yards away, the Pacific gently lapped the shore. Behind them, the forest stood as a green line over a black shadow. On the sand-washed lawn, Jane walked toward them.

"Yes," Anna said quickly, not wanting Matilda to see Jane's approach. "Yes, she was here. And yes, she is dead. A six year old shot her in the back with a silver bullet."

"Really! Well, that is fitting I suppose," Matilda said. "Speaking of silver bullets, what about this person?" The photo now showed Hattie.

"Ax in the head," Anna said. "Dolores did it."

"Wonderful. And Dolores has the pistols, then?"

"She...what? Who? I mean, Maybelle got it from Donny..."

"No, Hattie's pistols," Matilda said. "Dolores would have taken them when she killed Hattie. Where are they now?"

Why do you care about the pistols?

Anna said, "I don't know where they are. Dolores was captured after she killed Hattie. McCain probably took them back."

"Hmm." Matilda looked at Anna the way a snake watches a bird. "I do not think you are being entirely honest with me."

"I don't think you are being entirely honest with me, either," Anna said. The coppery taste bubbled up in her throat as she said it. "Why do you care what happened to those pistols? This isn't about Joseph and Dolores at all, is it?"

Before Matilda could answer, Sarah stepped out of the shell that had been The Saint Frances de Chantal Orphan Asylum. She carried a long, thin blade. As she approached, she sheathed the blade inside her parasol. Small droplets of blood stained the right sleeve of her dress. She spoke, in a voice identical to Matilda's. "There are no survivors."

"Hmm, very well," said Matilda.

Anna noticed a hole in Sarah's dress, just below the left breast. It had not been there a moment ago. The edges of the hole were darkened, and tiny black specks surrounded it, burn marks.

Matilda saw where Anna was looking and said, "Sarah, you seem to have torn a small hole in your bodice."

Sarah again glared at Matilda, cool death in her eyes. "It shall be no trouble to mend," she said. "It looks like our friend is back." Sarah walked past Matilda, blocking Jane.

Another hole had appeared in Sarah's dress, this one in the back, a bloodless exit wound.

"Anna, pay attention now," Matilda said, ignoring Jane. "We still have several photographs for you to identify, and a few objects to locate. I need Hattie's pistols and...a key? Yes, I believe Dolores gave you a key. We will be needing that, as well. If we can finish up in a timely manner, I can leave you in peace. Do you recognize this man?"

Anna didn't look at the picture. She was forming her own picture in her mind. It was a dark and ugly picture, with these two women standing at the forefront.

"You didn't send Dolores to free Joseph. That wasn't the real reason." Anna said." You sent her here to fight McCain."

"*I* did not send her at all," Matilda said, "the coven did – to right her wrongs, and to repay her debts. But that is none of your business. Did you see this man or not?"

The strawberry-copper syrup burned in her brain, but Anna still did not look at the picture. "What 'wrongs' and 'debts'? She was orphaned and tortured for your coven. She watched her brother die rather than give you up."

"Her brother did *not* die. And that *is* the problem," said Matilda. "We have been very careful, for centuries, to hide our existence. Our enemies had begun to believe they had wiped us out, or that we had never been real at all.

"Before Joseph, McCain had only a handful of nutty fanatics in her order. Once his existence became known, well, McCain had no trouble recruiting an army of witch-hunters. What Dolores did ruined hundreds of years of careful work and planning, and cost several lives."

"So you sent her here, all by herself, to do battle against your enemies?" Anna asked.

"No. I told you, *I* did not send her, the coven did. Enough, already! Look at the picture and tell..."

"You didn't even tell her what she was getting into, did you?" Anna asked. She felt the key in her pocket, her anchor, and clutched it tightly, fighting through the copper-strawberry bubbles in her brain. "She had no idea she would have to fight this army."

"No more questions!" Matilda nearly yelled. "I told you it is not your business, and you would not understand it, anyway. You have seen that we have power, to do good or to harm. I did not want to harm you, or your friends, but you *will* cooperate with my investigation."

"I will not," Anna said. "I will answer no more questions until we come to terms. And you will not take Dolores from us. She is *our* sister, not yours."

"What? What *terms*? What are you babbling about? Of course she is not your sister..."

"Before I answer another question, you will fix Donny, unswell his brain," Anna said.

"That is quite impossible..."

"You *will* do it," Anna said again. "You are lying. Somebody just shot your doppelganger, through the heart, and it didn't hurt her. She stitched up my back and she didn't even have a needle. I know you have the ability to fix him."

"No," said Matilda. "I will not waste my strength or time on an orphan boy."

"That orphan boy is the only reason Dolores didn't burn," Anna said. "But that isn't what you care about, so let me tell you something else, if not for that orphan boy, McCain would have killed Dolores long before all of her order arrived. None of them would have been killed. The only reason your sadistic little plan worked is because of that orphan boy."

"Be that as it may," Matilda said, "his fate is not my concern."

"Then you may leave now," Anna said, pointing to the silvery dinghy, "Because you will get nothing else from me. And you will not go anywhere near my girls."

"You do not want to make me your enemy, Anna," Matilda said.

"Lady!" Jane interrupted, in a voice that made Anna want to hide under a cot, "are you *blind* as well as stupid? Look around you. There used to be a fortress here. It stood here for a hundred years. It's gone now. You know why? Because it made Anna its enemy. If anyone ought to be scared, lady, it's you. There used to be a factory there, now it's just a hole full of sand and seaweed, because it tried to keep Anna on this island.

"Anna fought off an entire order of evil nuns, an army of mercenary witch-hunters, a pack of wolves and a—a—a Joseph-Thing, to rescue her girls and get us off this island. And now, you are going to just saunter up in your silly white dress and threaten her? I've seen a lot of moronic behavior since I've lived here, lady, but you take the cake. You are one dumb witch!"

Sarah's blade made the distinctive *snict* of steel on steel as she drew it. Matilda stayed her with a wave of her hand.

"McCain's order," Anna said, speaking as the thoughts came to her, "they didn't all die here. That's what you want to know, right? McCain was waiting for reinforcements. She was trying to hold off Joseph's attack until they arrived. It sounded like that was the larger part of her army. Do you think that rumors of Joseph stirred up trouble for your coven? Just think what this will do. You've made a martyr of McCain."

Matilda and Sarah exchanged troubled glances.

"In fact, the reinforcements are probably on their way as we speak." Anna made a show of shielding her eyes and looking out to sea. "I'm surprised they haven't arrived already. It seems to me that you would want to know which of McCain's order remains alive, to know who is still hunting you. Also, I don't think you would want them to find us, me and my girls. If you leave us behind, we could provide them with details you may not want them to have."

"You will tell them nothing," Sarah hissed.

"No, I won't," Anna said, "because you are going to help Donny, and then you are going to take us away from here."

Matilda studied Anna, then surveyed the horizon. Finally she said, "You are telling the truth."

Anna nodded.

"Sarah, see to the boy,"

"Matilda!" Sarah said.

"Do it," Matilda said. "Time is short."

Sarah whipped her blade from its parasol sheath. White-hot sunlight flared of its steel. She raised it above her left shoulder, then cross body slung it into the sand a Matilda's feet. "Do not think that I will forget this," she said. Her voice was ice and needles.

Matilda raised one eyebrow.

Sarah turned and marched toward the woods.

When she had gone, Matilda said, "I am counting this as a debt you owe me, child. I do not give favors. You will tell me everything you know about who was here, about who died and how, and about who was coming to assist McCain. And when you have told me everything, you will still be in my debt. When I come to collect, you had better be ready to pay."

"You help Donny, and take my girls somewhere safe," Anna said, her hand clutched the key in her pocket so tightly that her nails dug into her palm, but the strawberry copper taste was gone. "That is your end of the deal. My end of the deal is I saved Dolores from the army of witch-hunters that you set on her. That makes us even. I will give you the information I have as a favor to you. I owe you nothing."

"That is not the way I see it," said Matilda. "But we must go, now. Collect your girls. We'll hash out terms on the ship." She stooped and retrieved Sarah's blade from the sand. It glinted in the late morning sun.

Anna nodded, as solemnly as she could, but inside she felt a glowing, radiant hope. "You get nothing from me until Donny has recovered."

"Then we shall speak this evening," Matilda said in a cold, cold voice.

Anna turned toward the wood line and was surprised to see Jane standing there, had forgotten her completely. Anna rushed to her and threw her arms around the older girl.

"We're leaving, Jane!" Anna whispered, trying not to let Matilda see her excitement. "We are sailing away from here forever. On that clipper ship. We're finally free!"

"I know!" Jane whispered back. She and Anna started jogging toward their little camp.

"And Donny's going to be okay!" Anna gasped as she ran, "They're going to make him all better!"

"Anna, slow down," Jane said, still holding her hand. "You shouldn't be running."

"Donny's going to be okay!" The wood line moved away from her faster than she could run to it, but the ground came closer by the second.

"Anna!" Jane shouted. It was the last thing Anna heard before pitching forward onto the beach. She plunged through the sand into swirling darkness. It was a very familiar feeling, one she was becoming accustom to, like swimming in the ocean.

Chapter 28

ANNA AWOKE TO THE GENTLE side-to-side rocking of the clipper ship skimming across the sea. Sunlight streamed in through portholes, painting radiant oblongs on the floor. Reflections of saltwater scintillated on the ceiling.

Donny rocked in a hammock beside hers. He looked almost exactly as he had the last time she had seen him, his eyes and mouth hanging partly open. A slow buzzing sound hummed out from between his lips. Anna had the horrible idea that a fly was trapped in there. Then the buzz drew out to a rattle and Anna realized that Donny was snoring.

"Donny?" she said.

The snore abruptly changed to a snort. Donny's eyes popped open, bright and green, fully alive. "Anna!" he exclaimed, swinging his feet down from his hammock and rushing to her side. "We're on a boat, Anna, a tall sailing ship! You've gotta see this thing! It's amazing, flyin' across the waves..."

Anna threw her arms around him and hugged him so hard one of the stitches in her back nearly ripped out. "Shut up, Donny," she choked through her tears. It was all she could manage before a sob clenched her throat. She wept into Donny's shoulder until she wet his shirt with her tears. A clean white shirt, Anna realized, after she had soaked it. She clung to him while the clipper sliced through peaks and glided across valleys, rolling gently.

Finally, she let him go, not all the way, just to arm's length. "You're not going to get sick are you?" she asked, trying to smile, only a hint of mischief in her voice.

"Not this time," he said. "One of those funny ladies gave me something to help with sea sickness. Uh, and um, I'd appreciate it if you didn't tell...anybody about me being sick before."

"You mean you don't want me to tell Lizzy," Anna said.

"Nah, that girl would probably follow me around no matter what you told her." Donny paused then asked, "Anna, how'd we get on a boat? Last thing I remember, I was standing next to a bonfire, up to my knees in water, talking to you. Then, all of a'sudden I'm here. Jane says nobody's allowed to say nothing to nobody about nothing until you wake up."

"Donny," Anna tried to laugh, but it came out as a dry sob. She wiped at fresh tears running down her cheeks. "Donny, you got killed, by one of those crazy nuns. Then a witch brought you back to life."

Donny raised an eyebrow at her and whistled through his teeth, nodding. "Yeah, figured it was something like that."

This time Anna managed a real laugh. "No, you didn't," she said, bopping him on the shoulder. She let her feet drop from the hammock, wrapping her arm in his. "Can you take me to see my girls?"

Donny led her up a narrow flight of stairs onto the deck of the clipper. The ocean spread out before her, a brilliant blue, all the way to the horizon on every side. It sparkled in the near blinding sunlight. Salt water sprayed as the sea slipped by below them. The wind played with Anna's hair and cooled her damp cheeks.

As her eyes adjusted to the light, Anna took in the ship. Three tall masts, with all sails full of wind, rose from its deck. The deck itself was probably a hundred feet from stem to stern. One of the witches, Anna could not tell if it was Matilda or Sarah, stood at the helm, wheel in her hands. She still wore the white silk gown. No other crew was visible.

Anna turned and looked to the front of the ship. Below the fore mast, her girls sat in a little circle – Jane, Lizzy, Joan, Mary One, Norma, Lilly, Maybelle. They each wore a clean white dress, without a trace of grime on their faces. Jane stood as soon as she saw Anna, but made no move to approach. Maybelle jumped up at the sight of Donny, but Jane took her by the arm and gently sat her back down.

Between Anna and her girls, another figure in white lounged, her feet resting on the railing and a broad brimmed hat covering her face. Anna guessed who it was by the bandages on her feet.

As Anna approached, Dolores raised the brim of her hat and smiled. She extended her hand to Anna, and when Anna took it, Dolores pulled her in and wrapped her arms around her.

"You came back for me," Dolores said.

"I had to..."

"No. Anna, you didn't," Dolores said. "No one has ever come for me. I have always been alone. Do not discount what you have done. It is something no one has ever done before."

"Dolores, you're one of us, you are one of my girls. How could I have left you?"

Dolores was silent for a long time. When she finally spoke, she said, "I made sure that your girls were properly fed. They've also been bathed and clothed, as you can see. There's a washtub below, and clean clothes for you as well, when you're ready for them."

"Thank you, Dolores."

"Please," she said in a voice that sounded angry but wasn't. "Please don't thank me. It was the least I could do. I'm sorry, Anna, I – I have been alone for a long time, and I wasn't planning on being alive today. I'm having a difficult time...knowing how to behave. It may take me some time to remember how to be a friend."

Anna knelt beside her, trying to know what to say. She stared out at the sparkling waves. "Not a friend, Dolores, a sister. You are a fine sister. And we saved each other, I never would have made it out of there without you, nor would my girls." After a pause she added, "I think I like you better when you don't behave."

"*You* never did, did you?" Dolores smiled.

"No," Anna said, "I suppose not."

"Jane said you wanted to see the ocean," Dolores said after another pause. "I hope it is as wonderful as you imagined."

"It is," Anna said. "It's almost hard to look at. It just goes on and on forever, like it's not real. I keep thinking I'm going to wake up back in Saint Frances, or in the cistern."

"It's real enough, Anna," Dolores said, squeezing her hand. "You'll have plenty of time to adjust. Don't expect to see anything but ocean for several weeks."

"Weeks?" Anna said. "Where are we going?"

"What did you tell Matilda?" Dolores turned to her with a teasing grin and a little wickedness in her teary eyes. "She seems to think she needs you, seems to think you are too important to trifle with."

"All I said was that some of McCain's army was still..." Anna paused, then said, "I think maybe Jane might have over stated my role in McCain's demise."

Dolores smiled out at the ocean. "We're sailing to Australia, Anna. There's a school for young ladies in Perth. Matilda says you and your girls can stay there. 'Until you've grown' is how she put it."

"A school?" Anna said, flabbergasted. "We can live there?"

"Yes, Anna. Everyone except Donny. When you negotiated this deal, you insisted on a safe place for your girls, so Matilda is not obligated to provide anything for him," Dolores said, her eyes still twinkling. She watched Anna absorb her words, waited until Anna understood. As soon as Anna was about to ask what Donny was supposed to do on his own, Dolores added, "Fortunately for Donny, he has a friend in Perth who owes him a favor."

"You?" Anna asked.

Dolores lowered the brim of her hat and settled back in the lounge chair. "Yep," she said, "Somebody's going to have to look after me until my feet heal. I'll make sure he gets fed, and has a warm place to sleep. Maybe you can come by and visit sometime?"

"Of course I will, but..." Anna said, "But, Dolores? Australia?"

Dolores said nothing. Her smile broadened under the brim of her hat.

"Dolores," Anna asked, now in a hushed voice, "can I trust Matilda? You know that she set you up, right?"

Dolores's smile faltered. She lifted the hat brim to look Anna in the eyes. "Matilda will not lie to you. She agreed to heal Donny and she agreed to take you and your girls to a safe place. You can count on her to do those things. You must make absolutely sure that you uphold your end of the bargain. She is being extremely generous with you. That makes me think she wants more from you than you agreed to. I would recommend that you settle on exact terms sooner rather than later."

"What does she want from me?" Anna asked.

"Surely, I do not know." Dolores raised her eyebrows. "But, in as much as she seems to think that you singlehandedly wiped out McCain and half her army, my guess is she wants you to help her do battle with the other half."

"Dolores!" Anna cried. "I didn't do that, you did."

"Well don't tell *her* that," Dolores smiled. "Besides, I'll be around if you need a little help – And really, Anna, what else were you planning on doing with your life, now that you've seen the ocean?"

That thought struck Anna as so profound that she could find no words. Her future stretched out before her as sparkling and limitless as the ocean itself. A rushing vertigo swept over her and she sat back on her heels.

"Anyway," Dolores said, "This ship sails faster than any natural vessel, but it's still a very long way to Australia. You have plenty of time to wrestle with questions about the future. Eat. Rest. Dream. Oh, and you might want to go say hello to your girls, rumor is they are anxious to hear how you're doing...Donny, would you mind giving her a hand?"

Anna looked across Dolores, to the bow of the ship, where all the girls stood, looking toward her. Their faces were a mix of wonder and concern, amazement and bewilderment, and joy. She felt Donny lifting her to her feet, felt Dolores releasing her hand.

Anna floated across the deck, as if she were a hot air balloon and Donny was guiding her by a rope rather than by her hand. She looked back at Dolores as Donny walked her toward the bow. The hat hid the woman's face, except for one corner of her mouth, which turned up in a sly, contented grin.

Anna's balloon landed the second she touched the forward deck. The girls mobbed her, laughing and shouting and crying. She heard shouts about Australia, where they have raccoons with duck heads and rabbits that stand up as tall as a man. She heard shouts about a school where you can read as much as you like, where they feed you even if you don't make enough shoes. Someone kept asking if they have blackberry jam in Australia. Anna collapsed in a pile of hugs and tears.

At the ship's stern, the black haired woman still stood at the wheel, her white gown ruffling in the wind like a furled sail. Anna had unfinished business with that woman, but that would have to wait. At this moment, it didn't frighten Anna in the least. It seemed that just now, there was no room in her for fear. Her heart was too full with joy and wonder and love.

Author's Note

Thank you so much for reading Sisters of Sorrow. If you had half as much fun reading as I had writing, we are both the better for it. Many more hardships and adventures await Anna and her friends. If you'd like to be the first to hear about new releases, please sign up for my newsletter here by typing this link into your internet browser.

http://madmimi.com/signups/139439/join

I love hearing from my readers and welcome your feedback. If you enjoyed the story, please consider leaving a review on Amazon.com. Reviews are the real-world magic that keep stories like Sisters of Sorrow alive.

You can contact me directly by email at axblackwell@gmail.com. You might also find me flinging inane comments into the twitterverse at @AxelBlackwell or palling around with my writer buddies on Facebook.

About the Author

Axel Blackwell grew up in one of those small Indiana towns where the only fun is the kind you make yourself. Many ghost sightings and UFO sightings in the central Indiana area between 1985 and 1990, as well as several small fires, can be attributed to Axel and his brothers attempting to escape boredom.

Axel now lives with his wife in the Pacific Northwest. He still enjoys summoning ghosts and fires, but has learned to bind these creations within the pages of a book...most of the time.

Made in the USA
Lexington, KY
01 October 2016